BEFORE
I SAY
I DO

About the Author

Vicki Bradley splits her time between writing psychological suspense novels with being a DC with the Met Police. *Before I Say I Do* is her first novel and won the 2018 inaugural Write Here, Right Now open submissions competition run by Simon & Schuster UK, Darley Anderson Literary Agency and the Bradford Literature Festival.

To find out more, visit her website or follow her on Twitter.

www.vickibradleywriter.com
@vbradleywriter

BEFORE I SAY I DO

VICKI BRADLEY

**SIMON &
SCHUSTER**

London · New York · Sydney · Toronto · New Delhi

A CBS COMPANY

First published in Great Britain by Simon & Schuster UK Ltd, 2020

7 9 10 8 6

Simon & Schuster UK Ltd
1st Floor
222 Gray's Inn Road
London WC1X 8HB

Simon & Schuster Australia, Sydney
Simon & Schuster India, New Delhi

www.simonandschuster.co.uk
www.simonandschuster.com.au
www.simonandschuster.co.in

A CIP catalogue record for this book
is available from the British Library

Paperback ISBN: 978-1-4711-8524-3
eBook ISBN: 978-1-4711-8525-0
Audio ISBN: 978-1-4711-9155-8

Typeset by Palimpsest Book Production Ltd, Falkirk, Stirlingshire
Printed and bound in Great Britain by CPI Group (UK) Ltd, Croydon, CR0 4YY

MIX
Paper from
responsible sources
FSC® C013604

For Sylvia and Charles Richard Bradley.

Mum and Dad, thank you for encouraging us to question the universe and to follow our dreams.

Together at last and on your final big adventure.

Chapter 1

Julia Talbot

Sunday

My hands were shaking. I was terrified, but also elated by the promise of a new future: like waiting to be called for a job interview, but much, much more intense.

Outside, the summer sun was trying to push through the white clouds, and I willed it on, as if the light would bring me luck. The hotel grounds looked peaceful, not a single person around, but the surroundings did nothing to calm my nerves.

My palms were sweaty. Panic was building up in my stomach and rising to my chest. I took a long breath in, held it, and then I let it go. It was what my therapist had taught me to do.

'Not long to go,' Lucy said. She looked beautiful in her bridesmaid's dress. I'd asked her to make sure everything ran smoothly, and the pressure was showing. She was like a coiled spring ready to explode. She wanted everything to be perfect for me. It wasn't helping my rising anxiety.

'We're both ready,' I said.

Lucy nodded and then fussed with a loose strand of my hair, which had come free from my chignon and framed my face. She kept trying to tuck it back in, but it wouldn't stay. She knew my fine hair was unmanageable, but today she was refusing to give up.

'It's okay.' I moved away from her.

'Sorry.' She clasped her hands together. I wasn't sure who was more apprehensive: her or me.

I surveyed myself in the hotel mirror, checking every last detail, and smiled. My long blonde hair was staying up, a few delicate white pearls sprinkled throughout. My white dress fit perfectly, cascading around my feet. Lucy was reflected behind me in the glass, her brow creased with the strain of concentrating as she checked every detail too.

I smiled at her and made tiny adjustments to my flowers and dress. I took my time. I touched up the pink gloss on my lips; the colour made them fuller. This was my moment of transformation. No one was going to hurry me. I needed to get this right. Everybody would be watching me, including Mark's family. I had to be perfect.

'How do I look?' I grinned at her.

Lucy's brow creased and her lip wobbled.

'Come on.' I gave her a quick hug. 'We promised each other we wouldn't cry.' She was meant to be supporting me, but here I was having to carry her, on today of all days.

'I'm sorry.' She dabbed at her eyes, trying not to smudge her mascara. 'You look incredible.'

She composed herself and then wrapped her arms tightly around me, her auburn curls brushing against my cheek. I untangled myself and held her at arm's length.

I couldn't help but smile. Her curled auburn hair tumbled around her shoulders and her peppermint bridesmaid's dress made her green eyes glow.

'You look beautiful,' I said. 'It won't be long until it's your turn.'

'It's only been six months,' Lucy said, but a huge grin appeared at the mention of her boyfriend, James. I was glad to see her so happy. She'd had more than her fair share of pain over the years. 'Sorry he couldn't come today,' she said. 'He really did try, but he couldn't get out of the Dubai work trip.'

'Don't worry,' I said. 'You're here and that's what matters.' I gave her a twirl and she let out a little sob. Part of me suspected that her tears weren't all joyful. She'd never been sure about Mark and had been very vocal about it at the beginning. When she realized that I wouldn't give him up, she'd toed the line, but her concerns had always left me with a niggle of self-doubt. She'd known me my whole life; knew me better than anyone. I had found myself asking the same question over and over again. Was I making the right choice? But then Mark's lopsided grin would come into my mind and I told myself I'd never find anyone like him again. The day I'd met him I knew we were going to be married and live happily together, always.

'Come on, Miss Time-Keeper.' I tapped my wrist as if I was wearing a watch. 'Don't we need to get going?'

Lucy moved away. 'Sorry. Yes. They'll be here soon.' She wiped under her eyes with tissue and touched up her foundation before picking up her bouquet; it matched my larger bunch of peach and yellow roses.

I turned towards the door. As if on cue, there was a knock. A middle-aged man in a black suit marched into the room. He looked every inch the police detective, with his composed presence and the way he took control of the space. It made my heart stop.

'Miss Talbot, my name is Henry.' He thrust his hand towards me and I stared at it blankly. 'I'm going to be your registrar for today.' His hand hovered in the air uselessly and he tilted his head at me, a look of concern on his face.

'Of course, thank you.' I grabbed his hand gratefully, but shook it too fast in my relief. I caught a glimpse of my reflection glaring back at me from the large mirrors on the walls. I was frowning, and my shoulders were tense. I tried to relax. I was being ridiculous. Of course he wasn't from the police.

'First off, I need to check that you are Miss Julia Talbot,' the registrar said.

'I am.' I smiled at him.

'And have you ever been known by any other name?'

'No.' My skin prickled as I told the lie. Lucy's face didn't change but she gave a slight nod of approval. I could always rely on her.

'It's nothing to worry about,' the registrar said chirpily. 'Just part of the legal process. One always has to satisfy the law.' I suspected that he'd never been on the wrong side of it.

'I'm sorry.' I tried to relax. 'I'm all over the place today.'

'I've yet to meet a bride who hasn't suffered with nerves.' He patted my arm kindly, like a father would, and I felt pain needle sharp in my heart.

'Will anyone be walking you down the aisle?'

'No. I'll be walking down the aisle by myself.' My dad's face came into my mind, the last time I'd seen him. He was cradling his head in his hands, his whole body shaking with sobs.

'Right . . .' The registrar was flustered by my answer. 'And you've got one bridesmaid here.'

'Yes, that's me.' Lucy nodded at him. With Lucy stood beside me, I could do this.

'And who is your witness for the signing of the register?' he asked.

'Witness?' I looked at Lucy.

'When you and Mark sign the register, you'll have two witnesses,' the registrar said. 'I believe Mark has chosen his mother.'

'I thought his mother and father were going to be the witnesses?' I said. 'They both wanted to be involved in the ceremony.'

'Sorry, tradition dictates one witness should be from the bride's side.' The registrar shook his head at me and smiled. 'And I'm a stickler for tradition. What about your friend here?'

'Oh. Yes, Lucy.' There was only Lucy left on my side to be my witness.

'Or maybe a sibling, to get them a bit involved?' He clasped his hands together, waiting.

My chest felt tight and a sudden wave of dizziness hit me. I heard Rachel's childish laughter pealing through the trees, saw sunlight filtering through the woods.

I had to sit down or I'd fall. Lucy grabbed my arm. She guided me to the plush sofa in the middle of the room. My legs buckled under me and I collapsed onto it.

'Are you all right?' The registrar rushed forward; his already wrinkled brow was furrowed deep. He seemed at a loss as to what to do.

'She's fine.' Lucy bent over me, peering into my face. She turned to him. 'I can be the witness.'

'Do you need some water or something?' He shifted his weight from one leg to the other, not sure where to go.

'Great idea.' Lucy rushed to the table where a jug of water stood and poured me a glass.

'I'm all right,' I said. 'A little hot, that's all. This dress is too tight.'

'I have to ask . . .' The registrar leaned closer towards me. 'Is anyone forcing you to get married?'

'No, no one's forcing me to do anything.' I couldn't keep the irritation out of my voice. *Why was he asking me that?* I wished he would get away from me.

His face relaxed. 'I'm sorry – I have a legal duty to ask. It's one of the standard questions.'

'Of course.' I tried to control my breathing.

Lucy handed me the glass of water.

'I'll . . . I'll leave you to it,' he said. 'Thank you.' He hurried out of the room without looking back.

'Drink the water,' Lucy said. 'It's going to be fine.' She squeezed my shoulder gently.

Cool water slid down my throat. 'Do you . . . do you think they know about what happened?' I couldn't look at her as I said it.

'You're being paranoid.' She stood up straight. 'How could they know?' There was a sharpness to her voice.

'You're right. It's just . . . I hate being the centre of attention. Everyone staring at me again.'

She gave a brief nod but said nothing. We never talked about our past; it was our unspoken rule.

'We need to get going.' She handed me my bouquet and smiled at me. 'It's nearly two.'

I smoothed my dress and glanced in the mirror one final time. The colour was coming back to my cheeks. Today my life was going to begin with Mark. He had been everything to me for so long now and soon we would be married. I felt a flutter of happiness at the thought.

*

We waited outside the ceremony room – the point of no return. Once I crossed that threshold, everything would change, my life would never be the same again. I was ready.

But voices rumbled from inside the room; I'd expected silence. I glanced at Lucy, who was hunched over, fussing with my satin train.

I thought of Mark. How we'd talked about this day for so long. Now it was finally here it felt different. Strained, maybe. As if everything was pulled taut and a single thing could rip it all apart.

Lucy stood up and waited beside me. My feet were starting to ache and the underwire of my lacy bra was digging into my ribs. I tugged at my bodice.

Lucy turned to me. 'Shouldn't someone open the doors for us?'

'I would have thought so.' I tried to remember what my wedding planner had said would happen at this moment. The voices still rumbled on through the door.

'I can go in and find out what's happening?' Lucy suggested.

'No, everyone will see you. Let's give it a couple of minutes. David's probably lost the rings or something. I told Mark he'd be useless, but did he listen?' I'd never liked David. He seemed so superficial and didn't strike me as a good person.

'Tweedledum and Tweedledee.' Lucy muttered under her breath, but then saw my look and realized what she'd said. She knew I hated it when she compared Mark to David. 'I mean . . . you know, for friends, they're very alike. Same haircut, same suits. That's all. I didn't mean . . .' She blushed and looked downwards. I decided to leave it. Now was not the time to start arguing with my only bridesmaid.

'Sorry,' she said.

'It's fine.' It wasn't and she knew it. We waited for a few more minutes. 'I put one-thirty on the invites. They'll all be sat there waiting. This is embarrassing.'

'The bride's always late,' Lucy said.

'But I'm not late. I'm ready.' My patience was wearing thin. I'd never understood that tradition. 'Maybe you're meant to open the doors?'

Lucy peered through the tiny gap in the oak double doors, which were festooned with white ribbons and peach roses. 'They're all just sat there waiting.'

'Well, I can't stand here for ever. Open the doors.'

Lucy was still trying to peek through the doors, stealing nervous glances back at me. She turned to me. 'Surely someone should come out and open the doors for us?'

I wasn't going to stand here any longer. I set off towards the door with Lucy trotting behind me. She hurried in front of me and pulled open the doors, and then fell in line behind me.

The ceremony room was not as I remembered it. People filled the room, mostly sitting, but a few were on their feet. They weren't looking my way, and some were even blocking the aisle.

Mark was at the front, speaking with the registrar, his back towards me. I remembered the first time I'd met him, when he'd come into my little jewellery store. I'd known he was different. I couldn't stop watching him. He had a good eye for jewellery, selecting one of my favourite pieces for his mother's birthday. I felt at ease with him. When he discovered I was the jewellery maker and owner, he was amazed. Most people see jewellery as frivolous, but he said it was art.

He'd bought the piece and left, but the next day he

came in again. He'd claimed he needed to buy another present, but it became clear he wasn't there for the jewellery. I hadn't been able to stop thinking about him, and I couldn't believe he'd come back. I knew in that moment that one day we'd be married and now here we were.

I waved at the pianist to start playing and he frowned at me and shook his head. I mouthed '*play*' at him and he shrugged his shoulders and began the canon, filling the room with a rising crescendo. All faces turned towards me, but no one was smiling.

Gemma, a colleague of Mark's, loomed in front of me, blocking my way. 'Julia, you shouldn't be here,' she said. 'Elizabeth was supposed to talk to you.'

'What do you mean? Of course I should be here. It's my wedding day.' *Had she lost her mind?*

'Get out of her way.' Lucy stepped in front of me and pushed Gemma aside.

I saw a smirk play across Gemma's face as she shrugged her shoulders and turned away. I'd always suspected she'd liked Mark a bit too much. She'd certainly never been keen on me. Tears filled my eyes. Everything was blurred.

As I stumbled down the aisle, the people around me gawped. One of Mark's cousins put her hand over her mouth.

I concentrated on Mark; he was a few metres away. If I could get to him, everything would be all right. He was in a deep discussion with the registrar, their heads bent towards each other. Those standing were blocking my view. I couldn't get his attention without shouting at him and I wouldn't stoop to that.

Confusion spread through the room. The whispers grew. Elizabeth, Mark's mother, was hurrying down the aisle towards me, a strange look on her face.

Mark turned around to face me – but it wasn't Mark. It was David.

When Mark had joined the gym, David had too. When Mark changed his hair, David had too. I couldn't believe I'd mistaken him for Mark. Of course it wasn't him.

I brushed the tears from my eyes and checked the crowd either side of me, but Mark wasn't there.

David hurried towards me, meeting me halfway down the aisle just as Elizabeth reached me. He was the last man in the whole world I needed right now, but I was stuck with him.

'Your wedding planner was going to talk to you.' His eyes darted from left to right, searching for her.

'Where's Mark?' I grabbed his hands to make him focus on me.

'I don't know.' He pulled his hands from mine. He wouldn't look at me.

'When did you last see him?' It felt like I was free-falling as my stomach flipped in fear.

'Yesterday afternoon.' He glanced at me and then quickly looked away.

'But you were meant to be staying at our flat with him last night?'

'He didn't turn up. I just thought he was with you.' He pushed his hair back and his eyes searched the room, as if looking for an excuse to get away from me.

'You knew he wasn't with me,' I said. 'We told you we wanted to spend our last unmarried night apart. He was meant to be with *you*.' Mark had been missing for twenty-four hours and David hadn't told anyone.

'Sorry, what do you want me to say?' He put his hands up in surrender and moved away from me. 'Look, I'll try to call him again. We'll find him, don't panic.' He pulled out his mobile and put it to his ear.

My heart hammered inside my chest. Mark was gone. So, this is what it felt like. I'd been preparing myself for this for so long, imagined it enough times, but I hadn't expected it to feel like this. As if my insides had been scooped out. An emptiness.

Elizabeth, Mark's mother, was wittering on at me. She was wearing a ridiculous, pink and gold, frisbee-like hat, which was balanced precariously on top of her greying curls. Her dress was white with a matching pink and gold swirling rose pattern, too bridal for my liking.

'I thought you were going to tell her?' Charles, my soon to be father-in-law, was standing up.

'I thought the wedding planner had gone out to do it.' Elizabeth waved her hand towards me dismissively.

My cheeks burnt with shame. They all thought he'd left me. Snatches of gossip rushed at me. I felt my jaw tightening in anger. I wanted to scream for silence, but my voice had stopped working.

Above me there were white angel sculptures flying out of the top of the stone pillars, their shoulders bent under the weight of the oak beams they were holding up. The effect was meant to be ornate, but the angels were suffering under their burden. Their eyes stared down, pitying me.

I had come so close to happiness. I dropped my gaze to the tiled floor. God was getting me back for everything I had done. And I didn't deserve anything less.

Chapter 2

Alana Loxton

Sunday

Alana Loxton watched the hands move on the cheap plastic wall clock. Two hours to go until she could say she had survived her first week in Southwark borough CID. So far, she'd been assigned two gang stabbings, a domestic and a stranger sexual assault. Her head was spinning. It had been years since she'd had to deal with volume crime, but here she was, back in the trenches.

She took a deep breath and let it out. She rolled her shoulders back twice and tilted her head left and then right. The back of her neck clicked. She promised herself that she'd use her upcoming days off to book that long-awaited massage.

Her team was short, with one person off on long-term sick leave and another on maternity. Those that were there regarded her with suspicion, as if she was a spy from the Department of Professional Standards. She told herself they were just overworked and stressed; it was nothing personal. She should stop being paranoid. At least Kowalski had been friendly towards her.

If she could just keep her head down and wait out the storm, maybe she'd be able to return to the Murder

Investigation Team in a year or two. The constant shifting of roles in the police meant a department was unrecognizable every few years, and that suited her fine after what had happened in the murder squad. The demotion had hurt, but she wasn't about to quit. Murder investigation was what she excelled at; it was where she belonged. She couldn't imagine another path in the police force. She'd bide her time and then she'd reapply – this was just a punishment posting, after all.

DCI Winter marched into the crowded office dressed in an expensive dark blue suit. He stood out in the drab room as a man with ambition – the worst type in the police, from her experience. They were out to impress – not the troops below, but the bosses above.

She tried to make herself look busy, hunching over her keyboard and typing. She hadn't been introduced to Winter yet, and the frown on his face suggested that this was not the day for it.

Winter was scanning the room for something. His eyes fell on her and Loxton's stomach clenched. There must have been thirty people in the room. Why was he looking in her direction? She couldn't be in the shit already . . .

'You two – in my office now, please.' Winter nodded at Loxton and then Kowalski, who was sitting four desks over, halfway through a Snickers bar. Winter then headed back to his office, addressing a few detectives on the way.

Kowalski took one last look at his chocolate bar, placed it back onto his desk, and joined her. 'Come on, new girl,' he said. 'He doesn't bite – much.'

Kowalski was in his early thirties, and although his Polish accent had softened living among Londoners, it was still detectable. He was pale, with light blue eyes and short cropped brown hair. Instead of a detective, she thought he had the look of someone who should be on the Territorial Support Group carrying a riot shield.

Loxton gathered up her notebook and pen and hurried past the bank of desks. Detectives looked up at her, but none of them smiled. They all looked tired and drawn. Would she look like that after her first month, she wondered?

Winter's office was cramped and small. Pinned to the wall was a faded poster warning detectives to think forensically. Stacks of dirty cups surrounded his coffee machine. There were files discarded in one corner of the room, with different handwriting on the spines. It was like a dumping ground. Perhaps the DCI didn't distance himself from the mess after all; maybe he got stuck in.

'This afternoon a 32-year-old banker, Mark Rowthorn, was reported missing by his fiancée, a Miss Julia Talbot.' Up close, slight stubble was visible on Winter's face, and the dark bags under his eyes looked permanently shaded on.

Loxton jotted down the names.

'Rowthorn disappeared before their wedding ceremony. We have the thankless task of trying to find out where the hell he's got to.'

Loxton looked up from her notepad. 'Sir, is this a priority?' The DCI turned his cold gaze on her. She carried on anyway, knowing that she'd have to explain herself now. 'Shouldn't the uniform deal with a case like this? I mean, he's probably got cold feet. Does it need a detective to—?'

'That would be the obvious conclusion. What you need to ask yourself is *why* I'm sending two detectives to this call. Your ex-DI from murder squad warned me about you, but I wanted to make my own judgement. Don't disappoint me.' Winter had spoken to her former boss, and DI Taylor wouldn't have been kind; he was still furious with her. She dropped her gaze to the floor, drawn to the worn-out carpet tiles, which were frayed to a dull grey-blue.

'To answer your question, the missing man's father is the editor of the *South London Reviewer*. He called the Commander to ensure that this matter is dealt with efficiently. I wanted to send my finest and brightest, but they're up to their eyeballs in work. You two are all I've got left.'

Kowalski raised his eyebrows and Loxton tried to control her anger. Reporting a groom missing on his wedding day; it didn't get any more menial than this. She'd be a laughing stock in her old department if it ever got back to them.

'But police constables could complete all the initial enquiries,' she said. 'Then hand it over to us in the morning if he still hasn't turned up.'

She saw Kowalski's eyes widen briefly, but he quickly made his features impassive again. Loxton didn't care. She wasn't going to be taken for a fool; she had worked too hard in her career for that.

'I'm not sending uniform to report him missing, stomping their size eleven boots all over Mr Newspaper Editor's lovely cream carpets.'

'We've got it covered, sir,' Kowalski said. He was looking at her as if he was trying to decipher a forgotten language. Despite everything, Loxton wanted to get on in her new role, so she took Kowalski's cue and decided to drop it.

'I don't want us looking stupid in front of the press. It'll be the end of all our careers. I trust you, Dominik.' Winter turned his gaze to her. 'Loxton, don't mess up.'

'Understood,' said Kowalski.

'Good.' Winter handed them a print-out of the 999 call. 'The last confirmed sighting of Rowthorn was well over twenty-four hours ago at around one-thirty in the afternoon by his best man, David Steele.'

Loxton scribbled down *Steele* and circled it. In her experience, the last one to report seeing the misper alive was usually the reason no one else had seen them since.

'A hospital search and custody check have been completed,' Winter said. 'There's no trace of Rowthorn. There have been no transactions on his bank account since his disappearance, either. We need to be seen to be covering every angle.'

'Of course, sir.' Kowalski nodded.

Loxton hated the way the police responded to media pressure, but it was always the same. Media scrutiny ensured a gold standard service.

'You're to head to Rowthorn and Talbot's home address: Flat 39, The Jam Factory, Green Walk, Borough, if that's not too much trouble? The fiancée, Julia Talbot, will be there. Are there any questions?'

'Have intelligence checks been done?' Loxton asked before she could stop herself.

Winter stared at Loxton, and then turned his face to his computer screen. A look of surprise flashed briefly on his face. 'It seems that's not been done yet. I'll get someone to put Rowthorn and Steele through the system while you're on your way. Dismissed.'

'And the fiancée too?'

'Her as well.' Winter nodded at her.

Kowalski headed for the door and Loxton followed him.

'I don't think he likes me,' she said when they were out of earshot.

'This isn't the murder squad; you can forget about being treated like an adult here. You've got to learn to take orders.'

He was right. She needed to keep her mouth shut and try to fit in. You couldn't change the game if you weren't allowed to play. 'I just don't understand why he's wasting resources on a groom that's gone AWOL. There's at least twenty unsolved stabbings in this office, and he's sending us to deal with *this*?'

'He's got friends in high places, and sometimes they call on him for favours. It's best to keep the people at the top happy and off our backs. He's a good DCI. He's just about managing to keep this place going, which is no small feat.' Kowalski was searching his desk, which was piled high with files.

'Since when did the police become this political?' Loxton spotted his radio aerial peeking out from underneath some papers and handed it to him. She grabbed her case, which had everything packed neatly inside and ready to go.

'Everything is politics these days.' He slid the radio inside his jacket pocket. 'You need to remember that.'

She pulled on her jacket. 'Let's go looking for this runaway groom then.'

Chapter 3

Alana Loxton

Sunday

A colossal Victorian red-brick building loomed over Loxton. The Jam Factory. Gutted inside and adapted into trendy bachelor pads, a world away from the poor who used to work here.

She parked on double yellows, tossing the police logbook onto the dashboard and praying that she wouldn't get a parking ticket. She flashed her badge at the aged security man, who didn't look twice, and headed through the black-gated courtyard.

Kowalski made a low whistle, shaking his head. The flats must cost well over a million each. London's relentless sirens and screaming horns were muffled here and that was worth something. If Loxton worked for another 50 years, she still wouldn't be able to afford one.

'You take the lead on this case, murder squad girl,' Kowalski said. 'You can show me how it's done.'

'Make sure you're taking notes,' she said. To her relief, he smiled.

The front of Rowthorn's and Talbot's flat was floor-to-ceiling glass. Through it she could see two women stood up talking. One was in her early thirties, wearing a green bridesmaid's dress; the other looked like the mother of the bride, judging from the god-awful hat she was wearing.

She spotted Julia Talbot sitting on an armchair gazing into the middle distance. There were also two men in wedding suits, sitting on the sofa, looking uncomfortable. They were all waiting for the police to arrive and fix everything. Loxton wished it were that simple.

She pressed the doorbell, throwing Kowalski a glance. This wasn't the type of property they usually visited – not their usual type of people either.

Loxton steeled herself, expecting the bride to answer the heavy black door, but it was the woman in her late sixties who came and yanked it open. Anger and frustration seeped from the woman's every pore and her headwear was threatening to fall off her over-curled grey hair.

'I'm DC Loxton, and this is DC Kowalski. We're here to see Julia Talbot.'

'Please, come in, come in.' The woman ushered them into the flat and away from the front door.

'I'm Elizabeth Rowthorn. Mark's mother.' She showed them into the living room, which was large, with a beautiful wooden floor. Loxton noticed the woman in the bridesmaid's dress had disappeared and so had the younger man in the morning suit.

Julia Talbot was sat upright in an armchair, surreal in her wedding dress. Her blonde hair was twisted into an elegant chignon, pinned up with white pearl clips. It was as if she expected to be teleported back to the ceremony at any moment, but her face was grey and waxen behind her smeared bridal make-up.

'I'm DC Alana Loxton and this is DC Dominik Kowalski. We're investigating Mark's disappearance.'

Talbot looked up, but her eyes were glazed over. She stared right through them.

'We're here to establish Mark's last known movements,' Loxton said.

'We've done all that on the phone to the police,' Mrs Rowthorn said impatiently. 'What are you doing to find him?'

Loxton turned towards her. 'We're doing everything we can, Mrs Rowthorn—'

'You haven't started looking, have you?' Mrs Rowthorn said, ignoring her and addressing Kowalski. Loxton was used to being dismissed at the early stages. At twenty-nine, she was younger than people expected – and female, of course. She didn't fit the plastic mould that people expected of a police officer.

'We've contacted all of the local hospitals—' Kowalski managed, before he too was interrupted.

'I've already done that. There was nothing.' Mrs Rowthorn's voice had become shriller and she spoke faster. 'Is that all you've done? You have to find him. It was his *wedding* today. Do you know how much *money* it cost us?'

'Darling, I'm sure they're doing everything they can,' said the older morning-suited man who had remained – her husband, Mr Rowthorn Sr, Loxton assumed. He seemed embarrassed by his wife's emotional outburst.

'Charles, you're sitting there as if nothing's happened. Our *son* has disappeared. These people are supposed to be out there looking for him.' Mrs Rowthorn glared at them.

'Mrs Rowthorn, could I speak to you separately?' Kowalski moved towards the kitchen, but Mrs Rowthorn stayed put. *Nice try*, thought Loxton. It was what she was about to do.

'Anything you want to ask me you can ask in front of my family. We have no secrets.'

'Some of the questions might be upsetting,' Loxton said.

'Not as upsetting as my son disappearing.'

There was an awkward silence. It was broken by the woman in the bridesmaid's dress coming in carrying a tray loaded with cups, steam rising from them. Her auburn hair tumbled around her shoulders. She was the most overdressed tea-lady Loxton had ever seen.

'This is Lucy Webb, Julia's bridesmaid.' Mr Rowthorn made the introductions. 'This is DC Loxton and DC Kowalski.'

Webb handed out the cups of tea. 'Would you like one?' she asked. She had striking emerald eyes.

'We're fine, thank you,' Kowalski said.

Webb sat next to Talbot and held her hand. Talbot still didn't say a word; her entire focus was on something small cupped in her palm, but the way she was sitting blocked Loxton's view of whatever it was.

'Julia,' Loxton began softly. 'Can we speak with you alone for a moment?'

Talbot's hand gripped Webb's tighter and she looked at both detectives. 'Why?'

'We need to ask you some questions about Mark, and it might be easier for you to answer them if you're on your own.'

Talbot glanced at Webb and the people in the room, her eyes hovering on Elizabeth Rowthorn. 'It's fine to ask me here. Like Elizabeth said, we don't have any secrets.'

Loxton glanced at Kowalski – there seemed little else they could do at this stage but continue.

'Has Mark had any issues with anyone recently?' Kowalski asked Talbot.

'No, he's very popular,' Mrs Rowthorn answered. 'Since he was a little boy he's been very popular. He was voted head of his year in college, two years in a row.'

'Has his mood changed?' Kowalski asked.

'He was about to get *married*.' Mrs Rowthorn's voice had become shrill again, as if the question was an insult. 'This wedding was not your average affair. He was very busy. It required extensive planning. Didn't it, Julia?'

Talbot nodded in silence and her face became more drawn. Loxton wished she could get Talbot on her own. 'Mark didn't seem down to you, or agitated?' Loxton asked Talbot.

'What are you suggesting, officer?' Mrs Rowthorn's face was going puce. 'That my son was depressed and killed himself? Let me assure you that my son is perfectly happy.'

'We were happy,' Talbot added finally speaking. 'I don't understand any of this.' She covered her face with her hand and her whole body shook. Her other hand had unfurled and Loxton saw she was holding a gold and silver wedding band. The metals were mixed together to create an elaborate wooden grain effect. Loxton had never seen a ring like it.

Mrs Rowthorn turned her full attention to Loxton. 'Mark hasn't wandered off because he's a bit *glum*. He would never leave us all like this. Something terrible has obviously happened to him. You need to do your job and find him.'

'Mrs Rowthorn, I can't imagine how hard this is for all of you,' Kowalski said. 'We're just trying to make sure we don't miss anything.'

'That's what I'm trying to do too.' Mrs Rowthorn glared at him.

'Who are his friends?' Loxton asked. 'Is there anyone he might have gone to stay with?'

'His friends are all from the bank,' Julia Talbot said. 'He works such long hours, the bank's his life.'

'Is there a big drinking culture at the bank?' Kowalski asked Talbot.

'It's quite a high-pressured job,' Mrs Rowthorn added quickly. 'They need to let off steam.'

'Can you make a list of his friends?' Loxton asked.

Talbot nodded. 'The ones I know were all at the wedding. David, his best man, can help you with the rest of the City Enterprises lot. He's just gone to make a call.' She motioned towards the rear of the flat.

'It seems Mark was last seen yesterday at around one-thirty in the afternoon by David Steele. Can you tell me where you were yesterday after one-thirty? If you saw Mark after that time?'

'I didn't see Mark.' Talbot said sadly. 'I was in the Silver Tree Hotel at around two. I checked in and was getting things set up for the wedding.'

'I was helping Julia in the afternoon,' Webb said. 'And I stayed with her that night. In the morning we were getting ready for the wedding. Make up, hair, you know.'

'Thank you,' Loxton said. It seemed the best man was the last person to see Mark Rowthorn.

Kowalski carried on with the standard questions while Loxton took in the scene and the people discreetly. She doubted if anything terrible had happened. People went missing all the time, and they usually came back of their own accord.

Loxton scanned Rowthorn's living room; it was straight

out of a designer home magazine, spacious and bright. There was no clutter, and few clues about the man who lived here. The books on the shelves were about people management, banking and wine. All clinical.

Talbot herself appeared to have the magazine lifestyle. She was wealthy, young and beautiful, with a show-home London apartment. Research had shown she ran her own jewellery business. But none of that mattered now. Talbot was just like anyone else suffering, scared that it might be permanent.

'Do you think this could be related to your work, Mr Rowthorn?' Kowalski asked. The killer question. Loxton braced herself for Mrs Rowthorn's outburst.

'Charles?' Mrs Rowthorn put her hand to her mouth.

'No,' Mr Rowthorn said. 'We have threats all the time. People get upset about the odd article but there's been nothing recently. Nothing to merit this sort of scenario. Should I put out a press release?' Mr Rowthorn asked.

'Not yet, but I'll discuss it with the Commander,' Kowalski said. Loxton was surprised at his political insight. He was doing his best to make them believe this case was the police's top priority. In cases like this, either the family were the obvious suspects, or they were the last to know what was going on in their loved one's life. Loxton wondered if Rowthorn had a second life. Maybe a wife already, who he'd been hiding from his mother and fiancée? It was amazing what people could get up to. And it was more likely than a kidnap scenario.

'Miss Talbot, we need to speak with your family to make sure they haven't seen him,' Loxton said. 'What are their contact details?'

Talbot looked down towards the floor and Webb touched her shoulder.

'Her mother and father died in a car crash years ago,' Webb said.

'I'm sorry to hear that, Julia.' Loxton handed Talbot a pen and paper. 'Could you write down the names of Mark's friends on here, and their contact numbers, if you have them?'

Talbot nodded and stared at the pen and paper in her hand.

'We also need to do a search of your flat.'

'Of course,' Talbot said and carried on staring at the pen and paper.

'Is that really necessary?' Mr Rowthorn said exasperated. 'You can tell what sort of people we are. It's not like he's hiding in the bathroom.'

'I'm afraid we have to, sir,' Kowalski said. 'We'll need to ask David a few questions too, as he was the last person to see Mark.'

Mr Rowthorn nodded but he was frowning. He was used to being obeyed.

Loxton and Kowalski left the room and went down a narrow corridor. Before they reached the rear of the flat, Loxton could hear a man arguing in a low voice in one of the bedrooms.

'Do you think I'm crazy?' The male's voice was an angry whisper. 'I'm not going to tell them anything about that, so calm the fuck down. Don't threaten me.'

Loxton glanced at Kowalski.

'Look, I've got to go.' The man was whispering now. 'If I hear anything, I'll let you know.'

The man was in the master bedroom and jolted when he saw them outside in the corridor. He fumbled to end the call. Loxton went into the bedroom and Kowalski followed, closing the door behind him so they had the man alone.

'Hello, I'm DC Loxton and this is DC Kowalski,' Loxton said.

'Sorry, you gave me a start. You're as quiet as cats. I'm David Steele.' Steele was in his early thirties, tanned, and had short black hair which matched his dark eyes. His sandalwood aftershave was overpowering, and Loxton tried not to sneeze.

'Sorry, we didn't want to disturb you,' Loxton said. 'Your phone call sounded important.'

'Just a friend,' Steele said. 'We're organising a search party to check out Mark's usual pubs and things. In case he's gone there. Julia's going to start a Facebook page. This is all just so fucking weird.'

'We just need to ask you a few questions,' Kowalski said. 'You were the last person to see Mark?'

'Yes . . . Yes, I was.'

'When did you last see him?' Loxton asked.

'When we picked up the suits from the Yardsmen yesterday afternoon.'

'Yesterday afternoon?' Kowalski asked.

'Yes, he just said he had to go.' Steele shrugged. 'I . . . I thought he'd forgotten something.'

'Go where?'

Steele looked uncomfortable, running his hands through his hair repeatedly, and then crossing his arms in front of him to stop himself. 'I don't know. He just left.'

Loxton glanced at Kowalski. The body language was unmistakable, a repetitive tick – the first lie. 'Is that what you'd both planned?'

'No. He dumped all the suits on me. I had to take a cab on my own to get them back here.'

'Did he say where he was going? Who he was seeing?' Loxton asked.

'No.' Steele rubbed the back of his neck. 'He was a bit agitated. I thought maybe he'd forgotten to do something.'

'Had he been acting agitated before?'

'He was getting married. His mother and Julia had been butting heads about their perfect day. It's not been easy for him.'

'Did you see him again, after you split up at the Yardsmen?' Loxton said.

'We were supposed to be going for dinner and a few beers. I was meant to crash here with him last night. All that bad luck stuff.'

'And?' Kowalski asked.

'He never showed up.' Steele shrugged. 'I kept trying to call him, but it went straight to voicemail. I guessed he'd had last-minute nerves and gone for a drink.'

'And you didn't think it was odd that you weren't invited along for this drink?' Loxton glanced around the bedroom. She noted that, like the living room, there were no photographs or pictures on the walls.

'Sometimes he likes being on his own. He's always been like that. When it got late, I tried calling again, but his phone was off. I thought he was letting off some steam. I don't know.' Steele seemed lost as he looked at Kowalski and then Loxton. His mobile bleeped and he ignored it. 'I slept in the spare room. In the morning I tried again, but his phone was still off.'

'And you didn't tell anyone?' Loxton knew he was lying, but she wasn't sure about what or why. To cover for Rowthorn or to protect himself?

'I thought that maybe he'd convinced Julia that he could stay the night with her. When he wasn't at the hotel this morning, I didn't know what to do. I kept expecting him to turn up at any minute.'

'You waited until the wedding ceremony was due to begin before you told anyone. Why?'

Steele ran his fingers through his hair. 'I guess I'd convinced myself he was just running late. I didn't want to drop him in it, make a fuss. He's always late. It's no big deal, he's always there in the end. When the registrar wanted to speak to him before the ceremony, that's when we realized, his family and me, that no one had seen or heard from him. None of us could get hold of him. It was surreal.'

'Was he having problems?'

Steele squirmed under her scrutiny. 'The usual. Work's been tough at the bank. Settling down was scary. But nothing out of the ordinary.'

'Do you work together?' Loxton asked.

'Well, not exactly. We both work at City Enterprises. It's a trading bank in the City. It's huge.'

'And you said it's been tough?' She tilted her head to the side, wondering what he was omitting.

'There have been a few sackings.' Steele gave a half-shrug. 'Some money went missing, but that's not that unusual in a bank that size. The management have got pretty tough, but that's got nothing to do with this.'

'What do *you* think has happened to Mark?' Loxton watched Steele carefully.

'Honestly, I don't know.' Steele put his hands out as if in surrender. As soon as someone used the word 'honestly', Loxton knew they were being untruthful.

'People don't just disappear into thin air,' Kowalski said, disbelief palpable in his voice. 'There are signs. Problems. You're his best man. You must know something.'

'We won't tell his parents or Julia, if that's what you're worried about.' Loxton tried to look as friendly as possible. 'It'll be between you, us and Mark.'

Steele shook his head. 'Mark's like a brother to me. If I knew anything, I'd tell you. But I can't help you.'

'If you're covering for him, you need to stop, because this could be serious,' Loxton said, her voice harder than she meant it to sound. She couldn't help thinking that Steele was lying to her.

'I'm not covering for him,' Steele replied angrily, folding his arms across his chest. 'I told you, I've got no idea where he is.'

'What were you talking about on the phone just now?'

'That's none of your business.' Steele glared at her. He looked ready to hit her, but kept his arms folded. He had a temper.

'What was it you mustn't tell us?' Loxton asked.

'That was a private conversation and nothing to do with this.'

'I don't believe you.' Loxton stared at him. 'Who was threatening you?'

'I don't know what you're talking about and I don't have to listen to this.' He tried to manoeuvre around them, but Loxton remained in front of the bedroom door. She wasn't done with him yet.

Kowalski shrugged and stepped aside. Loxton threw Kowalski an annoyed look, but he ignored her. 'No one's asking you to stay,' Kowalski said. 'You're free to go. Thanks for your time, it was most helpful.'

Steele cursed under his breath and stormed out of the bedroom past Loxton.

'He's a shit liar.' Loxton closed the door behind him. 'We'll get his mobile number off Julia and get his phone records,' Kowalski said. 'See who he was just talking with. No point arguing with him, he clearly wasn't going to tell us anything.'

'I just can't stand people lying to me.' She pulled on blue plastic gloves and began rifling through the chest of drawers, pulling out socks and T-shirts.

'You might be in the wrong job . . .' Kowalski stood watching her.

'He knows something. If he cared about Rowthorn, instead of his own skin, then he'd tell us.'

'Life's not that simple.' Kowalski pulled on his own gloves and went to the wardrobe and started searching. 'Sometimes trying to get witnesses to trust you means they open up later.'

They continued in silence. It took her for ever to go through the top drawer of balled-up socks. Kowalski was tearing through the wardrobe, as if the whole exercise was a waste of time.

She pulled out the emptied drawer, checking along each side. Kowalski rolled his eyes at her. 'This isn't a drugs raid, Loxton.'

'You'd be amazed what people have hidden away,' she said.

He shook his head, moving on to the bed, pulling off the cream satin sheets.

Loxton turned back to the chest of drawers. The second drawer contained Talbot's running gear, folded neatly.

In the third drawer down she found a photo album. She pulled it out and flicked through the pages, looking for anything out of place among the photos of Talbot and Rowthorn. The pictures showed them on beaches and mountains and spa retreats. At parties with friends and dinners for two. They were a good-looking couple.

'What you got?' Kowalski said.

'I'm getting a photo for the house-to-house and missing posters. If it even goes that far.' Part of her hoped Rowthorn would turn up any minute, hungover and sorry, so she could get back to her stabbings. The other part of her felt something was wrong – very wrong.

Kowalski looked over his shoulder. 'They look pretty solid, don't they? You never can tell who's going to make it and who's not.'

She pulled a photo from the last page of the album: a close-up of Rowthorn and Talbot. 'This will have to do. There's never a photo of him on his own.'

'Lucky him,' Kowalski said.

Loxton hauled out the final drawer.

'This idiot will have turned up by tomorrow and this will all have been a waste of time,' Kowalski said. 'I hate missing person inquiries – a whole lot of nothing.' His brow furrowed, making him look more sullen than usual.

Loxton turned the heavy oak drawer over to check the bottom, her arms aching with the effort. Then her whole body tightened.

There was a mobile phone taped to the underside of the drawer. She pulled the masking tape off and took the phone. Kowalski's breath was on the back of her neck as he craned down to see. She touched the screen, holding her breath, but the lock screen flashed. An unread message appeared: '*I know what you did and you're going to burn.*'

All eyes fell onto Loxton as she entered the living room. 'Miss Talbot, we'll be getting out of your way now. But before we do, I need your permission to take a few of Mark's belongings. They could help us to find him. We need to take his mobiles, laptops and passport.'

'You've found something?' Talbot sat up in the armchair she'd been slumped in. *Not so vacant after all.* 'Please, is he all right?'

'We are treating Mr Rowthorn's disappearance as a missing persons case, which means we must take these types of items as standard procedure. Can you confirm that this is his mobile?' Loxton held out the hidden mobile so Talbot could see it.

'I haven't seen that one before.' Talbot pointed at the phone in Loxton's hand. 'This iPhone here is his work phone.' She pointed at an iPhone on the coffee table in front of her. 'He was going to leave it at home. He promised he wouldn't take it on our honeymoon.' Her lower lip trembled.

'Thank you.' Loxton took the iPhone and then crouched in front of Talbot. 'I need to take a photograph of him too. Is it all right if I take this one?'

'Please . . . can you make sure I get it back? That's from the weekend he proposed to me.'

'Of course. I need any other mobiles or computers he has here too.'

Kowalski picked up a silver Mac laptop from the coffee table. 'Is this Mark's laptop?'

'Yes, but you can't just take it,' Talbot said. 'He needs it. He's always on it.' Her hands reached out towards the laptop.

'We need to check it,' Loxton said. 'We'll bring it straight back.'

Talbot's gaze drifted onto the ring she still held. Loxton was losing her, and she needed a good rapport with this woman to help her find Rowthorn.

'I've never seen a ring like that,' Loxton said.

'It's my wedding band,' Talbot said. 'I made one for Mark too; he should still have it.'

'You made this?' The ring was exquisite.

'I'm a jeweller. The silver and gold are melted down and intertwined for ever. They can't be separated.' She held the ring up towards Loxton.

'It's beautiful,' Loxton said.

'They'll find him,' Webb said to Talbot. 'That's their job. We've got to let them do their job.'

Talbot looked at her friend and leaned back into the armchair, wrapping her arms around herself. She began to rock back and forth.

'We'll be in contact, Julia,' Loxton said. 'And if anything changes, we'll call you right away. I'm sure he's fine.' Loxton found herself telling the lie while thinking of what she'd already found. Lying was second nature to her. Eight years in the police had trained her well. She'd lied to the dying, promising them that everything would be all right, that they'd see their loved ones again. She lied to suspects, coaxing them to put their knives down, promising them she'd do her best to stop them from getting locked up. Lying was the bread and butter of her job.

Loxton headed towards the door.

Talbot stood up, as if to say something, but whatever it was, she thought better of it. Loxton had the nagging feeling that she wasn't the only one holding things back. Talbot was hiding things too.

Chapter 4

Julia Talbot

Sunday

I turned back to my strange party of guests.

David, uncomfortable in the corner of my living room, every few seconds checking his mobile as he sheltered beside the bookcase.

Elizabeth was wringing her hands, terrified, and kept looking at Charles. Lucy was looking at me, her eyes full of concern. I could tell she had so much she wanted to say, but not in front of the others.

I hated this.

Should I have told the police? It had nothing to do with Mark disappearing and would just confuse things, bringing suspicion on me that I didn't need.

'It's going to be all right.' Lucy patted my arm. I felt like I didn't have room to breathe. 'He'll be back soon.'

I nodded my head a little to stop her going on. That policewoman had looked concerned when she'd come back into the living room, as if she'd found something bad. What had she seen?

'Try to drink some tea.' Lucy pushed the mug towards me. She'd put extra sugar in it, which made it too sweet. I sipped it anyway, but it made my stomach churn more.

'Did the police talk to you, David?' I asked.

'Yeah, they just asked me a few pointless questions. They think he'll be back by tomorrow.' David shrugged.

'Did they say that?' I stared into his face searching for some sort of reassurance. I'd heard raised voices and seen David's face when he'd come back into the room. He hadn't looked happy.

'Not exactly, but they implied it. They thought I knew where he was, as if I have a clue.' He shook his head and rubbed his forehead with his fingertips, screwing up his eyes for a second. Then the old David was back as he ran his fingers through his hair.

'They think he's just gone off somewhere?' Elizabeth looked desperate.

'Well, I guess it happens a lot.' David shrugged again. 'There's a lot of pressure with these weddings . . .' David wouldn't look at me. He focused on Elizabeth.

'If I just knew he was all right . . .' I looked at the gold and silver band in my palm. I remembered melting them together on my kiln in my workshop and watching as it changed from burning red molten metal into a shining promise. Where had it gone so wrong?

'What shall we do now?' David asked. He was eager to get away from us all. Knock back a drink and forget all about it for the rest of the evening. I knew how he worked.

'You'll do the same as you always do.' *Pretend it's not happening.* I didn't say the last part aloud. Instead I closed my hand around the ring.

'What does that mean?' David stared at me, making me uncomfortable.

'If you'd told someone yesterday that you couldn't get hold of him, the police would have had an extra day to find him.' I couldn't hide my frustration.

'You can't blame *me* for this?' David pointed at his chest, as if I could be talking about someone else.

'Julia.' Elizabeth shot me a look. 'It's not about blame.'

'We should have been married by now.' I tried to hold in the tears.

'It's not my fault he's run off,' David said.

'What makes you so sure he's run off?' I couldn't contain my anger. He was keeping things from me, I just knew it.

David shrugged. 'What else could have happened? He's not in a coma in a hospital – Elizabeth's called them all. He's not been kidnapped by aliens.'

'Stop it.' Lucy stood up and looked at David and then me. 'This isn't helping anyone.'

She was right. She was always right. Arguing wasn't going to make this any easier. I couldn't look at him or any of them.

'It's been a long day,' Lucy said. 'Everyone's exhausted. Perhaps we should all try to get some rest? We're going to need to be strong for tomorrow.' She caught my eye and I nodded back at her.

Elizabeth snorted. 'I won't be getting any rest tonight, I can assure you. I won't sleep again until I know he's all right.'

'I agree we should call it a night.' There was David, pouncing on the chance to escape. It was fine by me; I couldn't stand to be around him.

'There's not much else we can do here now.' Charles was fidgeting with his mobile. 'I should go to the office, make some more calls. Make sure no one's heard anything. If there's any news, we can call each other straight away.'

David left first. He didn't wait for a cab – just walked out into the chill summer evening.

'Elizabeth, I can make up the bed in the spare room if you like?' I prayed that she'd decline. I wanted some space to breathe and to talk to Lucy in private.

'I can stay over.' Elizabeth's face softened. 'I wouldn't want you to be on your own.'

'I was planning on staying, so she won't be on her own,' Lucy said. 'If that's all right?'

'I don't mind,' I said. An embarrassed silence filled the room. 'You . . . you can both stay.'

'I'm going to the office,' Charles said. 'Make sure I haven't missed anything. Julia, the police will find him. Don't worry. Come on, Elizabeth, Lucy will look after her.' He nodded at Lucy, grateful that he didn't have to try to comfort me anymore.

I waved to them as their taxi pulled away, like I had a hundred times before. It was as if they were leaving after one of their brief visits. I shut the front door and turned around, but it wasn't Mark standing behind me in the hallway, it was Lucy. Her face was wan and her eyes sad. She put her arms out and I let her hug me, but I felt crowded.

'Where the hell *is* he?' I shrugged her off and went back into the living room, but I couldn't miss the hurt on her face. 'I can't believe this is happening.'

She followed me with her arms dangling by her sides. 'I know. It's crazy.'

'I'm sorry. I just miss him so much.' I sank into the sofa and wrapped my arms around me, wishing they were Mark's.

'It's going to be all right.' She sat next to me.

I pulled a face at her. I was tired of people telling me that when they had no idea if it was true.

Lucy sighed. She could see the tenseness in my

shoulders. The old worry. 'None of them know us now,' she said quietly.

'But they could have found me.' I tried to make her listen, but her face had closed down. She wouldn't look at me.

'You changed your name,' Lucy said. 'They can't find you.'

'You only changed your first name. They could have found me through you.' I pressed my palms into my temples to try to stop the banging in my head. Had Mark known before the wedding? Is that why it had all gone so wrong?

'You're being paranoid. No one will think we're still friends, not after all these years.' Her brow furrowed, but then it softened. 'I'm going to run you a hot bath. It's going to be okay, I promise.'

I was glad she was here with me. Without her I'd feel so alone. I caught a glimpse of myself in the wall mirror. I looked bizarre: sat in my living room, the lace trail of my wedding dress cascading around me, my make-up smeared. I noticed that my hands were balled into fists, as if expecting a fight.

I opened them and there, in the middle of my left palm, was my wedding band. No longer needed. I slipped it on anyway, next to my engagement ring; a perfect fit.

Chapter 5

Alana Loxton

Sunday

The police station was deserted. The corridors were black in front of Loxton, the lights flickering on as an afterthought as she and Kowalski set off the motion sensors.

One solitary corner of the CID office was lit, with four detectives huddled together, a stack of prisoner case files between them. They were the late-turn shift. They looked up as Loxton and Kowalski walked past.

'Nothing for you guys. Don't look so worried, Kanwar,' Kowalski said.

'Are you guys early turn?' Kanwar asked.

'Yeah, we've still got a bit to do,' Kowalski said. 'Is Winter here?'

'Even on a Sunday he's still here.' Kanwar pointed in the direction of Winter's office and went back to quarrelling with his team-mates.

Loxton hesitated at Winter's door. How was he going to react when she told him that this was looking less and less like a groom who'd gone walkabout?

'What's wrong?' Kowalski said.

'If it were up to me, we wouldn't have gone there. We'd have left it to uniform.'

'Well, we can't worry about all the "what ifs" and the "maybes" in this job. Reality keeps us busy enough.' He reached over her and knocked on the door.

'Come in,' Winter said.

Kowalski motioned for her to go first, and Loxton pushed open the door.

'Has he turned up yet?' Winter asked. The shadows under his eyes had grown.

'No, sir,' Loxton said. 'You were right. There's more to this case than a runaway groom.'

'Take a seat.' Winter leaned back in his chair, settling himself in for the story.

'I found a hidden mobile,' Loxton said.

'Is it his work one?' Winter asked.

'No, we've identified Rowthorn's work mobile – it's an iPhone. This one was taped under the bottom of a drawer in his bedroom. There was an unread message displayed on the screen. I saw it when I accidently knocked it.' Not true – there was nothing accidental about it. She'd been praying the phone was unlocked, but Winter didn't need to worry about every little misdemeanour that happened on a case.

'What did it say?' Winter didn't break eye contact with her.

'It said: "*I know what you did and you're going to burn.*"'

'Can I see this message?'

'The phone's locked, sir. After a few seconds the message disappeared and it won't come back up now. The mobile could be Julia Talbot's, although she denied ever seeing it before when I showed it to her.'

'What did the family say about the message?'

'We haven't told them yet.'

'Good. Let's see what we've got first before we go scaring them. They're all potential suspects at this stage anyway. I want that mobile taken to the lab and downloaded. Let's establish that it's Mark Rowthorn's and that that message was meant for him. In fact, take his work mobile and laptop too.'

'I'll do it now.' Loxton stood up.

'Not you. Get someone on the late shift to do that. I want you and Kowalski to go to his workplace first thing tomorrow morning. He works at City Enterprises in Canary Wharf. The managing director there is Timothy Benson. Poke around. If the message isn't from a family member, then maybe a work colleague We could be looking at someone trying to gain access to the bank through Rowthorn or we could be back to the runaway groom scenario. Go with an open mind.'

'Yes, sir.'

'I'll chase the intel department. Nothing's coming back on him yet, but they might not have done the full works. Something's not adding up here.' Winter glanced out of the dark window. 'This isn't going to be solved by morning. The Commander is not going to be happy tomorrow.'

'Have you pinged his outstanding personal mobile, sir, to try to see where he is? He must have it on him.' She couldn't help herself – she had to check everything was being done. She was used to directing cases.

'Triangulation of a mobile is expensive, Loxton. But I should be able to convince the superintendent with this threat and the fact that he's now been missing for over twenty-four hours. How the super will feel about a phone call at ten to midnight on a Sunday, though, I'm not so sure . . .' Winter looked tired. She realized that he must spend most of his time knocking on closed doors, only to be told there were no more resources coming anytime soon.

'Are you going to call the homicide team?' Loxton's throat tightened, making her voice sound strange. She wasn't ready to see her old team again so soon.

'No, Loxton. He could still have done a runner. I'll need a lot more than what we've got if we're to push it their way.'

'Of course.' The tension left her shoulders. 'But would he have left the secret phone behind if he'd *chosen* to disappear?'

'Maybe he had to leave in a hurry, or he's scared he'd be tracked through it,' Winter said. 'I'll assemble a team first thing. You two get yourselves off home now.'

She headed towards the door. 'Sir, there's one other thing.' She turned back to him. 'The best man's hiding something. He was cagey.' Winter looked at Kowalski.

Kowalski nodded once. 'Whether it's significant, we don't know yet, boss. I got the impression that he was on Rowthorn's side though.'

'Time will tell,' Winter said. 'Dismissed.'

Chapter 6

Jenny Hughes

Monday 24 July 2000

Last week at school, before the summer holidays started, Jonny had passed me a note telling me to meet him here. I'd been waiting for today all last week. I still had the crumpled note in my pocket. Maybe he'd ask me to be his girlfriend? All the other girls in my class would be so jealous when I went back to school.

I'd just known something was going to ruin it, though. Rachel.

'Is that all you've got?' Jonny glared at Rachel. We were all hot and bothered. We'd found shelter from the sun under some trees at the beginning of the wood, but the summer heat was relentless. Sweat stuck my turquoise T-shirt to the small of my back.

Jonny examined a green yoyo from Rachel's treasure pile. She'd won it at last year's summer fair. He tossed it back onto the pile. 'It's all crappy kids' stuff. How old are you anyway? Four?'

'I'm nearly seven.' Rachel's voice was small.

Jonny's hair was shaven and he was twice her size. Rachel was quiet around him; normally she never shut up.

'I don't want your baby toys.' He turned away from her and glanced at me. It was meant to be just the two of us, but I'd got lumbered with babysitting Rachel at the last minute. I'd begged Kayleigh to look after her for a few hours, so Jonny and I could be alone, but Kayleigh had refused and gone off to the shops. She didn't like Jonny.

'Please, I want to see where the children went missing,' Rachel whined. I still couldn't look at her without feeling resentful.

'I don't care.' Jonny pushed the toys towards Rachel. 'This is all shit.'

Rachel pulled Buzz Lightyear out of her pocket; it was her favourite toy after Bunny.

Jonny snatched Buzz Lightyear and turned the toy around in his tanned hands. 'I could get something for this. Holding out on me, eh? You're not as dumb as you look.' He pocketed the figurine and then glanced at me. 'Jenny, it's up to you if I take her?'

'Jenny, please can we go?' Rachel pulled at my arm, pleading.

'Don't be such a spoilt baby.' I shrugged her off. Her bottom lip trembled and I rolled my eyes, remembering too late that I was trying to be a better big sister. It was so hard when she was such a pain. 'Okay, but if you ever tell Mum and Dad, they'll never let you out again, or me. Understand?' Rachel looked like she was about to explode with excitement.

Jonny scooped up the toys, but I reached my hand out to stop him taking Bunny. For a moment our hands touched, and it felt electric. Rachel's face fell as she watched him pocket her treasured toys, but she snatched Bunny and held him tightly to her chest.

'What do you know about the children going missing?'
Jonny said.

'It was years ago, before we were born.' I shifted my
weight to the other side, so that I could better keep a
watch of the tree line where the wood began. It made
me nervous being this close.

'The children were all murdered in there.' Jonny pointed
towards the wood.

Rachel let out a squeal and clasped her hands over her
mouth. Why did she have to scream?

'She's too young,' Jonny said. 'You should take her
home.'

'No, she's fine.' Rachel was ruining everything. 'You
want to hear, don't you, Rachel?'

Rachel nodded, her hands still covering her mouth.

Jonny paused for a moment, considering, and then
leaned into our little circle. 'My uncle was in one of the
girls' classes at high school. He heard everything about
it. He told me everyone in the village was looking for
them. The police found them a week later.'

'Were they all right?' Rachel asked.

'Of course they weren't, you stupid baby. They'd been
murdered.' Jonny shook his head at her in irritation.

'Sorry.' Rachel looked at her trainers.

'All three bodies were by the brook. The oldest girl
was laid on her front, the top half of her body in the
water. She was completely naked. The policemen lifted
her out of the water and laid her down on the grass.
When they turned her over, one of the coppers threw
up.'

'Why?' I shivered despite the heat of the day.

'Her face was black and twisted in a silent scream.
She'd been burnt.'

Rachel let out a sob. I patted her arm. 'You wanted to hear what happened . . .'

Rachel sniffed and controlled her crying, nodding roughly.

Jonny leaned in closer to us. 'White flowers had been scattered around her body. Their petals were bright against the girl's burnt skin.' He finished, intoning the details like a campfire ghost story.

'What had happened to her?' My stomach was light, and my body was tensing.

'The police said she'd been set alight, her friends strangled to death beside her. Some sort of satanical sacrifice.'

'That's horrible.' I held Rachel's hand. She clung on tightly, her other hand wrapped around Bunny's neck.

'People said angels had laid the flowers around her, but others said that the killer did it.'

'Did they ever catch him?' Rachel asked.

We huddled into a tighter circle despite the heat, desperate not to miss a word.

'Police didn't have a clue,' Jonny said. 'No fingerprints or anything like that. Some people said a demon did it.'

We breathed out all at once.

'It wasn't a demon,' I said.

'But the angels . . .' Rachel said. I tried not to roll my eyes at her. She still really believed in all that God stuff. I'd stopped going to church last year. Mum was still furious with me.

'There's no such thing as angels or demons,' Jonny said. 'That's just shit they tell you to make you behave.'

'There are angels.' Rachel glared at him. I felt my face flush red with embarrassment. He'd think my family were bible-bashers.

'Grow up,' Jonny said. 'Santa's not real either.' Rachel glowered at him as her lower lip trembled.

'Santa's real,' I whispered reassuringly and squeezed her hand to calm her down before she became inconsolable and I'd have to take her home.

'People say the children's ghosts still wander the woods, waiting for their killer to be caught,' Jonny said.

'We should help them,' Rachel said. 'I bet we can solve the murder and set them free.'

Jonny craned his neck to look behind him towards Ashurst Wood. 'My uncle saw two of them walking through the forest. He called out to them and they vanished.' He lunged forward into the circle and we shrieked. Jonny barked out a laugh. It wasn't funny, but I laughed along with him anyway.

'It's all bollocks though,' he said. 'My uncle drinks too much.'

The wood was bathed in sunlight and it seemed impossible that anything bad had happened there.

'I want to go and help them.' Rachel clapped her hands together.

'I can show you where they died,' Jonny said.

I turned towards Rachel and frowned to try to look serious. 'You won't tell anyone that we went into the woods, will you?'

'Never,' Rachel said.

'Swear on Bunny's life.' I folded my arms and waited. Rachel looked at her blue-and-white polka-dot bunny. It was a big ask.

'If you tell, Bunny will get it.' Jonny thrust a finger towards Rachel's face.

'I swear on my life and Bunny's.' Rachel placed her hand on her heart, her face serious. I tried not to laugh.

'Okay,' I said firmly. Once I made my mind up, I stuck to it. If Rachel got scared, it was her own fault.

We climbed over the rickety fence that separated the playing fields from the wood. It felt dangerous, exciting. I peered into the darkness between the trees. A branch moved and a dark shape darted just out of sight. My eyes became blurry as I stared without blinking, trying to see if it moved again. The sun was too bright. I had to close my eyes, and when I opened them again, the shadow was gone; it might never have been there.

'Is it safe?' Rachel asked me.

'You're with me, aren't you?' Jonny was getting away. 'Come on, we don't want to get left behind.' Rachel had to run to keep up with me. I kept looking back, scared I'd lose her. I grabbed her hand. Jonny ran so fast.

Jonny stopped and opened his arms. 'This is where it happened.' He was enjoying being the guide and I was enjoying being led by him.

A brook flowed in front of us, noisy and angry. He pointed to a willow that hung over the water, its branches forming a green cage. 'Right there's where they found the girls. Any clues of who killed them will be here. Come on. The light won't last for ever.' Jonny grabbed a stick and started poking it into the river, mud swirling to the surface.

I started searching the riverbed near him. The water sparkled and I saw a fish dart away from Jonny's stick. Rachel came bustling over to me, wanting to help me look.

'Go find your own spot.' I shoved her away and she sloped off. It was just me and Jonny. Just like I wanted it to be. Butterflies fluttered inside my stomach.

Chapter 7

Alana Loxton

Monday

Mr Benson wore an expensive black suit with a white handkerchief in his top pocket. To one side of his oak desk were three plasma monitors, with graphs fluctuating like snakes in a basket. A set of crystal glasses and a decanter stood on a small desk to Loxton's side filled with dark blood-red liquid. The wine probably cost more than her monthly salary.

Loxton smoothed the cheap grey linen of her own suit and fussed with the cuffs of her cream blouse. Kowalski threw her a sideways glance, and she told herself to relax. People with money always made her nervous.

'I understand this is something to do with one of my employees,' Benson said. 'A Mark Rowthorn?'

'Do you know him?' Loxton leaned in closer.

'I'm the CEO of this bank.' Benson tilted his head kindly, as if he was explaining something to a child. 'I don't know every employee personally.'

'He was reported missing yesterday,' Loxton said. 'He never made it to his wedding.'

Benson froze momentarily, then nodded quickly. 'Missing? That's strange.'

'Do you have any idea what's happened to him?' Loxton asked.

Benson paused for a moment, weighing up his options. 'Anything from drink-drive to a pub brawl. My employees work hard, and they party hard too. I've had a few dealings with the police regarding the odd stray employee who ended up on the wrong side of the law. Missing is different though.'

'Do Mark's employee records show any issues?' Loxton knew it was a long shot, but they had to ask.

Benson tapped on his keyboard and scanned the screen. 'His last year's review was very good indeed.'

'No arguments with anyone?' Kowalski asked. 'No disagreements with clients?'

'Mark's an investment banker and we only employ the best here. We don't have disagreements with clients. He appears to be a very well-liked colleague.'

'We'll need his records,' Loxton said.

'I'm afraid I can't hand over employee records. We have strict policies, and there's the Data Protection Act. I can assure you, though, I've had a look, and there is nothing of interest to you in there.'

'Could I speak with his direct line manager? It would help us a great deal.'

'He's away on his summer holiday.' Benson shrugged his shoulders and gave her a sympathetic smile. 'Mark was about to get married, you say. Perhaps this is more of a domestic issue?'

Loxton frowned. Benson didn't want them poking around. He'd forced her hand. 'Mr Benson, if you don't co-operate, I can go to a court and get an order to force you to let us look at his records. But all of that wastes precious time, which Mark Rowthorn might not have, and it draws unnecessary attention to your bank, wouldn't you agree?'

Benson pressed his lips together. He regarded her as if he was trying to weigh up if she was serious. 'Look, this is completely confidential,' he said finally. 'I don't want this spread across the newspapers.'

'Of course,' she said.

He stared at her a moment longer and then sighed. 'We've been having some issues.'

'Issues?'

Benson nodded but dropped his gaze. 'We'd started to suspect some insider trading, which is of course illegal, but we didn't have any proof. Then the regulator brought it to our attention and Mark Rowthorn's name came up, along with a couple of others.'

'Which other names?' She tried to keep her voice calm.

'The other people have been ruled out.' Benson folded his arms. 'They're not relevant.'

'But who were they?' Loxton asked.

Benson shook his head in annoyance.

'Mr Benson, we need to know. One of your employees linked to this has gone missing.'

'Fine, but this is off the record. It was a Duncan Etherington, a David Steele and a Meredith Shaw. But there's no evidence to prove they had anything to do with it.'

Loxton sat up straighter at the mention of David Steele's name. She remembered the whispered conversation they'd overheard at Talbot's flat, how he'd been evasive when she'd asked him what it was about. What was it he'd said exactly? He'd promised someone that he wasn't going to mention something to the police. 'Are you sure those three employees have been completely ruled out?'

'They just worked on some of the mergers that Mark

Rowthorn did, and we've eliminated them from the investigation. Mark Rowthorn is the only one who's worked on every single merger where inside trading is suspected. His own private trading makes interesting reading too.'

'How much money are we talking?' Kowalski raised his eyebrows.

'Well, it's very difficult to say at this stage.' Benson dropped his voice slightly and leaned closer towards them, as if worried someone might overhear. 'We could be talking hundreds of thousands, maybe even more. Mark Rowthorn has a few investments, and they may be perfectly legal, but we're working with the regulators to establish if there was any wrongdoing.'

'Have you reported this to the police?'

'We are still conducting the internal investigation. At this stage it's more intelligence than evidence. We tend to go to the police only when we have something concrete to pass on to them.'

'Did Rowthorn know about the investigation?'

'I don't think so,' Benson said. 'Like I said, it was only intelligence that the regulator passed to us, and we like to eliminate innocent parties before we start taking action. As you can imagine, banks survive on their reputations, and we don't want to cause unnecessary damage if there's just been a simple misunderstanding.'

'Can you send us what you have?' She passed him her card with her email address on it.

'Yes, of course, but it's not a great deal at this stage.' Benson took her card and placed it on his desk without looking at it.

'Does Mark Rowthorn have life insurance?' Kowalski asked.

'Yes, I believe he does. All our staff do. We offer a very good package.'

'Who is listed as his benefactor?'

Benson turned to his computer and typed into the keyboard, studying the computer for a moment. 'A Miss Julia Talbot. She would receive Mark Rowthorn's life insurance pay-out in the event of his death. But that isn't the scenario we're looking at, is it?' Benson looked worried.

'There's nothing to suggest that at this stage,' Loxton said. 'How much would that pay-out be?'

Mr Benson looked uncomfortable. 'Well, our standard is four hundred thousand, and I can see that's the package Mark Rowthorn has opted for.'

Loxton tried not to look so surprised. That was one life insurance package. 'Mr Benson, have any threats or demands been made to the bank?'

'None. We have strict policies in place with regard to kidnapping scenarios. The first thing we would do, of course, is call the police. Is there anything to suggest kidnapping?'

'No, not at all,' Loxton said. 'I just like to cover all bases.'

'An employee disappearing is of great concern. Please keep me updated.' Mr Benson stood up. 'Now, I have some meetings scheduled that I can't miss. My PA will show you out.' Mr Benson pressed the intercom for his PA and smiled at Loxton, but was obviously desperate for them to leave.

'Thank you for your time.' Loxton stood up, it was clear Mr Benson wasn't going to help any further.

Loxton had trouble keeping up with Benson's PA, an attractive woman with red hair in a tight bun and four-inch black patent heels, clattering a few metres ahead of them.

'Do you think Benson's hiding anything?' Loxton whispered to Kowalski.

'You'd hope not,' Kowalski whispered back. 'But you're right, Benson doesn't want us poking around.' Kowalski nodded towards their escort, who was striding ahead but kept glancing back to make sure they hadn't wandered.

They reached the shiny lifts and the secretary turned to smile at them as she pushed the button.

Loxton decided to try her luck. 'Mr Benson said we could borrow a meeting room to interview a few employees this morning about an incident. Would you mind finding us a free one?'

The PA frowned but then nodded and showed them to a glass side room. 'Please, take a seat. We'll start with you, if you're free?'

'Of course.' The PA took her time sitting down, glancing at the door as if someone might come to rescue her.

'Could you tell us your name, please?'

'Emily Hart.' The PA glanced towards Mr Benson's office, unsure.

'Do you know Mark Rowthorn?' Loxton asked.

'Yes, he works in this office. He's one of the brokers.'

'He's been reported missing.'

'Is he all right?' Hart bit her lip, she looked genuinely concerned.

'We don't know yet, I'm afraid,' Loxton said.

'Mr Benson told us Mark was missing and that the police would be coming. He told us not to talk to you.' She motioned behind her towards the open-plan office. 'No one wants to be involved in this; they're all distancing themselves from Mark.'

'What do you think might have happened to him?' Loxton said.

'Did Mr Benson tell you Mark was about to be sacked?' Hart kept her voice low. She threw glances at the people in the office. Loxton was glad her back faced the office. It meant only Loxton and Kowalski could see the fear in her eyes.

'He said Mark was under investigation,' Loxton said. 'That it was at the early stages.'

She laughed bitterly and shook her head. 'Typical Benson. Look, please don't tell anyone I spoke with you. I could lose my job.'

'Any information, however small, might be what we need to find him. And we will do our best to keep anything you tell us confidential.' Kowalski was on full charm initiative, tilting his head in sympathy.

Hart nodded at Kowalski in appreciation. 'Thank you. Mark was known around here for being reckless. He took big risks, but he always got high rewards. His nickname was "the Legend" but his luck ran out in the last couple of months. A few bad deals. The company completed a review and discovered that he might have been involved in some insider trading. Maybe even laundering money. They take that very seriously. It damages their reputation, and what with the current banking climate . . .'

'How much money overall?' Loxton tried to keep her voice level. They were getting somewhere.

'Even Mr Benson doesn't know how much. They're still investigating. It will be hundreds of thousands for the regulators to have noticed. Mark was about to face a disciplinary board.'

'Did Mark know?'

'Mark was distraught about it, said he'd been set up, but there was nothing he could do. Once the management have any doubts about you, it's impossible to keep on working here.' Hart looked close to tears.

'How long have you known Mark?' Loxton wondered how close she was to him. He seemed to have confided in her.

'We've both been at the company for years.' She closed her eyes for a moment. 'Around six years. I've been here longer than him.'

'Why do you think Mr Benson didn't tell us Mark knew he was facing a disciplinary board?'

'Mark's father has already called here asking Benson if he'd seen Mark. The company wants to distance itself from whatever's happened. They don't want to be blamed if Mark's done something . . . stupid.'

'Benson's thinking suicide?' Loxton said.

Hart began to weep and covered her face with her hands. She managed a quick nod as she tried to gain composure.

'Thank you, Emily,' Loxton said. 'You've saved us a lot of time. And what was your relationship with Mark, if you don't mind me asking?' Loxton said.

'We were friends.' Hart's tears dried up and she folded her arms across her chest defensively. 'I've already told you that.'

Loxton nodded and handed Hart her card.

Hart stood up to leave but paused. 'I'm worried about him. All that money missing and now he's disappeared. I know he was having financial problems. He'd asked his father for money, but Charles said no because he'd already given Mark twenty thousand towards the wedding. God, poor Mark.' She clenched her fists and looked down. Loxton felt Hart might be more involved than she was letting on.

'We're doing our best to find him.' Kowalski stood up.

Hart nodded, wiping the tears from her face. 'Please tell me when you find him.'

'Of course,' Loxton said as she showed her out.

After another hour of interviewing City Enterprises employees, they had got no further. They had learnt Rowthorn had a talent for downing pints and was gregarious and well-liked by his colleagues. None of them had a bad word to say about him. And none of them knew what could have happened to him

Once they were out of the impressive building, Loxton felt herself relax at last. She waited until no one was near them and turned to Kowalski. 'I couldn't work out who was trying to protect themselves more: Benson or Hart.'

Kowalski nodded at her. 'None of his other colleagues mentioned the insider trading. Rowthorn seems to have only confided in her.'

'She was either in on it or she and Rowthorn were more than just friends. We should get intel checks done on her and keep an eye on her in case Rowthorn makes contact.'

Kowalski nodded. 'And let's see if the fiancée knows anything about the insider trading.'

Chapter 8

Julia Talbot

Monday

There was a buzzing in my head that kept repeating. It took me a minute to realize it was the phone.

I'd been staring at photos on Mark's Missing Person page on Facebook. I'd spent all afternoon creating it. I'd chosen an image of him where he was smiling his lopsided grin, the one that had made my heart melt. Had I picked that one just to torture myself? I didn't know how long I'd been staring at his face for. It was nearly six in the evening. Lucy should have been back from work. I hated being on my own right now.

I closed the laptop lid. I couldn't bear to see Mark staring at me anymore, his eyes seeming to accuse me from whichever angle I looked at him.

The phone was still ringing. I heaved myself up and lifted the receiver.

'Hello, Mr Rowthorn?' A female voice. She sounded mid-twenties.

'He's not here.' Why was this woman calling our landline? I felt the old suspicions rise.

'We need to speak with him urgently.' The woman sounded official.

'I'm his fiancée, Julia Talbot. What's this about?'

'Ah, Miss Talbot. It's regarding the missed mortgage payments. I'm afraid we have no alternative but to send out a court summons to you both.' Her voice sounded strained.

'A court summons?' I pulled the receiver closer to my ear. Had I misheard her?

'Yes. To repossess the property. The mortgage is quite clear: if you fail to make the repayments, we can repossess the flat. And you've missed seven.'

'But there must be a mistake. We're overpaying our mortgage every month.' The receiver was slippery in my hand. Anger bubbled up inside me. She must be wrong. This was the last thing I needed right now.

'We've been very patient, but you've failed to make any repayments for the past seven months.'

'That can't be right.' My heart thudded hard in my chest.

There was a long silence.

'How much are we behind?' My throat was tight, my voice small.

'Twelve thousand and seventy-five pounds.'

'You must be mistaken.' My voice came out as a whisper. It felt like my throat was closing up. How could we be in so much debt? Mark had never said a word.

'I'm afraid I'm correct. The summons will be sent today, but we wanted to forewarn you.'

'I didn't know about any of this. Why has no one contacted me?' I asked.

'We have been sending letters to your address in both your names.'

I hadn't seen a mortgage statement for over a year. I just thought they'd gone paperless, like everything else. Mark must have been hiding them from me. Hiding all of this from me. I felt sick. When had the lies started? Now I knew why he'd wanted the wedding to be on a Sunday, why he was trying to save money here and there.

'I didn't know about this. Please, can't I just renegotiate the payments with you now?' What was I going to pay with? I'd gone into my overdraft paying for the honeymoon and my credit cards were maxed out on the wedding items which I'd not budgeted for correctly. When anyone mentioned a wedding, the price doubled.

'You'll have to do that at the court hearing. Unless you can pay the outstanding amount now.'

'I can't pay it today,' I said. 'It'll take me a bit of time to get the money together.'

'Miss Talbot, I suggest you and Mr Rowthorn work out what you can afford and attend court for the hearing, which will be next Monday. The details will be on the court summons.'

She hung up on me, leaving me alone in my beautiful home which was about to be taken from me. I'd worked so hard to make this new life, to survive my past, and now it was all being ripped from me.

I dropped the phone back on its stand, but it went crashing to the floor. My hands shook with fear. Mark had been lying to me. How could he do this to us? And what had he been doing with the money I gave him each month for my part of the mortgage? My mind was racing through questions. I was so angry with him, but I felt sick with fear for him too.

I thought I'd be lying on a beach right now, sun rays soaking into my skin, my head on Mark's chest, his arms wrapped around me. Instead he was gone.

The phone – it was off the hook. I scrabbled for it, banging my elbow as I flung the receiver back onto its holder. What if the police called with information?

I froze. What if they called to say they'd found him – dead? I tried not to retch. I opened a window but the air outside was as warm as inside the flat.

There was a rapping at the door, and my whole body jolted. I took deep breaths in and tried to calm myself.

In my head I wished it was Mark. My Mark. Not this new Mark who lied to me. He'd be standing there, giving me that crooked smile of his. I'd know everything would be all right.

The rapping became a banging. I pulled myself up but the urge to be sick strengthened and I rested against the sofa to wait for my stomach to steady. The knocking continued, and I managed to reach the door, but my hand was shaking as I struggled to turn the latch.

It was Lucy.

'Where have you been? You said you'd be back at five,' I said.

'I told you, I was getting supplies. You need some dinner. You didn't eat anything yesterday,' Lucy said. 'I tried to be as fast as I could.' She dumped two straining carrier bags onto the floor. 'I got you some microwave meals.'

'Thanks.' I couldn't think of anything worse. A fresh wave of sickness hit me.

'I know, I know, but they're easy and it beats my cooking.' She pulled out a bottle of merlot but stopped in her tracks. 'I thought this might help, but you look awful. You should sit down.'

'The bank wants to repossess my flat.' I moved over to the sofa and sank into it.

'What?' Lucy sat down next to me, leaving the shopping by the door, a look of disbelief on her face.

'Mark's not been paying the mortgage.' I covered my face with my hands and shook my head. Saying it to Lucy made it real. 'We owe twelve thousand pounds. I don't have twelve thousand pounds. We hadn't even finished paying for the wedding and Mark didn't take out any wedding insurance.'

Lucy leaned over the sofa, grabbing the merlot from the shopping, and twisted the cap off the bottle. She poured some into the nearest mug and thrust it into my hand.

'How can you be behind on your mortgage repayments?' Lucy frowned at me. I could almost see her mind spinning behind her eyes. 'I thought he was loaded. And what about Julia's Jewellery? I thought you said your business was booming?'

'I thought so too . . . But I let Mark deal with all the finances.' I held my breath, hoping Lucy would help.

'You don't know about your finances?' The accountant in her was horrified. 'But you're a businesswoman?'

'Mark's the banker. That's more his strength.' It sounded weak when I said it out loud. I'd trusted him completely at the beginning. I'd never thought he was capable of lying like this.

'I told you to keep your accounts separate.' She shook her head. 'You're running a business; you need to keep on top of this.'

'We do have separate accounts. I just used to send him money each month for the mortgage.' I shrugged at her.

Lucy's usually carefree face was now creased with worry. 'I told you to do things properly. You should have paid the bank direct. What the hell's he been doing?' She looked angry, but she was doing her best to suppress it.

'I don't know, but just please stop.' I covered my ears with my hands.

She patted my arm quickly, seeing I was at breaking point. 'Don't worry, we'll find a way like we always do.'

I lowered my hands and tried not to cry.

'I'm sorry,' she said. 'I know how hard all this is for you.'

'How can you?' I said. 'Because James works abroad a lot? It's not just that I miss him because he's gone off on some business trip. He's *disappeared*. *Gone*. And he might never come back.' I felt bad for snapping at her, but I felt so useless.

'I'm sorry, stupid choice of words.' She poured herself some wine and took a swig. 'The police will find him.' She nodded firmly. I wished I could have her confidence.

'I keep thinking what could have happened to him.' And what had he done with our money?

'You'll drive yourself crazy doing that.' She sipped her wine, watching me carefully over the mug.

'What if someone has done this?' I played with the mug handle, unable to make eye contact with her.

'What do you mean?'

'Someone could have hurt him.'

'Who would want to hurt Mark?' she asked.

'No one.' I wanted to hurt him for lying about the money. I sloshed the red wine around my mug, watching it rise and fall like waves on a blood-red ocean. 'But there's plenty of people who might want to hurt me.' I stopped playing with my mug and looked at her.

'Like who?' She folded her arms across her chest, daring me to say the name out loud.

'Jonny.' She had to see; it made perfect sense. 'Jonny could have done this.' It'd been years since we'd talked about him. I'd tried to push him away, but I heard him in my head shouting at me from across the courtroom: '*You'll get yours.*'

'Why would he come for you now, after all these years?' She leaned closer to me as our voices became whispers.

'He was only released last year. Maybe all this time he's been waiting for revenge.' My throat felt suddenly dry, making it hard to say the words. 'Jonny might have taken Mark because of me.'

'This isn't your fault.' She put the mug of wine on the coffee table, placing her hand on top of mine. I jerked it away from her.

'We need to find out where Jonny is now. Make sure he isn't involved.' My stomach twisted in fear.

'No. You're exhausted, that's all this is. Forget about Jonny. He's still dangerous. People like that never change. We should stay well away.'

I needed her to help me – she was the only one who could. She was the only other person who knew the truth. My eyes began to sting as tears filled them and I looked away from her.

'That's it.' Lucy dug into her bag and placed a packet of pink pills onto the white coffee table in front of me.

'What are they?' I asked, brushing the tears from my cheeks.

'They're sleeping tablets. You need a good night's sleep. You take two in the evening. If they don't work, you can take one more. They work wonders.'

'I don't want them.' I pushed them away.

'I know you don't, but you're scaring me,' she said.

'These aren't that strong. My doctor prescribed them when I had some trouble sleeping.'

'When was that?' She'd never told me. We told each other everything.

'A while ago.' She shrugged as she looked at the floor. 'It didn't go on for very long. Those pills did the trick.'

'Why didn't you tell me?'

'It was after you got engaged. You were so happy; I didn't want to drag you down.'

Lucy reached over the table and grabbed my hands. I'd been repeatedly hitting the sides of my head without even noticing. Concern made the fine lines around her eyes stand out.

'This is all such a mess,' I said. Mark was gone and part of me missed him, but the other part of me was furious at him. I thought I'd known him, but he could still surprise me, even when he was missing.

She released my hands slowly but kept hers near mine. 'I'm sure this has got nothing to do with Jonny and the police can't find out about any of that. Leave it in the past.'

'But what if it's important? What if it could help them find Mark?'

'Jonny's not involved, but even if he were, going to the police now would be the worst thing we could do. If it's Jonny, he'll make contact, he'll want to talk to you, and then you'll know. Then you should go to the police.' She looked into my eyes; hers were filled with anxiety.

'Okay.' I didn't want to have to think about Jonny again. He was dangerous. He could destroy me. I prayed he was just getting on with his life and would stay far away from mine.

'Your past has got nothing to do with Mark going

missing,' Lucy said. 'You shouldn't be punished for him going off and . . . well, whatever.' She looked away, embarrassed when she saw the hurt on my face.

I kept seeing him in my mind, lying on the floor alone, a deep gash on the back of his head. He was slipping away and I couldn't help him.

The phone rang and I jumped.

'Miss Talbot, it's DC Loxton. Would you be able to come into Walworth police station now?'

'To the police station?' My voice was unsteady. I hadn't been in a police station for a long time.

'Yes. We're creating a timeline of Mark's last movements. It's nothing to worry about; we're getting everyone's accounts.'

My mouth was dry.

'Julia, are you there?'

'Of . . . of course,' I stammered. 'Have you found anything?'

'We're working on it.'

'Yes, fine.' I looked at Lucy, hoping she'd go with me. She shook her head apologetically and mouthed '*work*' at me.

'Thank you, Julia.' The line went dead.

'I've got a voice conference in half an hour, sorry,' Lucy said. 'A client's insisted and we can't lose this one.'

'It's okay. They want me to go through my account again at the police station.' I wished she could come with me. 'It's just they always blame the spouse.' Although I wasn't even the spouse. We hadn't even managed to get married.

'Now you *are* being paranoid,' Lucy said. 'The police are just doing their job; I'm sure it's just routine.'

I nodded, but the tightness in my body didn't subside. I never thought I'd be interviewed by the police again.

Chapter 9

Julia Talbot

Monday

'Thank you for coming today.' Loxton had faint black circles under her eyes and her long chestnut hair was hastily thrown up in a loose ponytail. 'I know this is an awful time.'

'It is.' I tried to keep my voice steady, to hold back the tears.

'Please, take a seat.' Kowalski motioned to a faded blue plastic chair, which was screwed into the floor. An unwashed musty smell lingered in the windowless room. How could they bear this every day? I sank into the offered seat.

Kowalski turned on a digital recorder and the room flashed onto a tiny screen. I could see a tiny version of myself, small and alone on my side of the table. They were videoing me. The police had moved on since my last encounter with them.

'Am I a suspect?' *Why did I say that? Stupid.*

'No, of course not.' Kowalski looked surprised. 'You're a significant witness in a missing persons case. It's normal procedure to record your account at this stage.'

'Okay, sorry. I just don't know what I'm doing. This is all so strange.'

'That's all right,' Kowalski said. 'We know this is hard for you.'

'I don't want my face in the media. I couldn't bear them harassing me on top of everything else.'

'This video is just for the police,' Kowalski said. 'It's not for the press.'

'Can you stop the press knowing who I am?' I was clutching my hands together, turning my knuckles white. I had to keep my face out of the news.

'We can try, but we can't control the press,' Loxton said. 'I wish we could for you. I'm sorry.'

My heartbeat grew louder in my head and I tried to stop panicking.

'We'll see what we can do,' Kowalski said. 'Perhaps Charles Rowthorn would have some influence too?'

I nodded. It wasn't a bad idea. Charles and the police might be able to put enough pressure on the press so that they wouldn't release my photo or focus on me. I couldn't risk that happening.

'Are you okay to start the interview?' Loxton looked concerned.

'Of course. I want to help.'

'I need to explain a few legal things to you,' Loxton said. 'Anything you say today is being recorded and could be used as evidence in court in the future. You could be asked to attend court as a witness. If you deliberately mislead the police, you could be prosecuted for perverting the course of justice, which carries a lengthy sentence. Do you understand?'

This was getting serious fast. 'I want to help you. Why would I lie?'

'Do you understand?' she asked, her gaze unwavering.

'Of course.' Sweat trickled down the back of my neck. I resisted the urge to run.

'Sorry about that.' Loxton's posture relaxed and she smiled at me. The smile transformed her face, and I realized that she was quite beautiful. 'It's just something we have to make clear. Please, tell us about when you last saw Mark.'

'At about eleven the day before the wedding in our flat. He left to meet up with David.'

'What did you do then?' she asked.

'Lucy met me at the Silver Tree hotel in the afternoon. That's the hotel where I was going to get married.' It hurt to say that out loud. There was a long pause.

'What time was that?' Loxton said.

'Does that matter?' I didn't like her tone, the way she was scribbling everything down.

'We're trying to get a picture of where everyone was.' Kowalski leaned back in his seat, as if we were old friends catching up.

'Of course.' I was perched on the edge of the chair, my shoulders hunched up and aching with tension. I needed to relax, appear innocent. I forced myself to lean back, mimicking his body language, dropping my shoulders. No one suspected me of anything. 'I got there about two and Lucy met me a little after that, probably two-thirty.'

'Did you speak to Mark?' Kowalski said.

'No. I didn't want any bad luck.'

'Superstitious?' Kowalski asked.

'I know it's silly, but I've not had much luck. I always expect the worst.' I shook my head. None of this was coming out right. I was starting to sound like a crazy person.

'I understand,' Kowalski said. I hated that. How could he understand?

'What did you and Lucy do then?' Loxton asked.

'Ok, well, I unpacked my things. Double-checked everything. I tried the dress on again to be sure there were no problems, like you do.' There was no ring on Loxton's slender fingers and no indentation mark. She obviously didn't know. 'I had a long bath. I called my wedding planner to double check a few details. Then Lucy and I went for dinner.'

'What time was that?'

'Around eight-thirty I think.'

'Where did you eat?' Loxton's pen hovered over her paper.

'A restaurant down the road from the Silver Tree. I didn't want to eat in the actual hotel in case I saw any guests.'

'So where, precisely?' Loxton narrowed her eyes at me slightly.

This woman liked detail. The trick was to be vague about everything until they gave up. It gave you room to breathe. The police could turn the slightest mistake into an admission of guilt, if you weren't careful. 'It was a pub, about a ten-minute walk down the road. I can't remember the name.'

'And Lucy stayed with you after dinner?' Loxton said.

'Yes, that night she stayed in my room. Tradition again. I had no idea there was a problem until . . .' I tried to think of something else, but I kept imagining David turning around and Mark not being there. I dug my nails into my palms to try to shift the image. 'Until he wasn't at the ceremony.'

'And what did you initially think?'

'I thought he'd been in a car accident, something like that. It's what I always think when someone's late.' I didn't want to bring up my parents again. Loxton's pale blue eyes were noting everything.

'Because of your parents?' Loxton's face softened. Had she lost someone? Was that something I could use? I nodded my head fast and allowed my eyes to moisten. I was going to have to play this carefully.

'I'm having trouble finding your parents on our system. You said when we first met that they'd been in a car crash?'

I hadn't expected the police to do checks on my parents. It felt like a sharp kick to the gut. 'That's right.'

Loxton frowned. 'Could you tell me their names? So I can find them on the system easier.'

My vision blurred as I tried to think. 'Their names were Margaret and Philip Talbot.' I dabbed at my eyes with my fingertips. 'But I'm not sure what they've got to do with Mark going missing now?'

Loxton handed me a packet of tissues from her pocket. Did she always have them on her for such occasions? Loxton threw Kowalski a look, but he shook his head slightly and remained relaxed. 'And what do you think has happened to Mark?'

'I don't know.' The tears were coming, but I tried to hold them back. I thought of the missed mortgage payments. What had Mark been doing with our money? 'He hasn't called.'

'How was he before the wedding?' Loxton had put her pen down and was staring at me.

'He was stressed, a little uptight.' It was hard for me to admit, but as the wedding drew nearer, Mark's mood had plummeted. He'd told me he didn't like being the

centre of attention, that the day had got too big, but it
had been more than that. Maybe he'd got into a financial
mess, perhaps that's why he'd been distant.

I looked at them both. 'You don't think he's done
something crazy, do you?'

'Sometimes the loved ones are the last to know.' Loxton
studied her hands. Kowalski glanced at her but then
looked back at me.

'Did he have any problems?' Kowalski asked.

I shook my head. The police had got it all wrong. I
couldn't believe it. They didn't know anything about
Mark. But, then, he hadn't told me about failing to pay
the mortgage.

'Any problems in your relationship? Work problems?
Financial problems? Health problems?' Kowalski fired
the questions at me.

'He never mentioned any problems to me, but I don't
know. He might have had some money problems. I'm
not sure. He dealt with all the finances.' I shrugged
helplessly. What sort of fiancée was I, that Mark hadn't
confided to me about his problems?

'Did you know he was in trouble at work?' Loxton said.

'What trouble?'

Loxton's face was unreadable. 'He was about to be
sacked for insider trading and money laundering.'

'That's not true.' They were both watching me, their
faces serious. 'Where did you get this rubbish from?' Why
would he be struggling to pay the mortgage if that was
true? It didn't make sense.

'We've been to his workplace.' Loxton said.

'He'd have told me.'

'It's the truth, Julia. He didn't tell you?' Loxton's eyes
bored into me.

'No . . . I . . . He never told me because it didn't happen. I don't have to listen to this.' The room was spinning now. I needed to get out of this stuffy, rancid place. I picked up my handbag and slung it onto my shoulder as I stood up.

'It looks like he might have been involved in insider trading, which is a way of stealing money from the bank. If it wasn't for the two of you, who was it for?' Loxton tilted her head at me, her eyes sad.

'What are you saying?' My stomach was heavy. I put my hands on the desk to steady myself.

'Could there be another woman?' Loxton said softly.

'I know Mark.' I thought of his lopsided smile, the way he used to make me feel like the only woman in the world. 'We don't keep secrets from each other. We're a team.' There was a stabbing pain in my stomach. I gripped the table edge, trying to focus on something solid.

'Have you bought your mobile with you?' Loxton asked. 'We need to download the contents.'

'I left it at home.' I lied. 'And I need it anyway. What if Mark tries to call me?'

'Are you sure you haven't got it with you?' Loxton frowned at me in confusion. 'It would only take a day to download it as a priority. We could go and collect it after this interview and have it back to you tomorrow morning.'

'I can't be without it, not even for a day. There's nothing on there that would help, anyway.' There was a pain in my abdomen now and I grimaced through it.

'Are you okay?' Kowalski asked.

'I'm fine, I just need a minute.' I tried to breathe slowly, but it wasn't working. The more of the stench of the room I took in, the worse it got.

'Why don't you sit down?' Loxton said. 'You've had a lot to take in.'

'I can't believe this.' I looked at them both in turn. I had to make them understand. 'There is no way Mark stole that money. The bank has safety measures in place to stop people from being able to steal anything. It's some sort of mistake. Maybe the bank's gambled it away and is trying to blame Mark, now that he's not here to defend himself? That's it, he's some sort of scapegoat. Ask David, he'll tell you.' None of this made sense. I'd already said too much. I needed to get out of here before I said any more.

'David and Mark work closely together?' Loxton asked.

'They sit next to each other. They're in investment. That's how they became friends.' Didn't they know anything? Loxton and Kowalski glanced at each other.

'Julia, we're sorry about these questions.' Kowalski smiled at me sympathetically. 'I know it's hard. Please, take a seat. We're just trying to find Mark.'

'I know you are.' I sat back down, focusing on my breathing. In and out, nice and slow.

'I know this is hard, but we're on your side.' Loxton said.

I nodded, trying to compose myself.

Loxton hesitated before she spoke. 'We need to ask about a hidden mobile we found in your bedroom. Is it yours?'

My handbag was on my lap, the strap still on my shoulder. Loxton wouldn't be able to see it under the table. I carefully felt around inside my bag for my phone. There – under my purse and lipstick. I tried to hide the relief from my face. I slowly removed my hands from my handbag and placed them back on my lap. 'No, it's not mine. I don't have another mobile.'

'There was an unread text on it.'

'What did it say?' I dug my nails into the palms of my hands – readying myself.

'It said: *"I know what you did and you're going to burn."*'

'Who . . . who would send that?' I asked.

'Do you know anyone who has a grudge against Mark?' Loxton asked.

Jonny leapt into my mind. The boy from the past I'd tried so hard to hide. I breathed in and out, but my stomach was cramping harder. I clutched at my abdomen, trying to stop the shooting pains.

'I'm not feeling that great,' I said. 'Can we do this some other time?'

Kowalski stood up. 'I'll get you some water.' His face loomed in front of me, his pale blue eyes and strong jawline suddenly out of focus. He was staring at me as if I was an animal trapped in a cage for him to study. His face separated into four, all rotating round and round me.

My stomach lurched as I threw up violently. There was a second of relief, and then I retched again, sick spattering onto the table below me. I wiped my mouth with the back of my hand. Kowalski looked down at his vomit-splashed shirt.

'I'm so sorry.' I held out the tear-soaked tissues Loxton had given me, mortified.

'No, it's fine.'

I gripped my handbag for something to hold onto.

'Is Mark in danger?' I could barely get the words out before I began to choke on my tears.

'We don't know.' Loxton's face softened.

'Mark didn't have enemies,' I said. 'I'm sorry, I don't

know who would send that. I . . . I need to lie down.'
The detectives began to fuss over me, as if a spell was
broken.

'We can finish this when you're feeling better,' Loxton
said. 'But it would really help if we could just download
your mobile today.'

I didn't have to give them my mobile. 'Mark might
call me. I'm sorry, but I know my mobile won't help you.'

Kowalski's brow creased in confusion, but he shook
his head at Loxton as he opened the door for me. The
sick must have been soaking through his shirt and onto
his skin. I cringed inside.

'Let me show you to the bathroom,' Loxton said. 'Then
we'll take you home.'

'Thanks, but I'll get a cab. I'd rather you were looking
for Mark.' I wanted to be as far away from them as
possible.

I hurried out of the police station, not daring to check
behind me until I was around the corner and striding
down a side street. No one seemed to have followed me,
but I quickened my pace anyway and kept stealing glances
over my shoulder. It felt like someone was watching me,
but every time I looked around me, there was no one
there.

Chapter 10

Alana Loxton

Monday

Kowalski dabbed at his shirt with tissue. 'I can't go to the shops looking like this.'

'You haven't got a spare in the office?' A spare suit had been essential in the murder team. You never knew when you'd be looking at a decomposing body and then have to meet their family. It was bad etiquette to still smell of someone's loved one's decaying corpse.

'Maybe in my locker.' He gave up with the tissue. 'Odd that Talbot wouldn't give up her mobile. I didn't expect that.' He went quiet for a moment.

'She really didn't want us to have it, even lying that she hadn't brought it with her. She's probably having an affair.' She hated that she was getting so cynical these days.

'Or she was hiding something worse,' Kowalski said. 'That secretary knew all about Rowthorn's work problems, but Talbot didn't seem to have a clue, unless she was pretending not to know. Maybe she found out and they had a row?'

'I don't think Talbot's involved.' Even as Loxton said the words, they didn't feel right, but she decided to keep quiet until she could properly formulate her concern. 'We haven't got enough to take her mobile at this point.'

'Agreed, but we'll keep an eye on her. We do need to revisit David Steele,' Kowalski said. 'He told us that he didn't work with Mark. And Benson said that Steele's name came up when Mark's did during the insider trading and money laundering investigation.'

'Benson still hasn't sent us much on that,' she sighed. 'Trying to get information out of that bank is impossible. None of Mark Rowthorn's team have talked to us, except to say Mark's a great guy. They've all closed ranks.'

They headed into the main CID office, which hummed with energy as the people gathered there were working on their own enquiries. They were all mentally preparing themselves for the case ahead, each with their own rituals. One DC was clutching her mobile as she warned her husband she'd be busy. She saw another one loading his drawer with crisps, cans of coke and pot noodles, anticipating the long unsociable hours when he'd barely have time to stop. They all knew this case was going to be big.

Loxton checked the full intelligence packages she'd requested on Rowthorn and Steele. Both clean. Not a single record for either of them. It didn't surprise her; they needed impeccable records to work at that level in a bank. Talbot had come back clean too, but she hadn't expected anything else.

'The data from Rowthorn's work mobile and hidden mobile are back,' Meera Patel said as she passed the records to Loxton.

'Any luck tracing the stolen money from the bank?' Loxton asked.

'Rowthorn had a hidden account,' Patel said. 'It took

the lab a while to find it on his laptop. He'd used encrypted software.'

'The bank should have known about this, even if they couldn't get into it,' Kowalski said.

Loxton shook her head. 'Benson knew more than he was letting on.'

'He's probably stalling disclosing until the bank is aware of the scale of the losses and has got its collateral damage protocol in place,' Patel said. 'Incidents like this can damage an investment bank's reputation on the stock market.'

'I'll ask Winter to call Benson and get the bank's full report,' Kowalski said.

'Well, I've found that Rowthorn's account had just under one hundred thousand in it, but on the day Rowthorn disappeared it was emptied.' Patel read from her notes. 'Looks like he used the dark net late in the evening to access it and purchase Bitcoin. There's no way to trace his IP address to find out where he was when he did it. He's bounced off different servers so he could be abroad, anywhere. Bitcoin is anonymous; that's the appeal. Untraceable.'

'So, Mark and one hundred thousand pounds disappear on the same day,' Kowalski said. 'Looks like he's running away. The insider trading case Benson's lot were looking into must have spooked him. I'm going to check that stops have been put on his passport so he can't leave the country, if he hasn't already.'

'Could someone else have emptied Rowthorn's account?' Loxton asked.

'It's possible,' Patel said. 'All you need is the password. There's no way to say for sure who emptied it.'

'I'll analyse the phone data.' Kowalski took the records

off Loxton. 'Maybe the answer will be in there. Loxton, can you review the CCTV around the Yardsmen? That's Rowthorn's last known location. Try to see where he goes. There's quite a lot of it, so get Kanwar to help you if it gets too much.'

'I'll put the kettle on,' Loxton said. It looked like they were going to be there all night.

Loxton's vision was going blurry as she peered at the CCTV playing on her computer monitor. She'd been studying it for the past ten minutes, rewinding backwards and forwards. Staring at the image of a handsome man with cropped brown hair, smiling.

Rowthorn.

The only image she could find of him. She wished she knew where he'd gone, but as soon as he left that shop, he'd disappeared into a CCTV blind spot and she hadn't been able to pick him up anywhere else on the high street. It was as if he'd disappeared into thin air.

Cell-siting Rowthorn's personal mobile had failed to locate him as it had been turned off, the last location being at the Yardsmen. There had been no bank transactions and no travel history since he'd left there.

She let the CCTV play one last time. Watched Rowthorn pay the cashier at the Yardsmen checkout. Rowthorn's smile looked genuine and warm. He was muscly under his shirt; anyone would take a second look. Steele was stood next to Rowthorn, straining under the weight of three suit bags.

Rowthorn turned from the cashier and marched towards the exit as a dark look flashed across his face, the smile falling from his lips. Steele rushed to keep up with him.

She paused the screen and studied the last image of

Rowthorn's face before he disappeared. She couldn't tell if it was fear or anger on his face. Whichever it was, he'd now been missing for over forty-eight hours and, although no one would say it out loud, suicide or even murder seemed possible. She hoped he had just escaped his problems and had somehow managed to avoid leaving any trace behind.

It was one in the morning and she was exhausted. Her eyes felt gritty. She should go home, but she knew she'd never sleep. Her mind was buzzing with questions. She thought of Rowthorn's fiancée, the lost bride, frozen in time. It was hard to imagine a wedding day going any worse.

Loxton needed to find him. She needed to prove to herself she wasn't a fuck-up. Her last case had nearly destroyed her – this one had to put her broken pieces back together. If she couldn't do that then there was nothing left for her to do but leave, and if she didn't have the police, what *did* she have?

She imagined Rowthorn's face now: lifeless, his eyes unseeing. She pushed the thought from her mind.

Patel smiled at her. 'How are you getting on?'

'Fine, thanks. You?' Where most policewomen avoided overt make-up, Patel's nails were painted hot pink and her glossy dark hair made her look like she'd sauntered out of a magazine shoot.

'Winter has still got me trying to trace the Bitcoin.' She sighed. 'It's all pointless, just dead-ends. There's no way I'll ever be able to find it.' Patel looked as tired as Loxton felt.

'That's not a one-person job.' Patel would be working the longest hours with that to do on her own. Loxton hesitated but then relented. 'I'll help you.'

Relief spread across Patel's face. 'Thank you, Alana. That'd be great.'

Loxton smiled at her.

'Which department did you come from again?' Patel tilted her head slightly.

'The murder squad.' Vague enough, Loxton hoped.

'I'd love to be on the Murder Investigation Team.' Patel's eyes lit up. 'Why did you leave?'

'I want to go for promotion next year.' It was a white lie. 'It's hard to get the acting-up experience on the MIT. You get more chance in borough CID. Anyway, I don't want to hold you up. Send me the Bitcoin stuff and I'll have a look at it later on, when I get a chance.'

'That'd be a big help.' Patel smiled. 'Us women have got to stick together, right?'

'That's true.' Loxton managed a smile. She felt bad about lying to her, but what else could she do? The truth was too painful to talk about and she hardly knew Patel. She didn't know any of them.

She looked back at Rowthorn's face on the screen but couldn't shake off the feeling of shame she felt.

'Still no trace?' Kowalski had come over. He held a crate of beers in his arms.

'No. After this image, he disappears. He's not been picked up by any CCTV cameras nearby, or on the buses or tube.'

Kowalski held the crate towards her. 'Beer?'

'Sure.' It was the last thing she needed, but she pulled a can out, not wanting to stand out anymore.

'*Na zdrowie.*' Loxton clunked her can against his.

'*Na zdrowie,*' Kowalski said. 'You speak Polish?'

'Not really. A few words.'

'Ah, right.' Kowalski looked disappointed. 'There I was thinking you had Polish heritage,' he said, walking away.

Loxton closed down the CCTV on her computer and pulled up the police database. She typed Julia Talbot's name in, trying different spelling variations, but still nothing appeared. It was as if Talbot didn't exist. There was no record of her parents' car crash either. Their deaths weren't listed in the fatal road accidents database.

It had been a long day. Loxton imagined curling up in her bed and closing her eyes. On the other side of the office, Kowalski switched on the TV. A female newsreader was going through the day's stories.

Rowthorn's face appeared on the screen. He was wearing a tuxedo, holding a cigar in one hand and champagne in the other. Everyone froze. They knew it would be coming, but it was still a shock to see their case on the national news.

'Mark Rowthorn, a banker for City Enterprises, has been reported missing after he failed to turn up to his wedding yesterday. Police have made Rowthorn's disappearance a priority.'

'Shit,' Kanwar said, choking on his takeaway pizza. 'How the fuck did they find all that out so quick?'

'They've been sniffing around the police station all day.' Patel sighed. 'Only a matter of time until someone let something slip.'

'Winter is *not* going to be happy.' Kowalski shook his head.

Loxton felt her old anger surface. She hated the press. When she'd been in the murder team, they'd come close to destroying her career, and she couldn't help feeling like history was repeating itself. This time it would be different though. This time nothing would distract her. She would find Rowthorn and make up for her past mistake.

Chapter 11

Julia Talbot

Monday

It was there, in front of me. I'd spent the best part of two hours trawling the internet for it while Lucy was in the living room with the TV turned low, thinking I was asleep.

I paused a moment to listen for her. I heard her voice. I couldn't make out all of the words, but it sounded like she was on the phone to James, which meant she'd be a while. He should be coming back from Dubai this week. I'd not met him yet, but now wasn't the right time. I was irritable and snappy with everyone. I dreaded him coming back – Lucy would want to see him, and I'd be left on my own.

I rested my back against the headboard and re-angled the laptop screen in case I'd got it wrong. I was ready to slam the lid down in a second if Lucy came in. I peered at the image in the gloom of my dark bedroom, but there could be no doubt.

I'd found Jonny Cane.

It had been a long time, but here he was. The photograph was of him in a dark nightclub, one arm coming towards the camera in a fist, the other wrapped around a mate's neck, dragging the drunken man closer for the picture. They were the same blue eyes I'd known all those years before, but so much had changed. He was a man now. I felt sick and angry all at the same time.

At least I knew where he was. His profile was sparse, but it said he worked in London. I'd hoped he'd be far away from me, far away from the police. But he was so close; it made it hard to breathe.

There was another photo of him in the driver's seat of a black matt-finish BMW. It looked like he'd done well for himself in the year he'd been out on licence. I couldn't imagine he'd got that car through legitimate work.

He was hard to track down. It wasn't until I'd used the app Swipebuster that I'd finally found him. All I needed was his name, age and area, plus a paltry three pounds to buy the app, and then I could find out if 'my man was cheating on Tinder'.

Thank you, Tinder.

I'd first used Swipebuster a few months back. I'd started to get suspicious of Mark, the late nights and the weekends away. I'd found nothing and felt awful for even doubting him. He'd asked me to marry him a month later and I'd felt even worse that I'd spied on him. I'd nearly confessed to him what I'd done, but decided that would be crazy. But perhaps my initial suspicions hadn't been so wrong after all. He'd lied about the mortgage payments – perhaps that wasn't all he'd been lying about. I was so angry with him, leaving me with all this mess and doubt, but then the anger changed to fear and guilt.

I looked at Jonny and the old feelings flared up. He'd been my first crush. He was still good looking, despite the years in prison. He was bigger than I'd imagined. He must have been working out. What should I do now that

I'd found him? Lucy was right – Jonny was dangerous. Perhaps I should leave him well alone.

Though maybe he was just getting on with his life. Maybe he never even thought about me at all. I had to hope.

I pulled up the Facebook appeal page Lucy and I had created for Mark. My time was better spent looking for *him* online. If the police checked my search history, it wouldn't just be Jonny Cane they'd find. I'd used the incognito setting on Google to search for him, but I didn't know if that would stop the police discovering it.

There were ten unread messages. One woman swore she'd seen Mark at Bank station in a suit, but she couldn't be sure; she was in a rush. She described him as having green eyes. Mark's blue eyes flashed in my mind. The way they lit up when he looked at me. I felt the weight of pain settle inside my chest, wondered if I'd ever feel normal again. If anything would ever be normal again.

Halfway through the messages was an odd one from a Chantelle Jones. She said that she had some information but she didn't want to talk to the police. She'd sent the page a friend request. I accepted. I peered at Chantelle's photo on Facebook. She was about my age, pretty. She looked like a party girl, her low-cut dress showing off cleavage, the lighting of the photo altered to make it soft and flattering.

A direct message suddenly appeared on Facebook Messenger. It was from her. I clicked on it.

'*I have some information. I don't want to speak to anyone but you. I'm sorry, I just can't deal with the police. Is that okay?*'

I stared at the words glowing on my screen. Who was she? '*What's the information?*' I typed back.

'*I can't write it down. I'll tell you in person, that's best. But I can't get involved, I'm sorry.*'

I didn't like this. DC Loxton had warned me about nut jobs, to tell her straight away if anyone made contact with possible information. I didn't want to deal with a nutter. I knew how dangerous people could be.

'*Why don't you want to get involved with the police?*'

'*I had a bad experience with them before and I swore I'd never go to them again,*' Chantelle typed. '*Look, we can meet in public. I want to help you, I just can't get involved. You'll understand when I meet you.*'

I typed the words out again. '*What information?*'

'*I can email the stuff anonymously to the police but it might cause you some problems.*'

The words burned on the screen. Might cause *me* some problems? Did she know about my past? Did she know something about Jonny? I couldn't trust the police, especially not with something as fragile as the truth. I needed to find out what Chantelle knew.

She was typing more but then the dots disappeared. After a moment they started again and the message popped up: '*Can we meet? Just you and me?*'

The text prompt flashed impatiently at me. What did she know? And why just the two of us?

'*Where do you want to meet?*' I asked.

'*The Night Jar Bar, Southwark. It's public. Tomorrow. 6pm okay?*'

'*Are you a reporter?*'

'*No, I'm not one of them. It's not like that. I want to help you find Mark. I'll be wearing a green dress.*'

'*Ok.*' I typed. '*Tomorrow 6pm. Please help me find Mark.*'

'*I will. I promise.*'

I let out a slow breath. I should take Lucy with me, but Chantelle expected me to go alone, and I didn't want to scare her off. I should tell Lucy about the meeting at least, but what if she tried to stop me going to see this girl? What if she insisted on coming with me? I needed to find out what Chantelle knew and what she was going to do with the information. She could be trying to blackmail me about my past for all I knew.

I closed my laptop and slid it under the covers. My legs ached as I moved them and I was tired to my bones, but my mind was racing. I wriggled down the bed, pulling the covers up to my chin. I closed my eyes, but I knew I wouldn't be able to sleep.

The wooden floorboards creaked as Lucy came along the corridor towards me. They were the familiar sounds of my flat, but instead of him, it was her making them.

'I thought I heard you get up. Still can't sleep?' She was frowning as she came in. She didn't put the light on, instead letting the corridor's light seep into the room. 'Those pills should have worked. Have you taken them?'

'I had a nightmare; it woke me up.'

She sat down on the edge of the bed. 'What about?'

'Nothing,' I said.

'Jonny?' She tilted her head at me, struggling to hide her concern.

'No,' I said.

Her frowned deepened. I was never very good at lying to her. She almost always spotted it. 'You need to stop thinking about Jonny. This isn't helping Mark. Or anyone.'

I knew she was talking about herself; the years of secrets weighing down on her as well as me. I wanted to pretend it had never happened too, but I couldn't. I didn't want to put Lucy through all of it again.

'It was just a nightmare,' I said.

'I know this is hard, but Mark will be back before you know it.' She patted my arm and smiled.

'The police don't think so,' I said.

'Why do you say that?'

'When they interviewed me, they were asking so many questions. They said he'd been stealing from the bank.'

'What? Why didn't you tell me earlier? Mark wouldn't do that. He's not stupid. I'm sure there's an explanation,' Lucy said. 'By the way, the police are going to come by my house tomorrow evening after work.'

Why hadn't they asked her to come to the police station, like me? My brain started to whir again

'You look like you haven't slept at all. You really need to try or you're going to make yourself ill.'

'I know.' She was right, I felt drained, and my head was so muddled, a few hours might make things clearer.

She leaned across and hugged me. 'If you need me, I'll be in the spare room.'

'Night.' I turned onto my side and closed my eyes. I heard her retreating footsteps on the floorboards and the door closing behind her.

It would be all right. Everything would be all right. I just needed to be careful.

Chapter 12

Alana Loxton

Tuesday

Loxton knocked hard on the red door. Had Webb forgotten they were coming? She glanced at Kowalski and he shrugged back, just as a flustered-looking Webb opened the door, a strand of auburn hair falling loose from her ponytail.

'Sorry, I can't talk long. Julia's been on her own all day.' Webb was itching to get back to her friend. People often reacted like this when the police came to their house, as if they were an omen that brought disaster with them. Sometimes Loxton felt like she was a curse.

'It won't take long.' She squeezed past Webb and into the cramped hallway.

Webb invited them into the living room and motioned at a sofa, unsure of herself. 'Sorry, first full day back in the office today and now this . . .' She smiled at them apologetically.

'We understand.' Loxton sat down, sinking into the ancient fabric of the cream sofa, which was crowded with a pattern of large pink roses. The arms were thread-worn from years of use. In one corner of the living room stood an imposing mahogany display cabinet with porcelain

Victorian figurines of pale children posing in neat rows. It was like a museum.

Webb perched on the edge of a matching cream and pink armchair crossing her legs and folding her arms. 'I doubt I've got anything useful to say.'

'We still need to ask. Where were you last Saturday afternoon?' Loxton asked.

'I headed to the Silver Tree to meet Julia.'

'What time did you get there?'

'I'm not sure. Sometime around two I think. It might have been nearer three.'

'What did you do?'

'Julia was quite nervous. She rang a few people to check on details, kept fussing with her dress. We didn't go to dinner until after eight, I remember being starving. I guess brides-to-be get used to feeling hungry in the fight to fit in the dress, but bridesmaids are meant to be a bit plumper, aren't they?'

Loxton smiled at Webb. She felt like they were breaking through with her, building a rapport.

'I can imagine,' Loxton said. 'How was Julia before the wedding?'

'Nervous and excited. She was besotted with Mark.' Webb smiled sadly. 'I know Julia sometimes comes across as cold, but she's had a traumatic life. When bad things happen, she tends to withdraw. I've seen it before.'

'Can you tell us about her parents? The car crash?' Loxton asked.

'We were seventeen. It was the summer holidays and her parents were going away for a weekend. The police said they died on impact. One minute Julia's life was perfect and the next everything just fell apart. Her parents' death left a massive void.'

'Seventeen's so young. How did she get by?' Loxton crossed her legs, trying to mimic Webb's body language.

'Julia inherited her parents' house.' Webb said. 'Her parents' life insurance took care of the finances.'

Loxton tried not to let her surprise show. Another big life insurance pay-out. And Julia Talbot seemed about to receive another one if Rowthorn never turned up. She was making a habit of surviving off them.

'Julia threw herself into her studies,' Lucy continued. 'University was her goal; it promised to take her away from that house and the memories.'

'I can't find any reports of the car accident.' Loxton leaned back, trying to look relaxed.

'That's odd.' Webb looked puzzled. 'It was in the local papers. I guess it pre-dated the internet though. The local paper should have a record.' Loxton had already checked that – nothing.

'How was Mark before the wedding?' Kowalski asked.

'I wouldn't know.' She shrugged. 'We've never hit it off. I don't know why. It's a shame really. I guess before the wedding he seemed distant, but that's normal for him. You can be talking to him and you know he's not really listening.' Webb's hands clenched on her arms.

That had hit a nerve. Loxton tried to keep the interest out of her voice. 'Distant?'

'Even when he was with Julia, it was like he was somewhere else. I'm sorry, I'm not explaining it very well.' She rubbed her face with her hands. She looked tired. Her friend's distress taking its toll. 'He was one of those people who struggled to be interested in other people. Everything always had to be about him.'

'What do you think has happened to him?'

'I wouldn't be surprised if he turns up in a few days with his tail between his legs.' Webb scowled at the thought.

'Please, go on,' Loxton said.

'He's never struck me as one for commitment. I was shocked when he proposed. Then he talked about them emigrating to America after they were married. I think it was his way of trying to ditch her, to be honest.'

'Why would America put her off?' Loxton asked.

'Her jewellery business is here . . . her friends. She'd never leave London.'

'You think Mark's run off somewhere?'

'He might have panicked the night before and now he's holed up somewhere trying to build up the courage to come home.' Webb pushed her hair behind her ears. 'Julia told me about the trouble he got himself into at work. Maybe it all got on top of him?'

'Do you think there could be another woman?' Loxton watched Webb's face carefully.

Webb's brow creased as she thought for a moment. 'I don't know. He seemed pretty smitten with Julia at the beginning. But recently . . . she'd said he seemed distant. I was hoping it was just wedding pressure, maybe something all couples go through. I wouldn't know personally.' She motioned at her wedding finger, where there was no ring.

'Would anyone try to hurt him?' Kowalski asked.

'Who would want to hurt him?' Webb looked from Kowalski to Loxton.

'Humour us.' Loxton dropped the fishing line, sure there was something to catch.

Webb unfolded her arms and inspected her burgundy nail varnish as if playing for time while she decided what to do. A moment passed. Loxton waited. People hated quiet moments; they were desperate to fill them.

'He worked hard,' Webb said looking up at Loxton. 'But he partied hard too. I saw him take coke a few times, that's all.'

'When did you last see him take coke?'

'Their engagement party. I didn't see him take it, but Mark and David went into the toilets together and came out hyper.'

'David takes drugs?'

'From what Julia's said, David's a real coke-head. He gets coke for Mark.' Webb paused and looked at them both. 'I thought you'd know all this?'

'We didn't know all of it,' Loxton said, but, in truth, she hadn't spotted this at all. Both Steele and Rowthorn had come back negative for any drug intel. 'Please, it all helps.'

'I shouldn't have said anything. David would be angry if he knew I'd told you all this. It's not my business really.' Webb began tapping her foot.

'Is he aggressive?' Kowalski asked.

'Hasn't he got a record?' Webb looked surprised; her foot stopped its nervous rhythm.

'Has he ever been violent when you've been with him?' Loxton asked.

'I hardly know him,' Webb said. 'I'm sure he's got nothing to do with all this.' She shook her head, annoyed at herself for saying too much.

'Have you ever taken coke?' Loxton asked.

'I can't stand it. Turns people into complete arseholes and some addicts. My father was an addict, though alcohol was his poison.'

'I'm sorry to hear that,' Loxton said.

'It doesn't matter now, he's dead.' Webb shook her head slightly.

'Does Julia take cocaine?' Kowalski asked.

Webb stared at Kowalski and then Loxton. 'Of course not. You don't know anything, do you? Look, I don't want it getting back to her that I told you about Mark's drug habit. I shouldn't have mentioned it.' Webb checked her watch.

'For us to find Mark, we need to know everything,' Loxton said.

'Julia's defensive when it comes to Mark. You can't say a bad word against him. She'd go ballistic if she heard me talking about him like this.' Webb looked down at her hands.

'How well do you know him?' Loxton asked.

'Not well,' she admitted. 'We haven't really got anything in common. He's a banker; I'm just a lowly accountant to him. I was never convinced he was the one for Julia if I'm honest. But what would I know?' Webb wrung her hands as if she'd said more than she'd meant to. 'Look, I need to get going.'

'We won't be much longer,' Kowalski said.

'You're her best friend.' Loxton watched Webb closely. She knew the woman was holding back. 'Why did you think Mark wasn't right for her?'

Webb glanced at the door, as if wishing she could make a run for it. 'Look, Mark has a bit of a temper.' Webb shifted uncomfortably on her seat, a pained expression on her face. 'Julia won't tell you this, but they argue a lot. He doesn't always treat her that great. Work comes first, his friends and family. She makes excuses for him all the time.' Webb was frowning now.

'Did you talk to her about this?' Loxton asked.

'I tried . . . a few times. But love's complicated.' Webb shook her head.

'You'll get no arguments from me,' Kowalski said.

'We fell out about it,' Webb said. 'I had to drop it, otherwise I'd have lost her.'

Loxton nodded and waited, but Webb didn't fall for the silent trick again.

'I don't mean to be rude, but Julia's on her own.' Webb glanced at her watch. 'I promised her I'd go straight over after this.'

'Of course,' Loxton said.

'Please, don't tell her what I've told you. I'm the closest thing to family she has right now. I would hate her to think I'd betrayed her.'

'We understand,' Kowalski said.

'We'll be gone soon,' Loxton said. 'We just need to look around. It's routine.'

'Routine?' Webb's frown deepened. 'He's not here. When you said earlier another woman . . . you don't think it's me, do you?' She looked hurt. Loxton didn't blame her. It wasn't nice, but it was something they had to consider.

'It'll be a quick walk round,' Loxton said. 'There are set procedures for missing persons. Can we start upstairs?'

Webb nodded but she didn't look happy. Loxton climbed the creaking stairs with Kowalski behind her. Webb followed them both.

The house was a two-up two-down Victorian terrace – not bad at all for a woman in her early thirties. The main bedroom at the front of the house was trapped in a time warp, though. A queen-sized bed dominated the room, leaving little space for other furniture. There was a dark dressing table with an ancient oval mirror parked in front of the bay windows. Upon it was an old jewellery box. Loxton couldn't help but shiver. She expected a ghost to drift past at any moment.

'My aunt left me the house in her will.' It was as if Webb had read her mind. She paused by the old jewellery box, opening the lid and listening to the tinkling music. 'She didn't have any children. I was like a daughter to her. People think I'm lucky to have this house, but I miss my aunt every day. She was always there for me and she had this brilliant sense of humour.' Webb smiled briefly and then realized who she was talking to. She closed the lid on the jewellery box, swallowed hard.

Loxton nodded. She knew what it was like to lose someone you loved and not be able to move on. The whole house was a shrine and it seemed Webb was unable to change a thing.

'This is my room.' Webb showed Loxton into the smaller rear bedroom.

A practical wardrobe and matching chest of drawers stood by the far wall. A framed photo of a handsome man was on the bedside table.

'My boyfriend, James,' Webb smiled when she looked at the photo of him, and Loxton felt a pang of jealousy. It had been a long time since she'd felt like that about a man. The last one had broken her heart.

Expensive stilettos were lined up against the wall along with some plain black ballerina pumps. There was a single bed shoved in the far corner with a green-and-white spotted patchwork quilt thrown over. One patch in the corner had been replaced on the quilt; it was sky blue with white dots. It reminded Loxton of the pink quilt her mother had made for her when she was a child.

'You said this is your room?' Loxton was surprised by the single bed.

'I've been meaning to get a double for ages, but I've just been so busy. I work such long hours, there's never any time for shopping.'

Loxton nodded in sympathy, knowing what that was like. 'That's a very pretty quilt.'

'My aunt made it for me when I was a baby.' Webb smiled at the memory. 'Every year she'd add more patches, so it grew with me. She tried to teach me, but I was hopeless at sewing.'

'My mum made me one,' Loxton said. 'I was useless at sewing, too.'

'I spilt cola on that corner when I was a teenager.' Webb pointed at the replaced patch and shook her head at the memory. 'The stain wouldn't come out. My aunt had to stich a new patch on; I couldn't do it myself. I remember being devastated because we couldn't find the same colour, like it was the end of the world. Silly really looking back, but it's the only thing she ever made for me, and I love it.'

Loxton opened the wardrobe but there was nothing unusual in there, just women's clothing, some still in dry-cleaning bags. She peered under the bed. Plastic storage boxes underneath stuffed with towels and bedding.

Loxton struggled back down the steep ancient stairs, wondering if Webb's aunt had ended her days falling down them. Webb followed close behind her.

As Webb and Loxton entered the living room, Loxton saw Kowalski shoving papers back into the sideboard drawer. He had the good grace to look embarrassed.

Webb peered around Loxton and her mouth fell open. 'What are you doing down here?'

'Sorry, just went into house-search mode.' Kowalski

cringed. 'We need to get going, Alana. Something's come up. Thank you for your time, Ms Webb, it's appreciated.' Kowalski slipped out of the front door fast.

'Thank you again, Miss Webb. Apologies for my colleague – he's used to drug raids, not missing persons cases.' Loxton smiled at Webb apologetically as she left.

'What were you doing?' she hissed at Kowalski as they hurried down the path, Webb staring after them.

'I thought you'd be a little bit longer upstairs finishing off a "Loxton search".' Kowalski made quotation marks with his fingers. 'Anyway, that doesn't matter. I've had two missed calls from Winter. He never calls twice. Something's happening.'

Loxton's mobile began to ring. She fished it out of her pocket: Winter.

'You need to divert to Surrey Docks.' Winter was talking quickly. Something had excited him. In police work, that never boded well.

'Why?' Loxton's heart sank.

'Uniform are there. I think they've found Mark Rowthorn. It's not looking good.'

'Understood.' Winter hung up on her. She felt a sadness settle on her, making her feel physically heavier.

Kowalski was watching her carefully. 'What's happened?'

'We're going to Surrey Docks. Winter thinks Rowthorn's turned up.' She handed him the keys and climbed into the passenger seat.

'*Kurwa*,' Kowalski's clenched fist slammed into the steering wheel.

'I know,' she said.

They both knew that's where the bodies washed up.

Chapter 13

Julia Talbot

Tuesday

The Night Jar Bar was quiet, but then I supposed it would be at 6pm on a Tuesday. It was next to a nightclub of the same name, which was promoted as an exclusive club. I scanned the room but couldn't see anyone in a green dress. I ordered a gin and tonic to steady my nerves and sat in the far corner, hoping Chantelle wouldn't spot me straight away. I wanted to at least figure out if she was alone.

I'd checked every social network site I could think of, but I hadn't found anything more about her, which was worrying. She had to be a reporter, about to splash my face across tomorrow's tabloids as the weeping fiancée. I should have known better than to come here, but my desperation to find out what she knew had got the better of me.

I forced myself to stop checking Facebook Messenger every few seconds.

Then the thought hit me: I was here on my own, and no one knew where I was.

My stomach knotted in panic. What if it really was some macabre nutter? What had I been thinking? I could get up and leave – but then I'd never know.

Each table was garnished with a trendy square glass vase filled with dark red snapdragons. The flowers reminded me of childhood summers playing in my back garden. The time before it had all gone wrong. I opened up a flower and let it snap shut.

'Jenny?' My old name. A man's voice.

I looked up so fast I was dizzy for a moment. His voice was different but the same.

Jonny.

It was like he'd been stretched out. He towered above me. His dark blue eyes were the same, but there was little else left of the boy he'd been. I couldn't speak. I was frozen to the spot. My two worlds were colliding and I felt like I was between them, being smashed to pieces. *Of course it was him who sent the message.*

I tried to get past him, to run, but he blocked my way, putting his hands out in front of him, silently telling me to sit back down again.

A warning.

I sank onto the chair. This man was dangerous. I could never escape that day and now Jonny was stood in front of me, wanting payback. I'd always known this day would come. I felt my blood turn cold and I swallowed hard, my throat suddenly dry and tight.

I couldn't see a weapon on him. I checked the bar, but no one was paying attention to us.

'Why are you here?' My voice sounded strained. Hoarse.

'Just to talk, that's all.' He sat down opposite me. 'I know you think I did it. But I'm innocent and I want to prove it to you.'

'You were convicted in court. Tell me why you're really here.' I was surprised by my own bravery.

'Because you framed me,' Jonny said. 'We both know that.'

'I didn't frame you.' If I shoved the table into him would it give me time to run? 'You're crazy. Please—'

'I know what you did,' Jonny said. 'And I get it. You thought it was me. You wanted me to rot in prison. So you planted the ring with my blood on it onto Rachel's body to make it look like it was me. I didn't blame you for what you did. The police were desperate to pin it on me. They must have pressured you. Except it wasn't me, Jenny.'

I could still picture the purple crystal of my ring glinting at me even now. My favourite colour back then. I'd thrown away anything purple after that day, refused to wear it. I'd never tried to frame him. I tried to think what he was talking about, but everything back then had been so confused, the chaos of tall policemen in the house and determined reporters following me to school. Everything had been a blur. 'You aren't meant to come near me. It's on your life licence. You'll go back to prison and never get out this time.' I had my bag on my lap. I inched my hand into it, searching for my mobile. If I could just find it, then I could dial the police.

'I may as well be in prison.' Jonny shrugged, his eyes angry. 'I can't get a proper job. If I have kids, they'll take them away from me. I'm deemed too big of a risk. I need to clear my name. That's why I'm here. I just want a life – that's all.'

'Clear your name?' He couldn't prove he was innocent. He was lying and I didn't know why. I clenched my mobile so tightly in my hand I thought it might break.

'Let me help you find Mark.' There was an agitated energy in him and he kept tapping his finger, as if trying to keep himself calm. 'Prove I've never meant you any harm.'

'How can you help me find Mark?'

Jonny scanned the room and lowered his voice. 'I have ways of finding people. Ways the police don't have. I do background checks for this guy, make sure his clients are who they say they are. I find out every single thing about them. If I can help you find Mark, then you tell the police what really happened that day in the woods with Rachel. Tell them it wasn't me. That you planted the ring. I would have grounds to appeal. They would clear me. Don't you want to know what really happened back then?'

I couldn't let him go there. He'd been found guilty, justice had been served, and I'd somehow managed to escape all of it. I couldn't get dragged back into a past I'd spent my life escaping. He was lying. 'I know what happened. You were convicted of murder.'

I wouldn't let this destroy my future with Mark. He didn't know about any of this. How would he feel if he found out I'd been lying to him for years? I'd paid enough. None of it was meant to have happened. She wasn't even supposed to be there.

'Jenny, there was someone else in the woods that day. Don't you remember? When I ran away I saw him, a figure running. There was a rough sleeper in the woods. It was him. You must have seen him?'

There'd been no one else. 'It was just us two, Jonny. You and me.'

He shook his head in frustration. 'Maybe you didn't see him, but I did. The police wouldn't listen to me. Look, if I can't find Mark, you'll never hear from me again.' Jonny bent towards me, desperate now. 'You can go back to thinking I'm a monster. But if I help you find Mark, then maybe you could think about helping me. That's all. No strings attached. Do you know anything about where Mark could be? What's happened to him?'

'I want to leave.' The door was just a few metres away.

'Look, I know you've tried hard to run away from it all. I don't want to have to drag you back there, but it's destroyed my life.' He'd started to tap his foot, his leg jiggling in agitation. 'I want to go straight, Jenny. Just give me one chance to prove that it wasn't me. I need this.'

I pulled my jacket closer around me despite the warmth of the bar. Seeing him brought it all back. 'Have you done something to Mark? Have you hurt him?' He was so much bigger than me.

'You knew me back then. I was just a normal kid. I would never have done that. Jenny, use your head for once. Stop listening to what everyone else has told you must have happened and think. There was a man in the woods that day.' His blue eyes bored into mine.

I sat dazed for a moment. This wasn't the adult Jonny I'd feared all these years, a violent thug, his face ugly with hate and murder. This Jonny was agitated but controlled, if a little desperate and sad. He had a crew cut, there was stubble across his jaw; he was handsome. He didn't look like a killer. He looked like the Jonny I remembered, the Jonny from before.

'I've got to go.' I pulled the strap of my bag over my shoulder, kept my mobile in my hand, and staggered past him. I was terrified, but I had to keep going.

'Wait.' He chased after me. 'Jenny, just wait.'

A few other patrons turned to look, but quickly dismissed us as just another drunk couple having a domestic. I rushed onto the pavement, people having to move out of my way, desperate to get some space between Jonny and me. He had to dodge past a man, jumping into the road, just to keep pace with me.

'If I'd done something to Mark, why would I come and speak to you? That would be crazy!' he shouted.

I spun round and faced him, my hands balled into fists. 'How did you know he was missing? And how did you know he was connected to me?'

People pushed past us. He looked around and spotted a closed shop entrance. He pulled me under its awnings, out of the way. I shrugged his hand off my arm, gripping my mobile tightly.

'Like I said, my job is to find information on people. When I was released, I needed to find you, to speak to you. Your new name was good, but Kayleigh wasn't as careful as you. I knew if I found her there'd be a good chance I'd find you. I checked out your life. Your fiancé. I didn't want to approach you blind. If I wanted to hurt you, I would have done it by now and you'd never have known it was me. I saw you'd set up a Facebook page because your fiancé had gone missing and I thought this was my chance to show you I'm not who you think I am.'

I wrapped my arms around myself. I'd thought I was hidden, safe, but all that time he'd known where I was.

'I'm not here to hurt you.' He clenched his fists as if he was frustrated. His voice became hard. 'I'm risking everything by speaking with you. I need to prove the police got it wrong back then.'

The rage inside me burned but I didn't know what to do with it. He was trying to play me. This felt like some elaborate game of revenge. Or did he mean what he said? Was he innocent?

'You can get me on Facebook Messenger. I'll let you know if I find anything. If you want, you can call the police right now. I'll be on the CCTV meeting with you. I've breached my licence. You can have me locked away again to serve out the rest of my sentence. You've got all the power, Jenny. I'm not messing with you.'

'I don't want anything to do with you. And if you make contact again, I'll call the police.' He must know I would never go to the police. I didn't want my old life catching up with me. I'd worked tirelessly to stop Mark from knowing who I really was. If I told the police I was linked to Jonny, the past would be splashed across the papers within twenty-four hours, and the future I'd dreamed of would be over before it had begun.

He pulled a packet of cigarettes out of his jeans pockets, lit one and took a drag. It was the same brand we'd smoked all those years ago. It was as if we were behind the bike sheds in school again, catching a precious ten minutes together.

'Want one?' He offered the packet to me.

'I don't smoke.' I pushed my hair behind my ears, my mind whirring, trying to figure out the man in front of me.

He laughed and pulled out a cigarette anyway, lit it using the one from his mouth and offered it to me. 'Look, no one can blame you for having one cigarette right now. You look like you need it.'

I shook my head. He shrugged, stubbing the offered cigarette out on the wall and pocketing it.

'The police will be watching you,' Jonny said. 'Be careful. They get a bit het up on spouses. And trust me, sometimes they get the wrong person.'

'You need to stay away from me.' I couldn't take my

eyes off him. I felt sick with him stood so close to me. All the old feelings of hate and disgust swimming in my stomach. I tried to figure out whether he was threatening me, or whether this was still part of his act of pretending to help.

'Laters,' he said as he walked away, and he glanced back over his shoulder at me, nodding a last goodbye.

This was the start of something dangerous. He was out to get me, I was sure of it. And I couldn't even go to the police for help. I'd had so many nightmares about Jonny Cane over the years. Him stood over Rachel, blood dripping from his hands. Him watching me as I smashed Rachel's skull in. Sometimes the dream was of him swinging a rock at my face. I would wake up dripping with sweat just before the moment of impact, my arms thrust forward, shielding my face.

I'd told Mark it was anxiety, brought about by losing my parents when I was seventeen. I couldn't tell him it was post-traumatic stress, brought about because my sister had been murdered. Because it was my fault she was dead. I had taken her into those woods to die.

Chapter 14
Alana Loxton

Tuesday

Surrey Docks was deserted. DC Loxton could hear the water lapping against the shore, the delicate sound amplified at this late hour.

The three police officers stood around the corpse of an adult male slumped on his back on the small pebbled beach; his mouth was wide open.

The water crept nearer to the strange group, as if wanting to reclaim the body that it had lost. Pieces of rubbish were strewn around them, washed up from the river. An empty red crisp packet, the label faded, was blown onto the dead man and skittered away towards the water's edge.

Kowalski stood opposite her, grimacing. Rain clouds hung heavy and the light was fading fast, bringing on an early dusk.

Loxton shivered as the wind whipped a strand of her chestnut brown hair across her face; she was grateful that the temperature was plummeting, but the smell was still overpowering her.

The uniformed police officer droned on, his voice background noise, the body demanding her full attention. She tried to focus.

'Have forensics finished up?' she asked.

'They've taken photographs and swabs at the scene.'

'I'll schedule the post-mortem,' Loxton said.

The corpse was blanched and the stomach bloated like a massive balloon. The face was puffy with a dozen tiny abrasions. She guessed fish had been feeding on it. The eyes were gone, black holes taking their place, mirroring the dark clouds above. The fingertips were nibbled to the muscle, the prints erased for ever.

Frustration overwhelmed her, and her stomach knotted. It would take days to identify the body as Mark Rowthorn's. She hadn't expected it to end like this: a rotting corpse belched out by the river. She'd hoped to find him alive.

The body was in such a state that it would be difficult even to ascertain the cause of death. The corpse was like a cheap movie puppet in a low-budget horror. If it wasn't for the foul stench, she wouldn't have believed it was real.

'Is it him?' the young policeman asked her. 'You said he was in his thirties and athletic, but you know how punishing the Thames is.'

'I'm not sure,' Loxton said.

'Have you searched him for identification?' She hoped that he had spared her that task.

'Just the pockets but there was nothing.' The young policeman shifted his weight from one leg to the other.

The three of them waited in silence for someone else to make the first move.

'All right,' sighed Kowalski. 'Let's get this over with.' He handed Loxton blue plastic gloves, and then pulled some on himself.

These were the moments in the job that Loxton loathed.

She turned to the flowing river, which was oblivious to the suffering it had caused. She forced her head up towards the black clouds above, inhaled the air blown from over the river, took a deep breath, and then turned back to the body.

They searched the corpse gingerly. There was nothing obvious to suggest foul play. No stab wounds or obvious bullet-entry sites. The back of the head was caved in, but that could have been caused during a fall into the river, hitting his head on a bridge rampart, or by the current dragging him along the bottom. The damage could all be explained away by the river and the scavengers that lived within. Or it could be that someone had hit the man with a blunt instrument and then disposed of his body in the Thames.

They had nearly finished searching when Loxton noticed a watch on the dead man's wrist. She unbuckled it. On the back was inscribed: 'To Mark, love always, Julia'. Loxton couldn't move for a moment, spellbound by the delicate swirls that formed the words. She dropped the watch into an evidence bag and showed Kowalski.

'Looks like our missing man is now a potential murder investigation,' she said.

Kowalski nodded. 'Once we've finished here and updated his fiancée, we'll need to speak to David Steele. At the moment, he's the only person we know of with a clear motive. Someone moved that one hundred thousand pounds from Rowthorn's account, and I don't think it was Rowthorn.'

Chapter 15

Julia Talbot

Tuesday

My doorbell rang. It was late. I'd only just got back in and managed to take off my make-up, throw on my pyjamas and dressing gown, before Lucy had come back from speaking with the police.

I'd wanted her to think I'd been at home all day.

I hated lying to her, but she kept looking at me like I was made of china and would break at any moment. She'd be so angry if she knew I'd gone off on my own. All I wanted to do was forget about Jonny, pray that he'd leave me alone.

The bell went again. I dragged myself up off the sofa and peeked through the spyhole. There was a handsome man in a smart suit. He was drenched; blond hair darkened by rain. He rang the bell again and then started knocking.

'Yes?' I opened the door part-way. He had a kind face and striking hazel eyes.

'Miss Talbot, I'm Alec Saunders from the News Association.' He put out his hand, but I crossed my arms across my chest. He withdrew it and I noticed he was also holding a notebook. How did he know where I lived?

I scanned the courtyard but there was no one else there. Were more journalists coming to harass me? I made a note to warn security.

'Why are you the only one here?' I asked.

'I make it my business to always be in the know.' He smiled at me. 'I used to work for your father-in-law, a few years back.'

Charles had never got to be my father-in-law. I didn't recognize this man and Charles had never mentioned him. 'I don't talk to journalists,' I said firmly. The chill evening started to seep into my hallway and I shivered. I tried to close the door, but he put his hand on it before I could manage to.

'I understand. This must be the worst time in your life. Can I come in? I won't take up too much of your time.'

'It's late.' I kept my hands on the door and wished he'd step back so I could close it.

He carried on speaking, but I refused to listen. 'Please, can you just go?'

'Of course, but I wanted to say I'm sorry for your loss. If you ever want to talk . . .'

'What did you say?' My voice was unnaturally high.

'I said I'm sorry for your loss.' He consulted his notes. 'Have the police asked you to identify the body?'

Everything seemed to stop. I felt dizzy. He must have noticed the blood draining from my face because when he spoke again he was stammering and less sure of himself.

'You . . . you didn't know . . . did you? The police should have told you by now. They found a body in the Thames.'

'No . . . no, it's not true.' My voice was raised as I tried to block him out and then Lucy was at my side. The journalist tried to say something to her, but she slammed the door shut in his face.

'What's happened?' she asked me, her face pale.

'They've found him,' I managed to gasp, as if I was drowning. I couldn't get enough air into my lungs.

'What?' Lucy reached her hands out to steady me.

'He's dead.' I gripped my wedding band tight, which hung on a chain around my neck.

'He can't be.'

I tried to speak but couldn't. My legs gave way and I sank to the floor. My vision blurred. *The police had found a body.*

The doorbell resonated through the fog.

Lucy hugged me and I sobbed into her shoulder. The letterbox rattled. The reporter was staring at us through it.

'Miss Talbot,' he said, sounding flustered. 'You've had a shock. I'm going to leave you my card. I'm writing a number on the back as an idea of the sort of figure we could offer you, if you'd share the story of your time with Mark.'

I stood up, aimed a hard kick at the door and watched his card flutter down onto my doormat.

'Oh my god, I'm so sorry.' Lucy held me but I wrenched free. Mark was really gone. I'd never see him again. Never hear him telling me he loved me . . . never hear his laugh. I'd prepared for this moment, imagined losing him a million times, expected a feeling of freeness when it happened – release. But of course it wasn't like that, it was never going to be like that. My nightmares were finally real and there was a crushing fear in my chest, stopping me from breathing, from thinking. He was gone and there was no coming back from it.

I opened the door, ready to scream at the journalist, but he was moving back.

Loxton and Kowalski were striding towards me. Their hair was wet and their clothes clung to their bodies. The evening rain drummed harder against the house, spattering dirty water into my hallway.

'I already know.' I went to push the door closed, but Kowalski was too quick and managed to hold it open.

'I'm so sorry,' he said. 'Let us talk to you. Explain.'

Loxton was arguing with the man from the press. She was furious. I was too shocked to fight, my mind numb. I had to get inside. I let the door go and retreated into the living room – anything to get away from the noise. My mind was racing, trying to understand what I'd heard. I imagined Mark's body being pulled from the water, but it couldn't be real. Lucy sank into a chair next to me.

'I can't believe it, Julia. I'm sorry.' Lucy was shaking, her eyes shining as tears gathered. At least I had her with me.

Kowalski crouched in front of me, his brow etched with concern. 'We're so sorry for your loss.'

Everyone was *sorry*. The word kept rattling around in my head. Useless and banal. Lucy took my hand and I clung to it. 'Please,' I said. 'Tell me what happened.'

'A man's body has been found in Surrey Docks; it appears that he drowned,' Kowalski said gently. 'We don't know for sure that it's Mark, but it is looking likely.'

'Mark can't be dead.' Lucy's hand tightened on mine.

'There was trauma to the back of the head. We don't know what happened yet.' Kowalski's arms moved a fraction towards me, as if he wanted to gather me up his arms and hold me. I would have let him.

Loxton joined him, her lips pressed firmly together as if she was in pain.

'I don't understand.' I closed my eyes and covered my

face with my hands. *Trauma to the back of the head*. I could see him, lying on the ground, brain and blood matting his brown hair. It felt like someone was squeezing my heart.

'This could have been an accident.' Kowalski's calm voice grated on me. I suddenly felt a flare of anger; his life was untouched. So was Loxton's.

'What happened to him?'

'We don't know yet,' Loxton said. 'We need to do a post-mortem and for the formal identification to come back.'

'But it is him, isn't it?' I said. 'Why else would you be here so late?'

'The male didn't have any ID on him, but he was wearing a watch. We were hoping you could have a look.' Loxton took out an evidence bag from her briefcase and held it up to me. Inside, suspended in the tight plastic, was Mark's watch. I'd bought it for his birthday.

I leaned closer and turned the bag over to read the inscription.

'Is this Mark's watch, Julia?' Loxton was watching me carefully.

There was no doubt. I'd inscribed it myself. I nodded through the tears.

'Thank you.' Loxton returned the watch to her briefcase.

'Did you find his wedding ring?' I asked as I touched my own. The past few days had made me question Mark's love for me more than ever, but if he had the ring, that proved our love had been real. I'd have that at least.

Loxton shook her head. 'Not yet.'

'I want to see him.' I stood. I needed to be with him. I owed him that much.

Despair crossed Loxton's face, making her look much older. She exchanged a look with Kowalski that I didn't like.

'I'm not sure that's a good idea,' Loxton said at last.

'I could identify him for you.' I knew every line on his face, every freckle on his body.

'It's not that simple, I'm afraid.' Loxton swallowed hard. 'You wouldn't recognize him. The river . . . it's . . . it's damaged the body. We're going to have to do a dental comparison or DNA for the formal identification.' Her gaze dropped to the floor.

'How can a river damage a body?' A surge of rage flowed through me. He belonged to me, and I needed to be with him, wherever he was.

'Do you know if Mark was wearing his watch when you last saw him?' Kowalski said as Loxton continued to look away.

I tried hard to remember the past few weeks. My mind was fogging over. 'I don't know.'

'Please, this has been a big shock,' Lucy said. 'Can't you see it's too much?'

'Of course,' Kowalski said. 'We'll leave you now.'

'But I need to be with him. Where is he?'

'It's not possible right now,' Loxton said.

I stood up, refusing to take no for an answer, but they all ignored me. It was as if I didn't exist. Lucy walked them out of the living room, and I could hear them talking in the hallway.

'Mark's parents are being informed now by our colleagues.' My heart sank. Poor Elizabeth and Charles.

'Thank you,' Lucy said and added in a whisper. 'Julia's in no fit state.'

Then they were gone.

It was as if I'd fallen into someone else's life. Everything was the same – the pictures on the walls, the sofa and cushions – but they weren't mine anymore. It didn't feel real. Something had come into my life and taken away the Mark I knew and replaced him with a stranger who'd been missing and now had been found.

Lucy was beside me, wrapping her arms around me, pulling me close.

'It's going to be all right, you'll see,' Lucy whispered, rocking me back and forth as if she could soothe my pain.

I closed my eyes. Her body felt wooden, as if it was a life sized doll. She wasn't real. The whole world wasn't real and no one else could see it but me.

Chapter 16

Alana Loxton

Tuesday

Loxton walked out of Talbot's flat filled with a useless anger. If they'd got there first, that meeting would have been different. Still hard, but they'd have had Talbot on side. Losing the family at this stage would compromise the investigation. She waited until they were in the car and away from prying ears before speaking.

'That was difficult.' She massaged her temples, giving herself a moment to relieve the tension.

'All we ever do is deliver bad news,' Kowalski said. 'Sometimes I hate this job.'

'What the hell was that journalist doing there already?' The memory of Alec Saunders outside the house caused a lump in Loxton's throat. He was the man who had ruined her career. She hated him more than anyone else on the planet. He'd nearly destroyed her.

Kowalski let out a long sigh and stared out of the window. 'I don't know, but we need to let Patel know the press might be on their way to Charles Rowthorn's house. Winter won't be happy this has been leaked so quick.'

'Shit.' She grabbed her mobile and spoke to Patel, who

confirmed that they were already at the Rowthorns' house
and there were no press there yet.

'Only you, me, the uniformed officer and Winter knew
about that body.' Kowalski turned on the car's heating.
'One of us is leaking information to the press. Winter
isn't going to blame himself, is he?'

'Great. That makes me suspect number one as I'm the
new girl.' Loxton slumped back into her seat. A pain was
screwing into her forehead, slow and relentless. So, this
was history repeating itself. She'd rightly been accused
of leaking information to the press before, but that was
through her own stupidity, which was the only reason
she still had a job – she'd been manipulated by Saunders.
But whoever had leaked the story on this case had done
it deliberately. For cash or for favours she didn't know,
but she would be the one to get the blame.

'I was with you the whole time,' Kowalski said. It was
small comfort; he didn't know about her past.

'It doesn't matter,' she said. 'We know it wasn't us.'
But it did matter. Of course it did.

'I'll handle Winter,' Kowalski said. 'It's the uniform.
He'll have told someone who's told three other people.
You know how it goes. I wouldn't worry about it.'

There was a light rapping at her window. Startled, she
turned to look.

It was Alec.

She opened the window, holding her breath. The rain
had eased, but there was still a light drizzle.

'I forgot to ask earlier, how are you keeping?' Alec
Saunders grinned at her.

She wanted to punch him in the face. 'Much better
now I don't have to deal with your bullshit. You're not
going to get a quote from us, Alec, so piss off.'

He laughed politely. 'Always the feisty one. I'm not here for a quote. I just wanted to see how you are.'

Loxton didn't know how to answer. Inside she was seething. She had so many things she wanted to say to him, but Kowalski's presence stopped her.

'How did you find out so quick?' Loxton asked. 'Who told you?'

'I never reveal a source.' Alec tapped his nose with a finger.

'You shouldn't have told Talbot about the body,' Kowalski said. 'That woman is more distraught than she needed to be, just because you're desperate for a story.'

'It's not my fault you're so slow.' Alec shrugged.

Kowalski frowned, his demeanour turning sour. 'Look, mate,' he said. 'We've got actual work to do, rather than profiting from other people's misery, so why don't you fuck off? You can quote me on that.'

'But police and journalists can work well together, can't they, Alana?' Alec said. 'We could help each other out here.'

Kowalski revved the engine. 'You should step back now. Wouldn't want to ruin your shiny shoes.'

Kowalski pressed on the accelerator and jolted the car forward an inch. Alec jumped backwards, his mouth open.

'Told you to step back, *ukłucie*,' Kowalski said over the growl of the engine.

'*Ukłucie*?' Alec frowned.

'It means "prick" in Polish,' Kowalski said as he surged the car forward.

'You crazy Polish twat,' Alec said. 'I'll have your—'

Loxton didn't catch the rest as the car raced forward, leaving Alec a tiny figure in the passenger mirror.

'How'd you know that idiot?' he asked.

'Press conferences . . .' Loxton lied. 'He had a few useful sources and could dig up things we couldn't. But that was a long time ago. I stopped working with him. Unreliable. His need for a scoop was more of a priority than protecting evidence.' She watched London whizzing past her window.

'Isn't that all reporters?' Kowalski threw her a sideways glance as he traversed the traffic.

'Some of them are good guys.' She couldn't look at Kowalski.

'But not that prick?'

'No. Not that prick.'

Kowalski drove in silence, back towards the nick, throwing her glances a couple of times, but she kept her eyes forwards watching the road ahead.

As they neared Walworth police station, Kowalski pulled into a side street a few roads away and parked up.

He turned to face her. 'If we're going to work together, Alana, you need to be honest with me.'

Kowalski's cold blue eyes bored into her. She squirmed in her seat and stared ahead, watching the wipers swishing across the windscreen.

'Alec Saunders is the reason I got shunted out of the murder squad.'

'Okay.' Kowalski folded his arms across his chest.

She took in a big breath and turned to face him. Dancing around it was painful. 'I met him in a bar. He told me he was an A&E doctor.'

'Christ.' Kowalski shook his head at her. 'You're not a probationer, Loxton.'

'We were together for a couple of months. He started

staying over more and more. Then we pretty much lived together; the relationship got serious fast. I fell in love with him. We'd talk about work. His patients, difficult decisions. And, eventually, I talked about my murder case.'

'And he printed it?'

'Not until my murder trial was underway. A husband had killed his young wife when she'd filed for divorce. The media went mad. She was a model whose career had just got going. Saunders's paper was going for a miscarriage of justice angle. "*Innocent man wrongly accused. Police desperate to get a result, no matter what.*"'

'And were you?' he asked.

'No, of course not. The suspect was guilty as sin, but he got off. And it was my fault. There was enough doubt tossed into the mix to throw the jury off. I would tell Alec everything – the decisions we made, the avenues we prioritized, the false intelligence leads we eventually wrote off as misinformation.'

'Are you sure your suspect did it?'

'Yes.' She put her fingertips on her temples and massaged them lightly. 'He reported his wife missing. He'd hired a professional hit on her, didn't want half his estate going to her when she filed for divorce. He'd made the body disappear, but the hitman had been sloppy with the crime scene. We had him.' She looked at Kowalski.

'So, the suspect had money. He could have hired Alec Saunders to go above and beyond his journalistic duty to get insider information, make sure the police looked bad in the press.'

'Yes.' She folded her arms across her chest.

'So this Saunders is baying for your blood?'

'We couldn't prove a connection between Alec and the suspect. All I could do was put in a complaint to the journalist bureau about his conduct and he got fired. He's had to go freelance ever since.'

'And he's desperate for the next big scoop.'

She nodded.

'Strange that Saunders turned up at the fiancée's address so quick and this just happens to be your case. We better tell Winter.'

So, telling Kowalski had been a mistake. 'I know it looks bad,' she said. 'That's why I don't want everyone knowing about this and gossiping about me. Alec has already ruined my career enough. Can you keep it to yourself?'

'Alana, you should tell Winter. Lying about it is only going to make it worse.'

'I'm not lying about it,' she said, frustrated. 'I'm just not going to mention it. You have to believe me, I didn't leak anything.'

'I know you didn't. I've been with you the whole time.'

'I just can't let that man hinder my career again. I won't let him.'

'All right, have it your way.' Kowalski said, but he stared at her for just a moment too long. He wasn't happy. He turned on the engine and they headed towards the police station in silence. It was a risk not telling Winter, yes, but it was an even bigger risk telling him. He might kick her off the case, and she wasn't ready to give up yet – she needed to find out what had happened to Mark Rowthorn. To prove to herself that she still could.

Chapter 17

Julia Talbot

Tuesday

I kept seeing Mark. Every single time I closed my eyes. There was no rest. It didn't matter how many sleeping pills I took, I couldn't knock myself out. I just couldn't believe I'd never speak to him again.

My mobile pierced the silence. A Facebook Message from 'Chantelle' flashed up on the screen. My stomach churned. Jonny.

Lucy looked up, a quizzical expression on her face.

'It's Elizabeth,' I said quietly. 'She's asked me to call her. I'll go in my room.'

Lucy pulled a confused face. 'But she only just called an hour ago? And it's getting really late.'

'She's distraught, maybe she forgot to ask me something. I don't know, I need to be there for her.'

'Yes, of course, you're right.' Lucy nodded at me. 'Sorry.'

I retreated to my bedroom, closing the door behind me. I took a deep breath in to calm myself and then read Jonny's message.

'I can't find your husband,' Jonny's message read. 'I've tried everything, but he's done a great job of disappearing. This will shock you, but I found out he owes a few drug dealers some money. A *lot* of money. Maybe he's had to do a runner?'

'Mark's dead.' I messaged back.

There was a long pause and then he typed. 'I'm so sorry. What happened?'

I pressed the video call on Facebook Messenger. I wanted to see him try to deny he'd killed Mark to my face. He accepted the video call.

'The police found his body in the river this evening.'

'I'm . . . I'm sorry.' His voice faltered and he looked genuinely shocked. I couldn't figure out if it was an act or not.

'You did this.'

'No, Jenny. I didn't.' He shook his head as if in disbelief. 'I'm sorry.'

'*You fucking did this and you're going to pay.*' I hissed, clutching the mobile tighter.

'No. Jenny, I swear. I didn't touch him.' Jonny's words rushed out of him, panicked.

'I don't believe you.' Tears pricked my eyes. I wanted this all to stop. I wanted him to leave me alone.

'He was in the river?' Jonny said. 'Did the police say what happened?'

'They don't know yet, but they'll find out.' Why was I even speaking to him? But once I started saying the words out loud, I just couldn't stop.

'I don't think it's suicide,' Jonny said. 'Mark was in a lot of debt. Sounds like he had quite a drug habit. Let me see if I can get you some names of the people he owed money to.'

'He didn't take drugs.' The lie was out of my mouth before I could stop it. *He did take drugs. You know he did.* But only at the weekends, as a social thing.

'Jenny, his drug debt died with— They won't bother you. There are rules.'

Tears choked me. I needed to keep him talking. Try to find out if he was lying or not. 'How did you find all this out?'

'I told you, I work for this guy who needs background checks done on people. I did some digging to try to find your fella, and this drug stuff came back. People were after him. I think they caught up with him.'

My back straightened. He'd let something slip he shouldn't have. 'You already know who he owed money to. Tell me their names.'

'I don't know their names, I just heard he owed people some money for drugs. But I'll find out who they are. I'm risking a lot here, though. These people are dangerous. If they ever find out I passed their names to you, they would kill me.'

'I don't believe you.' I should call the police right now. Tell them everything.

'Give me twenty-four hours and then you can go to the police,' he said. 'Just twenty-four hours and I'll get you those names. If I don't, then you can call the police. But it wasn't me. I wouldn't have contacted you if I'd killed Mark. Think about it, it doesn't make sense. Please. I'll be in touch soon.'

Then silence.

He'd managed to avoid telling me the names, if they were even real. But the police had talked about drugs and Mark hadn't been paying the mortgage for months. He'd been in trouble at work. Had he got into debt with drug dealers? Had it got him murdered? Mark had hidden all of this from me. I needed to look at our lives again, but with my eyes open this time. To find out what happened to him.

I needed to find the password for Mark's accounts. Would he have hidden them in the flat or memorized them?

I lay on our bed, trying to put myself in Mark's head, but I realized I had no idea. I rolled over to face his side of the bed. The sheets weren't ruffled, that half not slept in.

Grief seeped into the spaces where emptiness had been. I'd felt pain like it once before. When Rachel had died. Everyone I loved was stolen from me. I was cursed. But then the Mark I'd loved had never existed. He'd been a fantasy.

Now I had to work out where this stranger had hidden his bank passwords. Where he'd been spending his time when he'd told me he'd been working. It might lead me to his killer.

Jonny had asked for twenty-four hours. After that I'd tell the police about him. There was a chance he was telling the truth and I couldn't risk the opportunity of getting the names from him. I knew he'd never tell the police. What difference could twenty-four hours make?

Chapter 18

Alana Loxton

Wednesday

Southwark's mortuary was no different to any other Loxton had been in; the corridors were white and bathed in a cold, bright light, throwing every defect into the forefront. Beside her Kowalski checked the time on his mobile, turning the shadows under his eyes a deep purple. It was ten past nine in the morning, and they hadn't seen a soul since the receptionist had first let them in.

'Update from Patel,' Kowalski said. 'The mobile that sent the threatening text to Rowthorn has been turned off since Rowthorn disappeared, as has Rowthorn's personal mobile. Patel's getting the techs to download the historic cell-siting and phone data, but we won't get anything current until those phones are turned back on.'

'We might get an idea of the location of this person from the historic data.' Loxton doubted it, however. And if the mobiles were never turned back on, how would they ever find the person who had threatened Rowthorn? She didn't want to dampen Kowalski's enthusiasm, though; it was the only thing making the day bearable as she waited for the post-mortem to begin.

A bald man in pristine white overalls came over. He

looked in his early sixties. 'Here for the special post-mortem?' he asked.

'Yes,' she said.

'I'm George, assisting for today,' the bald man said. 'Right this way.'

Loxton and Kowalski followed George. For an odd moment, it was as if he was leading them to their table for dinner.

The comparison ended once the smell of rancid meat and formaldehyde hit her as she entered the next room. It was ice-cold and she shivered, pulling her coat tighter and buttoning it up. The room had several steel tables around its perimeter, on top of which rested the dead. No one had bothered to cover them up; this was their domain. She was both fascinated and repulsed in equal measure.

George strode past it all, not looking at the bodies once.

'You've got a lot in,' she said.

'Not much gets done at the weekends; they just shove the bodies in the fridges. Those porters haven't got a clue. If you're not careful, Mrs Miggins's cause of death will be prostate cancer.'

'Please tell me you're taking the piss?' Kowalski said.

'I wish I was,' George replied. 'Here's your one.' George stopped by the last table. In this sterile room, the body looked more surreal.

'Have you formally identified him yet?' Loxton asked.

'Waiting on the dental records to match up with your missing man. We tried fingerprints but all of the skin's been eaten away.'

'What about DNA?' she said.

'Your DCI declined DNA. Said it'd cost a fortune.

Dental's slower but it's all about saving money these days. The dead man was wearing your missing man's watch, wasn't he?'

Loxton nodded. 'Yes, but you can't tell on the last CCTV images we have of him that he was wearing the watch the day he went missing, as he had a coat on. And his fiancée couldn't remember.'

'Thorough, I like that.' George nodded his approval and then took hold of one end of the table the body was laid on. 'Whilst we're waiting for Dr Reynolds, might as well set up. Miss, could you grab that end of the table and help me wheel him to the post-mortem room?'

'Sure.' Loxton took the other end of the table.

George led them into a large rectangular room lit by fluorescent white lighting, giving the impression that they were all on stage. They pushed the trolley into the centre of the room where Reynolds was already waiting for them, snapping on his plastic gloves.

'Is this one your case, DC Loxton?' Reynolds said. 'Nice to have you back, you were missed.'

'It's good to be back,' Loxton said. She liked Reynolds. He was a good pathologist. Quick but thorough. And he had the grace not to mention her suspension and demotion.

'Excellent, we have the dream team assembled then. George, start the recorder. Officer, the hacksaw, please.'

Loxton passed Reynolds the hacksaw and he moved towards the head. She steeled herself for the smell. It was unbearable now, but it'd be worse when the body was split open.

'Trauma noted to the back of head. Unknown if this is the cause of death yet.'

Kowalski flinched beside her as the first incision was

made into the forehead. That was the worst bit. If you could get through that, you'd make it.

Loxton reached into her pockets and held up a packet of mints. 'Here.'

Kowalski took them and ripped open the packet. Loxton went over to George and leaned towards his ear. 'I'll be the exhibits officer.'

'Are you sure, Missy? It's a messy job.'

Loxton glanced back at Kowalski who was furiously sucking on the mint and George's gaze followed hers. 'Ah,' he said. 'For the best.'

The pathologist was already examining the brain and taking his samples. She hurried over and labelled the test tubes and exhibited them.

No one had told her when she joined the police that she'd be handling body parts. It had never occurred to her what an exhibits officer meant, until she'd gone to her first post-mortem. What a wake-up call that had been.

Loxton navigated through the post-mortem, Kowalski helping where he could.

'Interesting lesions to the brain.' Reynolds pointed out the scar tissue.

'Cause of death?' Loxton's eyes met Reynolds's.

'Oh no, he's had these for a while. Could be substance misuse of some kind.'

'Could it be from cocaine?' she asked.

'That would explain the lesions. He must've had quite a habit. Or it could be alcohol abuse. I'll know more when the toxicology report is back and I've checked the liver.'

'And the brain trauma at the back of the skull?'

'He was alive when that happened. I can tell by the blood that's gathered around the injury and the swelling of the brain. If he was dead, you wouldn't get this reaction in the brain material. The impact was a blunt trauma.'

'Consistent with hitting his head from a height?' she asked.

'Unlikely, but not impossible. I'd expect the neck to be broken and it isn't. Also the head trauma would be more severe and widespread.'

Reynolds looked perplexed as he carried on with the examination. He noted the preliminary findings for the cause of death as drowning and that the liver did have significant lesions. She knew they'd have to wait for toxicology and his final report before it was confirmed.

They stood by the car for a moment, taking in the fresh morning air, both relieved to be out of the morgue. She carefully packed the samples in the icebox for transportation to the toxicology laboratory.

'So there's still a chance our man jumped after a bit of Dutch courage?' Kowalski asked.

'He didn't jump very far. If you wanted to kill yourself, you'd pick a higher bridge. Drowning's one of the worst ways to go. He could have fallen in by accident, but we still can't rule out murder.' Loxton found herself more and more convinced that Rowthorn had been killed.

'Murder will be hard to prove.' Kowalski shook his head. 'Suicide's more likely.'

'He was in debt and about to lose his job,' Loxton conceded. 'And he was struggling with a drug addiction.' It was all laid out like a trail for her to follow. But it was too easy. She wasn't seeing all the other signs along the way.

Chapter 19

Alana Loxton

Wednesday

Loxton and Kowalski stared at the pages of highlighted phone data spread out in front of them. It was from Rowthorn's work mobile and the hidden one they had found. Loxton rubbed her face, tiredness making it hard to focus on the numbers. It was early afternoon, but she felt groggy from lack of sleep, her eyes hurting and everything aching in complaint. Kowalski pulled out a packet of Haribo from his desk and offered it to her. She shook her head.

'Only thing that's keeping me awake.' He popped one in his mouth.

She smiled at him as he popped another sweet into his mouth, then looked back at her papers. 'Rowthorn was getting through three grams of cocaine most weeks.'

Loxton thought of Julia Talbot, the permanent red eyes and circles underneath. How would she feel when she was told the man she had loved and was desperate to find had never existed? Mark Rowthorn had been a carefully constructed fantasy – devoted fiancé, perfect son and successful investment broker. That was all about to shatter.

'I've put the mobile number of the drug dealer supplying Rowthorn through the system,' said Kowalski. 'It was bought a month ago, unregistered pay-as-you-go.'

'Another nameless ghost,' she said. 'Can't be anyone high up the chain; they'd have known to ditch the mobile after a few days and get a new one.' Were they amateurish enough to still have the phone? Loxton hoped so; they were due a lucky break.

'The mobile that sent threatening texts is also unregistered,' Kowalski said. 'It became active three weeks before Rowthorn disappeared and was only used to send threats to him. "*You will burn.*"'

'Burn for what?' she said. 'Inside trading? A drug deal?' A headache bloomed deep inside her head.

'It could be anything.' Kowalski dropped the pages back on the desk as if he was done with them. 'I'll get the dealer's texts and call data from the phone company. This could be as simple as a drug deal gone wrong.'

'The best man still looks good to me.' Loxton flipped through the pages until she found what she was looking for. '"*I can't believe you'd do that. What's wrong with you?*" That's Steele to Rowthorn a week before the wedding. And the number that called Steele just before we interviewed him at Talbot's flat that first day has come back as a burner phone. It was only used for that one phone call.'

'So someone high up the chain to be that disciplined. We need to speak to Steele again,' Kowalski said.

'Agreed,' she said. 'He was the last person to see Rowthorn. And we need to ask him about the insider trading.'

'Better update the boss we're going to visit Steele.' Kowalski looked at Winter's office and then at her. She returned his strained look. They'd been avoiding Winter, but they couldn't hide anymore.

'We should tell him about the leak too, but we don't have to mention Alec Saunders's name. It's not really relevant.' Loxton looked at him, hoping he'd agree. She felt awful asking Kowalski not to mention Alec Saunders, but she knew she'd be treated differently, as if she was the one leaking police information.

Kowalski sighed and nodded. 'All right then, but that better be the last we see of Saunders.'

'I'm sure it will be.' She prayed that it was.

Winter stared at Loxton in amazement. 'You're telling me that Rowthorn was taking drugs and that he and Steele are linked to insider trading at City Enterprises. And just before Rowthorn goes missing, Steele has an argument with him?' Winter stopped pacing. 'This situation is out of control. Have you seen the press outside?'

Loxton looked at Kowalski, their eyes locked, neither wanting to take the lead.

'What?' Winter sank into his chair. 'Tell me.'

Kowalski placed his hands on the desk, as if bracing himself. 'There's a problem.'

'You're telling me. What now?' Winter sighed, his shoulders dropping.

'A journalist got to Talbot first. Told her about the body in the river.'

'Oh God.' Winter put his head in his hands. 'How the hell did the press get there before you?'

'We don't know, sir.'

'Why didn't you tell me this before?' Winter frowned at Kowalski.

'We . . . got caught up in enquiries.' Kowalski wouldn't meet Winter's gaze. The truth hung in the air. They had been avoiding him, neither wanting to have to mention Saunders.

'What was the journalist's name?' Winter asked.

'Alex something . . .' Kowalski said. 'He didn't give us his name. Some freelance guy.'

Winter frowned at them in turn. 'I'd better call the Commander. This means there's a leak, and I won't stop until I find it. What you've just told me doesn't leave this room, obviously.'

They nodded in unison. Loxton's throat was tight and she felt sick. She wanted to run out of the room.

'Charles Rowthorn will no doubt have already complained to the Commander.' He regarded them both in turn. 'Rowthorn's been demanding we stop the press from releasing Julia Talbot's photograph and details. The police press bureau has requested that the media not print her photograph out of respect, but it's only a matter of time until one paper does, and then they all will. And now a journalist has been at her house, giving her the death message before we could. You should have told me immediately.'

'I'm sorry, sir,' Kowalski said.

'You'd better get going.' Winter turned to his monitor.

'Going?' Kowalski asked.

'This Steele keeps coming up.' Winter's eyes darkened. 'Get in his face. Make him sweat. See what he does. I'll authorize a drugs warrant. Search his flat under that pretence but find this missing mobile if it is him.'

'We're on it.' Kowalski was out of the door nearly as quickly as Loxton.

Chapter 20

Alana Loxton

Wednesday

Steele's flat was on the twentieth floor and fitted every preconception Loxton had about bankers. The living room was bigger than her entire apartment. Every surface gleamed under the spotlights. She noticed Kowalski was gawping at the room. Was he trying to calculate how much it was all worth, like she was?

The London skyline glittered back at her, the Shard overlooking the city. The evening was cloudy, blocking out the stars.

'Thank you for seeing us,' Loxton said.

'I heard you found a body. Is it Mark?' Despite the sombre demeanour, Steele was wearing a tuxedo and his hair was styled with gel. He was holding a glass of what looked like whisky.

'It's not confirmed yet,' she said, 'but it's looking that way. We have a few questions.'

'I was just going out. The bank's had this fundraiser organized for months. I can't skip it. Will this take long?' He took a swig from his glass.

'It shouldn't do. Was Mark wearing a watch when you

last saw him?' She needed to ask him this question before executing the warrant and he closed down.

'You're kidding me.' Steele stared at them both in turn. 'I have no idea, sorry.'

'It was a silver Armani watch with a navy face.'

'I don't remember.' He put the glass down. His eyes kept sliding to the door.

'Did he mention losing his watch?' Kowalski asked.

'No.' Steele checked his own Omega, impatient.

'How was Mark in the weeks leading up to the wedding?' Loxton said.

'You've already asked me this.' He frowned at them. 'He was a bit jittery but that's what you'd expect from a groom.'

'Did you have any arguments with him?' Loxton wished, not for the first time, that she could read minds.

'No, not really.' Steele couldn't meet her eye. 'He did become a bit of a groomzilla, though. You know, everything had to be perfect.'

'David, we know about the insider trading in the bank.'

'That's got nothing to do with me.' Steele's voice became cold and his shoulders visibly tensed. 'I don't know anything about that.'

'Mark was facing a disciplinary board. He was your best friend and you didn't know anything about it? Everyone else at the bank did. The bank has passed the investigation to us and your name has come up.'

'I can't answer for Mark and I don't know anything about the insider trading.' Steele looked nervous, his eyes flitting about the flat, as if searching for a way to escape. 'I don't have to talk to you, I know my rights. Now get the hell out of my flat.' He glared at her and banged his whisky glass down on a side table and walked to the door.

'Actually, we'll be staying. We have a drugs warrant to search your premises authorized by my boss and signed by the magistrate.' Loxton took a copy out of her jacket to show him.

'This is a fucking joke.' Steele's voice rose, as he punched the wall; the crack of his knuckles reverberated through the empty space. He didn't even flinch at the pain. He was working himself up for a fight. He snatched the copy of the warrant from her hand and ripped it into pieces, scattering it onto the floor. 'You're not searching my flat.'

Loxton pulled out her handcuffs. She felt adrenaline course through her veins, anger and fear mixing together to put her on high alert. She kept her voice calm. 'Put your hands out in front of you, Mr Steele. This search is happening whether you want it to or not. Don't make it any worse for yourself.'

Steele stared at the handcuffs. 'You're not fucking putting them on me.' He shoved his head closer to hers, squaring up to her. His spittle hit her face, and the stench of stale whisky and smoke from his breath almost made her gag. Even his strong sandalwood aftershave couldn't cover it up. He must have been drinking all afternoon. Her stomach twisted in alarm. He towered over her by a foot.

'Calm down.' Kowalski stepped forward and put his hand on Steele. Kowalski was broader and a few inches taller, but Steele was not deterred. His pupils were pinpricks.

Loxton was losing patience with this dickhead. 'What have you taken?'

Steele shoved her backwards towards the front door. 'Fuck you, bitch.' Her leg collided with the sofa behind her, throwing her off balance, but she managed to steady herself.

Kowalski lunged at Steele and dragged him away from her. She grabbed Steele's wrist, but he pulled back, forcing her towards him, even while Kowalski was trying to restrain him. Steele's strength was terrifying.

'Don't even think about it.' Kowalski was still holding tight onto Steele's shoulders. 'You touch her again and you'll regret it.'

Steele span around to swing at Kowalski with his free arm. 'Get off me, you cunt!' It was as if he was possessed. Drugs?

Kowalski grappled with him as Loxton kicked down onto the back of Steele's knee. Suspects always underestimated the female officer. Steele's leg gave way and he collapsed. Kowalski stepped to Steele's side, twisting his arm behind his back, and used Steele's weight against him to push him downwards. Steele let out a feral growl as he crashed hard onto the floor.

She crouched down, trying to pin one of Steele's shoulders to the floor, but he thrashed about, trying to lift himself with his free arm. Kowalski shifted his grip, causing Steele to cry out.

He tried struggling through the pain but eventually gave up. 'All right. You're fucked up, the pair of you.' He relaxed his arm and Loxton grabbed his wrist, clicking the metal cuff onto it and then the other one.

Together, Loxton and Kowalski managed to help Steele onto his feet. Her breath was ragged and her muscles were starting to ache as the adrenaline wore off.

'You've broken my fucking arm,' Steele said.

Kowalski rolled his eyes. Loxton checked Steele over

but all he'd have in the morning was minor bruising –
like they would.

'You'll live,' she said.

'You two are about to lose your jobs.'

'If I had a pound for every time I'd heard that,'
Kowalski said as he searched Steele, 'I'd be nearly as rich
as you.'

'You are going to be in so much shit,' Steele said
through gritted teeth.

'You're under arrest for assaulting an officer.' Kowalski
still had hold of him. 'You do not have to say anything,
but it may harm your defence if you do not mention
when questioned something which you later rely on in
court. Anything you do say may be given in evidence.'

Steele shook his head in annoyance. Kowalski searched
him, retrieving Steele's mobile phone from his pocket and
putting it into a plastic bag. That was probably Steele's
main mobile, and they knew he hadn't used it to send
threatening texts to Rowthorn, if it was him who'd sent
them.

'You search the flat, Alana,' Kowalski said. 'You've got
a knack for it. And why don't you take a seat, Mr Steele?
We're going be here a while.'

Loxton was glad of Steele's lack of substance. The flat
was minimalistic, and she searched through Steele's living
room and bedroom quickly, looking for any hidden
mobiles while she searched for drugs. She was sweating
by the time she found something – underneath a loose
floorboard beneath the bed.

Wrapped inside a plastic shopping bag were clear
plastic snap bags with white powder inside. Cocaine. Not
the mobile she was hoping for, but better than nothing.

Loxton headed to the en-suite. She pulled off her gloves

and placed them carefully on the white sink. Her hands were sticky and the fresh air was good on her skin. She bent down to splash her face with cold water but stopped.

There was something on the white bathmat. A tiny dark reddish-brown stain. She knelt down to take a better look. Dried blood. She'd seen it enough times to recognize it. She put her gloves back on and gently lifted up the mat. More traces of blood. Someone had tried to cover it up.

Looking closer, she saw there were more tiny drops of red on the grouting between the white tiles by the sink. Someone had wiped most of it away, but hadn't been very thorough. But whose blood was it? Could this be the last room that Rowthorn had seen?

She dialled Winter's number. She was going to need a full forensic team.

Chapter 21

Julia Talbot

Wednesday

Sunlight poured in through the living room windows, intensifying the heat in the room. I wiped the sweat from my forehead as I took a moment to catch my breath. It was two in the afternoon and a sweltering hot summer's day. I'd thrown all the windows open, but if anything it seemed to make the room hotter.

I could have done with Lucy's help, but she was at work, and then she had to pick up James from the airport. She'd said that she could come over afterwards in the evening, but I'd told her she should see James. Elizabeth and Charles were coming over later for a few hours to discuss the funeral, and it was best if it was just the three of us.

I'd heaved another big box into the living room and dumped it onto the floor. I'd been working all morning. I was fast running out of boxes. I still hadn't found any clue as to what had been going on in Mark's life. The police said Mark had been stealing money from work, but then Jonny had said Mark was in debt to drug dealers. I needed to know what had happened to all of this money.

There was so much crap hidden about our flat it'd taken me four hours to get this far. It was hard to believe what we'd been carrying about with us for all this time. Everything from old tax bills, birthday cards and my school paintings were scattered around me. I'd kept my school art to show my children one day – our children. That would never happen now.

How could something so sure end up like this? I guess I'd never really known Mark and he'd never known me. I'd been meticulous in my lies to make sure to keep my secrets hidden from him. I'd told him my parents were dead. I'd pretended I'd always been Julia Talbot. And I'd never told him about Rachel.

It had never occurred to me that he'd been keeping his own secrets from me. We'd projected different people onto each other, and we'd tried to become them. That's where we'd gone so wrong. If we'd just been honest with each other, maybe he wouldn't be dead now. But that just wasn't how I operated. I was always lying. Always hiding. Never letting anyone in.

I cried silently as I carried on my search. The box in front of me was different from all the rest, in that it was solely Mark's. Nothing of mine was mixed inside. There were folders full of paperwork, but a cursory glance showed me that it was his old university junk.

There was a photo of Mark graduating. He looked so young and handsome. There was a university group shot, too, but I didn't recognize anyone. I'd never met any of Mark's university friends. I was starting to realize how little I'd known about his past.

I dug through the rest of the papers and, right at the bottom of the box, was an envelope with my name in Mark's handwriting. The envelope was bright white and it stood out against the yellowing papers around it. I struggled to tear open the envelope in my panic. I pulled out the letter and saw Mark's neat handwriting running across the page.

It was his last will and testament.

I stared at the words. He had left me everything. With our finances the way they were, that wasn't much, but his life insurance was worth four hundred thousand pounds, and I was set to inherit all of it. There was a separate note inside with the details of a hidden online crypto account.

I followed Mark's instructions to check the hidden account, first downloading TOR and then bouncing off different servers. But it looked like the account had been emptied the day he went missing. One hundred thousand pounds – gone. So, Mark must have been murdered for money. Or that was what someone was trying to make it look like. And the only person who stood to benefit had been me. Had the police seen this will? Did they know about his life insurance?

I went back to the box and saw that I'd missed something. There was a business card right at the bottom. I picked it up, the glossy dark blue highlighting the words *The Night Jar Bar* in swirling white italics across it. The figure '50,000' was scribbled across the nightclub's card in Mark's handwriting. My hand shook as I held the card, staring at the numbers. This was the nightclub Jonny had met me at.

I put the card into my jeans pocket and tried to steady my breathing. A wave of nausea rose in my throat. Had Jonny lied to me? Had he known Mark? I grabbed my keys and headed for the door. His twenty-four hours were nearly up.

Chapter 22

Alana Loxton

Wednesday

'Mr Steele, would you care to tell me about the cocaine I found in your flat?' Loxton sat opposite Steele in the interview room, only the small plastic table between them. So far, all of his replies had been, 'No comment'. Anger radiated off him. She was glad Kowalski's large bulk was beside her.

Steele looked to his solicitor, the overweight Mr Harrington, whose cobalt three-piece suit and ridiculous red tie wouldn't have looked out of place at a wedding. Mr Harrington shook his head slightly.

Steele replied again: 'No comment.'

The solicitor was good. He'd spotted Steele's temper and decided it was best he said as little as possible. She sighed. There would be no coaxing anything out of him now.

'Ever given cocaine to Mark Rowthorn?' she asked.

'No comment.'

'We know you both took cocaine together socially.'

'No comment.' Steele narrowed his eyes at her.

'This is your interview, Mr Steele,' Loxton said. 'Your solicitor won't be standing in the box with you if this goes to trial. You'll be facing the music – alone. He gets paid whether you get off or not.'

'I'm not a child.' Steele sneered at her.

Kowalski, whose tall frame had been threatening to topple the flimsy plastic chair he'd been leaning back on, moved suddenly forward, forcing the front legs to bang back onto the floor. Steele flinched momentarily. Steele and Mr Harrington's chairs were screwed to the floor.

Kowalski scribbled onto Loxton's notebook so that only she could see: 'This one's a real prick.' It broke the tension of Steele's angry gaze and Loxton relaxed.

'Let's cut to the chase shall we, David?' she said. 'We found blood in your flat.'

'Blood?' Steele's voice sounded panicked.

'A lot of blood.' She kept her voice steady.

'Where?' Steele crossed his arms in front of him defensively, but he couldn't hide that he'd gone pale.

'It's your flat; you tell me.' Loxton shrugged and waited.

Before he could answer, Harrington interrupted. 'Officer, you didn't disclose this to me before the interview.' He was frowning. 'And what has this got to do with possession of cocaine and assaulting a police officer? Is it your blood?' He scanned her face and body and pulled a puzzled face at her.

The bruise on her leg throbbed as she remembered the fight in the flat. 'I don't need to disclose every last detail of the police's case before I begin an interview,' she said. 'We're here to record and test your client's account. And no, it's not my blood. Now come on, Mr Steele. I haven't got all day.'

'The bathroom.' Steele waved his arm dismissively. 'I cut myself shaving.'

'You must have hit an artery,' Kowalski said. 'There

was blood everywhere.' He swept his arms wide, indicating the whole room.

'There wasn't a sea of blood this morning,' Steele threw a glance at his solicitor, then turned his full attention back to Kowalski.

'Maybe not to the naked eye,' Kowalski said. 'But once the area's been sprayed with luminol, our UV lights can pick up the blood spatters, and there was blood everywhere in your bathroom.'

Steele frowned but there was a flash of something else. Fear.

'It's time to tell the truth, Mr Steele,' Loxton said.

'I . . . I remember now.' Steele's gaze darted between the officers. His voice had risen and the words tumbled out of him in a panic. 'I had a nosebleed. That's what happened. It was bad.' Steele started to pick at the nail on his index finger, tearing shreds of skin off.

'Some nosebleed.' Loxton shook her head at him in disbelief.

'I've always had bad nosebleeds.' He ripped a shred of skin away and a drop of bright red blood blossomed. He fixed on it, not meeting her eyes.

'Occupational hazard, shoving this up your nose.' Loxton tossed the packet of cocaine onto the table.

Steele's eyes flicked onto the bag.

'Talk me through this terrible nosebleed.' She wondered where he was going to try and go with his lies.

Steele couldn't look directly at her, so instead he focused to the right of her. Loxton recalled being taught in training school that people who are lying often looked to their left, accessing the part of their brain that imagines, as they thought up a lie on the spot. 'It . . . it started in the living room. Wouldn't stop. I went into the bathroom to clean up. Managed to stop it with cold water.' He smiled triumphantly.

'Did you go to the doctor afterwards?' Loxton said.

'It was just a nosebleed,' Steele shrugged.

'Quite a serious one from all the blood,' she said. 'When did this happen?'

'I don't know.' Steele looked to his solicitor and then back at Loxton. 'Saturday evening, I think.'

'I thought you were meant to be at Mark's flat on Saturday evening, not yours?' she said. Steele raked his hands through his hair and glared down at the table.

'So just around the time Mark went missing, lots of blood appears in your flat,' she continued. 'I wonder if the blood in your bathroom will come back as Mark's . . .' Loxton knew it would take the lab a few days to compare it to Mark Rowthorn's DNA, but she didn't have time to wait. She could only keep Steele in for twenty-four hours.

Steele's eyes widened and he turned to his solicitor. Not such the hard man after all. Sweat trickled down Harrington's fat face but he still shook his head at Steele.

'Won't take the lab long at all,' Loxton said. 'All we need to do is compare it to Mark Rowthorn's DNA, which we took from his toothbrush, and bingo, I bet we'll have a match.'

Steele swallowed and reached for the plastic cup on the table, taking several sips.

'Better start talking,' Kowalski said. 'Or you'll be sitting in a cell for a long, long time.'

'Fine.' He sat straighter, a cold look in his eyes. 'After we picked up the suits from the Yardsmen, Mark and I went back to *my* flat. And he was fine when he left.'

'You told us he left you at the Yardsmen and you never saw him again. We've been looking in the wrong place thanks to you.' Kowalski was struggling to keep his temper. 'Why not just say you went to your flat when we first talked to you?'

'Mr Steele, I'd advise you to answer "no comment" from now on,' Harrington said.

'I couldn't find him on the CCTV on the high street. How did you get to your flat?'

'We drove,' Steele answered, ignoring his solicitor's advice.

'And you're maintaining the blood is yours?' Loxton asked.

Steele sneered at her. 'Like you said, nosebleeds are an occupational hazard. So yes, I had a nosebleed. Mark and I took cocaine in my flat, but the blood's mine.'

'And then Mark goes missing and is found in the river,' Loxton said. 'How inconvenient for you. He can't back up your story.'

Steele closed his eyes for a second, as if realizing how ridiculous this all sounded.

'Why didn't you tell us this before?' Kowalski asked.

Steele shook his head at Kowalski. 'What a great mate I'd be. "Yeah, Mr Policeman, last time I saw Mark he was taking coke in my flat." He wasn't meant to be there. We were meant to be in his flat.'

'You lied to protect Mark?' Loxton said. 'I don't buy it. What if Mark overdosed and died in your flat? You panicked. You had to get rid of his body. You cleaned him up in the bathroom and then threw him in the Thames? He was meant to sink, but it didn't work out like that.'

Steele's eyes looked panicked as the enormity of his situation hit him. 'You . . . you can't think I've got anything to do with his death?' He looked from Kowalski to Loxton, as if searching for an ally. 'That's insane. I was his best friend. I don't know how he ended up in that river, but it wasn't anything to do with me.'

'Officers, you did *not* tell me this was a murder enquiry,' Harrington barked. 'This is an abuse of process. I shall make a formal complaint.'

'It isn't a murder enquiry,' Loxton said.

'But what you've just said—'

'I've just described concealing a dead body. You're the one who introduced the word murder; do you know something I don't?'

The solicitor scowled back at her and then started scribbling on his notepad.

'This is unethical.' He shook his head at her in disgust.

She turned away from him and looked at Steele. 'Do you see the problem we've got? You've lied consistently to us, telling us you last saw Mark outside the Yardsmen, but you last saw him at *your* flat. Why did you do that? We know you had a serious argument days before he disappeared – it's on his mobile. Your name is all over the insider trading, just like Mark's. There's blood in your flat. You don't have an alibi for the day he went missing. In fact, you were the last person to see him alive – and now it turns out it was at your flat.'

'Shit,' Steele put his head in his hands. 'What the fuck happened to him?' He ran his hands through his hair, pulling at the roots. It wasn't what she'd been expecting, but she also knew that Steele was a practised liar.

'That's what we're trying to find out,' Kowalski said.

'I wasn't the last person to see him alive. I mean . . . I wasn't on my own. Mark's dealer can vouch for me. We were all in my flat together.'

Harrington's voice rose in exasperation. 'My client will not be answering any further questions until—'

Steele turned to him. 'Why don't you shut your stupid fat face?' he shouted. 'They're trying to pin a fucking *murder* on me and you're telling me to go no comment?'

'Mr Steele, it's for them to prove—' Mr Harrington said.

'Next you'll be telling me miscarriages of justice never happen.' Steele turned back to Loxton, visibly calming himself.

'Tell me what happened, from the start.' Loxton tried to keep her voice neutral. As alibis went, this was up there.

Steele had stopped picking at his index finger. 'After we picked up the suits, Mark started getting nervous; wanted to take the edge off. He called his drug dealer. Said he wanted to buy some coke. His dealer picked us up in his car from the Yardsmen, we sat in the back of his car. He and Mark were friendly. He was always doing favours for Mark. I thought it was a bit weird, personally.'

That explained why Rowthorn's travel card and bank card hadn't been used since the Yardsmen. It was how he'd disappeared, and why she hadn't been able to pick him up on CCTV after that. There'd been a blind spot outside the Yardsmen of about twenty metres and the road itself wasn't covered well by the shop cameras.

'Why didn't you just tell us?' Kowalski folded his arms in front of his chest.

'I couldn't tell you Mark had got into a drug dealer's car.' Steele leaned towards them. 'He was in enough fucking trouble with the bank as it was without me telling them he hangs out with drug dealers. I thought he'd just done a runner. I guess it doesn't matter, he's dead.' Steele pressed his lips together, as if trying to control his emotions – or at least make a show that he was.

'What car did the drug dealer use?' Loxton hated these elaborate alibis, which would take time to disprove. 'Do you remember any of the registration?'

'Not the reg.' Steele shrugged at them. 'But I think it was a BMW . . . maybe an M3. It was matt black. I remember thinking, *This isn't bloody discreet.*' Steele ran his hands through his hair again, calmer now, more in control.

Loxton made a quick note. She would check the CCTV later, see if she could identify the car. It seemed to her that Steele was playing for time, hoping to get bail while they had to track down this imaginary car. Was he going to try and run for it?

'Go on.' Kowalski nodded at Steele.

'Mark got the dealer to drive us all to my flat. I wasn't happy about it, but Mark didn't want to go to his place, in case Julia turned up for some last-minute reason. The dealer sold Mark a few bags of coke. I bought a couple.' He pointed at the bags on the table. 'We both snorted some, just to test the purity before we bought it. The stuff was pure. I mean really pure. I got a nosebleed. That's never happened before. I'm cleaning myself up in the bathroom and Mark gets this WhatsApp, says he has to go. I know he had a woman on the side. I thought it was that. Me and the dealer were left in my flat and he ran out. It was bizarre.'

'A woman on the side?' Loxton couldn't help staring at Steele.

'I know I should have told you, but I just didn't want it getting back to Julia. In case Mark wanted to try again with her. I just thought he'd gone off with his other woman. I didn't know it was going to end like this.'

'Who is this other woman?'

'I have no idea. He kept pretty quiet about it. I only guessed – it's not like he ever admitted it.'

Loxton didn't believe him. 'Can you tell me more about this dealer?'

'I don't know.' Steele shrugged. 'His name was Jack . . . No, wait, Jonny. I never knew his surname.'

'Can you show us his mobile number on your phone?'

Steele shook his head. 'He was Mark's dealer. I never had his number and I think Mark contacted him through WhatsApp. I didn't want anything to do with him. He was a bit weird around Mark. Over-friendly. Wanted to be his mate. That was strange. But you get people acting like that around bankers. Money groupies.'

'Thanks for your cooperation. We'll be seizing your phone as evidence, David. This interview is terminated.' Loxton sat back. She watched Steele nervously running his hands through his hair, glancing at his solicitor as if to check he'd done enough. She didn't like Steele. She could tell all he ever did was lie.

She felt her mobile vibrate in her pocket. She stepped outside the interview room and Kowalski followed her.

'Good afternoon, DC Loxton. It's Dr Reynolds here.'

'Afternoon, doctor.' She put the phone on speaker so Kowalski could hear.

'The dental comparison has just come back on the body in the river,' Dr Reynolds continued. 'It's not Mark Rowthorn. It's come back as a Robert McGregor. I've emailed you the report.'

Loxton shook her head and looked at Kowalski in confusion. There must be a mistake. 'Are you sure?'

'I triple checked,' Dr Reynolds replied. 'It's not your missing man.'

'*Gówno.*' Kowalski's brow furrowed.

Chapter 23

Alana Loxton

Wednesday

'I can't keep Steele in for Mark Rowthorn's disappearance on this.' Winter dropped Loxton's report onto his desk. He looked at them both. 'I'll have to let him go.'

Loxton's heart ached with frustration. 'Sir, we know that Steele and Rowthorn had a row and I bet it's Rowthorn's blood in Steele's bathroom. Steele was the last person to see Rowthorn alive and that was at his flat. He lied to police. We should at least show it to the CPS.'

Winter tossed a file onto his desk. 'Loxton, you don't even have Rowthorn's body. The man found in the Thames is this Robert McGregor. And you've told me Steele thinks Rowthorn was having an affair.'

Loxton skimmed the report. Robert McGregor had been reported missing one week ago.

'Where the hell is Rowthorn then?' Kowalski said.

'And why was this missing person wearing Rowthorn's watch when he died?' She rubbed her face with her hands, trying to shift the tiredness she felt. If McGregor had been murdered, the MIT wouldn't be far behind. And they would bring her secrets with them. It would be out in the open for the whole team to know.

'I'm getting an intel package done on this McGregor,' Winter said. 'If there's a link between them we'll find it. I've sent Patel and Kanwar to Julia Talbot's home to tell her that her fiancé may be alive yet. Let me focus on McGregor, you track down this drug dealer "Jonny" that Steele mentioned. And try to find out about this other woman, if she even exists.'

'What are we going to do about Steele?' Kowalski asked.

'Charge Steele for possession of cocaine and assaulting a police officer. The court will give him bail in the morning, but there's nothing we can do about that. Get his phone downloaded and see if there's anything on it to do with Rowthorn's disappearance.'

Loxton didn't wait to be told twice. She headed straight out of the door, Kowalski jogging to keep up with her.

Chapter 24

Alana Loxton

Wednesday

'I've found it!' She couldn't hide the excitement in her voice, shouting across the office to Kowalski.

Kowalski came over, carrying a coffee cup with him. 'Found what?'

She pointed at the monitor. 'I've found the matt black car. It's here. You can make out there's two passengers in the back. That could be Mark Rowthorn and David Steele.'

'So, who's the driver?' Kowalski peered at the image.

'It's impossible to say,' she said. 'The angle from this shop isn't great. We're lucky it captured the car at all.'

'Can you see the reg?' He took a sip of his coffee.

'Not from this camera, but maybe on the CCTV from the bank on the corner.' She brought that up, scrolling to the correct time and hitting play. The matt black car soared past, so fast she couldn't read. She rewound the footage and moved it along frame by frame, pausing as the car drove away. She smiled. 'XV66 MGH.'

Kowalski plonked himself in the chair next to her and pulled up the Police National Computer database on the monitor next to her. He typed in the registration and they waited.

'I'll be damned,' he whispered, as if he didn't want to jinx it by saying it out loud. She read the returned hit. The car was registered to a Jonathan Cane, Flat 5, Ledbury House, John Ruskin Street, Walworth, London.

'That's just down the road.' Loxton looked at Kowalski and he shook his head at her in disbelief.

Kowalski frowned at the screen as he completed a few more checks.

'What's up?' she asked.

'He's got a conviction for murder, back in 2000. He's a lifer.'

'A life licence from prison? Does it say any more about the murder?' She felt her heartbeat quicken.

'No, it's too far back.' Kowalski shook his head. 'We'll have to request the old files and a full intel profile to be done on him.'

Loxton packed her CS spray in her covert harness. You didn't deal with someone on a life licence too often.

'We can arrest him on suspicion of drug supply and see what's in his flat and what he has to say about Steele's alibi.'

'And we should take his phones. See if they back up Steele's story.' She picked up her grab bag full of evidence bags and exhibit labels. She put on her stab vest, the weight of it pushing her down. Kowalski called Kanwar over and told him to follow as back up, in case anything went wrong.

So, this was Jonathan Cane's flat, Loxton thought. He lived alone inside a tiny bedsit that he'd been renting the past six months. The landlord had let them in with a key when they'd shown him the search warrant they'd got en route.

The wallpaper was peeling in the corners, and damp patches sprawled across the ceiling. The smell of smoke and cannabis was overwhelming.

The single bed had a grey duvet crumpled on it and on the bedside table was some paperwork. Loxton leafed through it. A probation meeting scheduled for Thursday at 10am. She took the name and number of the probation officer.

Kowalski opened the fridge. There was the smell of something off and when he picked up the milk it was two weeks out of date.

'Doesn't come here often?' Loxton offered, wondering where Cane spent most of his time. She began searching the rest of Cane's meagre possessions.

'Bingo.' Kowalski had pulled the small fridge away from the wall and found several envelopes stashed behind it. Kowalski dropped them onto the cheap side table, next to the overflowing ashtray, which they had to move aside.

Each envelope was crammed with piles of photographs. 'Looks like an old Kodak disposable,' Kowalski said as he studied the camera he had found in a kitchen drawer.

'I guess he didn't want to have to get these developed or have any of this on his phone.' Loxton held a couple of the photographs up. Then she froze for a second, hardly believing what she was seeing.

They were all of Julia Talbot.

In one, Talbot was walking along a high street in a blouse and skirt, a handbag swinging from her arm whilst she talked on a mobile.

In another, she was in a jewellery store, talking to a customer. The photo was taken from outside, through the display window.

There were hundreds of them, all of Talbot in public, oblivious that she was being watched.

Loxton took in a sharp breath. Had Jonathan Cane been threatening Mark Rowthorn? Blackmailing him to launder the money and using Julia's safety as his motivation? Had Cane become obsessed with Julia Talbot after meeting Mark? Had he murdered Rowthorn in a moment of jealous rage?

'Look.' Kowalski handed Loxton a photograph in which Rowthorn was speaking to David Steele outside the entrance to City Enterprises.

They pulled the flat apart and found more photographs. Some of the ones of Julia were creased and folded, as if Cane had been carrying them around with him for a long time. One was through Talbot's living room window late at night. She was curled up on her sofa in a cream chemise, checking her mobile, the soft blue glow of her TV illuminating her features.

Loxton shivered. The thought of being stalked for months and having no idea made her stomach twist. She felt sick.

Her hand tightened on the photograph. 'Where is he? We need to question him about all of this.' She motioned at the photographs scattered across the table. 'And the drugs, the money laundering, and Steele's alibi.'

'Well, since he's obviously not here often,' Kowalski said, looking at the empty flat, 'let's put him out as wanted. We can do some more digging to find out where he operates from. Who he works for. A little bit of pressure and they might tell us where he is.'

Loxton nodded and gathered up the photographs into evidence bags.

Kowalski's mobile rang. 'Hi, Meera, what's up? . . .

Okay – slow down. Have you tried Webb?' A pause. 'Keep trying them both. When we've dropped this off at the station we'll try to get hold of her too. She needs to know the body wasn't Rowthorn.'

Kowalski's eyes met Loxton's. 'They can't find Talbot. She's not at her flat and she's not answering her phone.' He looked worried. Having found these photographs, she could understand why.

Chapter 25

Julia Talbot

Wednesday

Coming here alone was the stupidest thing I'd ever done. My hand clenched tightly around my mobile as I stood in the queue for the nightclub, jittery and alone. I could still call Lucy to come and join me, but she'd go mad as soon as she saw Jonny, and I needed to be discreet.

I got lucky in the Night Jar Bar queue. There was no sign of Jonny and the bouncer let me through without taking too much notice. All he seemed to care about was the twenty-quid entrance fee.

Inside I was hit by darkness and noise as the music pounded through the club. It was bigger than I'd imagined, and I could see a sign pointing to the Night Jar Bar where I'd met Jonny only yesterday evening.

It was busier than I'd expected for a Wednesday, and I was glad of it. If Jonny did work here, then I didn't want him to spot me on an empty dance floor.

Women in their twenties were throwing themselves at middle-aged men in suits who passed the girls little snap bags of white powder. The girls giggled and sauntered off to the ladies' room in pairs, and a few minutes later stumbled back arm in arm looking the worse for wear.

The DJ was playing electronic music which went on and on, and about forty people were writhing about on the dance floor, off their faces. Groups of businessmen kept coming in, shouting to each other over the music. More young women would come from a door beside the bar and start mingling with the groups of men. *Had Mark really been in here?*

I spotted Jonny in the VIP section, a collection of sofas and low tables on a raised platform to the right of the dance floor. He was wearing a dark blue shirt and fitted dark jeans with black trainers. He was sat up straight, his eyes scanning the room. He did work here.

An older man all in black stopped to talk to him, and then sat in the VIP area with some dodgy-looking men who wouldn't have looked out of place in a Tarantino film. Were these the drug dealers? Or had Jonny made all of that up? I was out of my depth, but I didn't care. I needed to find out what had happened to Mark. He'd been here. Maybe this was where he'd met his killer.

I ducked away from Jonny and fought my way into the crowd congregated by the bar. A few people grumbled and one girl swung her sharp elbow into my ribs. The pain radiated through my right side, but I resisted the urge to elbow her back. I was deep enough in to be blocked from Jonny's view.

My breathing was ragged as I waited for a tap on the shoulder, but it didn't come. When I got to the bar I bought a gin and tonic and found an empty table to sit at in a dingy corner with the dance floor between us. Jonny hadn't spotted me, and I intended to keep it that way. I sipped my gin, trying to figure out what I was going to do.

The day Mark disappeared, someone had emptied his

crypto account of one hundred thousand pounds, and I knew that someone wasn't me. Somebody here must know something, but they weren't going to tell me anything if I just came out and asked them.

I noticed that people kept going over to the man in black and talking in his ear. He would then instruct them and they would go through the staff door and out of sight.

I saw women come out of the back with trays of shots, mingling with the crowd, passing them little snap bags in exchange for cash. When their trays were empty of drinks, they dropped them off at the bar and went through the doors again. If I could get in the back, maybe I could find something on Mark – CCTV or paperwork or something.

I headed to the ladies' bathroom and reapplied my make-up to match the girls' heavy eyeliner and heavy lipstick, unbuttoning my top to reveal more cleavage. I pulled out a cigarette and lighter and then headed back to the bar, collecting some empty glasses on the way and placing them on the side and slipping through the doors. The barman didn't look twice at me; he was too busy trying to serve the crowd.

I headed down a corridor and went past the kitchen. A heavy-set man came out of a side office.

'What you doing down here, darling? Bar's that way.'

I laughed. 'I've not seen you before, where've you been hiding? I was just going to sneak out the back before the boss notices. Is that okay with you?' I held up my lighter and cigarette and smiled at him. Starting smoking again after all these years had its benefits.

He laughed. 'Course it is, darling. Just be fast.'

Men seemed to fall for my deceptions so quickly.

'I promise.' I winked at him and hurried down the corridor, turning the corner. My heart was racing. That had been too close. I saw a fire exit at the end of the corridor, but on the right was another office door. I held my breath and tried the handle. Inside was a neat office, with metal filling cabinets along one wall, and an imposing wooden desk with a laptop open opposite me.

I prayed the laptop was unlocked. I touched the cursor, but there was just a picture of a snow-capped mountain with the username and password section blank.

I closed my eyes for a brief second. There was no way in a million years I'd be able to unlock it. Perhaps I could grab the laptop and make a dash through the fire exit, get one of those dodgy stalls to hack into it. But the fire exit was probably alarmed, and I didn't fancy my chances against the bouncer I'd passed earlier.

My palms were clammy as I reached out and tried the drawers of the desk. It was a big oak thing and seemed stubbornly secure, but I gave the handles a yank anyway. Unsurprisingly, they didn't budge.

This had been a waste of time. Who the hell did I think I was? It was time I got out of here before I got caught. I crept to the door, paused by the metal cabinets and listened for a moment.

Silence.

No one was nearby. I waited a little longer to be sure, scanning the room one last time before I left. I spotted that there was a key still left in one of the locks of the clunky drawers in the metal cabinet. Someone must have just been here. I pulled open the drawers and flicked through the files, as quickly as I could. I'd been here too long; I should go, but I might never get this chance again.

Four drawers down and I spotted a file labelled 'MR

& DS'. I pulled it out. Pages of numbers were inside, almost like records of a loan. The numbers were staggering, rising rapidly. Sometimes large sums went in, only to have more added on the next row.

'*Mark*' was scribbled in the margins next to some payments and '*Dave*' at other points.

MR – Mark Rowthorn.

DS – David Steele.

David had lied. Whatever trouble Mark had got into, David had known all about it. From these records, I could see they owed the club two hundred and fifty thousand between them. A red circle had been drawn around the figure and there were no more entries after it.

I took a photo on my phone and dropped the file back in the cabinet. This was the evidence I needed that Mark had been involved in the nightclub, the same nightclub that Jonny worked in. It also showed David knew more than he'd said, and I didn't want him to escape justice. He wouldn't charm his way out of this and blame everything on Mark. I needed to call Loxton. I shut the cabinet door and slipped out of the room, heading back along the corridor to the bar. The man dressed all in black was striding towards me. *Shit.*

'Perfect,' he said, looking me right in the eye. 'Could you come with us into my office? We'll be making some drinks orders.' He pointed towards the office that I had just come out of. I opened the door and stood aside so he could enter. Jonny was behind him and looked startled when he saw me, but followed his boss into the office without saying a word. *Why hadn't he said anything?*

'Please, come in,' the man said to me. He sat himself behind the ornate wooden desk and motioned towards the drinks' cabinet. Could you make us two Old Fashioneds?'

I moved slowly over to the bottles and opened the cabinet, trying to steady my breathing. I sneaked a glance at Jonny, but he was looking at his boss, not me. They were talking about the security rota.

What would they do to me? Would they make me 'disappear'? I felt sick as I tried to focus on the gleaming bottles. There was whisky, gin, vodka . . . So many spirits I didn't know what all of them were.

My hands were clammy as I took out two glasses. I knew whisky went in an Old Fashioned but after that . . . I poured a healthy measure in both glasses and got some ice from the freezer. Then I just added a few random spirits, hoping they weren't watching me. Maybe Jonny wouldn't say anything? Maybe it would be okay.

'I do like a good Old Fashioned,' the man said as I put the glasses in front of them, trying hard not to drop them in my panic. I headed slowly towards the door. 'Don't leave. I wanted to ask you before you go why you've been searching through my files? I've been watching you on our CCTV. I want to know who you are.'

I froze at the door. I could run but Jonny was just there. He could reach out and grab me in a second.

'I'm not with the police,' I said. My mind was whirling from one scenario to another, but there was no way I could lie my way out of this one.

'I gathered that. Who are you, then?' His voice became harder. He motioned to Jonny, who stood up and grabbed me by the arms, manoeuvring me into his seat. He stood by the door with his arms folded.

'Are you getting soft in your old age?' The boss asked Jonny.

'No,' Jonny looked anxious. 'It's just . . . she's a woman.'

'Never stopped you before.' The boss turned his cold gaze on me. 'Best start talking or this could get unpleasant. What's your name?'

'I'm no one.' I tried to keep the tremor from my voice.

The boss slammed his fist into the table. I flinched despite myself. 'I asked you your name.' His eyes bored into mine. 'You get one more chance.' He tried to keep his voice steady, but it shook with anger. He sat back down and straightened his tie.

'I'm Julia Talbot. Mark Rowthorn's fiancée. He's been murdered and I found this club's business card in his things.' I held his gaze, refusing to look away. I didn't want to show this man I was petrified.

'So, you broke in and searched for his killer in one of my filing cabinets?' His voice was unnervingly calm again as he motioned at the metal cabinets, all neatly closed.

'I know he was in debt to you. I want to know what you've done to him.'

'*Done* to him?' The man sat back in surprise. And then he laughed. Jonny laughed along, looking from his boss to me. I had no idea what the joke was, and I didn't think Jonny did either. Anger began to bubble up in me, mixed dangerously with fear.

'I haven't *done* anything to him,' the man said. 'He and his mate owed me two hundred and fifty thousand pounds, as you saw in the ledger. All legitimate of course. Mark threw a lot of office parties here. And between you and me Mark liked to gamble. Big. He told me he was going to get the money and I believed him. I'm still waiting.' He put his hands out, as if expecting me to produce the money from thin air.

'Bullshit. You've killed him.' I was losing control, but

I didn't care. I hated this smarmy man and whatever shit he had got Mark into.

'Now that sort of accusation I won't have.' The man's face darkened. I knew he was no longer playing. 'I don't want to ever see you here again. I haven't killed your boyfriend, which is lucky for you, because if I had you'd be joining him. If the police come sniffing round here, I'll be sending someone to your door. Take her outside, Jonny.' He waved his hand as if dismissing a naughty child.

'No problem, boss.' Jonny seized me and dragged me towards the door.

'Make sure she understands.' His eyes fixed on Jonny's, who nodded his agreement.

Jonny marched me along the corridor and towards the fire exit. I didn't dare breathe. He flung open the fire door and pulled me outside. It was a secluded alleyway. There were large metal waste disposal bins near to the door. Jonny pushed it closed.

'What are you fucking playing at?' He was right in front of me. There was no way I'd be able to get away. 'Do you know how much shit you could have got me in back there? He's dangerous.'

'You lied to me about Mark.' I glared at him, the rage making me brave. 'You said you didn't know him. But he was here. He owes money to your boss. You've killed him.'

'I haven't touched him.' He paced up and down in front of me. 'I don't know what the fuck happened to him. I only ever tried to ruin your life . . . like you ruined mine. I'm not a killer.'

'What did you do?' I should have called the police after I'd first seen him. I'd been an idiot. He was still as dangerous as he'd ever been.

'You stitched me up, Jenny. Sent me to prison by planting that ring on your sister. I was a kid at the time, I didn't understand what was happening at the trial. It took me a long time to realize what you did. So when I came out of prison the plan was simple. Ruin your life like you'd ruined mine. You were set to marry a wealthy banker. I figured if I could corrupt him, then you'd end up wasting your life on him, just like the best years of my life were wasted in prison.'

'I . . . I don't understand.' I could barely get the words out; my throat was closing up with fear. The pure hatred in his eyes was scaring me.

He rolled his eyes at me. 'I introduced myself to Mark at one of the city bars. Told him and his mate there was this private poker game. Lots of influential people. Brought him to this club. They loved it. Flirting with the girls. The drugs. The gambling. When he got himself into debt, like they always do, that's when the boss offered him and his mate a solution. He had them sell him inside information from the bank to pay off their debts.'

I felt sick. The way he'd stalked and set out to destroy me.

'I got to watch Mark dig himself deeper and deeper into the shit, knowing he was about to marry you.' He smiled at the memory but then the smile vanished. 'But then he disappeared and so did the money he'd been paid. The boss wants it back. And because I brought him to the club, it's my job to get it back. I didn't want to contact you, it was too risky, but I thought you might know where he'd gone. I had to come up with that story about clearing my name to see if you knew anything. I don't know how he's ended up dead. I don't care. I just

need the fucking money back or the boss will kill me.'
His spit hit my face as he shouted at me.

'I don't know where it is,' I screamed back at him. It
didn't matter what I did. I knew then that he was going
to kill me here in this alleyway, just like he'd killed Mark,
and Rachel. That story was just more lies. I had to get
away. I tried to turn away from him as tears stung my
eyes.

'Hey. You don't get away from me that easily.' He
grabbed my arms and pulled me to him. His hands gripped
my shoulders and his face was close to mine 'You
destroyed me back then. You got to walk away, but I
fucking didn't, did I? You know I could've made something
of myself. I wanted to run my own business. But then
that day happened and everyone blamed me. Do you
know what it's like being called a child-killer and my
parents still having to live round Ashurst Wood? It ruined
their lives. And prison's fucked up my head.'

'Of course I know what it's like to be called a child-
killer.' I hated him. 'That's why I could never go back to
it. I wasn't found guilty but that didn't stop people judging
me. I was the one who was meant to be looking after
her. She was *my* sister.'

I tried to wrench myself free from his grip, but it was
no good – he was too strong.

'You don't get to walk away this time. This time you're
going to fucking pay.' His right hand tightened around
my arm, while his other hand jabbed at my face. 'I won't
let you pin murder on me again. I didn't kill him.'

'You're insane.' Anger and fear coursed through me,
making everything brighter. Jonny was trying to blame
everything on me, like he had in the past. This had all
been a game and he'd been playing it for years. I tried

again to back away from him, but his hand held me so close I could smell the stale cigarettes and cheap lager on his breath.

'No, you've got to be punished for what you did. How do you want to be punished?' His other hand was trying to yank down my jeans.

I struggled against him. 'No.' I couldn't look him in the eye – too afraid of what I'd see. 'Get off me.'

'You did me over once and you're doing it again. I should kill you.' His spittle hit my face and trickled down my cheek.

'Don't—' I was shaking violently and my breath came out jagged.

'Stop fighting.' He slapped me hard across the face. 'You owe me. All those wasted years because of you.'

My skin stung where he'd hit me and for a moment I was stunned, but then I came back to my senses. 'I'll go to the police,' I shouted.

'You heard the boss. You go to the police and he'll kill you.' His hand moved up my waist to my breast.

'Stop.' I tried to push him off, and my open hand struck his jaw.

He looked shocked for a second and then his fist slammed into the side of my head. Dazzling pain stabbed into my brain, pulsating and sharp.

'Don't ever fucking try that again – you got that?'

I put my hands up in defence, as a wave of nausea washed through me. I dry-retched and he finally pushed me away, disgusted. 'Don't fucking puke on me.'

I knew that if I screamed, he'd silence me. I tried to slow my rapid breathing, to get control, as I tried to think what to do, how to get out of this . . .

'I won't let you and your stupid fiancé get me killed.'

He lifted his fist to the level of my face. 'I want that hundred and fifty thousand in cash tomorrow or you'll be fucking sorry. And don't contact the police, they won't be able to protect you if you do.'

'And what if I don't care what you do to me.' I spat the words at him. In that moment I didn't care anymore. He killed my sister and Mark.

'What about Kayleigh? Do you care about her?'

Lucy. Would he hurt her? My legs were shaking. I lifted my hands up in front of my body to ward off any more blows. 'Okay,' I said, although I knew there was no way I could get that sort of money. 'Please . . .'

'Don't ever show up here again or the boss will have you killed and then me. You don't know what you're playing with.' He glowered down at me. 'And you fucking better get that money to me tomorrow . . . or Kayleigh dies.'

Something in my mind snapped. I rushed at him, shoving him backwards with all of my body weight. He fell backwards towards the dumpsters, his hands grappling at the air, trying to steady himself.

There was a cracking noise as the side of his head collided with the sharp corner of one of the bins, and it knocked him sideways, where his body and head smashed into the concrete floor beside the metal container. Blood dripped from an open gash. I tasted bile in my mouth as I looked at the torn skin. At what I'd done in my anger.

'Jonny?' He didn't move.

I inched nearer and whispered 'Jonny' again, but he stayed motionless on the floor. Unconscious or maybe worse. I tried to ignore the rising dread I felt and the need to scream. Instead I looked up at the CCTV camera. It was still pointing at the fire escape. It wouldn't have captured me pushing him. All I'd done was push him when he'd threatened Lucy.

My phone started ringing and I fumbled through my pockets. The noise was deafening. I saw it was Lucy calling and stabbed at the mute button with my shaking finger. Quiet at last. I glanced back towards the fire exit and scrabbled behind the metal bins in a panic, crouching down so no one would see me. There was silence except for my own ragged breathing. I stayed there trembling in the dark, waiting, but no one came.

My phone vibrated silently in my hand. Lucy again. After a while it stopped and I saw she'd tried to call me earlier, when I'd been in the nightclub. There were also several missed calls from the police. I closed my eyes. What was I going to do?

Chapter 26

Julia Talbot

Thursday

'You did *what*?' Lucy was trying not to get angry, but she was pacing. It was one in the morning and she looked exhausted, her auburn hair scraped into a ponytail. She'd picked me up a few streets away from the bar and had driven me home. I'd told her about the money that Mark and David owed the club owner and that Jonny was involved. She'd been furious. I couldn't tell her I'd pushed Jonny, left him there on the floor bleeding. What would she think of me? She was all I had left. The police wanted to see me and were coming to the flat. It had to be serious this late at night.

'It was stupid . . . but Jonny contacted me. I didn't know it was him at first.' I dropped my gaze to my hands. The diamond on my engagement ring gleamed in the light.

'I shouldn't have left you on your own. Not after the news about Mark. I'm sorry, this is my fault.' She stopped in front of me, worry replacing the frustration as she looked at the bruise on my temple.

'Jonny kept saying that it was my fault he was convicted. That I planted the ring with his blood at the scene. He was convinced. He said if he helped me find Mark, then maybe I'd know he wasn't evil, and I'd help clear his name.'

'And you *believed* him when he said he'd help you?'

'No, of course not. I told him to stay away from me. But he didn't listen. He sent me information about Mark. He seemed to know things. I thought I could find out if he was involved in Mark's death.' It sounded so stupid when I said it out loud, but when I'd found that business card I wanted to know if Jonny was involved. I'd had to find out for myself. Always trying to deal with things on my own.

'I don't understand why you wouldn't tell me about him making contact?'

'He told me not to tell anyone. I thought he knew something about Mark. Now I think he killed him.'

'Why didn't you tell me or the police?' She shook her head at me in disbelief. 'I can't believe you'd go there alone.'

'I wasn't thinking straight. Jonny ruined my life all those years ago. I needed to know if he'd done it again. I thought I could find the answers, and if I couldn't, I'd at least get him to tell me what happened. I knew he'd never talk to the police.'

'You should tell them everything you've just told me. This is getting seriously out of control, Julia. You could have been killed.' She tried to inspect my bruise but I brushed her off. I couldn't meet her eyes. I'd tell the police about Jonny and the messages, and what his boss had said, but I couldn't tell them we'd had an altercation and I'd left him there. I was scared he might be dead.

'I'm sorry,' I said. 'You dismissed me when I mentioned Jonny, didn't want me bringing him up again.'

'So, because I didn't listen you decide to go all Rambo and confront him? You could have *died*,' she said again.

Tears coursed down my cheeks and I couldn't stop them. I wished I could confide in her what I'd done to Jonny, but I couldn't. She didn't deserve all this. I turned away from her.

Someone knocked on the door. Lucy wiped the tears from her face as she peered through the spyhole. 'It's the police.'

'Are you sure?' Fear made it difficult to breathe and I spotted a drop of Jonny's blood on my jeans. I tried to rub it away with my hand, but it didn't budge. I retreated to the sofa, pulling a cushion across my lap to hide the spot.

'Julia, I'm sorry it's so late.' Loxton scanned the room, looking at Lucy and then at me. She frowned as she looked at the bruise on my face, her eyes flicking back to Lucy briefly, and then finally settling on me.

'We couldn't get hold of you,' she said.

Kowalski looked worried. I felt like a child being admonished by a parent.

'I'm sorry, I was asleep,' I lied. 'I've been taking these tablets. And Lucy was picking up James from the airport.'

'Of course,' Loxton said, softer now. 'We have something we need to tell you.' She sat on the armchair to my left, while Kowalski stood to my right. I was hemmed in.

Lucy nodded at me, but I clutched the cushion tighter, my knuckles going white. She frowned at me and then said. 'Julia needs to talk to you too. There's something she didn't tell you.'

I pressed my lips together. I couldn't run away from my past any longer.

'What do you need to say?' Loxton looked at me intently.

'You go first,' I said.

'I'm sorry for the late call. The news I'm about to tell you will come as a shock.'

I nodded at her to go on.

'The body we found in the river isn't Mark. I'm sorry we implied that it was.'

Bile rose up my throat. *It wasn't Mark.* So where was he? What had they done to him? If I could find the missing money like they'd asked, would I get Mark back? A million questions raced through my mind but Lucy only had one.

'Then who the hell is it?' Lucy asked.

'A Mr Robert McGregor. Does that name mean anything to you?'

'No . . . no, it doesn't,' I said. Loxton was watching my face, noting my every reaction. Her gaze hovered again on my injury.

'Lucy, do you know a Robert McGregor?' Loxton asked.

Lucy shook her head. 'Never heard of him.'

'You said Mark was dead.' My eyes began to well. It wasn't Mark. The relief was overwhelming. Then fear started to slither inside my stomach, growing inside me, making me feel sick. *Where was he?*

Loxton nodded. 'I know. I'm sorry. McGregor was wearing Mark's watch; we're trying to find out why.'

'If you'd let me see him, I would have told you straight away it wasn't Mark.' They exchanged glances, as if willing the other to take the lead. Was Mark's watch on the dead man a warning to keep my mouth shut or he'd be next? I had to be careful.

'I'm sorry you have to go through this,' Loxton said finally. 'And that we gave you the wrong information.'

She looked like she wanted to wrap her arms around me, but instead she clenched her hands together on her lap.

'Can you tell me when you last remember seeing Mark wearing his watch?' Kowalski asked.

I pictured it in my mind. It had been an extravagant present I couldn't afford at the time. 'He normally wears it to work but he leaves before me. I'm not sure.'

'Did he tell you he'd lost it?' Kowalski asked.

'No . . . I think he was wearing it the weekend before. We went for dinner with his parents.' I was sure he was wearing it.

'Thank you.'

'David might remember if he was wearing it,' I said.

Loxton and Kowalski exchanged looks.

'David was arrested earlier today. We think he knows more about Mark's disappearance than he's letting on,' Loxton said. 'He's on bail and he's not allowed to contact you.'

'David Steele?' I was glad the police were on to him. He was linked to the missing money. They already had him figured out, it seemed, but how much was he involved? 'You think he's involved?' I asked, playing dumb.

'We don't know yet,' said Kowalski. 'This McGregor might have something to do with it. Are you sure you don't know anyone of that name? Mark's never mentioned him?'

'No . . . I don't think so.' I knew a lot of Mark's friends and work colleagues, but I was sure he'd never mentioned a McGregor.

'Did Mark ever introduce you to a friend of his called Jonny Cane?' Loxton asked.

My stomach dropped. Lucy was staring at me, her lips

pressed together in a firm line. I focused on the detective. 'No – why?' I couldn't tell them about Jonny, what I'd found. Jonny and his boss had warned me off talking to the police. Jonny had threatened Lucy and they might hurt Mark. And I'd left Jonny in the alleyway, unconscious or maybe worse. What would they think if I told them he'd killed my sister all those years ago? They'd think I'd hurt him on purpose; after all, I'd gone to the nightclub in search of him. I had to think. One wrong move and I could make it all worse.

'We need to speak to him.' There was a light in Loxton's eyes. She'd seen something in my face.

'Are you sure you don't know Cane? This is a recent photograph of him.' She showed me and then Lucy the photo. It looked like one taken in a prison. Jonny was glaring at the camera.

'Never heard of him.' I looked to Lucy quizzically, praying she would back me up. There was a brief moment and then she shook her head back at me and shrugged her shoulders.

Loxton looked disappointed. 'Could I speak to you alone for a moment, Julia?'

This felt like a trap, but I nodded to Lucy to go.

'I'll put the kettle on,' she said and closed the kitchen door behind her.

I tried to keep my breathing steady, to try and not look anxious.

'What did you want to tell me earlier?' Loxton asked.

'Oh. Just something on the Facebook appeal page. Someone thought they'd seen Mark near the Thames but it's just another mistaken identification.'

'Who hurt you?' Loxton's voice was softer, and her eyes fell onto the bruise on my temple.

'This.' I raised my hand to my face. 'It's nothing.'

'It doesn't look like nothing,' Kowalski said.

'I banged my face opening a kitchen cupboard. I was tired.' My voice shook, but I managed to keep my eyes on Kowalski as I said it, willing him to believe me.

'Did someone do that to you?' Loxton peered at the mark. 'That's only just happened.'

I shook my head, trying hard not to cry. 'Just me. I was rushing.'

'Was it David Steele?' Kowalski asked.

'No. It was just an accident. I'm fine.'

'Julia, this Jonny Cane had some photographs of you and Mark in his flat. Do you have any idea why?'

'No.' I shook my head, managing to keep the shock from my voice. Jonny had said he'd been stalking me since his release from prison. He'd been setting a trap for Mark and me and now he could be dead on the floor of that alleyway I might never find out the truth. It was best to keep playing dumb until I knew more. Mark could be alive and I needed to figure out how to help him.

'We're going to arrest him. Until then, do not let anyone into your flat. Only open the door if it's someone you know. Call 999 if you feel threatened or you see this man.'

I nodded. 'I'll . . . I'll check through the spyhole first.' I clasped my hands together over the cushion still trying to hide the stain of blood. 'You said you checked his flat, but he wasn't there?' I saw Jonny again in my mind, lain on the floor, perfectly still.

'He wasn't there, but don't worry, we'll find him,' Loxton said.

'Thank you,' I managed.

'Julia, call us anytime if you think of anything else.'

I let them out of the flat and then closed the door, double bolting it as Lucy came back into the living room. She waited a beat until we heard their footsteps fading. 'Did you tell them about Jonny?' she whispered.

'No,' I whispered back. 'It wasn't Mark in the river. He could be alive. If I tell them about Jonny and he is involved, he might do something to him. He kept going on about the missing money Mark owed his boss.'

Lucy went to the window and looked outside for the two officers, but they were gone. She shivered and wrapped her arms around herself as she turned to me. 'You need to tell me everything. Then we can decide what to do next. Together. Like we always do.'

'You should get back to James.' I got up from the sofa and headed towards the door to let her out. 'This isn't your problem.'

She hadn't moved and was giving me one of her looks, the one that meant that was never going to happen, and I felt stupid for trying to push her away.

'We need to find out who took the money from Mark's bank. You're an accountant – if you look at the crypto account, you might be able to work out who took it. I have the password.'

'I can have a look, but the police would surely do a better job?' Lucy looked doubtfully at me.

'We've got to try ourselves first. It might be Mark's only chance. If we go to the police and Jonny's lot find out, then they might hurt him.'

Lucy sighed and then nodded. 'Okay, but if we don't get anywhere you need to go to the police.'

'I will.' I nodded, but all I could think about was Jonny

bleeding and what I'd done. When I thought Mark was dead, I didn't care, but now there was the possibility he was still alive, I could have made things much, much worse for him and for us.

Chapter 27

Alana Loxton

Thursday

Loxton looked around the Night Jar Bar. It had been a shabby nightclub best avoided a few years back, but a lick of paint, some distressed wood and dim lighting had turned it hipster. And made the prices soar to astronomical heights. To her it would always be the dodgy nightclub with the highest stabbing rate in Southwark, with an owner who had a reputation for using extreme violence to solve disagreements.

Rowthorn's credit card statements had shown he frequented this place every couple of weeks and he spent hundreds when he was here. She dreaded to think where the cash went. There was one intelligence hit that Jonny Cane worked here, even though he was registered as unemployed and was on jobseeker's allowance.

Kowalski was arguing with a man with a shaved head behind the bar. They were both well over 6 foot and heavily built, but the barman was stockier compared to Kowalski's more athletic figure. She wasn't sure Kowalski would win in that fight.

'We're looking for Jonny Cane,' he said. 'He's not in any trouble, we just need to speak to him.'

'There's no Jonny working here.' The man's eyes were blurry and he had stubble on his face.

'Can you give me the manager's number, then? We need to speak with him.'

'He on holiday.' The man shrugged. 'You want drink?' He poured himself a large vodka, despite it being only 10am.

'We're going to need your CCTV footage,' Loxton said.

The man glared at her and downed his vodka in one. He had a thick scar under his chin which she hadn't spotted until he tipped his head back. 'It's not working. We're waiting for man to fix it.'

'Let me have a look. I have a knack for these things.' Loxton smiled at him and tried to pretend she didn't know he was playing a game.

'I don't know. You could break it.'

'I thought it was already broken? What harm can I do?' She smiled sweetly.

He sighed and stomped towards the side door. 'I don't know why you people never believe me.' He shook his head and grumbled to himself in his mother tongue.

He led them into a corridor with side offices on either side and into a tiny office. It was difficult for the three of them to fit in there. The CCTV was high tech and she struggled through the options, but couldn't get it to work. She checked around for a manual, but there wasn't one in sight.

'Told you.' The man folded his arms in front of him. 'A man is coming to fix it.'

'You've said that,' she muttered.

She tried a few more buttons and nearly jumped for joy when the screens sprang to life, showing different angles of the building.

'Looks like it's working fine.' She smiled at the man, who didn't seem as happy as she was about her managing to turn the machine on. She flicked through the cameras to see how many there were. She counted ten covering the back offices and five in the actual club, three of those covering the tills. Seemed like the owner was more worried about his takings than the punters' safety. There were another two covering the main entrance and one on the back.

'We're going to need to take the hard drive,' she said. 'I can't download it now.' She'd had enough trouble checking to see if it was working.

'You can't,' he said. 'We need for tonight. What happens if there's a fight or we're robbed?'

Loxton doubted anyone would dare to burgle this place. 'Okay, well we can download the data we need onto this stick.'

'I don't know how, but there's a manual somewhere.' He shrugged at her and half-heartedly opened drawers. Loxton rolled her eyes.

'I need around fifteen hours' worth of footage, here are the different days and times.' She pulled out her notes of the times and dates Rowthorn's credit card had been used in the club.

'Fuck.' The man stopped his search and sank onto his seat. 'That's impossible. I've got things to do.'

'We need it urgently and as part of your licence you need to comply. Or we could just take the hard drive back to our tech guys, as I say, and they could download it for us overnight? We'll get this back to you first thing tomorrow morning. What do you say?'

'Take it, then.' He looked annoyed.

Kowalski pulled on his gloves and stepped towards the

CCTV recorder. 'Won't take me five minutes to package this up.'

'Great,' she said. 'I'm just going outside to make a call. You all right here?'

'No problem.' Kowalski turned off the CCTV. 'Could you give me a hand with this? Don't want to break it.' He smiled at the bouncer as he took hold of the CCTV recorder to put it into a large exhibit bag.

Loxton slipped out of the office and walked down the corridor. She listened outside the doors but there was no noise. She tried the handles. One was a stock cupboard stacked with alcohol bottles; a couple of metal baseball bats propped up against the wall.

There was a kitchen the next door along. The last door was locked. There were stairs at the end of the corridor and a fire exit. She heard a man talking on the floor above and his voice grew louder. He was coming towards the stairs. She pushed open the fire exit and slipped outside, leaving the door slightly ajar behind her. She found herself in an alleyway with industrial grey bins on wheels. The smell of alcohol and rotting food hit her, as if it was an invisible wall.

She heard the man coming down the stairs. 'Boss, the pigs are here . . . I don't know. I saw them on the CCTV monitors upstairs. Valon took them into the CCTV room and they've turned it off. They're taking it . . . I don't know. Maybe Rowthorn's girl called them . . . I don't know, boss. We'll get rid of them as quick as we can.' There was silence for a moment. 'Wait a sec, the fire exit's opened.'

She ducked between the bins and crouched down, trying to quiet her breathing. She heard footsteps coming towards her and then they stopped before retracing their path back to the club. Had she heard right? *Rowthorn's girl?*

'Fucking Valon's left the fire exit open again. He does it every time he goes out for a fag.'

The fire exit slammed shut. She text Kowalski to warn him that there was another one incoming. As she put her mobile in her pocket, she noticed something sticking out from behind the dumpster, jammed between the wall and the lower part of the bin.

A pair of black trainers. But then, as she craned her neck, she saw legs.

A knot tightened in her stomach. It didn't matter how many dead bodies you'd seen; it never got any easier. She tried to close down her emotions, hardening her for what was about to come, as she stood up and pulled the bin towards her. First she needed to check if the guy was still alive. The body rolled forward onto its side, into the recovery position. But there was no recovery for this man. She climbed alongside the body and brushed the rubbish out of the way, revealing a man's torso and face.

Jonathan Cane.

He had a nasty gash on the side of his head. It looked like he'd been struck by something sharp. His eyes were half-closed. They looked like glass: too still to be real.

Loxton touched the waxen skin on his neck but there was no pulse. The skin was cool, the texture strange with no blood flowing beneath. A shiver rippled down Loxton's back. It felt like Cane's ghost was stood right behind her, demanding justice.

Loxton's skin crawled and a surge of irrational fear overwhelmed her. The primeval part of her brain told her to run as fast and as far away as she could from the unseen danger. Instead, she counted for five seconds, waiting for her logical brain to kick in, and began to assess the scene.

There was an empty syringe beside his arm. Jonathan Cane had a shaven head, and his dark blue shirt and jeans were designer. She didn't like to make quick judgements, but it looked like a typical night out overdose. Southwark was a busier borough than she'd expected. It was a strange place to get high, though. Open to the elements and at risk of being found by teenagers messing about. And how had he got the wound to his head? She checked his arms but there were no track marks. Not a regular user, then.

She pulled on two pairs of blue plastic gloves. She patted his pockets and found his mobile still there. She checked the number and called it in to Patel.

'We have a few hits on our intel systems,' Patel said. 'The most recent is an intel report linking this mobile to your missing persons case.'

'The drug dealer contacting Rowthorn?'

'Yes, you got it.'

So now they had evidence that Jonathan Cane was Mark Rowthorn's drug dealer. Steele hadn't been lying. She glanced at the body, wishing it could tell her Cane's secrets. She stood up and took five steps backwards, surveying the scene again. She crouched down next to the corner of the bin. There was blood on the edge, turning brown but still wet.

She pulled out her own mobile and called Kowalski. 'You free to talk?'

'Give me a second. The CCTVs in the boot. I was just taking a statement from Valon here and his friend who's just turned up. Two minutes, my friends, urgent call.' There was a pause. 'Okay, shoot.'

'There's a body in the alleyway. It's Jonathan Cane. Looks like an overdose but I don't buy it. He has a nasty cut to the side of his head, and there's blood on one of the dumpsters. His body's been deliberately hidden, but they've tried to make it look like he's fallen and banged his head, crawled behind the bins and died, and then the dumpsters got pushed into the wall without anyone realizing. Can you get Winter to call the murder team?' Her stomach clenched as she thought of seeing her old colleagues. She knew she couldn't hide for ever, but she thought she'd have longer than this before she'd have to face them again.

'Not sure there's enough to call out the murder team,' Kowalski said. 'Are you sure about this? Perhaps Winter should come down first.'

'I worked murder for five years, Kowalski, and I'm telling you this doesn't feel right to me. Cane was dealing drugs to Rowthorn, had those photographs, and now he's got a head wound and his body's been stuffed behind dumpsters.'

'Okay, I hear you. I'll call them. You need a hand up there?'

'No, you hold onto those witnesses. The other one mentioned that Rowthorn's girl might have called us. I want to know what he means. I don't want them disappearing or trying to clean anything up when they realize what we've found.'

Kowalski stretched and rubbed the back of his neck with his strong hands as he stood with Loxton near the body. Her shoulders and neck ached, and she longed for a hot shower and then to sink into her bed. That wouldn't happen for hours now. Winter was on his way, eager to try to convince the murder team that this was their job and to take it off his already strained CID.

'It looks like an overdose,' Kowalski said. 'Like he's taken too much and at some point cracked his head on this.' Kowalski motioned towards the large metal bin.

'This man isn't a regular user.' Loxton pointed at his arms. 'Dealers normally aren't.'

'So, he wasn't used to taking drugs and took a little bit too much?' Kowalski shrugged at her. 'Maybe something was troubling him?'

'Or Cane was blackmailing Rowthorn, who couldn't pay, so Rowthorn took things into his own hands and killed Cane.'

'Not such a straightforward overdose then. You can be a real killjoy sometimes, has anyone ever told you that?' Kowalski shook his head at her.

'Plenty of times.'

'One thing's for certain,' Kowalski said. 'It does look like our Rowthorn's cursed. Everyone he comes across dies. First McGregor and now Cane.'

'Perhaps we shouldn't try so hard to find him.' She smiled at Kowalski. 'One of the henchmen said Rowthorn's girl had been here.'

'Julia Talbot?'

'Unlikely. Maybe this other woman Steele mentioned. Maybe she worked here? The CCTV might help.' She pointed at the camera.

'It only covered the fire exit. It didn't cover the bins.' Kowalski sighed. 'If the body was brought out of the club we'll have a great image, but if the killer came up the alley and dumped the body behind the bins the CCTV doesn't stretch that far.'

'There's something we're missing. If I—'

She was interrupted by footsteps from behind her. She flinched at the sight of DC Tim Bale from her old team striding towards her. Heat prickled her skin as she remembered their last encounter a few months ago. The look of disgust he'd thrown her as she'd swept her belongings into two cardboard boxes and fled the murder squad. She'd hoped she'd never have to confront him again, now that she was in CID borough. Just her luck it was him that was called out. Or had he come looking for her to gloat?

To her surprise, Bale looked right through her, as if she didn't exist. She was shocked by how much his dismissal annoyed her. He addressed Kowalski. 'DC Bale, MIT south on-call team. Your DCI gave us a heads-up and I wasn't far, so I thought I'd take a look for myself.'

So, he *had* come out of his way to gloat.

'Adult male,' Kowalski said. 'Looks like an overdose but it doesn't feel right to us. See the gash on the head?'

'Got a name?' Bale asked.

'Jonathan Cane,' Kowalski said. 'The mobile on him is a drug dealer's phone and he's been dealing to a missing man we're trying to find.'

'You brought me here for this?' Bale shook his head. 'He's died of an overdose. Even the uniform would be able to call it.'

'Bale, that's not going to work with us, so drop the act,' she said. 'His body was jammed behind the dumpster and he didn't get there himself.'

'You disturbed the crime scene?' His voice was indignant, and he had that righteous look on his face which signalled he was about to launch into a rant.

'I needed to check his vitals. I couldn't do that with just his feet sticking out.'

'Our DCI's on his way,' Kowalski interrupted. 'We might have to join up a bit for this one. It's got links to the high-profile missing person we're working on – Mark Rowthorn.'

'The missing banker hitting the headlines?' Bale rolled his eyes. 'That's all we need. The press are going to love this.'

'They won't know it's linked,' Loxton said.

'Don't be naïve,' Bale said. 'Of course they'll know. They always find out, don't they, Alana?'

She opened her mouth to challenge him, but nothing came out.

'Your DCI can keep this whether he likes it or not.' Bale shrugged at her. 'It's just an overdose.'

Loxton turned as footsteps approached. DCI Winter strode up the alley towards them and he wasn't smiling. 'They train you murder officers well. You haven't even checked the body and you know it's an overdose? Impressive. We have a high-profile missing banker which the press are all over, and people who have been in contact with him keep turning up dead. Jonathan Cane was a suspect in our case.'

Bale looked to Loxton and then Kowalski in confusion.

'Rowthorn's watch was on the wrist of a Robert McGregor, a missing man who washed up from the Thames three days ago,' Kowalski said.

'Rowthorn's fiancée believes he hadn't lost the watch before he went missing,' Loxton said. 'And now Rowthorn's drug dealer is found dead outside this club and we suspect he might have been blackmailing Rowthorn. And one of the staff said Rowthorn's girl called us, so we need to find out who this other woman is and what she knows.'

Bale's eyebrows knotted together. He threw a furtive glance at DCI Winter, who was still glaring at him. The job was everything to Bale and upsetting the bosses was the last thing he wanted. Loxton still remembered the mortified look he'd given her as she'd been ousted from their murder team.

'I want Robert McGregor's plunge in the Thames raised to a murder investigation.' Winter stared at Bale, as if daring him to argue. 'And I want Jonathan Cane's death to be treated the same.'

'If we had all the resources in the world, sir, we would definitely oblige you. But we don't. You're going to have to hold onto these two until it's confirmed that they're murders. I'll see what my boss says about lending you a few extra officers, though.' Bale moved away from them, pulling out his mobile to put the call in.

There was a painful silence.

'I'll get Cane's mobile downloaded straight away and get Patel to prioritize exchanges between him and Rowthorn,' Loxton said.

'Good. We don't want to miss anything obvious. And I definitely don't want egg on our faces in front of the MIT,' Winter said. 'Especially not in front of that arrogant dick.' He nodded towards Bale. 'If he causes you any trouble, let me know.'

'Of course, sir.'

Loxton took out her mobile.

Chapter 28

Jenny Hughes

Monday 24 July 2000

The sunlight filtered through the woods, a fairy den of colours and light. Jonny was bored. Rachel was still digging about looking for clues. She thought it was for real, that she would find some clue that would solve the murders, and she kept bringing us bits of rubbish that she'd found.

We couldn't get a moment alone.

Now she was crawling through the bracken, still searching. I didn't even think there'd been a murder; I was sure that all the girls had been found safe and well, if not a bit scared. My mum had told me the story to keep me out of the woods.

Jonny looked through the trees towards home. 'This is lame. I'm going to the shops. Someone's bound to be there.'

My heart sank. 'Sorry. I didn't want to bring Rachel. My parents just asked last minute.'

'She's such a baby,' he said.

I looked down at my feet, not daring to meet his eye. 'Sometimes I wish I could lose her for ever.' A big part of me meant it.

'Great idea!' Jonny's eyes lit up. 'We could lose her for a little bit. It'd be funny. She's such a spoilt little brat.'

I nodded. 'Okay. Let's teach her a lesson.'

'How?' Jonny asked.

My mind was racing. 'Why don't we play hide-and-seek. Let her win, then we run away as far as we can, and wait until she loses it.'

'Then she'll come running towards home and we'll leap out on her.' Jonny's face broke into a grin. 'It'll be hilarious.'

I nodded excitedly as my heart skipped a beat. Jonny announced the game and Rachel's head popped out of the fern.

'I love hide-and-seek.' She ran over clapping her hands. Jonny started as It and Rachel and I hid. I stood behind a tree, making sure to leave my arm sticking out. Rachel ran straight back to the fern where she'd come from.

Jonny made the pretence of counting and then strolled over to me. I tried not to giggle too loudly as he shouted, 'Found you!'

I pointed to where Rachel was crouched in the ferns and Jonny tagged her. She stood up and saw me already caught.

'I win! I win!' She danced about.

'Yes, Rachel, you win.' I smiled despite myself. 'Now are you going to count to twenty while we hide?'

She nodded excitedly.

'Okay then,' I said. 'Let's see if you can break Jonny's record. No peeking.'

I made her turn away and face the brook. She began to count, and we moved away from her. When we were out of earshot, we ran as fast as we could. After a few minutes of running we stopped and fell about, Jonny laughing until tears trickled down his cheeks.

'*She totally fell for that.*' He grinned at me.

'*She'll come running this way any minute, and when she does . . .*' I lunged at him and he laughed. Even Rachel would find it funny in the end. We sat down and Jonny offered me a cigarette out of his pocket.

'*Want one?*'

'*Sure.*' I took the cigarette and held it in my hand. I'd only smoked a couple of times, but I tried to copy the stars in the films. '*You got a light?*'

'*Yeah.*' He pulled out a postbox-red lighter; it looked so grown-up.

'*Suck on it when I light it.*' He came nearer to me. The flame jumped into life and hovered in the air. I sucked hard and the end glowed. I started to cough and splutter; my throat was dry and felt burnt.

Jonny laughed. '*You'll get the hang of it.*'

I shook my head, unable to speak. My face grew hot and I knew I'd be bright red.

'*You must get fed up having to look after Rachel all the time.*'

'*Yeah, she's a real drag.*' I felt bad as I said it, but Jonny was looking at me intently. At last it was just him and me. '*I don't know why mum couldn't look after her, it's not my job.*'

'*I thought your boring mate was going to take her?*'

'*Kayleigh? I asked her to, but she wouldn't.*' I wished she had.

'*Your mate doesn't like me much, does she?*'

'*She just doesn't like boys. It's like she never left primary school.*' I rolled my eyes at him.

He laughed and then took another drag of the cigarette. '*Have you ever made out properly with anyone before?*'

'Yeah,' I lied. I thought we'd been making out properly when we kissed behind the bike shed. 'You?'

'Plenty of times. I had my first girlfriend in the first year. She was lame though; wouldn't do anything.'

'Like what?' I asked.

'She wouldn't let me touch her. How can you be going out if you don't touch each other? You might as well be friends.'

'Yeah, I know what you mean.' Everything I knew, I'd read from my Just Seventeen magazines.

I felt sweaty and hot as Jonny inched closer to me. I could smell his Lynx aftershave. He put his arm round my waist.

'You're pretty.' He turned me around to face him.

'Really?' I'd been desperate for this moment for so long, and now he was finally going to ask me out. I'd fancied him for ages. He was the year above. It had seemed impossible.

'Yep,' he said. He brushed my hair with his hand. 'And you're blonde.' He leaned forward and put his lips to mine, and a tingling travelled through my body. But then his hand went from my hair and down to my chest, cupping one of my boobs. I didn't know what to do. I didn't like it.

His other hand trailed the waistband of my shorts and then started moving downwards.

I pulled away from him, but he leaned forward, following me. I tried to push him off, but his grip on my boob became harder, his kiss fierce. He pushed himself into me. I felt a bulge down there. For a moment, fear made me freeze, and then it turned to anger. I pushed him away with both hands and he fell backwards, confusion spread across his face.

'What the fuck?' He panted. 'You said you liked me?'

'I do.' I felt stupid. My cheeks were burning with shame. I had said I liked him and now he looked hurt.

He took a step towards me. 'What's the problem, then?'

'I just don't want to.' I put my hands up as if to stop him. I didn't want him touching me again. It made my stomach turn.

'Cocktease.' He shook his head at me, disgust curling his lip upwards. 'You've got me hard now. You can't just do that.'

'I'm not some slag,' I said.

'Didn't seem that way a minute ago.' A nasty smirk played across his lips. 'Everyone at school will think you're a slag when I tell them that we shagged.'

My heart sank. If Mum and Dad heard about this, they'd kill me.

'Why don't you just give me head?' His hand moved to his jeans buttons and he began to undo them. 'I won't tell anyone.'

I shook my head and stepped back. I didn't want to do that. I'd read about that in magazines and that was for when you were older and in proper relationships. Not for now. 'I don't want to.'

'My last girlfriend didn't make all this fuss.' He rolled his eyes. 'God, you're just like all the rest of them. All talk and then nothing.'

I'd never said I was going to do that, I thought.

He moved towards me, a dark look on his face. A need. Panic made me want to run. He tried to grab me, and I scratched at his face to stop him, catching his cheek. He looked shocked as the blood trickled from a fresh cut.

The purple stone in my ring had caught him.

He touched his face and stared at the bright red blood on his fingertips. Blood kept dripping down his face.

He shook his head, his eyes wide. The cut looked like it stung. He didn't look so big now, more like a little boy who'd grazed his knee.

'You're mental.' He stepped back and then turned and ran.

For a moment I stood there, my own blood roaring in my ears. I knew he wouldn't say a word about it to anyone. He'd be too embarrassed by being hurt by a girl.

As I stood there panting, the fear I'd felt moments before turned into anger and something else. My fingertips were sore where they'd clawed his face and his blood was under my nails. He'd tried to make me do it, but I'd shown him. It felt good. I felt strong. He'd deserved it.

I felt free in the woods. Alive. I was alone. No mum and dad to tell me what to do. No friends to make me worry whether they liked me or not. No Jonny pressuring me.

No one but me.

I groaned out loud as I suddenly remembered Rachel, tipping my head back and looking up at the black branches high above me, which were stirred by the summer breeze. The sky was darkening. She would be freaking out, probably still by the willow, crying. She hated being left on her own. She hadn't even tried to find us. She was so useless.

When she was hysterical, she was hard work. Impossible to calm down. She'd tell Mum that I'd brought her into the wood and left her on her own while I went off with a boy. She'd do it just to get me in the shit.

'Rachel!' I called. 'Where are you?'

Maybe I could scare her into keeping her mouth shut too.

Chapter 29

Alana Loxton

Thursday

Loxton rubbed her face with her hands, trying to shift the tiredness. It was 4.30pm, but it felt so much later. The case had taken it out of her, but there was no time to stop.

'Here's your full intelligence package you requested on Jonathan Cane.' Kanwar barely looked at her as he handed her the file, before rushing off to answer a phone.

Loxton took the package and leafed through it.

'Jonathan Patrick Cane,' she read out. 'Also goes by "Jon" and "Jonny". Cane's on a life licence for murder, as we already know. He maintained his innocence in prison, which delayed his release for a few years because he refused to show any remorse. He eventually told the Parole Board he was sorry for his part in the murder and promised that he was a new man. He's got recent form. Possession of cocaine in the past year. He did well not to get recalled back to prison.'

'Let's not forget the prisons are full to the bursting,' Kowalski said. 'Does it say any more about the murder?'

'Murder of a child in 2000,' Loxton read out. She stared at the words. They still shocked her. Child murderers were rare, despite the news reporting them as if there was one living on every corner.

'That was a long time ago,' Kowalski said. 'How old would he have been?'

Loxton checked the DOB at the front and quickly did the maths. 'Fifteen,' she said. 'Just a kid himself.'

'He had a recent conviction for selling drugs and the current intel is that he was still involved in supply. There must be tonnes of people in his current life who wanted him dead.'

She nodded as she glanced at the summary of the murder in 2000: *Defendant killed child in Ashurst Wood using a rock*. So much horror contained in one sentence. What had made Cane kill a child? From that moment, his life had been mapped out in front of him. All Loxton felt was sadness. 'I'll get the murder case file sent to us.'

Kowalski looked surprised. 'That can't be relevant now. This will be to do with drugs. He might even be involved in the insider trading. Perhaps when Rowthorn went AWOL, Cane's boss decided to tie up some loose ends.'

'Maybe . . .' It seemed unlikely a crime committed so long ago could be the motive for Cane's death, but in a murder like that, of a child, there would be a lot of hate. And people could be patient. 'I still want to check. Curious, I guess.'

'The post-mortem results should be in by tomorrow afternoon. You never know, it still might have been just an overdose.'

'Or perhaps we'll find Rowthorn's DNA at the crime scene,' Loxton countered. 'When will the forensics be back for that?'

'It could take a couple of days,' Kowalski said.

She focused on her monitor and saw that an email had

arrived from Met Intel with attachments of everything they'd found on Robert McGregor.

Loxton read his missing persons report. McGregor was homeless. He'd failed to turn up for a rehousing appointment, which meant he'd lost his chance at a home. He was normally pretty reliable, so the homeless charity working with him had reported him missing three days ago.

McGregor also had over a hundred convictions. Mostly shoplifting, pickpocketing, street drinking and petty assaults. Nothing exceptional.

'Let's look at the recent police stops of McGregor,' Kowalski suggested, leaning across her and tapping at the unopened email Patel had sent. His boundless energy amazed her; he didn't seem tired at all.

'He got stopped twenty times by police on the Southbank last month alone,' she read aloud. Most of them were for suspected possession of drugs and begging. That didn't surprise her. The homeless population had exploded in the past few years. Where in the past you'd see a couple of older men at most, now she saw dozens of young men and women already so hopelessly lost.

'Lots of tourists in the day to beg from,' he said. 'And in the evening, drunk people who make easy targets.'

Something began to irritate her. 'Rowthorn could have gone to the Southbank for a drink and got more than he bargained for,' she said.

'It's possible,' Kowalski agreed. 'Or maybe *McGregor* got more than he bargained for and Rowthorn had to disappear.'

'You think Rowthorn put his own watch on McGregor's wrist to try to trick us?' Loxton tried to keep the disbelief out of her voice. It was important to always keep an open mind.

'Stranger things have happened.' Kowalski shrugged. 'There's lots of CCTV there; we should go and check it now while we've got time and see if Rowthorn shows up on any of it.'

She pulled up a map of the Southbank on her phone. It was the location that was playing on her mind. That particular part of the Southbank. She had a feeling she'd looked at it recently.

'Ready to go?' Kowalski asked. 'Might as well check this lead out while we wait for Cane's post-mortem results, forensics and the CCTV from the nightclub.'

'Give me a minute.'

'I know where the Southbank is,' Kowalski said, pointing to the map. 'I don't need that.'

'It's the location,' she said. 'There's something about it.' Where had she seen it? A couple of the roads stood out, and she couldn't take her eyes off it.

'You're thinking of a previous job. I get that all the time.'

'No, it's to do with this case.' The glare from her phone's screen was starting to hurt her eyes. She zoomed further out. It was just there, in the corner of her mind.

The Southbank was busy at 5pm. Tourists took pictures and office workers surged towards the pubs. Kowalski was noting the CCTV camera positions. Loxton couldn't focus. She was flicking through her notes. The Southbank had come up before. She saw a homeless woman huddled in a blanket by a cash machine on the wall. Loxton crouched next to her.

'Got any change?' The woman's eye bored into

Loxton's. Her face was grubby and pock-marked, the skin sagging with premature age.

Loxton dug into her pocket and pulled out a tenner. She gave it to the woman and her eyes lit up.

'Have you seen this man?' Loxton showed the woman a picture of Robert McGregor on her mobile.

'Why do you want to know?' The woman scowled at her, the light diminishing, fear replacing it.

'I'm his daughter. I just wanted to speak to him.'

The woman pressed her lips together until Loxton pulled out a twenty.

'He puts his head down a few roads back from here, under the railway bridge at Redcross Way.' She pointed down the road. 'I used to sleep down there, but it got too crowded. I haven't seen him around for a few days, though.'

'Thank you.' Loxton watched the woman gather up her blanket and scurry off.

Loxton checked the bridge on the map on her phone and frowned. The thing that had been niggling her was right in front of her eyes. Why hadn't she seen it before? She looked up at Kowalski. 'I know why this location is important.'

'What?' Kowalski said.

'It's here.' She pointed at the map. 'The research on Emily Hart puts her living two minutes' walk in that direction, which is seconds from where McGregor was sleeping under the railway bridge.'

'Emily Hart?' Kowalski asked.

'The secretary from the bank.'

'And?' He shrugged. 'She's got to live somewhere.'

'The secretary who seemed to know more about Mark's financial situation than his own fiancée did. If Rowthorn had come across McGregor here, don't you think it's a bit of a coincidence that he disappears within walking distance of her place?'

Kowalski raised his eyebrows at her, clearly thinking it was a stretch.

'She's just down here, off Redcross Way.' Loxton dodged through the crowd to head towards the side road. 'Maybe Rowthorn met up with Hart after he left Steele. What if that's what he had to sort out?'

'She'll still be at work,' Kowalski said.

Loxton hoped he would follow her anyway. She turned down the side road and into the small estate. After a call to Patel, she had Emily's flat number: fifty-five. Emily lived in a new-build block still shiny and unscathed.

'I'll do the talking,' Loxton said. 'A woman-to-woman chat.'

'And I'll try to be invisible.' Kowalski shook his head at her, and she smiled back at his large frame.

'Do your best.' She punched in the number on the intercom.

'Hello?' It was a woman's voice. She sounded like she'd been crying.

'Hello, it's DC Loxton. Miss Hart, I spoke to you the other day about Mark Rowthorn.'

'Yes?'

'Can we come up?' she asked.

There was silence. Loxton wondered if the intercom was broken.

'Yes . . . yes, but I'm a bit under the weather.' There was a click as the door released. They climbed the stairs, reaching the third floor. Hart's flat was down a long, cream corridor lined with bright, white circular lights in the walls. It must be like living in a spaceship.

When Hart came to the door, she was wearing a lilac dressing gown wrapped tightly around her small frame. Her face was gaunt and her skin blotchy. She looked like she had the flu.

'There's a virus going around work.' Hart coughed into her sleeve.

'I'm sorry to hear that,' Loxton said.

'Please come in.' Hart led them inside. Her flat was cluttered; every available space was covered in empty takeaway boxes and diet-coke bottles. There was the occasional half-empty vodka bottle, too. 'Sorry about the mess; it's been a rough few weeks.'

'That's all right, you've not been well.' It looked like it had been a rough few *months*, not weeks. The flat smelt of stale air and Loxton was shocked at the mess, but she kept her face neutral. She'd seen worse, but she hadn't expected it from the glamorous Hart. The flat itself was nicely decorated with expensive furniture; the mess was obviously a new addition. Loxton moved a plate of congealing sweet and sour chicken from the sofa and sat down. 'We have reason to believe that Mark went missing from this area,' she began.

'Really?' Hart fidgeted with her red hair, winding it around her index finger.

'Do you know this man?' Loxton held up her mobile screen showing the photograph of McGregor.

Hart peered at the picture, taken three weeks ago. 'I think he's one of the ones that begs near here.'

'We think he might be linked to Mark's disappearance.' Loxton held the photograph nearer to Hart.

She blinked rapidly at it and then suddenly burst into tears. Kowalski threw Loxton a look and she knew exactly what he was thinking. Hart was more than just friends with Mark Rowthorn. She had fallen apart since his disappearance. Loxton held her hand up towards Kowalski. It was better to coax than bulldoze here.

'Did this man hurt Mark?' Hart wiped tears from her face using her sleeve. Grief was never pretty.

'This man was wearing Mark's engraved watch when he was found in the river. We're trying to find out why.'

Hart looked sheepish. 'I wouldn't know anything about that.'

'We think this man might have attacked Mark and stolen his watch.'

'I don't think so.' Hart shook her head.

'Why?'

'Sorry, I . . . Mark lost that watch a few days before the wedding.'

'Are you sure?' Loxton was frowning.

'He told me he'd lost it.'

'His fiancée's pretty sure he had it the weekend before he went missing.'

'She's wrong.' Hart's voice became harder at the mention of Talbot.

'Emily, it's important that you're honest with us.' Loxton tried to keep the frustration out of her voice. It was these little white lies that often threw everything off the correct course. 'We'll waste a lot of resources on this lead, but it may not be a real one.'

'He lost his watch about a week ago and he didn't get it back.' Hart's voice was certain.

'Was he visiting you when he lost the watch?' Loxton asked.

Hart turned her face away, her lower lip quivered. 'Why does it matter?'

'It matters, Emily.' Loxton held her breath.

Hart covered her face with her hands.

'We won't be able to find Mark if we don't know what happened to him. The last few hours are crucial in an investigation like this.' Loxton reached her hand towards Hart instinctively but held back. It was as if there was an invisible wall between them, one she'd never be able to break through. She put her hands on her lap, feeling useless. She couldn't do anything for the woman falling apart in front of her.

Hart was crying in short, rasping gasps. Kowalski looked pointedly at Loxton, and she sighed. She didn't know what to say any more than Kowalski did.

'You were in a relationship, weren't you?' Loxton asked softly.

The crying grew louder, and Hart nodded her head, still hiding her face in her hands.

'We're not here to judge; we understand that life is complicated,' Loxton said. 'We're here to find Mark.'

'Please find him.' Hart's body was trembling, but she lowered her hands from her face and met Loxton's eyes.

'We need your help to do that, Emily.'

'Will Julia find out about the . . . affair?' Hart gazed down at her hands.

'Don't worry about that. Finding Mark is the most important thing.' Loxton leaned forward and patted Hart's hand.

'I didn't mean it to happen.' Hart gave a sad shrug of her shoulders. 'You spend all your time at work . . . it becomes your life.'

'Did he come here?'

'Yes. He'd pretend he was working late. It became routine. We had a row a couple of days before his wedding. He kept saying we should end this, but I didn't want to. It hurt like hell when he talked about me like I was a problem to be got rid of before his wedding. After the row, I threw all his things into a bin bag and chucked it out onto the street.'

'He had belongings here?' Kowalski said.

'Sometimes he'd stay over if Julia was away for the weekend, or he'd pretend he was away on business.' Hart's cheeks coloured.

'And when you threw his things out, that included his watch?' Kowalski said.

'I think so.' Hart glanced at Kowalski. 'I was angry and I'd been drinking. In the morning when I looked outside the bags were gone.'

'McGregor might have taken them,' Kowalski said.

'Mark was so angry when he found out what I'd done.' Hart shuddered at the memory. 'He was worried about who'd taken the bags. That maybe it would get back to Julia. It's all he seemed to care about.' She looked close to tears again.

'What happened then?' Loxton asked, trying to focus Hart on the next part of her story.

'He wouldn't return my calls or WhatsApps that week.' Hart looked utterly heartbroken and again Loxton had the urge to reach out and hold her.

Hart continued: 'Then when he came over the day before the wedding, we argued again, and he told me it was over. I couldn't believe it.' She wiped the tears from her eyes and shook her head, as if trying to free herself of the memory.

'You saw him the day before the wedding?' Kowalski's eyes widened.

Hart's face clouded over.

'Emily,' Loxton said. 'This is really important.'

Hart's cheeks coloured and she looked down at her hands. 'I WhatsApped him. I was losing my mind. I had to know whether he was going to go through with the wedding. I love him. I still do. It was killing me watching him marry someone else. I thought maybe I could convince him the wedding was a mistake. He came over and told me to leave him alone. He said it was all getting too much for him; it was destroying him. "But what about me?" I said. How could he marry someone else when he loves me?' Hart looked up again and her face was puffy and blotchy from crying. She looked desperate.

Loxton looked at Kowalski. She waited a moment, but Kowalski didn't say a word.

'What happened then?' The room was still. Loxton didn't dare move. Had Hart lashed out at Rowthorn? It seemed unlikely, given her small frame, but adrenaline could be a powerful hormone in the human body.

'He called me a bunny-boiling bitch and left.' New tears rolled down Hart's cheeks. 'I thought he loved me. I was such an idiot. But when he went missing, I thought that maybe he couldn't go through with the wedding after all.' She looked at them both, hoping to get the answer she wanted.

'What time did he leave?' Loxton said.

Hart's shoulders dropped. She thought for a moment. 'He left around six. He said he had a dinner to go to or something.'

'Is that the last time you saw him?'

'Yes.' Hart's eyes dropped to her hands. Either she was trying hard not to cry again, or she was attempting to avoid Loxton's gaze.

'Emily, did you send him threatening texts?' Loxton said.

'Mark asked me that too, but I didn't. I told him to his face he was making a mistake marrying her. How could I threaten him? He knew I'd never contact Julia or anything like that. I love him.'

Hart was a bad liar and had said far too much as it was. But the killer instinct was missing. Loxton glanced at Kowalski, and he gave a slight shake of his head, and she was relieved that he wasn't about to arrest Hart either.

'We need to search your flat and take your mobiles.'

'Why?'

'To verify that you didn't send those texts.'

Hart nodded; she didn't put up a fight. 'Are you going to tell Julia?' she whispered, her face pale.

'Not unless it becomes relevant,' Loxton said. 'Thank you for being honest with us.'

'If you tell her and my work find out . . . It's all I've got left.' Hart began to cry again.

'I understand,' Loxton said.

Hart wiped the tears from her face with her sleeve. 'I've lost everything. Please, find him.'

Loxton dropped Hart's single mobile into an evidence bag; she would analyse it when they got back. Before they left, she spoke to the security guard, who was happy to let her view the CCTV.

Kowalski stood behind her as she loaded up the footage from the reception on 6pm on Saturday 15 July. The day before the wedding. She fast-forwarded until, at 6.07pm, a man came out of the lift and pressed the green exit button, releasing the locked front door to the block. She froze the frame as his face turned to the camera on the front entrance door. There was no doubt. It was Mark Rowthorn.

She swapped cameras and watched him walking away out of the block, alone, then past an old man who was sat near the front entrance.

'Is that who I think it is?' Kowalski moved closer to the screen.

Loxton examined the image. The footage was good – no expense spared for the modern private block. She rewound and played it again. It was Robert McGregor sitting on the floor. She saw Rowthorn pause and drop a couple of coins into McGregor's open hand before continuing onwards and out of the CCTV's view.

'That's McGregor all right,' Kowalski said.

A minute later, Robert McGregor struggled to pull himself upright. He shuffled after Mark Rowthorn until he was also lost from the CCTV.

'I wish the camera angle was just a little wider,' she said.

'I know,' Kowalski agreed. 'What happened to him that he ended up in a river?'

Neither of them wanted to say it, but she couldn't help herself. 'I think *Rowthorn's* what happened to him. One way or another.'

Loxton took a week's worth of CCTV; two days before and all the way up to today. She'd check it when they got back to the station to make sure Rowthorn hadn't been back. For now, she was content that Hart had been telling the truth.

Chapter 30

Julia Talbot

Thursday

I couldn't sleep. I hadn't slept since the police told me the body wasn't Mark. The afternoon light seeped in through the curtains and my head whirred with images. Jonny Cane and his anger towards me, the gash on his head after I pushed him.

When I started to drift off, I would be jolted awake by fear. Sweat cooled on my skin and the sheets seemed determined to tie me in knots.

I went to the kitchen and poured a glass of water, popped another sleeping tablet. If I could sleep, then I wouldn't feel so dead. I sank onto the sofa waiting for the tablet to kick in and turned the TV on. I lowered the volume to a whisper, the harsh noise too much for my tired brain.

Eerie white light flickered on the walls as I skimmed through the channels. The usual daytime rubbish. I ended up on the news, hoping the relentless bulletins would make me drowsy. I settled myself down, wrapping my dressing gown tighter around me, trying to distract myself from the yawning ache in my chest.

The London news came on and a familiar view sprang onto the screen.

The Night Jar Bar.

I sat upright. A man had been found dead there this morning by the police.

Fear made my heart thud harder in my chest. There was an appeal for witnesses. They'd identified the body as that of Jonathan Cane. His family had been informed.

I picked up a sofa cushion and held it tight to my face, biting into it to stop me from screaming. So Jonny Cane was finally dead. The police had confirmed what I'd already feared. All those years of being scared of him, and now I was free. But at what price? I'd killed him. Would they believe me when I said it was in self-defence? I'd left him to die in that alleyway, not getting any help for him.

What had I done to deserve this? But, of course, I knew exactly what I'd done. This was my punishment. My punishment for Rachel.

I was shivering and I couldn't stop. Terror ballooned inside me, growing bigger and bigger.

My vision blurred and the room around me began to dance. Rachel and Jonny were spinning in front of my eyes, holding hands. She was laughing and her head was flung back. She was in her late twenties, the age she would be now if she'd lived, her hair still golden and long. He was the carefree boy I'd spent so many hours dreaming about as a girl. They looked happy as they spun round and round my living room. I wished I could join them.

I was losing my mind.

I glanced towards my front door. The police would come knocking soon when they discovered that I'd been in contact with Jonny. I covered my face with my hands as I sobbed.

There was a chance my DNA wouldn't be identified. I'd been arrested as a child, but that DNA would surely be destroyed by now. There were time limits now on how long they could store people's DNA, especially if they hadn't been convicted of anything. I'd read up on it recently.

Maybe the CCTV in the Night Jar Bar hadn't been recording. I should wait and pray that they never linked me to his death. There was nothing else I could do.

Lucy was going to lose it when she saw the news report. She'd want us to go straight to Loxton. But I couldn't tell Lucy I'd killed Jonny. She was the only person I had left. I couldn't bear to see the disgust on her face.

Sickness gripped my stomach and I tried to breathe in and out through my nose. I peeked from behind my fingers. Rachel and Jonny were looking straight at me. I shivered and my breathing came out ragged. What were they going to do to me? Their lifeless eyes were all I could see. I reached out for them, but before I could take hold of them, they were gone.

It was as if they'd never even been there.

Lucy had promised me we would check Mark's crypto account when she got back from work tonight and try to find where the money had gone. She'd told me to try to get some sleep. But part of me didn't want to wait for her. I felt like going back to the nightclub right now and speaking to the boss. He'd said he hadn't *killed* Mark. What if he had him locked up somewhere? But going it alone hadn't worked out so far. I'd wait for Lucy, go through the crypto account with her. And if we found the money, we could try to get Mark back. Without it, the police were my only option. But I couldn't confess to Johnny's murder when his boss might still have Mark. He might kill Mark in revenge.

Chapter 31

Alana Loxton

Friday

Loxton's sleep was always bad during the first week of a case, but this was worse than normal. It didn't help that every lead had been a dead end, with no finish line in sight. Cane's death had left them with more questions than answers and she felt helpless.

Could it have been David Steele, trying to pin the insider trading on Rowthorn? Making sure Jonny Cane was in the frame for that and seeing to it that neither man could give their side of the story? Or had Rowthorn just decided to walk away, realizing that he didn't love his fiancée or his mistress?

And why had Cane got all those photographs of Talbot, Rowthorn and Steele? Was he framing Rowthorn or threatening to hurt Talbot? Loxton wasn't sure how to broach it in a way that would guarantee that she got the truth from Talbot. She struck Loxton as someone holding back. But through fear or self-preservation? That was the real question.

Loxton looked at her watch. Ten past four in the morning. The rest of the world was sleeping.

But maybe not everyone. She thought of Julia Talbot,

alone in her bed, waiting for her fiancé to come home and afraid he never would.

Loxton sat up in bed, propping up her pillows, and pulled her laptop from her bedside table. It was still on when she opened the lid. There was one unread email in her inbox sent a couple of hours ago from Kanwar on the night shift. She opened it.

'Hi Alana, these case papers came into the CID inbox. The night shift's been crazy, two stabbings already, so we won't get around to looking at it tonight. It's something to do with the dead bloke you found at the night club. Thanks, K.'

Reviewing case papers was the last thing she wanted to do at four in the morning, but it was clear no one else was going to do it and it wasn't as if she was sleeping anyway. She took a swig of water from the glass on her bedside table and opened the document. It contained scanned documents, yellowing pages which had been handwritten. There was a letter at the front:

'*Urgent: FAO DC Loxton. From General Registry – Requested Case file relating to the murder of Rachel Hughes.*'

She opened the file and realized that she was looking at Jonathan Cane's murder case. She hadn't known who the victim was when she'd sent off her request. The murder team were convinced Cane's death was an overdose, but Reynolds was still waiting for the toxicology results to finish his post-mortem report. She'd learnt in her career never to leave any stone unturned. Ever.

Her brow furrowed as she read DC Neil Fraser's report. He'd been the officer in charge at the time. Rachel Hughes's sister, Jenny, had been arrested in the early stages. Something pulled at the edges of her mind, almost too ridiculous to entertain.

Loxton had never found anything on Julia Talbot's early life – no evidence of the car accident that killed her parents, not even their death certificates.

This murder had happened on Monday 24 July 2000, during the start of the summer holidays. Three children had gone into the woods and only two had come out alive. The murder weapon had been a rock.

Rachel Hughes had suffered a devastating blow to the back of her head which would have left her unconscious, if not dead. She had been struck two more times after that. From the angle and force used, the pathologist had surmised that it was most likely a child who had carried out the frenzied attack.

The two children had been arrested. The police had focused on the boy, Jonathan Cane, because he was a bad kid from the wrong side of the village. Jenny Hughes was described by DC Fraser as distraught. In her statement she said that her and Jonathan Cane had started to hang out a little at school. The day they went to the woods was the first time they'd been alone for a long amount of time. Jonathan Cane had tried to sexually assault Jenny Hughes, before he ran off towards where they'd left her sister. Jenny Hughes had then found her sister dead.

Cane had been in trouble with the police before: petty theft, criminal damage and arson. A local troublemaker. Cane's blood was found on the victim. It was a straightforward case.

She flicked to the witness statement section, but the statements weren't there. She re-read the letter from General Registry again. This was just the basic file, the officer's case summary and the pathologist's findings. The

General Registry were looking for the original statements and evidence in the case, but it could take a few weeks. There was a backlog. It would all be buried somewhere in the massive General Registry warehouse, if it hadn't been thrown away. Evidence was kept more securely now; back then, things weren't as organized.

She sighed; this would have to do for now. Loxton typed *Jenny Hughes* and her DOB into the Police National Database, and it began its slow search across the country.

Loxton stood up and peeked through the curtains onto the waking world below. She'd always loved the vantage point her bedroom window had given her, a good view down the road, so she could see what was coming from either side. She'd picked a second-floor flat as they were rarely burgled, with neighbours on either side and above and below. She'd felt sheltered from the chaos outside.

The sky was lightening, and the street below deserted, giving it an apocalyptic feel. In a couple of hours it would be pulsating with traffic and people on the commuter conveyor belt. But in this moment the world belonged to her.

She turned back to the screen. There was a hit waiting for her. She clicked on the record. Jenny Hughes, DOB 20.06.1986, had been arrested for murder in July 2000. Fourteen years old. Jenny Hughes's parents' details were there too: Carol and Michael Hughes.

There were no other police records for Jenny Hughes. She'd never come to police notice again.

A few more clicks through police systems showed her Carol and Michael Hughes's current address in Milton Keynes. They'd reported a burglary last year.

She punched a number into her mobile and waited. It took for ever for him to answer.

'Hello?' Kowalski's voice was groggy.

'It's me. We need to go to Milton Keynes.'

'What time is it?' Kowalski yawned.

She checked the time on her laptop. 'It's four twenty.'

'In the morning?' Kowalski said.

'Obviously.' Why were men so bad at waking up?

'Can it wait?' She heard the pleading in his voice.

'No, I need you. I've found a new lead.' She couldn't work this out alone. She needed a fresh pair of eyes. His eyes. She had to know what the connection was between Jonathan Cane and Julia Talbot. There had to be one. Julia had paled when she'd mentioned the name Jonny.

There was silence on the other end of the line.

'It might be big,' she said. 'You won't want to miss this.' Loxton was sharing her break with him. He was beginning to irritate her.

'Fine. I'll be there in an hour – but this better be good.'

Chapter 32

Alana Loxton

Friday

'I want to visit Rachel Hughes's parents,' Loxton said.

'Rachel Hughes. Is that name meant to mean something to me?' Kowalski rubbed his face as he stood in Walworth CID office, the dull early morning light bathing everything in grey.

'No, but the boy convicted of Rachel's murder will mean something to you – Jonathan Cane.'

His eyes widened in amazement. 'You found the parents, after all these years.'

'They're not far. Only in Milton Keynes. Steele and Jonathan Cane were two of the last people to see Rowthorn alive and now Jonathan Cane's turned up dead. Cane was stalking Talbot and Rowthorn. We need to find out what the link is. I think it's the key to everything.'

'I'm not sure this is relevant, Alana.' Kowalski spoke slowly, as if he was talking to a child. 'That murder was when Jonathan Cane was fifteen years old. How could it be linked? I like the insider trading angle more. Steele, Rowthorn and Cane working together, and when the bank realized what they'd done, all of them panicked, turning against each other.'

'This enquiry will only take the morning. In the murder squad we're told to profile everyone: the suspect, witnesses and victims. Learn their whole life history and leave nothing to chance. Jonathan Cane is a suspect. This murder was the most significant moment in his life. We need to check it out.'

'Okay.' He put his coat back on. 'Let's clear this one up and then we can focus on the bank angle. Best not to leave any avenues ignored, especially if we go to court.'

Patel walked in, her face confusion when she spotted them both. 'You're in early?'

'We've got an enquiry in Milton Keynes,' Kowalski said. 'Are you night turn?'

'Just finishing off before the early turn arrive. Alana, I reviewed that CCTV from the Silver Tree Hotel you asked me to. You need to see it. I was going to leave it on your desk, but as you're here . . .' Patel motioned for Loxton to come over.

'Can it wait? This enquiry's urgent.'

'It won't take long.' Patel unlocked her laptop. 'Dominik, you'll want to see this too.'

Kowalski joined them.

Patel's screen was filled with a car park, half-full.

'Where is this?' Loxton asked.

'The Silver Tree Hotel's car park on Saturday 15 July. The day before the wedding.'

Loxton nodded, her eyes focused on the screen. She checked the time: 8pm. A car pulled up. The driver stayed in the car for a minute and then climbed out. She pulled a small case out of her boot, paused for a moment, and then pulled her coat off and threw it into the car, slamming it shut and then clicking her key fob. Then she wheeled the suitcase towards the hotel entrance. She had long dark hair on the black-and-white image and was wearing a smart work skirt, white blouse and heels.

'Lucy Webb?' Loxton peered at the image.

'Exactly.' Patel switched the camera and they saw Webb checking into the hotel with the receptionist. She looked flustered.

'Talbot and Webb told us Webb arrived at 2.30pm on the Saturday,' Kowalski said. 'She's five and a half hours late – no wonder she looks a little hot and bothered.'

'I checked all of the CCTV,' Patel said. 'Julia Talbot did arrive at the hotel at 2.10pm, and it doesn't show her leaving. But there's no CCTV on the rear entrance, so Talbot could have left without being captured.'

'So Talbot doesn't have an alibi after all.' Loxton closed her eyes for a second as it sank in. 'Why would they lie?'

'Maybe Talbot didn't want any awkward questions about that afternoon,' Kowalski said. 'She wouldn't give us her mobile, which we both said at the time was weird, unless she was having an affair too. It's possible she was seeing someone at the hotel she shouldn't have been, and she didn't want it getting out.'

'And Webb covered for her?' Loxton thought for a moment. 'That's a good friend.'

'She was her bridesmaid, so they must be pretty close,' Patel said. 'I didn't recognize anyone else entering the hotel, but there were plenty of people coming and going. Any one of them could have been seeing Talbot. I think she has a little explaining to do.'

'Can you give her a call?' Loxton said. 'Get her to come in for an update and then we'll ask her. Thanks for this, Patel.'

'No problem. But there's something else you should know. I've checked the CCTV from the Night Jar. The

footage isn't the best quality, but it looks like Julia Talbot
– same size, fair hair. If it is her, she was there the night
Cane died.' Patel loaded up the CCTV from the Night
Jar.

Loxton peered at the grainy black-and-white image.
The woman's features were blurred, but it could be Talbot.

'*Rowthorn's girl.*' Loxton shook her head in disbelief.
'It was Julia Talbot after all.'

'And she tricks her way into the back. And a few
minutes later Cane and the owner follow her.'

'Thanks, Meera. When she comes in for the update,
we'll arrest her.'

Meera nodded. 'And just so you know, after exiting
with Cane, neither of them come back into the club or
into the camera's view.'

Loxton was glad they'd set off from London so early; it
meant they'd managed to escape the worst of the London
rush hour. Gridlocked traffic on the other side of the
carriageway tried to edge its way into London. All those
people crawling towards an already bloated city, Loxton
thought.

Michael and Carol Hughes had moved from the small
village of Ashurst Wood where their youngest daughter
was murdered and were now living in a large, anonymous
new-build estate, nestled on the outskirts of Milton Keynes.

Their house was a pretty semi-detached. There was a
small front garden, the lawn dark green and kept short.
On either side of the front door were two small patio
pots with miniature conifers. It was like a Lego house.
Loxton knocked gently on the white door.

A man in his fifties opened it a crack and peered at
her through the gap.

'Hello, Mr Hughes,' Loxton said. 'I'm DC Loxton and this is DC Kowalski. Can we come in?'

Michael Hughes narrowed his eyes at her but nevertheless opened the door wider. 'Yes, of course.'

He led them into the living room and offered them a seat. A woman came in and looked at Hughes with a confused expression. She was skeletal and grey, her skin hung from her emaciated frame. When Michael Hughes explained who Loxton and Kowalski were, she went white. 'Is it Jenny? Is she dead?' the woman asked.

'No, Mrs Hughes,' Loxton said. 'We're not here about Jenny as such. We're dealing with a Julia Talbot and a Mark Rowthorn, who seem to be linked to Jonathan Cane. I know this will be hard for you to talk about, but I wanted to ask you some questions about your other daughter, Rachel.'

Michael Hughes took his wife's arm and led her to an armchair.

'Do you have any photos of Jenny?' Loxton asked once they'd all sat down. She held her breath. She'd barely let herself imagine that her theory was right, but now she was here, she became hopeful.

'I threw them all out.' Michael Hughes jutted out his chin, as if challenging anyone to criticize him. 'She cut us out of her life, so I cut her out of ours.'

'I've got some.' Carol Hughes's voice was very small. Her hand fluttered to her mouth as if she wanted to put the words back in. Michael looked at her but said nothing. Carol disappeared upstairs, as quiet as a mouse.

They sat in an uncomfortable silence while they waited. The tick tock of an old-fashioned carriage clock on the mantelpiece made the wait feel longer. Loxton had never been able to find a single record of any fatal car crash involving Talbot's parents. In fact, she'd hardly found out anything about her. It was as if she'd materialized out of thin air at the age of twenty-one with an art degree.

Carol appeared clutching a white shoe box. She placed it on the coffee table carefully.

'May I?' Loxton asked. Carol nodded and stood there staring at the box. Her husband reached his hand out towards hers and guided her back to the sofa.

Loxton slid the lid off and lifted the photographs. There were photos of a tiny baby with large blue eyes nestled in the arms of a much younger and happier Carol. Then a bright little blonde girl holding hands with a red-haired girl with green eyes, both beaming at the camera clutching ice-creams. Another baby photo, but this time the little blonde girl was stood next to Carol, holding the baby's hand and smiling at the camera. The little girl seemed unsure of herself. And, finally, a dejected teenager with her blonde hair tied back, a lost look in her eyes, as she stared out at the sea on a grey day. She wasn't smiling in this last photograph.

There was no mistake, Jenny Hughes was Julia Talbot. Kowalski leaned over, studied the photograph of the teenager. He shook his head in disbelief, muttering something quietly in Polish to himself. Loxton knew how he felt; she couldn't believe it herself. Here was the link between Talbot and Jonathan Cane. Julia Talbot had known Jonathan Cane. He'd killed her sister.

'Mr and Mrs Hughes, your daughter, Jenny, she changed her name to Julia Talbot,' Loxton said gently.

Carol and Michael looked at Loxton in confusion.

'Is Jenny in trouble?' Carol's eyes widened in panic.

'She's the fiancée of Mark Rowthorn,' Loxton continued. 'A banker who's gone missing from London.'

'I saw that on the telly. It's been all over the news,' Carol Hughes said. 'Is that our Jenny? They didn't show a photo of the bride on the news.'

'That's because we asked the press not to.' Now Loxton knew why Talbot had been so distressed about her photo being published.

'They said on the news the groom just didn't turn up on the wedding day. What's happened to him?' Carol asked but she couldn't meet Loxton's eye. She swallowed nervously as her hands shook worse than ever. Michael patted her arm.

'He went missing the day before their wedding.' Loxton said. 'We don't know what's happened to him, but he's not been seen since.'

'She never even contacted me to say she was getting married.' Carol Hughes wrapped her arms around herself for comfort. Her husband continued to pat her arm.

'When did you last have contact with Jenny?' Loxton asked.

'Not since she went to university,' Carol said. 'She went and never came back.' She stared into the distance.

'And why was that, if you don't mind me asking?' Loxton willed her to go on.

'Things were strained after Rachel died.' Carol's lower lip trembled but she carried on, her hands gripped tightly together. 'It was such a hard time for us . . . Some days I didn't eat . . . I couldn't do anything. Jenny was only fourteen, she still needed bringing up, so I had to pull myself together. But I wasn't the mother I used to be.'

'There's no easy way to deal with the death of a child,' Kowalski said.

'Jenny didn't cope very well.' Carol was staring off again as if she'd gone back in time to that dark part of her life. 'We had to get her psychiatric help. It was awful.' She covered her face with her hands and began to cry.

'That must have been difficult,' Loxton said.

'It was,' Michael said, taking over for his wife. He clenched his fists and the muscles along his jawline tightened. 'The psychiatrist said that Jenny couldn't accept that she'd taken Rachel into Ashurst Wood and just handed her over to her killer. It left Jenny distant from us, prone to lying, making up fantasies of a completely different life. The psychiatrists said Jenny couldn't deal with her reality. Preferred a fantasy world. To escape. That fucking boy took both our daughters away that day.' Michael shook his head.

Loxton didn't know what to say. The Hughes's pain was still so raw. Perhaps Talbot had blocked her past out of her mind to survive, which is what had made her such a convincing liar.

'I can't believe it's going wrong for her again.' Carol closed her eyes. 'She never gets a chance to be happy.'

'The day Rachel died was the first time Jenny had had to babysit Rachel.' Michael shook his head as if he couldn't believe what he was saying. 'Normally we paid a babysitter. Jenny was jealous of Rachel. Everyone said it was normal sibling rivalry, but it seemed more than that. And on that bloody day, we couldn't get hold of the babysitter. We thought Jenny would be all right with Rachel.' His voice shook.

'If I'd just said no to work . . .' Carol said. 'I worked at a doctor's surgery and the other receptionist had gone off sick. I didn't want to let them down.'

'Do you think Jenny hurt Rachel?' Loxton had to ask.

'It wasn't Jenny.' Michael Hughes spat the words out. 'It was that animal. It was all him. Jonny Cane killed our Rachel. *He* did it.' Michael Hughes's whole body was shaking, years of repressed hurt seeping up and out through his skin. Loxton felt drained in his presence, as if she was being pulled into his pain.

Loxton looked at Carol. 'Who do you think killed Rachel?'

Carol glanced at her husband, then back to Loxton. 'Jonathan Cane was convicted. It was him.' She began tugging at her sleeves, worrying the material.

'We have some news for you both,' Kowalski said gently. 'You should prepare yourselves.'

Michael held his wife's hand.

'Jonathan Cane is dead,' Kowalski said.

'Dead?' Carol put her free hand to her mouth.

'We can't go into the details, but we thought you should know,' Loxton said.

'How did he die?' Michael's eyes were eager.

'We don't know yet,' Kowalski said. 'There needs to be a post-mortem.'

Michael nodded. 'I hope it was slow and painful.'

'You don't think Jenny had anything to do with it?' Carol's voice shook with fear.

'What makes you say that?' Loxton hadn't expected that reaction. Had Carol seen something in her daughter she didn't want anyone else to know about? Something dangerous?

'Well, I don't know really. I know Jenny took Rachel's death hard. We all did. It ruined Jenny's childhood. None of the other kids would play with her. Only Kayleigh Webb. They'd been best friends for years. Kayleigh was always a very sweet girl, never followed the crowd. But Jenny was bullied by the other children. Badly at times.'

'Kayleigh Webb?' Loxton asked.

'Here,' Carol held up the photograph of Julia as a little girl holding hands with the red-haired girl with green eyes. 'That's Kayleigh.'

Lucy Webb had auburn hair and green eyes. How long had they known each other for? Loxton took the photograph and studied the little girl's face. It looked like Webb. She took a photograph with her phone camera and handed the precious photograph back to Carol.

'We're sorry that you have to go through it all again,' Loxton said.

Kowalski stood up ready to leave, energy pouring off him. She could tell he was desperate to chase this lead. This discovery had changed everything.

'Poor Jenny.' Carol's voice was shrill, and it startled Loxton for a moment. 'Talbot's a funny surname to pick. You'd have thought she'd have used my maiden name, or something that meant something to her.' For a moment, there was stillness, and then Carol began to cry again – deep, croaking sobs that shook her whole body. Michael pressed his lips together. He looked at Loxton, his eyes pleading.

'Here's my card.' Loxton held it out towards them. 'Call me any time.'

'Please – will you tell Jenny we love her?' Carol managed through the tears.

'Do you want her to know that we've been here?' Loxton asked.

Carol looked torn. 'She must be devastated. I can't believe her fiancé disappeared the day before her wedding. And then that monster being found dead. It's awful.'

Michael took the card from Loxton. 'Thank you, officers.' He walked them to the door, leaving Carol on the sofa muttering to herself.

Michael lowered his voice. 'My wife's very fragile. I'm not sure she can take all of this. Please don't mention us to Jenny. We're easy to find if she wants to contact us. We haven't changed our names.' Michael glanced back towards the living room.

Loxton closed the door behind her as they left. When she was in the car, she rubbed the back of her neck with both hands; it was knotted and it was going to take much more than that to relieve the tension.

'That was awful.' She felt drained by their loss, helpless to ease their pain.

Kowalski shook his head in disbelief. 'I can't believe Jenny Hughes is Julia Talbot. Did you know?'

'No, I suspected,' she replied. 'Jenny and Julia had the same date of birth. It just seemed like too much of a coincidence, what with Cane stalking Talbot.' She knew something hadn't been right in Talbot's past and here it was. Julia Talbot had to change her entire identity to escape her history. To start again. Loxton could sympathize with that. What she couldn't understand is why Talbot had kept the lie going, despite everything that had happened.

'And I thought you were wasting your time chasing Cane's historic murder,' Kowalski said. 'Talbot had me fooled.'

'She had us all fooled,' Loxton said. Talbot had lied to her about everything – her identity, her parents being dead and that she hadn't known Jonny Cane. It took a certain type to lie that convincingly to the police and Talbot's lies had seriously hindered the investigation. Loxton suppressed the anger and frustration.

'Interesting that the day Rachel died is the first time Talbot ever babysat her,' Kowalski said. 'Do you think she was involved in her murder? Some sort of weird pact with Cane?'

It sounded ridiculous. 'From what I've read, Jonathan Cane was acting alone. Julia wasn't involved. She helped to convict him. This could be simple revenge on his part. He killed one sister and got caught, perhaps he was determined to destroy the other. Killing Rowthorn before Talbot's wedding day is particularly cruel.' It seemed plausible but then anything could have happened. Loxton's head span with all the possible scenarios.

'So Talbot found out Cane killed Rowthorn and has taken matters into her own hands?' Kowalski said. 'We need to get her back in for interview.'

Chapter 33

Julia Talbot

Friday

The police station was crowded, like a doctor's surgery, with people sat staring into space – their own troubles playing in their minds. Lucy and I headed to the receptionist but there was already an agitated man speaking to her.

'I want to talk to a real police officer,' the man said. 'My rucksack was stolen and all you can do is take a report?'

'Sir, there was a murder last night.' The receptionist looked tired. 'The police officers are dealing with that. I've reported your bag on the system and I've given you a crime reference number. Someone will be in contact soon. That's all I can do for now.'

Lucy gave me a furtive look. They were talking about Jonny. My gut twisted in fear. The lady on the phone had told me they wanted me to come to the police station to give me an update about the case. But was *Jonny's* murder why they'd really called me here? Had they found my DNA on his body already? I clasped my hands together and tried to breathe steadily.

'Don't look so worried,' Lucy whispered to me. 'It's all

right. We'll just tell them everything we know. They'll be able to work out the crypto account; I'm sorry I couldn't.' She didn't know what I'd done to Jonny, though. She just thought I'd spoken to him at the nightclub.

The receptionist looked relieved when the man with the rucksack stomped away. She turned to me. 'Can I help you?'

'I've been asked to come in for an update. DC Alana Loxton's been dealing with my case.'

'I'll call her for you now.' The receptionist picked up her phone.

I looked at Lucy and she gave me an encouraging smile.

'I can't get hold of DC Loxton,' the receptionist said. 'Are you okay to wait for a bit while I track her down?'

'I . . . I can wait, I suppose.' I turned away and dug my nails into the palms of my hands to keep me from screaming. I felt the walls of the police station closing in on me. This didn't feel right. I couldn't speak to the police now. I'd called Jonny with my mobile; they would link him to me. And my DNA was bound to be on his body. How had I been so stupid? I had to get out of here. I headed towards the door.

'Where are you going?' Lucy followed me, putting her hand on my shoulder. 'We agreed. This is the time to tell the police everything.'

I looked at her puzzled face, but my throat felt dry and I couldn't speak. I'd lied to her about Jonny. I hadn't told her that I'd pushed him. That I'd killed him. Would she ever look at me the same, once she knew I was a killer, that I'd kept it from her? It was too late now.

I heard the entrance door open and Loxton and Kowalski strode in, their eyes searching the room until they found me.

'I was . . . I was told to come in.' I swallowed, seeing the hardness in Loxton's face. 'But they said you weren't here.' I motioned towards reception.

'You don't mind if I sit in for the update too?' Lucy asked. 'For moral support.' Her voice faltered as she looked at Loxton and Kowalski's strained faces.

'Julia Talbot,' Loxton said. 'You're under arrest for kidnap and murder.'

My legs felt like they were going to give out from underneath me and I put my hand out to Lucy, who steadied me. All I could do was stare at them.

'You're arresting her for *murder*?' Lucy's voice was raised. 'You can't do that.'

'I'm afraid we can,' Kowalski said. 'We need to interview her. And I'm sorry, but you can't be there.'

'I'm staying with her,' Lucy's voice rose in anger. 'You've got this all wrong.' Her hand grabbed mine and tightened around it.

'Lucy, it's all right.' I gave her a quick hug. 'I'll meet you afterwards. It won't take long. This will all get cleared up. There's been some sort of mistake.' I doubted I'd be leaving the station, but I couldn't bear to see her so upset.

Loxton and Kowalski ushered me inside and Lucy was left standing in the reception staring after me. She looked so lost without me. I hated that I'd dragged her into all of this.

Chapter 34

Alana Loxton

Friday

Talbot had declined a solicitor. So far, she was sticking rigidly to her story that she'd been with Lucy the day before the wedding. Kowalski leaned back in his chair, relaxed, as if they were all just having a chat despite the cramped surroundings of the interview room.

Talbot was sitting opposite them. The bench was an inch lower than the blue plastic chairs, making her appear smaller. She'd gone downhill since Loxton had last seen her. Her usually shiny blonde hair was scraped back into a greasy ponytail. She was fidgeting with her engagement ring, twisting it agitatedly round and round her finger.

It was time for Loxton to start taking Talbot's story apart. 'You said Lucy was with you Saturday afternoon?'

'Yes. Why do we have to go over this again?' Talbot closed her eyes and rubbed her temples.

'We've checked the CCTV from the hotel. Lucy didn't turn up until 8pm.'

Talbot faltered. Suddenly she didn't look tired anymore. 'There . . . there must be a mistake.'

'There's no mistake. Lucy arrived at 8pm. The CCTV

shows you checking in at 2.10pm. It doesn't show you leaving, but there's a back exit not covered by CCTV.'

The CCTV showed Rowthorn leaving Emily Hart's block at 6pm, but if Talbot had found him there, anything could have happened.

'I didn't leave. I was there all afternoon.'

'Did you meet up with Mark before Lucy came to the hotel?' Loxton asked. 'Was he angry? Did you have a row?'

'I didn't see him. He went off with David to collect the suits. That was the last . . . the last time I saw him.' Talbot eyes were shining and her breathing was coming in shorter gasps. 'He told me he loved me and that he'd next see me walking down the aisle.'

'Why did you and Lucy pretend she was with you in the afternoon?'

Talbot wiped her eyes. 'When you first came to the flat and asked me where I was the afternoon Mark went missing Lucy panicked. She was meant to be with me that afternoon, so when you asked, she just lied and said she was with me. She was trying to protect me from you. She was worried you'd waste your time on me if I didn't have a proper alibi and she was right.' Talbot waved her hand angrily at the interview room as if it proved her point. Loxton didn't believe her.

'Where was Lucy?' Loxton asked.

'She called me that afternoon as she had to go into work. Someone had messed up on an account. She said she'd be as quick as she could. She works at Bailey's Accountants.'

'They were open on a Saturday?' Loxton asked.

'Yes, they often pull her in at weekends. Especially when there's been a mistake. She supervises accounts.'

Talbot shook her head frustrated. 'She should have been with me. She felt bad and that's why she pretended she was with me. It was silly but once it was done it was too late.'

'Let's talk about your parents, shall we?' Loxton said and waited.

A startled look spread across Talbot's face, but it soon became neutral again. She fidgeted with her long blonde hair, tugging at the end of her ponytail.

'You've gone quiet?' Loxton said.

'My . . . my parents are dead.' Talbot pulled at the wedding ring on her necklace and for a moment Loxton thought the chain would snap.

'They're very talkative for dead people.' Loxton sighed. She was starting to tire of this game.

Talbot lowered her head, dropping her eyes to the tabletop.

'Why did you lie about your parents?' Kowalski asked.

'We're estranged. They might as well be dead. For all I knew, they were.' Talbot looked pleadingly at Kowalski.

'Everything you've told us is a lie,' Loxton said.

'I'm sorry, but it has nothing to do with Mark going missing. I fell out with my parents years ago and I got into the habit of telling people they were dead. It was easier than telling them that—' She paused. 'It was stupid,' she continued, 'but I got stuck with it. Even Mark thinks they're dead.'

'You changed your name to Julia Talbot,' Loxton said. 'An interesting choice. Talbot's an old surname, it means messenger of destruction. Why did you pick that name?'

Talbot looked at Loxton, then sighed. 'Because I always feel like bad things follow me, no matter what I do. That's all. And I wanted to escape my parents.'

'It's also one of the commonest surnames for Oxbridge graduates. You had high ambitions when you picked that name.'

'I just wanted a fresh start. That was all.'

'Let's begin again, but this time we want the truth.' Loxton tilted her head at Talbot, unsure if she knew *how* to tell the truth.

Talbot crossed her arms across her chest. 'I've told you the truth.'

'You told us everything was fine between you and Mark.'

'It is – I mean, it was until he went missing.'

'Did you kill Mark because you found out about the affair?'

'Affair?' Talbot was frowning.

Loxton waited, letting a few beats pass.

'There was no affair.' Talbot's body was quivering with anger. 'You can't make up rubbish to upset me.'

'Mark was having an affair.' Loxton turned the pressure up.

'With who?' She threw her hands wide, glaring at them both in turn.

'We're not going to disclose that to you.' Loxton's eyes bored into Talbot's.

'You're making this up.' Talbot shook her head.

'Was it for his life insurance? Did he try to call the relationship off? You were set to receive four hundred thousand pounds in a lump sum. Not bad. People have killed for a lot less.'

'I didn't know about the life insurance.' Talbot was pale.

'We know all about your past,' Loxton said. 'You were arrested for murdering your little sister and now we're investigating you for possibly murdering your fiancé.'

'Have you found Mark?' Talbot's face had gone a sickly grey.

'We're asking the questions. Let's talk about your sister, shall we?' Loxton said.

'That's got nothing to do with this.' Talbot slammed her fists on the table. 'You have no right bringing her into this. Tell me what's happened to Mark.'

'I think it has everything to do with this.' Loxton put both of her hands on the table. 'It shows your propensity to kill when things aren't going your way.'

'I wasn't found guilty of anything.' Talbot glared at Loxton.

'But you were arrested.'

'Jonny Cane was convicted, not me.' A flicker of fear danced across her face, but then it was gone.

'I'm glad you've brought up Jonny Cane,' Loxton said. 'What were you doing in the Night Jar?'

Talbot stood up, as if desperate to get out. 'I want a lawyer, right now.'

'I bet you do. The time is five forty-five in the evening. This interview is terminated while we get Miss Hughes – apologies, Miss Talbot, a solicitor.' Loxton turned off the recorder. She hated being stopped mid-flow. Talbot would have plenty of time to compose herself now and she'd be coached by a solicitor.

'Sit down or we'll have to take you to your cell,' Loxton warned.

Talbot was wild, her eyes wide.

'I didn't kill my sister. I haven't done anything to Mark. You have to believe me. You're wasting time.' Talbot reached her hand across the desk towards Kowalski.

'Miss Talbot, you'd better wait for your solicitor.' He pulled his hand away from her.

'Please, has something happened to Mark? This is torture.' She started sobbing, tears trickling down her face. Loxton had a sudden pang of guilt.

'We can't discuss the case off the record, Miss Talbot,' Kowalski said. 'We'll have to wait for your solicitor.'

'You're disgusting.' Talbot burst into tears again, covering her face with her hands.

The wedding band hanging from Talbot's neck caught the light.

'Where's this bloody solicitor?' Loxton folded her arms. 'It's giving Talbot time to think.'

'He's probably got five other prisoners to get through before he even comes here.' Kowalski massaged the back of his neck with his fingertips.

'When did it get this bad?'

'About five years ago. You were shielded away in the murder squad so you wouldn't know, but things are getting third world down here. We spend most of our time waiting. Government cuts in the criminal justice system.' He rolled his eyes.

She and Kowalski were huddled in a corner of the custody suite as the bustle of normal police work went on around them. Two tired uniformed officers were booking in an obese drink driver, who was booming out the national anthem and waving his arms about. He was going to be blowing well over the legal limit.

'I think Talbot's cracking,' Loxton said.

'But has she got anything to do with Rowthorn's disappearance?'

'I don't know.' Loxton rubbed her eyes as a headache threatened. No one had told her that joining the police would leave her questioning every decision she made, that everything would ride on her opinion. She looked at Kowalski and sighed. 'This is the second time she's been arrested for murder. She either has really bad luck, or . . .'

'I don't believe in coincidences either,' Kowalski said.

A man in his fifties, with short, white hair, strolled into custody. He was wearing a cheap black suit, which strained against his massive bulk.

'Solicitor's arrived,' Kowalski said.

Loxton settled herself, picking up her pen and preparing her notes. They'd had a one-hour break and she had lost her stride. She straightened out her notes, but it was more to distract herself from the solicitor sitting opposite her.

William Fitzpatrick was one of the best in the business. Loxton had worked with him before. To Fitzpatrick it was all a game and a great money-maker. The pawns were the deprived and the vulnerable; their pain wasn't real to him.

Loxton turned on the digital recorder. 'Julia, we'll continue the interview. It's now six forty-five in the evening on the same day. Remember, you're still under caution. The same people are present, but there is also now your solicitor, William Fitzpatrick. Can you confirm we haven't talked about this case while the recorder's been switched off?'

'We haven't talked about it,' Talbot replied.

'Now, Julia, we suspect that you became aware of Mark's affair and became jealous,' Loxton said.

'I didn't know anything about an affair,' Talbot said. 'I don't believe you.'

'My client needs more information than that.' Fitzpatrick

stared at Loxton, as if they were the only two people in the room. He was trying to put her off her game. She ignored him.

Kowalski slid some printouts towards Talbot which contained WhatsApps between Emily Hart and Mark Rowthorn. They'd downloaded them from Hart's mobile. 'We've taken out the female's name for her protection and her mobile number. Take your time.' Kowalski sat back in his chair. 'You too, Mr Fitzpatrick.'

Fitzpatrick scanned the message in a moment and pushed them away. Talbot pored over them.

'Officers,' Fitzpatrick said. 'Is this really the way to break this affair to my client? She is the victim in all of this.'

'Actually, Mark Rowthorn is our victim,' Kowalski said.

Talbot's lower lip was trembling and she began to cry. She pushed the papers away and closed her eyes.

Kowalski picked up the papers. '*Sexy, need to see you tonight,*' he read out. '*Tell her you're working late.*' He paused and let a moment go by. 'That must have hurt, Julia. You must have been broken-hearted – humiliated.'

'I didn't know.' Talbot's eyes were red-rimmed and bloodshot.

'Did you find these WhatsApps on his mobile?' Kowalski said. 'What did you do?'

'I loved him.' She wiped the tears from her face. 'I thought he loved me too.'

'And now?' Kowalski asked.

Talbot burst into a new fit of tears.

'Officer, is this fair? You've asked my client your questions. She denies any involvement in Mark Rowthorn's disappearance. Shouldn't you be talking to this other woman? Isn't it more likely he's run off with her and is fine?'

'He hasn't run off with her,' Loxton said. 'The mobile Mark used to send these WhatsApps has never been retrieved. I assume it was on him when he went missing. What did you do with his mobile, Julia?'

'I never saw those WhatsApps. I didn't know he had so many phones. I just thought he had his work one.'

'Where were you on the afternoon of Saturday 15 July?'

'I was at the Silver Tree.' Talbot's voice was strained as she tried to control her anger.

'Ah yes, and you waited for Lucy to arrive, leaving you on your own all afternoon until 8pm.' Kowalski leaned towards Talbot. 'The same timeframe, coincidentally, in which Mark disappeared.'

'I don't know what's happened to him.' Her voice shook and she was tugging at the end of her hair now, her eyes full of fear. Was it for Mark or for herself?

'You're not helping yourself. You should tell us the truth. Explain your side of the story.' Loxton wished she could make the other woman tell her what had really happened.

'I *have* told you the truth.' She sounded frustrated. 'I was in the hotel.'

'Did he abuse you? Was it in self-defence? This is your chance to give your account.' Loxton needed to cover any future defences.

'He never hurt me,' Talbot's face twisted in disgust at the thought. 'He wasn't like that.'

'The only motivation for my client is this affair, and she's clearly just found out about it now,' Fitzpatrick said. 'Is that all you have?'

Loxton picked up the bundle of papers, which she'd had under the table, and dropped them in front of Talbot. She flinched at the bang. Talbot eyed the yellowing folder suspiciously. Loxton opened the old case file and leafed through the pages until she found what she was looking for.

'You've been arrested for murder before, Julia.'

'I've never killed anyone,' Talbot said.

'You wanted to teach your little sister a lesson. It was a fatal lesson. You abandoned her in the woods, and when things went wrong between you and Jonny, you went back to her. You took your anger out on her. Things got out of hand. And then you tried to blame Jonny Cane.'

'She was dead when I found her.'

'Maybe I've got it wrong. Maybe you and Jonathan Cane killed her together? Did he take the blame for you?'

Talbot winced at the mention of Cane's name. 'No.'

'You're good at getting people to lie for you. This time it was Lucy Webb, but she won't do it for ever when she realizes what you've done.' Loxton was running out of patience. They should have kept Webb in, heard what she had to say when confronted with the CCTV of her arriving at the Silver Tree hotel at 8pm. What had Talbot told Webb, to convince her to lie to the police for her?

'I didn't kill Rachel and I haven't hurt Mark. Jonny Cane was convicted, not me.'

'Jonathan Cane, the local nuisance. He was found dead yesterday at the Night Jar. Do you know anything about that?' Loxton watched Talbot's face, trying to spot any more cracks in the mask. This might be her one chance to decide if Talbot was a killer.

Talbot looked away for a moment and then her eyes met Loxton's. 'No.'

'Julia, have you had contact with him recently?'

'I didn't kill him.' Talbot put her head in her hands.

Fitzpatrick looked alarmed momentarily and tried to catch Talbot's eye. 'You don't have to answers these questions, Miss Talbot. They'll be asking you about Jack the Ripper next. Ridiculous.' He was sweating.

'Have you seen Jonny recently?' Loxton repeated the question.

Talbot seemed to gain her composure and looked up. 'I've not seen him since the court case.'

Kowalski opened a laptop and played the CCTV of the woman in the night club. It showed her go into the back being followed by two men. Then it flicked to the woman and one of the men leaving the club by a fire exit. They disappeared off shot a few seconds later.

'Is that you?' Loxton asked.

Talbot shook her head. 'I've never been there.'

'We'll be checking, Julia. Has Lucy – or Kayleigh – seen Jonny?' Loxton asked.

'No.' Talbot shook her head firmly.

'Where were you on the evening of Wednesday 19 July, the night that Jonny Cane died?' Loxton asked.

'I was in my flat.'

'Julia, the police went to your address twice and couldn't get hold of you that night. Where were you?'

'I was fast asleep. That's why I didn't hear them knocking. I'd taken sleeping tablets. Lucy will tell you.'

Loxton frowned. 'Was Lucy there?'

'No, she had to pick James up from City Airport. But she'll tell you I took the sleeping tablets before she left. I couldn't do anything after that.'

'Lucy's not exactly a reliable witness, seeing as she's lied for you once already.' Loxton sighed. 'We're going to take your DNA after this interview to compare it to the crime scene. Will your DNA be on Jonny Cane, Julia?'

'No.' Talbot kept her head down, refusing to meet Loxton's or Kowalski's gaze.

'We'll be examining your mobile, too. You refused to hand it over voluntarily early in the investigation. Why was that?' Loxton asked.

Talbot looked stressed. She glanced at her solicitor, but he said nothing.

'You say you haven't had any contact with Jonny, but he's been watching you since he's been out of prison.' Loxton took out a stack of photographs of Talbot and Rowthorn. 'These are copies of the photographs I told you about that we found in Jonny's flat. They're mostly of you but around thirty are of Mark and a couple are of David Steele.'

Talbot's face paled at the sight of the photographs. Her hands shook as she reached out towards them.

'When were these taken?' Loxton pushed the photographs towards Talbot.

'I . . . I don't know.' Talbot leafed through the photos, slowly at first, and then faster and faster. She looked up at Loxton, her voice shaking. 'There are so many . . .'

'Are they recent?' Loxton wondered how long Cane had been stalking Talbot.

'I think so. Wait, no. This one.' She held up a photograph of her outside her jewellery shop holding a coffee. 'I haven't got my engagement ring on. That must be over six months ago.'

'And you're telling me you haven't had any contact with Jonny Cane? If he threatened you and something happened, you should tell us.'

Talbot paused for a moment, but then shook her head.

'I haven't heard from him. I don't know why he had these. I wouldn't want to see him. He killed my sister. I'd call the police if he contacted me.'

'If you know anything about Jonny Cane's murder, you should tell us now.' Loxton looked for some glimmer of remorse from Talbot, but there was nothing. 'We'll be talking to Lucy about these sleeping tablets, too.'

'I haven't done anything.' Talbot was shouting now, her hands on the table, the photos scattering onto the floor. 'Jonny killed Rachel. You lot wasted time thinking it was me last time, when I was only a child, and you're doing it again now. Can't you see that Jonny's done something to Mark? Now Jonny's dead and you'll never find Mark. You're useless.' Talbot clenched her fists.

Loxton put her hands up, open-palmed.

'Mark's out there.' Talbot pointed towards the door. 'Something's happened to him. I can't believe I trusted *you* to find him.' She spat the words out, her voice shaking in rage. 'I should have known better.' She stood up. The tears had stopped, but her cheeks were turning a darker red and she was trembling.

Loxton got up as a shiver ran down her spine. Her body was preparing for Talbot to lash out; a surge of adrenaline pumping through her.

Fitzpatrick jumped to his feet. 'My client will not be answering any more questions. She's helped you enough. Julia, no comment from now on.'

Talbot stood glaring at Loxton, hate radiating from her like heat from a roaring fire. Loxton was taken aback by it.

'Thank you, Julia.' Kowalski stood up and put his hand on Loxton's shoulder. 'That will be all for now. I'm terminating this interview.'

Chapter 35

Julia Talbot

Friday

The door slammed shut, the vibrations echoing in the tiny space I found myself in. I was left alone. Fear snaked up from my stomach into my chest, wrapping itself tight around my heart. I was trapped and I couldn't get out. Not until DC Loxton let me. I tried to keep my breathing steady, take a full breath, but short sips of air were all I could manage.

Not again.

I'd promised myself I'd never find myself in one of these cells again, but here I was. My pulse throbbed in my head. I felt dizzy.

I'd used up my one call from custody trying to speak to Lucy, but she hadn't answered my landline. The police hadn't let me access my mobile to get her number. They explained it was seized as evidence. They had told Lucy to wait at home for me as I could be in here for some time. I'd left a voicemail message on my answer machine for her, but I guessed she was on the underground still heading to my flat.

When they did open my mobile, Loxton would know I'd been lying – again. I'd called Jonny just hours before he was found dead and I'd been searching for his nightclub on my mobile. Would it show up that I'd been there? I was on the CCTV; and with my mobile they'd be able to prove it was me.

I twisted the ends of my hair into a knot and pulled at it, the sharp pain a release.

Mark had been having an affair. It was like someone was digging into my insides and spooning them out. I'd thought I was being paranoid, doubting him, checking to see if he had a Tinder account or if there were any messages on his mobile. I'd thought I was ill, always out to sabotage my life, fuck it up. My way of punishing myself.

But all the time I'd been right.

He'd been sleeping with someone else. When had it started? When had he stopped being mine?

Had he been preparing to leave me while planning our wedding? My head was replaying our time together – our engagement, lazy Sunday mornings in bed. I tried to spot the cracks. Work out when it had all gone wrong. I thought he'd loved me. I thought he was the one thing I could rely on and it had all been a lie.

All the happiness I'd felt had been fake. I was never going to find peace.

And who was this woman? A colleague from work? An old friend? Did she look like me or was she completely different? I couldn't bear it.

I closed my eyes, wishing the thoughts would stop. Instead I saw Jonny, laid by the bins, the cut to his head bleeding. He'd been stalking me for six months at least. My past coming back to get me. It made my body feel numb. What had he been really planning to do? What had he *done*?

I was glad he was dead.

I sank onto the white bench, a thin blue roll mat thrown on top of it, which did nothing to stop the cold and the hardness of the concrete. The air con was blasting freezing air into the room, shifting the rancid smell around so that it wouldn't settle. Opposite me was a silver toilet basin without a seat. I glanced at the CCTV camera. Were they watching me now?

I lay down on the concrete bed and closed my eyes. My head was pounding and I felt sick, as if I was in the belly of a ship that was rolling from side to side. I pressed my fingertips to my temples, trying to stop the pain with sheer willpower alone. For a brief moment it all ceased, but then the sickness came back tenfold.

I ran to the toilet and vomited, sick spattering the inside of the bowl. I dropped to my knees, clutching the seat as I vomited again. My whole body shook with the effort. The sour acidic smell made me want to throw up again, but there was nothing left. I wiped the bile from my mouth with the back of my hand and tried to calm my breathing.

I couldn't hide from it any longer. Mark had been cheating on me. I wished I could speak to Lucy; she would know what to do. I couldn't rely on the police. They weren't telling me anything.

Perhaps this other woman knew something. I needed to find out who she was and get her to tell me everything she knew.

Chapter 36

Alana Loxton

Friday

Winter was sitting behind his desk, his arms folded and his face stony, a screwed-up newspaper on his desk. The man looked like he hadn't slept in days. Loxton wondered if she looked as bad.

'Sir, we need a surveillance team. We can keep Talbot in overnight, and then, when she's released in the morning, they can follow her. She might lead us to Rowthorn. And if she doesn't, we can at least see if anyone else is watching her. I know she's the key.' She regretted leaving Kowalski to chase up Talbot's mobile's cell-siting while she tried to convince Winter of her plan. Kowalski had warned her he wouldn't go for it – too much money, no guarantee of a result, lots of risk. She hoped she'd convinced him.

'In all my time in the force, I've never been as disappointed.'

'I know we haven't got a result, but if you'd give us a bit more time, a surveillance team could find us the evidence.'

'You think this is about a result?' He stared at her, his anger visible.

'What else?' She didn't know where this was going, but the atmosphere in the room couldn't be worse.

Winter picked up the crumpled newspaper and slung it at her. She threw her hands up in time, catching the open pages before they hit her in the face. She dropped the paper onto the table.

'What the hell's going on?' *Had he lost his mind?*

'Read the front page, Alana. It's tomorrow's headline. The paper has forwarded it to me to ensure that it doesn't jeopardize our investigation.' He was shaking with rage. She had never seen a senior officer this angry before.

She glared at him, but turned the paper over, reading the headline on the front page:

Missing Groom Case: Police Arrest Innocent Bride.

She looked at Winter. 'You think this was me?' Anger made her voice sound shrill.

'Read the reporter's name,' he said, looking away from her in disgust.

She glanced down the page, finding the name in small print at the end of the article.

Alec Saunders

Her ex-lover. Her throat clamped up. She couldn't believe it – not again.

'Don't deny it.' Winter put his hand up to quieten her. 'I knew you'd compromised a case for this man in the past, but I thought you were the victim there. This will be the last time this happens, though. You're suspended.'

Winter had known the details of her move all along. Embarrassment made her look down, but then she raised her gaze, meeting his. This time she hadn't done anything wrong. 'I haven't spoken to him.' Panic rose inside her chest. He couldn't suspend her. Not when she was so close.

'Someone leaked the body in the Thames to the press

and who shows up at Talbot's flat? Your ex-boyfriend, Alec Saunders. You neglected to mention it was him when you told me about the reporter. I was an idiot to give you a second chance and now my job is on the line.'

All she could do was shake her head at him. How could this be happening again?

'Do you think I'm such an idiot that you could play me like this? Or is the money they're giving you too good to turn down? Or perhaps it's true love? Let me tell you something for free, Alana: that man doesn't love you. He's using you and you've just ruined your career for him. You could end up in prison for this.'

'Why would I do this when I know I'd be the first person you'd blame? Can't you see this wasn't me?' Hot tears of anger welled up in her eyes. She hadn't leaked this story, someone else had, and that person was going to get away with it. She would lose her job instead of them.

'Your warrant card, please.' He held his hand out. 'You're suspended from the office of detective constable while we investigate this leak.'

She flung her warrant card onto his desk, barely able to control her anger. 'I didn't leak this.'

'I don't want to hear it.' He took her warrant card and dropped it into a drawer, slamming it shut.

Tears rolled down her cheeks. There was no coming back this time.

'The DPS will be in touch. They're already pulling your phone records so don't bother deleting anything. And your login details won't work on our systems now. I'll call someone to escort you off the premises.'

He picked up the receiver. She couldn't have them walk her out like a criminal.

'Don't bother, I'm leaving.' She charged out of his office, leaving his door wide open.

'You're to wait here.' Winter shouted after her.

She ignored him and managed to keep it together until she reached the toilets. Luckily, she hadn't passed a single officer as she rushed through the long winding corridors. She was grateful for that. She locked herself inside a cubicle and sat down, wrapping her arms around herself, rocking back and forth. The police force was everything to her. Her old friends, her work, her dreams. There was nothing else.

She had to calm down. Someone had leaked the information, not caring that she would be the collateral damage. The obvious suspects were Kowalski or Winter. Only they knew about the body in the Thames and that Talbot had been arrested. Though news travelled fast in a police station. And all the communications flowed through the control room. It might not be them at all. *Please don't let it be Kowalski.*

She stayed there for a few minutes, trying to steady her breathing. This was no time for crying. She had to find the leak, solve the case. She splashed some cold water onto her face to try to take down the puffiness, cleaned away the mascara from under her eyes, then checked herself in the mirror. Her stomach became a tight knot as she failed to calm her rage. It was time to talk to Kowalski.

'This is it.' Kowalski was sitting at his desk, the smell of fat and grease around him. 'I got you a Big Mac from next door.' He motioned at the brown McDonald's bag next to him as he finished off his fries.

He barely looked at her as she walked up to him,

trying to keep her breathing steady, her anger controlled. The rest of the CID office was deserted at this late hour.

'The techies have pinpointed within one hundred metres the location of where the threatening texts were sent from.' He was pointing at the computer screen with a fry.

She leaned over, trying to get a glimpse despite herself. 'Where?'

'The phone was cell-sited on the Bricklayers Arms Roundabout mast.' He shifted over to let her see. 'Talbot's flat is right in the centre of the one-hundred-metre perimeter. We've got her.'

There it was. Loxton couldn't believe it. 'How could she be that stupid?'

'I know.' Kowalski hit the print button. 'But that should be enough to charge her. Whether it would stand up in court is another matter.'

'Charging her isn't going to help us find Rowthorn,' Loxton said. 'We should get that surveillance team behind her.' But, of course, it wasn't 'we' anymore.

Kowalski nodded in agreement before looking her up and down for a moment. 'I guess it didn't go well with Winter? He'll have to go for it now, though.' He stood up and grabbed the printout. 'Cheer up. You were right. Now, let's go and convince him together and you can tell me you told me so later.'

'Let's not see Winter. He's already said no to surveillance. We can follow her ourselves.' *What the hell was she doing?*

'This is compelling evidence, Loxton. Winter needs to see this now. The surveillance team was your idea. Winter will change his mind when he sees this.' Kowalski's brow had furrowed.

She wasn't going to be able to convince him. She sank back into the chair. 'I've been suspended.'

'What?' Kowalski sat down next to her, his face filled with concern. 'Why?'

He looked shocked. She'd been with him the whole time when they'd dealt with the body in the Thames; he couldn't have had a chance to give Saunders a tip-off about it. It had to be Winter or someone else who'd told Alec Saunders. She couldn't believe Winter would have done it – he was the DCI.

'Call custody first. Make sure Talbot's not released.'

Kowalski nodded, looking at her like she'd gone mad. He picked up the phone and dialled. 'Can you make sure Talbot's bedded-down? We've got extra evidence we'll need to re-interview her about in the morning.' Kowalski's face greyed. 'What the fuck? . . . On whose authority?'

'What's happened?' But she already knew.

'Winter has given her bail. She's already gone. I can't believe it.'

'You're joking.' Sickness swept over her. He must have called custody straight after she'd left his office. He'd dismissed everything she'd said, too busy worrying about the political fallout if Talbot was still in custody when that story hit the morning papers. It made it less likely that he was the one leaking the information to Alec.

'I need to get out of here before Winter's henchmen catch up with me. Can I tell you on the way to Talbot's house?'

'Talbot has gone, Loxton. We haven't got the authority to follow her. It would be criminal.' Kowalski frowned at her. 'You need to tell me what's going on.'

'It's Alec Saunders. He knows Talbot's been arrested and the story's being printed tomorrow. Someone is leaking information to him.'

'And Winter thinks it's you?'

She nodded, trying to hold the tears back.

'Shit.' Kowalski shook his head. 'We should have just told him about Saunders when that weasel first spoke to us.' Kowalski's mobile started ringing. 'Winter,' he said, looking at the screen.

'You should answer.' She wasn't going to drag anyone else down with her.

'I have a good idea what it'll be about.' Kowalski leaned towards her, resting his elbows on the table. He was an intimidating sight. His bulk alone would make anyone think twice about pissing him off. 'Did you leak this story to Saunders?'

Anger rose in her chest. 'I can't believe you're asking me that.' She knew he would never believe her. Why should he? He'd known her for all of two weeks.

'Okay, so who is the leak?' Kowalski said.

'That's the question.' She stared at him for a moment too long as she racked her brains trying to figure out if it was him.

'Innocent.' He placed his hand over his heart. 'We're a team. I would never do that to you. Not to anyone.'

'Sorry,' she said. 'My trust in men has taken a bit of a hit recently.'

'Saunders did a real number on you.' He shook his head. 'Fucking prick.'

She shrugged. 'Doesn't matter what he is. I'm off the case.'

'Yes, you are,' he said.

They sat for a moment in silence, letting the weight of her suspension settle in.

'Do you know I'm a trained boxer?' Kowalski asked.

She ran her eyes over his physique despite herself. 'Are

you going to knock Alec Saunders out for me?' She smiled to show that she was joking, but the idea was appealing.

'My father taught me to box. Everyone thinks boxing's about landing that sucker punch. The knock-out. But most fights don't end that way. Most are a hard slog until there's one man who comes out a little on top. Boxing is all about being able to roll with the punches and learning how to get back up. Even when you've got nothing left.'

She was silent, wondering where he was going with this.

'Alana, don't stay down. Get back up. Don't let them beat you.'

Her face felt hot. 'I need to find out who's leaking the information to Saunders, prove I'm innocent.'

'And we need to find Rowthorn,' he said.

She met Kowalski's eye for a moment. '*We?*'

'You don't strike me as the type who gives up on a case at the first wall she hits, however big it is. If you find anything out, just let me know, and likewise I'll do my best to keep you in the loop. And be careful.'

'I will,' she said. At least she had Kowalski in her corner. He reached over and gave her a hug. With it came a rush of relief; someone believed her.

Kowalski's mobile rang again. He pulled away from her and answered. He frowned in confusion. 'Are you sure? . . . Of course, sir. I'll come to your office straight away.'

'My suspension?' she asked, as Kowalski put his mobile in his pocket.

'Not just that. Talbot's been bailed because the blood in Steele's flat wasn't his. The forensic report has just come back. It was Rowthorn's blood all along. Steele lied in interview. Looks like we've got our man.' His eyes were bright as he said the words in a rush.

'What about Jonathan Cane?'

'We haven't had the post-mortem results yet and Talbot denied it was her in the CCTV. We need something concrete. DNA or her mobile placing her there. That will take a while.'

She nodded, pleased at the progress, but it was bittersweet as she watched Kowalski head towards Winter's office without her.

Chapter 37

Julia Talbot

Friday

I'd rushed out of the police station not daring to look back. I couldn't believe it; they'd let me out. The outside air was chilly and I breathed it in gratefully. I wrapped my coat tighter around me and noticed that the sky was darkening; evening was setting in.

The police still had my phone and I felt stranded. I couldn't even call Lucy, not knowing her number.

I struggled through the throng of people trudging home late from work or the pub. Most heads were down, barely looking at me. Others were laughing together and chatting loudly, recalling who had drunk too much and what gossip they'd picked up.

I quickened my pace as I scuttled to Kennington tube entrance. I threw furtive glances behind me, but all the faces swarmed into one. There was a middle-aged businessman jostling past me, another late one at the office. A twenty-something girl with blonde hair, her high heels swapped for trainers as she staggered precariously after one too many cocktails. All of them looking forward to getting back to their homes.

And how long would I have in mine? The detectives

seemed convinced I was guilty. It was only a matter of time before Loxton charged me for Mark's disappearance and Jonny's death. All she had to do was check my mobile history.

Instead of getting off the Northern Line at Borough, I stayed on. I wasn't heading home. I needed to find out who Mark had been having an affair with and the best place to start was near his work. I might discover what he'd been doing for the past couple of months. How he'd got into this mess.

I swapped carriages along the way, but no one seemed to be following me. I got onto the Jubilee Line to Canary Wharf and popped into the nearest Boots and bought some dry shampoo, heavy foundation, lip gloss, chewing gum and body spray. I used the last of the cash from my purse to buy them and then darted into a pub's toilets, the bartenders too busy to notice me.

I tried in vain to cover up the bruise where Jonny had hit me, but it was still visible, even with the dark-tinted foundation. After a rushed job trying to make the rest of me look less of a wreck, I headed to Gaucho on Canary Riverside. I remembered fishing Gaucho receipts from Mark's trouser pockets before I'd slung them in the washing machine. He'd taken me there once when we first started going out. It had been a perfect evening, great food and rich red wine. He'd made me laugh so much other diners had turned to look at us.

A chic waitress wearing a black shirt, trousers and heels showed me to a table, but I didn't sit down.

'Excuse me, this is a bit awkward, but I'm not here to eat.' I beckoned her closer. 'I'm a private detective. I'm trying to find this man.' I rummaged through my handbag and held out the photograph of Mark that I kept in my purse.

She nodded slightly, her face clouding over, but she didn't take the picture. 'Are you another journalist?'

'No . . . no, I'm not.' I put the photograph on the table facing her. 'My client is his brother. This man's gone missing. The police are winding down the case, but you can understand that my client is still desperate to find him.'

'A private detective?' The waitress looked me up and down, her eyes lingering on my bruise. She wasn't buying it. I could always tell when I was losing someone.

'I used to work for the police, but the pay wasn't that great. I earn a lot more doing this.' I motioned at Mark's photograph. I tried to emulate Loxton's posture, standing taller. 'Of course, it can get heated.' I touched my bruise and her eyes widened.

'What's your name?' she asked.

'Sarah Jones.' I tried to keep my face neutral but even I wasn't convinced by the bland name.

'Have you got a card?'

'I don't carry cards. I'm normally chasing cheating spouses, which requires an element of discretion.' I tapped my nose.

The waitress leaned towards me, as if we were conspirators. 'I bet that's interesting.'

'It really is. And so far, every cheating spouse case has proved right. It goes to show that people's instincts are usually right when it comes to this sort of thing.'

'People can be bastards.' She shook her head.

'They certainly can.' I tapped Mark's photograph, drawing her eyes to it. 'Have you seen him?'

'Yeah . . . he used to come in for lunch a lot. Him and his girlfriend. But I haven't seen him for over a week. Not since they said that he disappeared on the news. I've been keeping a lookout, too.'

This 'girlfriend' must be the woman he was having the affair with. I'd only been here once, a few years back. It made it real. I tried to keep it together, to stop the hurt from showing in my voice. 'His family and fiancée are distraught,' I said. 'I'm going back to all the places he frequented, trying to see if anything's been missed by the police. Can you describe this woman to me?'

'You don't think he was having an affair, do you?' The waitress twisted at her apron and leaned in, eager for news.

'In this line of work, nothing surprises me. What did this woman look like?'

'She's pretty. Auburn hair. Pale. She must work nearby. They used to come in at lunchtime mostly.'

It was as if someone had punched me in the gut. Everything was knocked out of me. I only knew one girl with auburn hair. 'Yes . . . yes,' I managed. 'I think his fiancée does work around here and she fits that description.'

'It's so awful.' She seemed to be enjoying the tragedy now, warming to the attention. 'They were so in love. They used to hold hands across the table. Imagine your groom not turning up on your wedding . . . She must be broken-hearted.' She shook her head slowly.

'Did you see anything unusual? Did he have any arguments with anyone whilst he was in here?'

'No. He was polite. Always tipped well.' That didn't surprise me at all. The waitress was very attractive. I suddenly wanted to get out of there. I couldn't do this anymore.

'Thanks for your time.' I managed to hold the tears in until I'd left the restaurant and turned into a side street. It was too much. I put my arm against the wall to support myself, coughing ugly tears.

The police had told me Mark had been cheating on me, but maybe it wasn't with someone I didn't know. Maybe it was with Lucy. Auburn hair and pretty. I couldn't believe it. I rested my forehead against the cold brick. They'd put on an incredible show of not getting on, but had they been lovers all that time? I dry-retched, my stomach cramping hard.

If I didn't have Lucy, I had no one. I'd been alone before and I couldn't bear it again. Rage ripped through me. I couldn't even confront Mark. He always managed to avoid the fallout.

A stabbing pain gripped my body and I clutched at my lower abdomen.

I felt hot and cold all at once. Something was wrong – seriously wrong. I felt lightheaded and the world grew dimmer. I put my hand in my pocket but there was nothing there. I remembered again that the police had my mobile. I staggered back towards the restaurant.

'Please, can you call an ambulance?'

'Are you okay?' The same waitress I'd spoken to earlier ran towards me, helping me onto a chair.

'It's my stomach.' I was burning up. Then, suddenly, I was shivering, freezing. Sweat trickled down my back.

'I'll call one now.'

I hoped she'd be quick. I wrapped my arms around my abdomen, doubled over on the chair. The pain radiated upwards until I was a bundle of nerve endings screaming with agony. I squeezed my eyes shut, the pain overwhelming me until it became fuzzy background noise, and I fell from the chair into blackness.

Chapter 38

Alana Loxton

Friday

This was wrong, but what other choice did she have? Loxton tucked her hair behind her ears and tried to fake the confidence that she was lacking.

A man in his late fifties opened the door to her. He was tall, wearing an ironed shirt and trousers. Retired Superintendent Neil Fraser. The man who'd investigated the Rachel Hughes murder all those years ago, back when he was a young detective constable.

If he asked to see her warrant card, she was in trouble. She'd rehearsed a spiel about leaving it at home, but she didn't think it would work on him.

'Hello, DC Loxton.' He shook her hand, his grip firm and strong. 'Please, follow me.' She followed him into the living room. There was dust everywhere, making all the colours dull and the room drab. There was the familiar musty smell of stale air and unwashed upholstery.

'How's retirement treating you, Mr Fraser?'

'Please, call me Neil.' He offered her a seat on a tired looking armchair while he sat opposite her. 'I gave the police the best years of my life. My marriage, my mental health, everything.' He smiled sadly. 'And then when I'd done my thirty years, I was shown the door, just like every other copper before me. I'm a police officer through and through. What am I supposed to do now?' He looked lost in his domestic setting, the buzz of the office no longer around him.

She knew how he felt. There was a strange space where her warrant card used to nestle in her jacket pocket beside her handcuff key. Her shoulders were lighter without the covert harness she normally wore underneath her jacket. She was a civilian now – but she couldn't stop being a police officer at heart.

'I think you're meant to travel the world,' she said. 'Enjoy yourself.'

He laughed. 'That may be so, but who would I go with and where?'

There was no wedding ring on his finger. No photos on the walls. 'Anyway, you're not here on a social call. You mentioned an old case on the phone. How can I help?'

'Anything I tell you . . . it's confidential.'

'Of course,' he said.

'You dealt with a murder twenty years ago. The victim was a child – Rachel Hughes.'

Fraser's face dropped suddenly. 'Not that case. Anything but that one.' Loxton recognized the tone. Every cop had this – the case they weren't sure about. The case that left them questioning everything that came before it and went after.

'Jonathan Cane is dead,' she said. 'It looks like he died of an overdose.'

He shook his head sadly. She hadn't expected that reaction.

'That doesn't surprise me,' Fraser said. 'He was never

going to make old bones; I knew that when I first met him. He was feral. Those types always live fast and die too young.' She thought she saw relief flicker in his eyes, and she realized that he was hoping that's all she'd come for, to tell him Cane was dead.

She wasn't sure how much to tell him, but, then, they'd suspended her. If they wanted to treat her like a civilian, then she wouldn't be bound by the same rules as an officer. Loxton knew she would have to tell Kowalski everything. He'd wanted her to keep working on this case, but she hoped this wasn't a step too far, that he'd understand why she hadn't been able to leave it alone. She needed to understand what had happened in the past before she had a chance of figuring out the present.

'Jenny Hughes's fiancé has gone missing.'

'Really?' Fraser's complete attention was on her while she told him about the case. He didn't utter one word as she spoke. Like all police officers, he was an intense listener.

'I've read your old case papers,' she said. 'I have a few questions that I just need to clear up in my mind.'

'That case makes me sick just thinking about it. That poor little girl. You wouldn't beat a rabid dog to death like that. That's the one case I got wrong.'

Loxton frowned despite herself. 'Wrong?'

'I was a young detective, desperate for a result.' Fraser looked into her eyes and whatever he saw there made him relax. His shoulders dropped as if he was finally letting a heavy burden go. 'I retired as a superintendent a couple of years back. That case made me . . . but it broke me first. Looking back now, I think an innocent boy went to prison.' He pulled a large bottle of whisky out of a drawer. There was a quarter left. 'Fancy one?'

'Why not?' she said, after all she wasn't working anymore, and it might help him to trust her.

He poured her a generous measure and then one for himself. 'Jonny Cane was a bad kid, everyone said so at the time. The psychiatrists said he was blocking out the trauma – that's why he never admitted to the crime. The pathologist said he was the right size. His blood was found under the purple stone on the ring Rachel was wearing. I remember it hardly fit onto Rachel's finger. It had been her sister's ring.'

'Her sister's ring?'

'Yes. Jenny said she'd decided to give Rachel the ring as she'd always loved it. The ring proved Jonny had been at the murder scene, that an altercation had taken place.'

'Did Jonny have any of the victim's blood on him?' This was the question Loxton needed answering.

'No. No, he didn't. But the pathologist explained that away. In a knifing incident, you get spattering, as you well know. And if the knife hits an artery, well, blood goes everywhere. But in a blunt impact injury, like Rachel had, the blood spatter can be quite small. Contained. And it tends to go sideways, like squashing an orange with a rock, no spray upwards as it's blocked by the impact weapon.'

'But Jonny didn't have a single drop of the victim's blood on him?' Loxton couldn't believe it.

'It's not as odd as it sounds. He went straight home from the woods, took a shower, and then threw all his clothes onto a makeshift bonfire in the back garden. He'd poured half a bottle of vodka on it and it was smouldering when we got to him.'

'Why?'

'Cane said he'd been terrified Jenny was going to accuse

him of rape and he panicked. He said he'd left her and a few minutes later he'd heard this awful screaming. He thought she was hysterical and was going to make something up out of revenge, because, in his words, "he'd come on to her a bit strong". He kept saying he hadn't touched her, and it was her that scratched him, causing the cuts to his face. He said he never saw the little sister after he left Jenny. Said he didn't know how his blood had got on her ring. It was a ridiculous story; it didn't make sense that he'd burn his clothes like that. Jenny said he'd kissed her, wanted to do more but she'd told him she wasn't interested, and he'd become angry and then ran off towards where they'd left Rachel. Jonny's story was discounted as a teenager trying to come up with a defence and failing badly.'

'So, it was Jenny's word against Jonny's.'

'At the time I accepted it all, but now, looking back, I don't think Jonny ever had that in him. He didn't kill that girl. I watched him in prison and after he was released. There was a nagging feeling I had about the whole thing. He was no angel, that's true, but he wasn't a sadistic sexual predator. He always maintained his innocence, even when it meant the parole board wouldn't release him. I started to think I'd got it wrong.'

'I read his psychiatrist reports from prison,' Loxton said. 'The theory was that he attacked the older sister but lost his nerve, so then went after the younger sister – an easier target. In the moment he lost control and killed her. But in prison his behaviour was normal, no indications that he was a predator. He was out on licence for over a year and there was nothing involving attacking women.' *Except for the photographs*, Loxton thought to herself. Stalking Julia Talbot. But then he blamed her for his conviction – perhaps he'd tried to blackmail her and Rowthorn into helping him with his appeal. 'But if it wasn't Cane, who did kill Rachel Hughes?'

'That's the question.' He stood up and went over to his bookcase, pulling out a large leather-bound scrapbook. He sat down and opened it. 'I kept going back to that case. Got a pathologist friend a few years back to look at the special post-mortem notes, unofficially. He said that the assumption it was a teenager was just that – an assumption. An adult could have crept up behind her, crouched low to make sure they hit her. Perhaps it was their first time, so they hesitated. The blows weren't particularly hard, but a child's skull is fragile.'

'The parents?'

He leafed through his scrapbook. 'Alibis, both of them. Good ones, too. They were both working. The father worked at the council offices in town planning; colleagues vouched for him. The mother was a receptionist at a doctor's surgery. Her colleague had to go home sick, so she got called in last minute. The doctor confirmed that she was there from late morning until seven in the evening. That's why the parents had to get Jenny to look after Rachel at such short notice.'

'Did anything stand out as odd?'

'At the time I just believed everything Jenny said. She was a good kid. Never in trouble. But when I started to look back at the case, I began to doubt her account of what happened.'

'You think Jenny did it?'

'Jealousy in siblings can have tragic consequences. Jenny didn't seem the type; she was bright, well brought up. She was known for exaggerating, according to her parents, but we didn't think she'd have lied about her sister getting *murdered*. But, then, there was always something about her . . .'

'What do you mean by that?'

'I don't know who that girl was, what was really going on inside her head. She always had a mask on. At first I thought it was shock, but she never showed much emotion. She seemed to bury everything inside, so deep that even she couldn't find it again.'

'I know what you mean.' Loxton thought of the first time she'd met Talbot. How she had been so quiet and closed off.

'Cane was obsessed with Jenny. He thought she could help set him free. He was convinced it was a tramp living in the woods. There was evidence of a rough sleeper in Ashurst Wood, but Jonny's blood was on the ring Rachel was wearing, and he had a deep cut to his face and scratches. He kept on that Jenny did it to him, but she denied it and she didn't have a mark on her.'

'It sounds like you had a strong case against him,' Loxton said.

'There was some concern when he was released on life licence. Jenny Hughes had chosen not to be informed by probation; she wanted to stay out of it. To all intents and purposes, she'd done a great disappearing act. The parole board deemed him safe to release.'

'Did the authorities find her?'

'No. They asked Kayleigh Webb, I mean Lucy Webb; she started using her middle name when she became an adult. Suppose she wanted to distance herself from it all. Anyway, they asked her if she knew where Jenny Hughes was and Kayleigh claimed that she didn't. The parents didn't know where she'd gone either. The parole board decided that Cane wouldn't be able to find her either.

He'd turned over a new leaf by this point, talked about his future, seemed excited. All thoughts of Jenny seemed to have been forgotten.' Fraser sighed.

Loxton thought of the hundreds of photographs in Cane's flat. 'Do you know how he got on after he was released from prison last year?'

'I've been retired for two years. I kept an eye out for the first six months but lost track of him after that. My mind's not what it used to be.' He held up his empty glass.

She nodded and stood up. 'Thank you for your time.'

'No problem. And here's some more free advice.' He poured himself another glass but didn't offer her one this time. 'You need to watch yourself, Loxton.'

'What do you mean?'

'After you first called me, I gave your nick a ring,' he said. 'Found out you've been suspended. There's very few cases you need to walk away from, but this is one of them.'

'Why?' Loxton asked.

'As I say, it made my career – but it destroyed my conscience, my marriage, my life. At the time I was so ambitious to progress and Cane's head was served to me on a silver platter. Everyone wanted it solved. We all needed justice for Rachel. Someone to blame. I didn't question the case enough, test the evidence properly. Inexperience, I guess. Ambition.'

'And me?' she asked.

'You're the opposite of me. You can't stop worrying about the evidence; picking at it as if it's an old scab. You need to let it go or this case will ruin any chance you have of saving your career. I don't know what trouble you've got yourself into already, but interviewing witnesses when you're suspended isn't going to help.'

She nodded slowly. 'What did you tell the officers who you spoke to?'

'Said I must have got the name wrong and that I hadn't heard back from you. They told me not to speak to you if you did come by.'

'You don't take orders well.'

'Nope, and neither do you.' He paused. 'Here, take this. I don't want to have to hold onto it anymore.' He passed her a photograph and stared into his whisky.

It was of a little girl holding a blue-and-white polka-dot rabbit. 'The mother gave me a copy of it. That's the last photograph ever taken of Rachel alive. She was a bonny little thing.'

'Thank you.' Loxton was drawn to the girl's sky-blue eyes. So full of life.

'What happened to the rabbit?' she asked.

'Funny you should mention that,' Fraser said. 'She had it the day she died, but we never found it when we searched the woods. It had disappeared.'

Loxton put the photograph in her pocket.

'Don't tell me what happens,' Fraser said. 'I like to pretend sometimes that I didn't get it wrong.'

Chapter 39

Julia Talbot

Friday

The Royal London Hospital Accident and Emergency was chaos. Beds were shoved against walls and every available chair was taken. Drunk people argued with hospital staff and security had to come and march the worst offenders away. I'd had blood taken, had to urinate in a plastic beaker. I'd used the name Sarah Jones, although I suspected I wasn't fooling anyone. I'd been waiting on a trolley in the triage ward for three hours for a bed.

Another doctor came in and stood over me, scanning her clipboard. She looked about my age. Her curly black hair was tied up in a hurried ponytail.

'How are you feeling?' she asked.

'Better.' The pain had subsided.

'May I?' She reached her hands to my abdomen and pressed one side and then the other. 'Any pain?'

'Not really. It aches but the sharp pain's gone.'

'That's good. I've booked you in for an ultrasound to check everything's all right. How far along are you?'

'What do you mean?' My shock made my mind go blank.

'How many weeks pregnant are you?' She smiled at me, as if I should be pleased.

'Pregnant?' My heart stopped in my throat. 'There must be some mistake.'

She glanced at her notes and then back at me. 'There's no mistake. Your hCG hormone levels from your blood test confirm that you are pregnant. I'm sorry, I assumed you knew.'

I placed my hands on my stomach. I'd put on a little weight, but I'd put that down to stress and living off microwave meals for the past week.

'I'm on the pill.'

She nodded sympathetically. 'It's not a hundred per cent effective, I'm afraid.'

I couldn't be a mum. My life was falling apart. Mark was gone. How would I cope? I felt claustrophobic in the curtained little cubicle.

'What other medicine are you on?' She was frowning down at her clipboard.

'Nothing else . . . Actually, sleeping tablets. Do those count?' I wasn't sure what she was getting at.

'How long have you been taking them for?' The doctor was looking at me strangely.

'A week, maybe.'

'You've got high levels of Benzodiazepine in your system. That's what appears to have brought on your collapse.'

'Are you sure these are my results? I don't know what Benzo . . . what that is. I've only just started taking sleeping tablets – hardly any, and I'm sure I'm not pregnant.'

'You are Sarah Jones, aren't you?' She was frowning at her clipboard again.

I paused for a second, confused, but then nodded quickly.

'And what's your date of birth?'

Shit. What had I registered when the paramedics had booked me in? I'd been in so much pain. I stared at her stupidly. 'God, I'm having a mind blank.' I put my hand on my stomach and tried to look pained.

'The sixth . . .' She waited expectantly.

'Sixth of November 1992,' I finished quickly. I'd given them Rachel's date of birth. Why the hell had I done that?

'Then these are your results.' The doctor was looking at me sceptically; I couldn't tell if she thought I was lying or just mad. 'Have you got these sleeping tablets with you?'

I fished them out of my handbag, trying to hide my cigarettes from the doctor. I passed the packet to her and waited while she peered at the words.

'I skipped my last period but just kept taking the pill.' I'd actually skipped my last two periods to avoid my skin flaring up on my wedding day. 'Could that have made the results funny?' I asked.

'No.' The doctor shook her head as she read the packet. 'How many of these are you taking a day?'

'My friend gave them to me.'

'How many have you been taking?' she repeated.

'Mostly two.' I'd been taking three, although her scorn put me off admitting to that.

'These are prescription only and the maximum dose is one a day and not when you're pregnant. They're more for anxiety disorders or severe insomnia.'

'I didn't even know I was pregnant when I took them.'

'Taking two of these a day could have serious side

effects: confusion, severe lethargy and abdominal pain.'
She motioned to my stomach as she said the last one.
'They can cause paranoia, depression and they're highly
addictive.'

I stared at my hands in stupid silence. Lucy must not
have realized. I felt sick and shaky.

'What's your friend's name?' The doctor's frown grew
even deeper.

'It was a mistake. I remember now. I misheard her. She
did say take one, but I thought they were harmless. It's
my fault, I'm sorry to have wasted your time. I'll stop
taking them right away.'

'Is there anyone I can call to come and be with you?'
Now she was looking at me pityingly.

'No . . . no. It's late and I'm fine.' This was going
wrong. Did she think I'd tried to hurt myself? 'You said
I need an ultrasound? Is my baby okay?' Saying 'my baby'
sounded so strange.

'You shouldn't be taking Benzodiazepine when you're
pregnant; the truth is we don't know if it would harm a
foetus. The amount you've been taking makes it likely
that what you experienced today are just side-effects of
the drug. Your blood pressure is low which is what you'd
expect with this dosage of sleeping tablets. I'd like to
keep you in until it's back to normal.'

'Is that necessary?'

'It's precautionary. We need to do an ultrasound in any
case, to work out how many weeks pregnant you are.
You haven't put down a next of kin?'

'Oh . . . my husband. He's working abroad in Dubai.'
It was easy to mix Lucy's life and mine up. The best lies
always had some truth in them.

'How did you get the bruise to your face?'

I touched my temple where Jonny had hit me. 'I bumped into a door when I was tired. Stupid really.'

She leaned away from me slightly as if to examine me. 'Okay, well it doesn't look serious, just bruising. I'm going to go and book in your ultrasound. Let your husband know you need to stay in overnight. And have a look at this.' She handed me a leaflet – *How to Quit Smoking for Good* – and then strode away. I waited five minutes and then grabbed my handbag and opened the curtains. There was no sign of her.

'Excuse me, where's the nearest bathroom?' I asked a passing nurse. She pointed down the corridor and I set off towards it. I glanced back but the nurse had already disappeared. I walked past the toilets and headed towards the ward's exit, forcing myself to go slowly.

The doctor was standing with her back to me by the desk, talking to a nurse.

'There's something not right going on. She's got a nasty bruise on her face from being punched with force and she's been overdosing on Benzodiazepine. I think it could be domestic violence. Can you call the police for me?'

I backtracked to the toilets and ducked inside, locking the door behind me. I had to get out of here. If the police were called and found out I'd been lying, I wouldn't get bail again. But if I was going to get past that desk, I had to act normally.

I unhooked my hair from my ears and tried to cover my bruised temple as best I could. It wasn't great but there was nothing else for it. I opened the door and walked towards the desk, plastering a serene smile on my face.

The doctor had gone but the nurse was still there. She was talking on the telephone in hushed tones, but

I heard her say 'domestic violence'. She put her finger up to me to indicate she'd be with me in a moment and stepped away from the counter to try to stop me from hearing what she was saying. She barely looked at me. I hovered for a moment as if I wanted to ask her something and then mouthed that I'd come back later. I forced myself to walk slowly as I headed to the exit.

When I got through the doors, I felt immediate relief – but what now? I needed Lucy, but then I remembered the sleeping pills. Why had she told me to take two to three tablets a day? And was she having an affair with Mark? Was this her way of stopping me from realizing, making me clouded and distracted? I should go to the police, but they already thought I was involved with Mark's disappearance and Jonny's murder.

But this could be a mistake. It sounded ridiculous and the doctor had said a side-effect of the tablets was paranoia. Lucy was besotted with James and there was no way she would ever try to hurt me. She'd always been there for me. When I'd first moved to London, not telling my parents where I was going, Lucy had let me stay with her in her aunt's house. She'd lent me money from her aunt's inheritance to set up my jewellery business. She'd been there every step of the way, encouraging me to follow my dreams.

She'd been my best friend, counsellor, sister and mother all rolled into one. Everything that I'd lost. She meant the world to me and she was the only person who could make me laugh until I cried. She was the only one who really knew me. This wasn't Lucy. This was someone else.

Chapter 40

Jenny Hughes

Monday 24 July 2000

I couldn't find Rachel. I was alone. Jonny had run off and now the dark was starting to set in. We'd been out here too long. We'd missed dinner and I knew I was going to be in real trouble when I got home.

An animalistic howl crashed through the trees, pulling me back to the moment. What was that? A fox? Jonny?

'Rachel!' I ran forwards but I wasn't sure where the scream had come from. It seemed to echo all around me, bouncing off the trees.

God, where was she? I kept calling but there was no response. All thoughts of trying to scare her disappeared. I just wanted her to be all right.

I wanted Mum to shout at me for taking her to the woods and for missing dinner. I didn't even care if Rachel told Mum I'd gone off with Jonny. Anything but this sick feeling that was twisting inside my stomach like a snake.

I ran towards where I thought the noise had come from. The trees loomed above me. I dug through tangled thorn bushes, my arms ripped and bleeding, but I couldn't find her. Where was she?

I waded into the water, peering upstream and down,

but there was no trace of her. My legs were wet and cold, my trainers squelching as I scrambled back up the bank.

I called her name again and again but there was no answer. I begged for her to come out. That I was sorry. That I'd be a better big sister.

The sky was darkening and I didn't have a torch. 'She can't be far,' I kept telling myself over and over again. I searched frantically until I was out of breath and there was a stabbing pain in my chest. Where was she?

The sun sank beneath the tree line turning everything grey and black. God, she could have been taken by someone. I tried to hold back the tears. What was I going to tell my parents? I couldn't go home without her.

I'd found the willow tree, which was leaning over the brook, as if crying into the dark water.

I wiped my own tears from my eyes. The temperature was dropping. I'd look one last time and then I'd have to give up. I prayed she'd somehow got past me and was waiting for me at home. That must be what had happened. Mum and Dad would be furious.

On my last search I forced myself to go slowly, peering into the darkness. I used a stick to whack at the ferns. I walked further from the brook, beyond the tree line. Nothing. I turned to come back.

It was then that I spotted it. A small mass on the forest floor in the clearing, opposite the willow tree.

My body froze.

I stood there for what felt like hours, my body shivering in the chill evening air, and then I managed to inch towards the shape. The size of a child.

As I got closer, I could make out her favourite Care Bears T-shirt in the gloom, but it was spattered with black-red liquid. *She was lying on her front. I couldn't see her face. The back of her head was matted with blood.*

I turned away. It couldn't be real. It couldn't be. My stomach lurched and I threw up onto the grass. My chest and throat burned. I sank to my knees and sobbed. *The wood was spinning above me.*

Somehow my legs and arms began moving and I pulled myself up and staggered over to her. Maybe it was worse than it looked? Maybe she was just unconscious? *I told myself as I dropped to my knees beside her.*

My hands were clammy and cold. *Everything was still spinning. I gently rolled her over towards me. Her eyes were open, but she wasn't looking at anything.*

'No,' I whispered. *Her eyes were doll-like, as if made of glass. Her lips were slightly parted, and there was dirt and moss in her mouth. Her skin was marble-white, her cheek cold to the touch.*

She was dead. And it was my fault. I had brought her here. I wished I could take it all back. I wished I could give her life again.

I didn't know how much time had passed but it was so dark it was hard to see past a metre. I shivered beside her. I didn't know what to do. I couldn't leave her, but she was too big to carry; I'd never make it home with her.

I should get help, but when I looked around me, everything was black. The woods looked different and I couldn't work out which way was home.

I stroked Rachel's soft hair, whispering to her that I was sorry. I took my ring off and put it onto her finger. She'd loved the purple stone, begged for me to give it to her. I'd said it was too big, and it was.

I knew I should try and get help, but I couldn't leave her. Rachel hated being on her own.

Who had done this?

And then it came to me.

Jonny.

He'd looked so angry when he'd come towards me, that dark look in his eyes. When he'd run away, he must have come across Rachel. Poor Rachel.

I felt a sharp pain and realized I'd been tugging at my hair. There were blonde clumps of it in my hands, but I couldn't stop. This was all my fault. Why had I left her in the woods alone? And I'd made Jonny angry.

Rachel looked so little among the trees. I didn't want to ever be apart from her. Deep sobs shook me; I couldn't breathe properly. I closed my eyes and prayed this was all some sort of nightmare. When I opened them, Rachel would be laughing at me, a game she'd been playing. And she'd properly tricked me. I would laugh with her. But when I did finally open my eyes Rachel was still lifeless on the grass.

I gazed into her face. I hit my head with my hands, again and again. It had to stop. Please, someone make it stop.

Adult voices filled the air. They were calling our names.

'We're here!' I stood up. 'Over here!'

The voices were far off. Strange. I didn't recognize them. Two men calling. With a sudden vice-like fear gripping me, I realized that they could be the killers. They'd come back looking for me. Somehow, they knew I was still here.

I was so stupid. I scrabbled to the nearby fern and ducked into it. My stomach reeled. My whole body was shivering. It was as if I'd been in a freezing bath and had just got out. I didn't think it'd ever stop. I held my breath, trying not to cry in case they heard me. I peered through the fan-shaped leaves.

A man came crashing through the undergrowth. 'Girls, where are you?'

He stopped dead when he saw Rachel. He put his hands to his mouth and let out a low, strangled moan.

More men appeared.

My dad pushed himself forward through the crowd of men. I ran to him. Nothing else mattered but reaching him. I threw myself into his arms sobbing.

I squeezed my eyes shut. Dad was here. Everything would be all right. I longed for him to put his arms around me, but he didn't. I looked up into his face, which was pale, his eyes full of horror as he stared down at me.

'Jenny, what did you do?'

Chapter 41

Julia Talbot

Friday

Bailey's Accountants was in a beautiful steel and glass high-rise tower near London Bridge. The reception was stunning, all polished white marble and glass walls. It was 6pm but the place still looked busy, with people sat on the plush armchairs having meetings. Lucy was meant to be working late tonight to catch up with the audit and her time away supporting me.

I'd tried to call my landline when I was in the police station, but she hadn't answered. She must have gone to work. I needed to see her. To ask her about the sleeping tablets, get it straight in my head. I was sure her doctor had got the dosage wrong, or she'd got confused when she gave them to me. I also needed to talk to her about Jonny. I was in real trouble, and without her help, the police would be charging me with Mark's disappearance and Jonny's murder very soon. Lastly, I needed to ask her about whether she'd been having an affair with my fiancé.

I walked over to the receptionist, pushing my hair behind my ears and smiling at her.

'Hello, how can I help you today?'

'I'm trying to get hold of Lucy. Could you let her know I'm here? My name's Julia Talbot, she'll know who I am.'

'Lucy? Do you know her surname and which business she works for? We have a lot of companies in this building.' The receptionist smiled at me.

'Lucy Webb. She's with Bailey's Accountants.'

She looked back down at her monitor. I glanced at the people around me, all in fitted suits or business dresses, and I tried to smooth out the crumpled T-shirt that I'd been wearing for the past few days.

The receptionist looked up at me. 'Lucy Webb's not coming up I'm afraid.'

'Really?' I tried to lean over the counter to see. 'It's Webb with a double "b" at the end.'

There was more tapping. 'Still not coming up,' she said. 'We've got a Lucy Robson; she's the only Lucy we have at Bailey's Accountants.'

'No, it's not Robson. Could you try Kayleigh Webb?'

'We've got no Webbs here in this building at all. Do you want me to put you through to Lucy Robson at Bailey's Accountants?'

'No. No, thanks. I must have got her name wrong . . . or the wrong building. Sorry.'

The receptionist looked at me, evidently confused, and I turned and hurried away. I fought the panic that was threatening to overwhelm me. I pulled out my cigarettes but then remembered – the baby. As I went outside I dumped them into the nearest bin.

This was the right building. I'd met Lucy here for her birthday drinks last year. We'd gone to a cocktail bar around the corner.

I racked my brain, but I couldn't remember a single time I'd met one of Lucy's colleagues. Even on her birthday drinks it always ended up being just her and me. Lucy would say that someone had cancelled last minute because they were ill, another had childcare issues and another had to stay late because of work and might join us later. They never did.

Something inside was irritating me, like a loose thread that I couldn't tie off.

Had she been made redundant and hadn't told me? She hadn't told me about needing sleeping pills either. Was her own life unravelling, but I'd been so caught up in mine I hadn't even noticed?

I hadn't spotted Mark's affair or that he had a serious drug habit. My whole adult life I'd been obsessed with guarding my own secrets. Had I been so closed off to everyone else's pain, their own problems, that this is how I'd ended up here?

Once this was over, I was going to change. I was fed up of this. From now on I was going to stop running from everything. And I only knew one person I had left who could help me to do that.

Chapter 42

Alana Loxton

Friday

Mamuśka Café was busy, the waitresses rushing to serve the evening crowd. Loxton checked her mobile again. Kowalski had told her nine o'clock, but it was now ten past. Maybe he'd changed his mind, realized what a mistake meeting her would be.

She sipped her coffee; it was hot and burnt her tongue. She glanced again at the doorway as someone came in. Not him. He wasn't going to show. She was surprised by how ready she was to give up. She was tired and perhaps Fraser had been right; it was time to walk away. She could just email Kowalski what she'd found.

But then the door banged to and she saw him striding into the café. She felt relief and her spirits rise. A couple of women sitting near the entrance watched him with interest, but when he sat down opposite Loxton, they went back to their conversation, disappointed.

'Sorry I'm late. Finding a parking space around here is like trying to work out what's happened to Rowthorn. Impossible.'

She smiled as he checked the menu, which was adorned

with photographs of the food. The waitress came over and smiled at him.

'*Poproszę o kawę i gulasz wieprzowy z cebula*,' he said.

She wrote it down and turned to Loxton. 'Anything for you?'

'No, thank you,' Loxton said.

The waitress went to get Kowalski's order.

'You should eat,' he said. 'Polish food is the best and you're getting real skinny.'

'I'm not hungry.' Her stomach was jittery and the idea of food was unimaginable. 'Any developments with the case?'

'Reynolds is now sure that Cane was murdered,' Kowalski said. 'He'd had a lethal dose of ketamine injected into him.'

'Whoever killed him knocked him out and then administered the overdose?' She thought of the gash to his head.

'It looks like it. A user wouldn't put that much into their system; they'd know it would be lethal.'

'It's not a gang killing. No big show of retribution as a warning to others . . .' Loxton shook her head. 'Someone wanted to silence him and avoid detection.'

'DC Bale also got the results of Cane's and Talbot's phone downloads. It shows that Talbot was in contact with Cane after Rowthorn's disappearance on Tinder and Facebook Messenger. And that's not all. Talbot's been pinpointed by her mobile's GPS to the Night Jar Bar around the time of Jonny Cane's death.'

'So, she killed Jonny Cane.' She shook her head. She wasn't sure Talbot was a killer, but Fraser had his doubts.

'Maybe, or maybe she had help. We know the blood in Steele's flat has come back as Rowthorn's. Turns out

Steele was as involved as Rowthorn in the insider trading and money laundering. He and Rowthorn fell out about a week before the wedding, Rowthorn threatening to come clean to the investigators, and Steele furious at Rowthorn that he might drop him in it. We'll be able to charge him with Rowthorn's murder and the trading, once we get hold of him.' Kowalski smiled at her, excitement in his eyes. She knew what it felt like when the pieces all started coming together.

'You think they were all about to get caught and things got ugly between them?'

Kowalski nodded at her. 'It's looking that way. I think Cane wanted to ruin Talbot by corrupting her fiancé. Get him sent to prison, like he was. It looks like Cane stalked them both before approaching Rowthorn about the money laundering. Rowthorn got Steele involved and then the bank started investigating them. Our latest theory is that somehow Talbot found out about Cane's involvement and maybe she did kill him out of revenge. We'll know more when forensics is finished and we can arrest Steele and Talbot. She's disappeared with the same diligence and skills as her fiancé, but we'll catch up with her eventually.'

'What about us trying to find Rowthorn? Talbot and Steele need to be followed. They might lead the surveillance team straight to him.'

'Winter hopes Steele will crack, once he's re-arrested. No one believes Rowthorn's still alive.'

'He's underestimating him. He won't crack.'

'You don't need to tell me that. I've never known two people lie so convincingly.' The waitress placed a coffee in front of Kowalski, smiling at him.

'*Dzięki*,' he said to her.

'*Nie ma za co*,' she said and lingered a little longer before moving off.

'Thanks for meeting me,' Loxton said. 'I know what you're risking.'

'Sorry it turned out like it did.' He stirred his coffee. 'Winter has partnered Kanwar with me, so I have to put up with him gloating. It's like he's the only officer working these cases.'

The waitress bought over Kowalski's food and he tucked into it hungrily.

'I called you here because I have some new information,' she said. 'I'm not sure how relevant it is though.'

'Go on.' Kowalski managed through his mouthful of pork stew.

Loxton put the photograph of Rachel Hughes on the table. 'I know this is going to sound crazy, but just look at this photo.'

Rachel was smiling at the camera, her blue-and-white polka-dot bunny dangling from her hand. Loxton had seen that pattern before. 'Retired Superintendent Fraser, the lead investigator back then, told me that Rachel had the toy in the woods the day she died but that they never found it.'

'And? That case has been solved, Alana.' Kowalski had briefly glanced at the image before continuing to eat. She guessed this was the first thing he'd eaten all day.

'When we went to Lucy Webb's house, she had a quilt on her bed.'

Kowalski looked dubious.

'It was green and white, but one patch stood out. It was this exact shade of blue with white polka dots.' She tapped the rabbit in the photograph.

'That's weird.' Kowalski frowned. 'Maybe Webb got it to remember Rachel by?'

'Or maybe the patch came from the rabbit.'

'You think Talbot killed Rachel and kept the rabbit? And she gave a piece of the material to Webb for her quilt? Why?' Kowalski frowned at her.

'I don't know. What I do know is that I don't think Jonathan Cane killed Rachel. Neither does Fraser.'

'You're right. You do sound crazy.' He shovelled more food into his mouth.

'Please, just humour me. I can't get hold of Webb to ask her about it. I contacted Bailey's Accountants to speak to her, thinking she might be at work, but they told me they don't have a Lucy Webb working for them – never have. And they told me a Julia Talbot turned up a few hours before I called looking a state and asking for Lucy Webb.'

'I'm not sure about this whole rabbit thing, Alana.'

'DC Fraser now suspects Julia killed Rachel, and he was the lead investigator at the time. He's had a long time to mull over this case. I could be wrong. Maybe the patch is just a way for Webb to remember Rachel Hughes. But maybe Talbot gave it to Webb, some twisted way to keep a souvenir, but not have it too close?' She could tell she was losing Kowalski.

'But what's any of that got to do with now?' Kowalski stopped eating and was looking at her like she was crazy.

'Maybe Steele didn't kill Rowthorn. Maybe Talbot confessed to Rowthorn the night before they were getting married and he didn't react the way she wanted. Maybe he called the whole thing off, threatened to go to the police. Or maybe Talbot discovered the affair and she's decided Lucy Webb is the mistress. I don't know, but we need to find Webb before Talbot does.'

'I should head back to the station for when Steele's arrested and to lead the arrest enquiries for Talbot.'

Kowalski didn't believe her. He thought she was going mad.

'I just thought I should tell you what I found.' She felt silly now, but she couldn't let it go. It was so frustrating being suspended. 'I know I'm not making much sense here, but something's not adding up. I know it.'

Kowalski studied her for a moment. Finally, he said, 'You couldn't get hold of Webb. All right, I'll admit, that's worrying. If Talbot's dangerous, as you say, we'd better find Webb and warn her before Talbot gets to her.' Kowalski pushed his half-eaten food away and stood up.

'But . . . Winter. I'm suspended.'

'Winter isn't here, is he? You are, and I'm not going looking for Webb on my own. You coming or what?'

Chapter 43

Julia Talbot

Friday

My knuckles ached from knocking at Lucy's front door for what felt like hours. I'd called my landline from a pay phone and there was still no answer from Lucy. She clearly wasn't at work. She had to be here.

I knelt near her front door, checking the plant pots under her front window. There were a few tired-looking geraniums dropping in the heat. It had to be here somewhere, and as my fingers dug into the soil, I found it. The spare key her aunt used to leave when we were children, in case we arrived early and needed to let ourselves in. It was caked in dirt and rusty, but I scraped off the worst of it.

I slipped the old key into the lock, praying that Lucy hadn't changed them in all these years. It was stiff and it wouldn't budge, so I forced it to turn, hoping it wouldn't break in the lock.

Click.

The key turned. I froze for a moment. I hadn't come here in years. It had always been easier to meet centrally or at my flat in Southwark. When I crossed that threshold, I'd be betraying my best friend's trust. But then a horrible image of Lucy and Mark's naked bodies tangled together filled my head, and I forced my guilt away.

Paranoia was setting in, the doctor had said the sleeping pills could do that. I felt like I was losing my mind. Lucy had always been there for me and she'd dropped everything when Mark went missing. I didn't deserve her. I had to get this out of my head now.

I crept inside, pulling the door shut behind me.

I was hit by the familiar smell of cinnamon. Lucy's favourite. She adored the cinnamon cookies my gran used to make, and we'd baked hundreds together after she had died. I spotted a large candle squatted on a stand by the front entrance, the cinnamon smell overpowering.

The place hadn't changed since Lucy's aunt had lived here. In the living room the collection of hideous pale porcelain children stared out at me from behind their glass prison. Lucy used to joke about them when we were kids. She used to say that we should set them free.

In the cramped kitchen, still shoved in the corner was the small kitchen table with the single chair. The ancient cooker dominated the space. Old-fashioned flowery plates still hung on the walls.

I tried to remember when I'd last been here. It must have been years, but it hadn't changed a bit.

I thought we'd grown up. Clearly, I was wrong. There wasn't a single photo of her as an adult, but it was festooned everywhere with photographs of us as children. Lucy riding her silver bike, her long red hair trailing behind her, and me running after her. Lucy and me outside the cinema on her tenth birthday.

I peeked out of the front windows but there was no sign of her. The sky had darkened and a single star twinkled back at me. She'd said she had to work late tonight, but where was she? I was starting to feel like I didn't know anything about her.

Upstairs in the small bathroom was a single toothbrush, strawberry shampoo and conditioner. No sign of a man, but James was supposed to be back from his work trip and staying here.

I padded into Lucy's bedroom. Her old single bed stood in the centre, meticulously made with a quilt pulled taut. Had Mark and Lucy been in there together? A wave of sickness hit me and I turned away. I couldn't bear to look at the bed. It couldn't be true. I was going insane.

In the wardrobe were row after row of beautiful women's suits, all inside laundry bags with the pink raffle tickets still attached to the outside of them. On the far left, there were a few plain black polyester skirts and some dark blue shirts with *Spring Fresh Dry Cleaners* sewn in canary yellow on the right breast pocket.

This was a uniform. Lucy worked at a dry cleaner's.

I was rooted to the spot, my fingertips touching the coarse fabric of her shirts. She'd been wearing other women's expensive clothes to pass herself off as a successful accountant. But for how long?

I wasn't sure how long I'd been stood there, holding the cuff of her sleeve, but suddenly I needed to get away. Panic threatened to tear me apart. I couldn't breathe in the room. In the house.

As I turned to leave, James's photo on her bedside table caught my eye. He looked like a model, smiling into the lens with his bright white teeth. I tried hard to think of the photos she'd shown me of him on her phone and on Facebook. Looking back, I didn't think there had ever been a single one of the two of them together. She'd been seeing him for six months and I'd never met him, never even be allowed to speak to him on the phone, but she said he was 'the one'. Her excuse was always that he worked abroad a lot, was busy and in a different time zone, but she would tell me all the stories about him, their romantic dinners and lazy weekends in bed together.

She'd flown out to Dubai for a week recently to be with him. The more I thought about it, the more I came to realize – I'd never met a single one of her boyfriends. In our twenties it had been a joke between us. That men didn't like funny women and Lucy was the best comic I'd known. After I met Mark, she'd started to mention boyfriends, but they never lasted long enough for me to meet them.

I staggered down the stairs, my vision blurring, and collapsed onto the bottom step. This was where we used to huddle as children to dream up the day's mischief when we stayed here in the summer. I sobbed, long and hard. My throat was constricted and my eyes stung with tears. I was losing everyone I loved.

I heard a muffled voice nearby; moaning. It sounded like children next door, mocking me. I didn't care. The Lucy I loved didn't exist. The successful accountant, making her mark in a man's world, was all fabrication. Her handsome boyfriend she was sure was the one, and couldn't wait to introduce me to, probably wasn't even real. Instead Lucy was alone and lost. How had I not noticed before? I'd been wrapped up in my own life – Mark, the wedding – never paying much attention to Lucy's world.

But that didn't mean she had anything to do with Mark going missing. A heaviness filled my chest as I thought of her, alone and depressed, frightened to tell me the truth about her life. I'd been neglecting her and she'd got herself caught up in lies, trying to hide her pain from me, from everyone. If anyone could relate to that it was me. I would help her, once all of this was over.

When had Lucy started to lie about her life? I tried to pinpoint the moment. Which boyfriends had been real, which ones imagined?

A muffled noise. I waited. Then there it was again. The smallest noise, like someone groaning as they lifted a heavy weight. It wasn't the neighbours. It was coming from deep within the house.

The cupboard under the stairs.

Lucy's father would sometimes lock her under the stairs when she was a child and wouldn't let her out for hours. But that had been years ago, when she'd lived near Ashurst Wood in her father's old house, before she'd inherited this place.

She'd always kept the cupboard locked. I tried to open the door, but it didn't budge. I put my ear to it. The noise was louder, clearer. It was human, all right. Someone grunting. There was someone down there.

I used a breadknife from the kitchen, wriggling it into the gap by the lock, and jemmied it in hard. The wood splintered and the old lock gave way.

Darkness and silence.

I stepped inside and fumbled for a light switch. It took for ever to find, and when I did, light filled the cramped space. Steep stone steps led downwards. Lucy had never told me she had a cellar. I crept down, wishing I could run away.

I shivered as the temperature dropped. I was under the earth and it was cold, like a cave. The concrete walls all around me reminded me of a prison cell. There were wooden support beams holding the ceiling up and a stone floor covered in a thick layer of grey dust. Fresh footprints in the dust led deeper inside, but I couldn't see where they went. It was too black down here. The light from the top of the steps barely reached down. My eyes adjusted but it was still impossible to see anything more than a few steps in front of me.

It smelt like an old garage. Paint and something else. I fumbled for my lighter, desperate to see something. My breathing was ragged in the dark. What was in there? I clicked the lighter on and a weak flame flickered in the dark. I swept the dim light across the room, hardly illuminating anything. I thought I could see something in the corner – a figure, huddled. I squinted my eyes, but it remained a dark formless mound.

My breathing quickened and my legs trembled. I inched toward it slowly. As I peered at the shape it mumbled. I was too frightened to go nearer. One lunge and it could grab me. What the hell was someone doing down here, anyway? I finally plucked up the courage and spoke.

'Hello . . . Who's down here?'

Nothing. I found myself creeping slowly backwards.

A voice I knew almost as well as my own moaned in the darkness and my heart stopped.

'Mark?' More silence. 'Mark, it's me.'

The figure jerked painfully and its face spun towards me. The features were ghoulish in the weak orange light. It took me a moment to recognize him. Mark had the beginnings of a beard and his face was gaunt. His hair was matted.

He was sitting on the floor, his legs stretched out in front of him. His shirt and jeans were tattered and torn. His eyes were dull and he squinted towards me and into the light as if I wasn't even there. His hands were wrenched backwards, tied together around a concrete pillar. A filthy rag gagged him.

I rushed over to him, crouching next to him. 'It's me.' No response. 'Julia.'

Then Mark's eyes locked onto mine.

I heard another groan and saw a shape stirring further back from us. This figure lay sideways on the floor with its ankles and knees bound together, its hands tied in front of it. The head moved upwards to try to see me. The weak light illuminated a mass of auburn hair, covering a bloody face.

Lucy.

She whimpered.

Then I saw that there was a figure stood behind her in the shadows. I raised myself up slowly.

'Who's there?' I asked, my voice cracking with fear.

The figure stepped backwards further into the gloom. I heard a scratching noise. A spark flashed and a tiny flame danced into life. I peered into the darkness, but I couldn't even tell if it was a man or a woman. Then I realized the smell of paint was mixed with something else – petrol.

'Wait!' I thrust my hand forward.

Before I could stop it, the lighted match was tossed into the air, spinning in slow motion until it struck the floor.

Fire leapt up and roared along a thin trail, straight towards Lucy. Her whimpers turned into shrieks as she wrestled in vain to escape the fire. I rushed towards her as the fire raced me, suddenly splitting in two, one trail leading to Lucy and the other on its predetermined path towards Mark.

The burning petrol was overpowering, scorching my

throat and lungs, making me choke on the thick smoky air. As the fire reached Lucy, a red-hot heat knocked me off my feet and onto my back. The blaze towered above me. It was a dancing wall between me and Lucy. The roar of the fire sounded as if there was a dragon in the basement.

The flames suddenly dropped as the petrol was eaten up and I could see Lucy behind the shroud of red and yellow that covered her. I could almost touch her, but the heat was too fierce, blistering my outstretched fingertips. Desperation and panic exploded in me and it felt like my heart was going to rupture.

'Lucy!' The crackle of the fire drowned out my voice. The heat of it made me dizzy.

I could try to put her out with my jacket. Drag her to the stairs. But I wouldn't be strong enough to get her out. The smoke would overcome me.

I couldn't risk helping her. My baby. The fire was too strong. Then her hair caught light and her screams pierced my ears.

I turned away and got down on my hands and knees to escape the black smoke, her cries echoing in my ears.

I crawled towards Mark, who was bathed in an eerie orange light. His eyes were panicked, and he was writhing about, trying to free his hands from the ropes. He had managed to scrabble backwards from the fire's path, but it inched closer and closer to him.

I had to save him for our baby.

Terror swelled in my chest, threatening to rip me apart. The pain of hearing Lucy's screams behind me made my vision blur. I should go back. Help her. But I knew it was already too late. I was aware of footsteps racing up the stairs and the bang as the cellar door closed.

'I'm getting you out,' I shouted to Mark. My hands shook as I tried to get a good grip on the tight loops of rope around his wrists, but they wouldn't budge.

Lucy's screams turned to low, animalistic moans. I looked back as she clawed at her face and bits of skin slewed off, hissing as they dripped into the fire.

Mark tried to shout at me, but the gag muffled his words. He jabbed his head towards the front of the cellar and a metal box. I scrabbled towards it. The fire was hungry, tearing shards off the wooden beams that threatened to split open, dropping the ceiling on top of us.

Thick black smoke hung heavy above, wanting to smother me. The heat made my eyes water and the skin on my face prickle. The tool box was heavy. I dragged it over to Mark. My hands fumbled for the latch.

Inside were screwdrivers, nails and bolts. Buried at the bottom was a hammer. I jammed the sharp claw part of the hammer head into the knots, but the rope stayed taut, defiant. The fire rolled towards us from all sides. We were surrounded.

I dug deeper into the box. Bolt cutters. My hands were slippery with sweat as I groped for them, my fingertips screaming in agony. I fastened the cutters onto the thick rope and closed them with all my might. A few threads snapped. I tried again and again until my hands shook with pain. Finally, the rope tore.

I lifted Mark up and he tried to head towards Lucy, but I pulled him back. It was useless. I dragged him towards the stairs. He ripped his gag off, shouting something at me, but the roar of the fire stole his words away. His legs shook with the effort of moving, wincing with every step we took.

Lucy thrashed around in the flames. When she'd needed me, I'd doubted her, and now I'd left her to die. I'd never forgive myself; this guilt would burn inside me for ever.

'I'm sorry,' I shouted the useless words to her. I wanted to scream and scream. Anything to block out her howling. Then she started to whimper, and I longed for the screams. The white heart of the fire embraced her, swallowing her up, as my heart ripped in two.

I dragged Mark up the remaining stairs. The black smoke followed us, thickening the air, making it impossible to see anything. My airways were blocked with it. I kept my head lower, bending down as we reached the top of the stairs. The heat blistered my back and legs. It was like being inside an oven.

I let go of Mark, he clung to the bannister, and I threw the door open. My lungs threatened to rip with the effort. Fresh air rushed at us as the black smoke billowed out. I staggered forward.

A punch.

My head snapped sideways and I sprawled onto the floor. Something warm and sticky oozed down my face. The edges of my vision darkened. I could see Mark at the top of the stairs, reaching towards me, before the cellar door was slammed shut, separating us. I tried to turn my head – it looked like Lucy was standing above me, her eyes filled with tears – but the world flittered away.

Then there was nothing.

Chapter 44

Alana Loxton

Friday

The street was deserted as Loxton got out of the car. There was nothing but silence. She tried the front door, but it was locked. She peered through the window into the dark room, but there was no movement inside.

She knocked again. Nothing.

'No one's in.'

Loxton pulled her mobile out of her trouser pocket. She put the mobile to her ear and waited. 'I still can't get through to Webb.'

Kowalski pinched the bridge of his nose. She felt uneasy. Something big was happening and they were in the dark.

'There's no way in from the back?' she asked.

'Not unless you want to jump a few six-foot fences,' Kowalski said.

There wasn't time for that. She knocked on the door again. Still nothing. Kowalski stared back at her, the same fear reflected in his eyes. What if they were too late?

It was the calm before the storm. She peered into the front room again, but all she could make out were stationary shapes. One looked like a tall man playing frozen statues, but as her eyes adjusted to the gloom, the man became a door left ajar.

She knocked louder; a persistent banging. Her knuckles were sore from hitting the wood too hard. Something was wrong. She tried calling Lucy again but her mobile was still switched off or out of signal.

Kowalski put his foot against the bottom of the door and it creaked under the strain.

'She hasn't double-locked it,' said Loxton. 'She must be in.'

Kowalski glanced left and right.

'Wait – what about Winter?' Loxton said. 'You haven't got a warrant. There's not enough for a section 17 entry.'

'The door was already broken when I got here.' Kowalski lifted his right foot and then smashed the sole of his boot into the bottom of the frame. There was a crack and Loxton turned away in time to avoid the splinters that flew at her. She turned around as Kowalski put his foot through the bottom edge of the door and it gave way.

'They don't make doors like this in Poland. Terrible workmanship.'

Loxton checked around them, but the street was still deserted. It was getting late and the first stars were appearing as the evening closed in. 'Hurry up, then.'

Kowalski kicked the door once more, forcing the gap wider, and Loxton squirmed through the tiny space.

'Wait.' Kowalski was wrenching at the door to make the gap wide enough for his broad chest. She ignored him and ran into the living room and then the kitchen. Nothing. She came back through and Kowalski was in the house, drawing his baton.

She checked the master bedroom but the door was

closed. She took a deep breath and flung it open, charging into the room. She had her arms up in front of her face, protecting herself, but there was no one. She checked under the bed and inside the wardrobe. Where the hell was everyone? She rushed back to the hallway.

'You got anything?' she said.

'There's no one here,' Kowalski replied.

On the wall was a photo of Talbot and Rowthorn, arms around each other as they beamed into the lens. They were stood in front of a palm tree grove and the sky was a brilliant blistering blue.

Then it hit Loxton. 'Webb said something about her boyfriend getting back from Dubai this week. Maybe Webb's gone back to her address to see him. Talbot might have gone there looking for her when she couldn't find her at work or here.' Loxton's stomach turned. She'd thought they were both staying at Talbot's flat, so Lucy Webb would be here at least, even though Talbot had disappeared. They needed to get hold of her to warn her Talbot might be looking for her, to ask her questions.

Kowalski closed his eyes and whispered, '*Gówno.*'

'Come on, we're not far.' She rushed to the door and he followed her.

Once they were outside, they sprinted to the car past a few elderly residents who had come out for the noise.

'Police, don't worry.' Kowalski waved his warrant card and the residents relaxed.

'What about the door?' she asked as she climbed into the passenger seat, pulling the door behind her.

'Call it in on your mobile. Withhold your number,' he added.

'Innocent passer-by. I like it.'

'Just make up a good name and hope those residents

have forgotten we were ever here.' Kowalski started the engine.

She punched in 999 as they sped off towards Webb's house. They'd gone way over the line and it was too late to back-track now.

Chapter 45

Julia Talbot

Friday

My head span as I opened my eyes. A searing pain throbbed in my left eye lobe, and as I lifted myself into a sitting position, the pain intensified. I reached my hand gingerly to my face while trying to remember where I was, what had happened to bring me here.

I'd been laid next to a door. There was banging.

Lucy. Mark. The fire.

The pain in my eye was surpassed by a ripping deep inside me. They were both dead. Between them, they'd been my whole world.

There was a rattling noise. The cupboard door behind me was closed. The handle to the basement door was turning repeatedly, a chair jammed under it, stopping Mark from escaping. He was still alive.

There was a figure in front of me, watching my movements. I looked up and saw an unharmed Lucy, staring down at me, silent. I shook my head, tears of relief making my vision blurry. Was she really here?

'You . . . you died?' My lungs burnt with the effort of speaking. 'Down there.' The pain I'd felt watching her burn, hearing her scream, it had felt like dying. The smell of her flesh. I must be dreaming.

'That was Emily Hart.' Her fists were clenched. 'You don't even recognize your best friend.' Lucy shook her head at me. She had a large carving knife in her hand.

A growing fear replaced my sorrow. Lucy was alive but she was different. I'd never seen her like this, with her eyes filled with malice.

'What the fuck's going on?' The throbbing in my head became a dull ache. Emily Hart?

'I wanted to see if you'd choose Mark over me, even when it really mattered. I got my answer.'

'What did she ever do to you?' Emily was Benson's secretary. Mark had mentioned her a few times, but I'd never met her.

'She was having an affair with him.'

'Were you jealous?' Fear made my heart thunder in my chest. I thought I'd escaped the fire, but she had been waiting just behind the door. There'd never been a chance that my baby and I would make it out alive.

'Me? Jealous?' She laughed. 'You've got to be kidding. You have really awful taste in men.' Mark was banging on the door. He was going to die if I didn't do something.

'You've got to let him out.' I tried to stand up, but she brandished the knife at me. I shrank back in fear.

'No. Sit down. He's not going anywhere.'

'Please, I'm pregnant.' I put my hands up in surrender. Something deep inside me screamed, *Not my baby!* 'He doesn't even know he's a father.'

'Pregnant.' She was quiet for a moment. Why had I told her that? She wouldn't like it. She didn't like anything that took my attention away from her. She'd always been like that and I'd just accepted it. Why had I not spotted this anger in her before?

She moved the knife nearer to my face and I leaned as far away from it as I could, the door against my back. 'That's not my problem,' she said.

Mark was rattling the handle and hammering at the door now. I could hear his shouting getting frantic.

'Why are you doing this?' I couldn't hide the tremor in my voice. The knife was so close.

'This was all for you,' she said.

'You've murdered Emily and Mark's going to die. You think you're doing this for *me*?' I had to get away from her.

'I can't believe you sometimes,' she said. 'You don't even know what's good for you. Mark and Emily would have destroyed you eventually. I couldn't let you waste your life on him.'

'This isn't good for me.' I reached my hand up towards her. 'Please, Lucy. Stop this.'

Her voice grew louder. 'You were going to marry that man. Your life would have been over.' She slashed at the air in front of me.

I pulled my hand away from the blade. 'You're right. You showed me.' I tried to hide the tremor in my voice. Make her believe me. I had to live for my baby. Lucy was insane. *When* she'd gone mad, I didn't know, but somewhere along the way she'd lost herself. I inched sideways away from the blade.

'I'm always having to sort out your messes,' she sighed.

'Let Mark go.' I stood up slowly, trying to keep my voice calm, when all I felt was terror. 'It doesn't have to be like this. We can say the fire was an accident.'

'I'll kill you first.' She lifted the knife higher.

'You wouldn't.' I had no idea what she was capable of. This wasn't my Lucy.

'You'll end up like your sister,' Lucy said.

Something dark skittered across my mind like a beetle uncovered from a rock. My whole body shook. 'Please, Lucy. Haven't I lost enough?'

'She was ruining your life. You said so yourself. You wished her dead daily.'

There was a tightness in my chest as if my heart had stopped. 'It couldn't have been you. You weren't even there. It was Jonny.' Blood rushed to my head and there was a roaring in my ears. *Why was she talking about Rachel?*

'Why did you bring her along that day?' Lucy asked. 'Why did you take her into the woods?'

'My parents asked me to look after her. I was jealous of her because my parents doted on her . . . but I never wanted her dead. She was a kid. We were all just children. I didn't mean any of it.'

Lucy shook her head at me. 'You said you hated her. That I should have been your sister.'

'I never wanted her dead.' I'd wished Rachel dead a hundred times, but I hadn't meant a single one.

The ringing in my head grew louder and her voice became muffled. None of it made sense. She was just trying to hurt me. 'Jonny Cane was convicted.'

'Cane? Please. Why would he kill Rachel? Come on. Someone had to go to prison and it wasn't going to be us.'

'What?' *Lucy* had killed Rachel? But she'd been the reason I kept going after Rachel died. The one who got me through it all. It *couldn't* be her.

'Forget Rachel.' She stepped towards me, the knife

coming closer to my face. Cold fury filled her eyes. 'You just let me burn to death down there.'

'You wouldn't hurt me.' I whispered, but tears trickled down my cheeks. Now I wasn't so sure.

'It won't hurt,' she said. 'Nothing like burning to death anyway.'

'Please . . . the baby.' I tried to edge away from her but there was the hot door behind my back. 'Let me go.' I thought I'd known her. I didn't know anything. I was going to die.

'I can't do that.' She shook her head.

'Why not?' The tears blurred my vision.

'Because you failed the test. You saved Mark over me.'

'You've not been well.' I reached out my hand towards her, terrified of the blade. 'I didn't realize because of the wedding, but I see it now. I'm going to help you.'

'Too right I haven't been well. Imagine having to watch you run around after that cheating, coke-snorting, soulless dick.' There was only a weak rattle at the cupboard handle now.

'But you've shown me,' I said. 'You've saved me.'

'Maybe I'm fed up of trying to show you, Jenny. My whole life I've been looking after you, putting you first. Helping you to achieve everything you've ever wanted. And do I get any thanks? No. You forgot about me. Cast me aside for him.' She waved the knife towards the door. Black smoke crawled from underneath and started to drift into the space around us. The rattling stopped.

'I'm sorry.' I wiped the tears from my face. 'I did forget about you. That was wrong of me. I'll never do it again.'

'*You won't ever do it again.* I'm sick of your endless excuses. When that baby comes along you won't think twice about me. It's taken me a long time to realize that no matter what I do, you're never going to see me. I gave you everything. I was always there helping you succeed. I was convenient. But I won't be ignored any more. Not by you, not by him, not by anybody.'

'I won't ignore you ever again.' It was all I could manage.

'Everything I've done for us, all the sacrifices, and you pretend not to remember.' She jabbed the knife towards me. All I could focus on was the sharp point. The damage it could do. She started to cry.

It hit me that Lucy had loved me, all these years, and she'd never said a word. I closed my eyes, wishing I could make it all go away.

Then I had an idea. I looked straight at her. 'Please. Stop for a minute.' I had my hands out in front of me. I could try to grab the knife if she went for me, but it would slice through my fingers easily. 'I love you. Don't you know that? How can you question what we have?'

Her face was unreadable.

'It hurts,' she said. 'It always hurts. My head never stops banging. I wanted to be happy, I really did, but I can't be. There's nothing here for us but pain. Tonight, that ends.'

'I'm not ready to die.' I was shaking uncontrollably. Smoke surrounded us.

'It's okay to be scared.' She moved towards me, one hand in front, as if she was trying to calm a wild animal. 'I was scared once. But it'll all be all right. I'm here. Don't worry.'

'Please.' My voice croaked. My throat was tight, panic taking hold.

'Close your eyes,' Lucy soothed. 'It'll be quick, I promise.'

'The baby. You can't kill the baby.' There was nothing around me to use as a weapon.

'If you'd taken the sleeping pills like I'd told you, you'd have fallen into a deep sleep by now. This would be painless.'

'You were always going to kill me?'

'Only if you failed the test. If you hadn't, I could have made this look like Mark had killed Emily. A lover's tiff. We could have disappeared together. But you don't love me. You wouldn't have let me die if you loved me.' Her eyes became dead and her face impassive. She stepped towards me.

I took my chance and lunged at her, pushing her backwards hard. She hadn't expected it. Her arms went upwards as she tried to catch her balance, the knife slashing my forearm before it went flying, skittering across the floor. Pain took my breath away.

Lucy regained her balance. 'You're going to die in here.'

My right forearm was bleeding heavily, the pain a cold white heat. She turned away from me, scrabbling for the knife. If she reached it, I was dead. She spotted it a metre from her and rushed towards it, her hand grasping for it.

I charged forward, grabbing her shoulders and yanking her backwards from the blade. She shrugged me off, flinging her fist into my face before I had a chance to stop her. I staggered backwards, raising my hands to my face, feeling hot blood on my hands. Then pain splintering across my cheek.

She darted to the knife, reaching down, but I ran into her and shoved her forwards with my weight. We tumbled down, landing hard on the ground. My knee exploded in pain and the wind was knocked out of me.

Silence.

I blinked rapidly, the world coming slowly into focus. Lucy was laid beside me, her eyes half closed. Blood pooled around her head. The joy I felt was momentary. The black smoke crawled over her and me, turning everything dark.

I didn't know which way was which. Panic made my heart race and my head spin. The smoke was everywhere and my head was getting light. The floor seemed to move underneath me. I scrabbled forwards on all fours to where I thought the cupboard was, trying to ignore the pain in my knee.

I had to save Mark.

Chapter 46

Alana Loxton

Friday

Loxton smelt noxious burning petrol before she saw the plumes of smoke darkening the sky. Thick and black it billowed high above her, like a thunderous storm cloud, covering everything below it in shadow. She craned her neck to see where the smoke was coming from. *Please not Webb's address*, she thought.

Kowalski put his foot down, racing towards the smoke. He thrust his radio towards her. If she called on the radio, Winter would know she had been with Kowalski. She pressed the button as Webb's address came into view. There was smoke flowing through the upper windows.

'Fire at 157 Lower Road, Surrey Quays,' she said. 'Unknown casualties, get LFB and LAS running.'

The car screeched to a halt and she was out, racing up the pathway, Kowalski right beside her. The front door was locked. Kowalski started to kick the stoic oak door but this one was not giving up as easily.

She grabbed Kowalski's baton from his harness and went to the living room window. She flicked the baton sideways, locking it open, and then smashed it into the pane, sending fine splinters running up the glass. She hit the window repeatedly, but the glass wouldn't smash. Her arm was aching and her breath ragged from the force.

Kowalski took the baton from her and moved her aside. He shattered the glass on his third attempt and scraped away the sharp pieces stuck in the frame with the baton. She climbed through the hole he'd created and he followed.

She was stunned by the dirty smoke twisting and curling above her, obscuring the living room ceiling. It hovered above them, as if about to strike. All she could hear was the roar of the fire deep inside the house, which made her body shout at her to cower in a corner.

A man's screams pierced the room. The voice was inhuman, making Loxton's stomach drop. She couldn't bear it. They followed the noise through the smoke, crawling on the floor, with their stomachs on the wooden boards to avoid the heat and fumes above them.

She couldn't tell which room was which and she tried desperately to remember the layout from when she'd searched Webb's address a few days before. The noise had stopped as soon as it started. It could have come from anywhere in the house.

Moaning started up again from her left and she moved towards it. The heat here was as if she was trying to crawl into an oven. There was a door with a chair jammed under the handle.

Kowalski kicked it away and used his baton to push down the door handle and open the door. Toxic smoke rushed out of the space, making it hard to see. A figure on its knees fell forwards. Orange light flickered up the walls towards them.

'We've got to get out of here,' Kowalski shouted into her ear over the crackling fire. He reached down and grabbed the figure under the arms and together they dragged the person back the way they had come. The smoke made it hard to breathe.

She forced herself to take a step at a time as she helped drag the figure towards the living room window. Black smoke forced itself into her lungs, choking her. Her eyes streamed from the heat.

She tried to shout over to Kowalski, but her lungs wouldn't fill with air. The blackness around them grew. She couldn't see Kowalski, couldn't see anything. Her strength ebbed. The casualty next to her seemed to grow stronger, scrabbling with her towards the light and air. She hauled herself onwards, pulling him towards the window, every inch harder.

She wanted to check Kowalski was with them, help the man out, but she had nothing left – to stop and check now could be deadly.

She threw herself through the small gap in the window, landing on the grass outside. The fresh air burnt into her lungs and she couldn't breathe.

She dragged herself away from the smashed window and rolled onto her back. She watched the window for what felt like a lifetime, but there was no one there. Where was the casualty? Where was Kowalski? She tried to move but her vision became blurry and dark at the edges.

She tried to call Kowalski but all she could do was take painful sips of air. Soon the burning in her chest subsided and her vision became clearer. She forced herself upwards onto her knees and peered through the broken window.

Kowalski was lifting the man towards the gap in the window. Tears welled up in her eyes. She couldn't believe they were alive.

She took in a deep lungful of air and managed to stand

to lean through the window. Through the grime she recognized the man as Mark Rowthorn.

She stretched her arms out as Kowalski pushed Rowthorn up towards her. She managed to haul him through the window, using her weight as Kowalski pushed. He tipped forward onto the grass and collapsed in front of her.

She didn't check to see if he was breathing, instead turning back towards Kowalski. She reached through and he grabbed at her hands. She managed to get a grip of one and pulled as hard as she could, using her full weight. Kowalski struggled onto his feet and was dragged through. Loxton landed heavily on her back and the wind was knocked out of her. Kowalski fell on top of her, crushing her, but she didn't care. Black smoke rose above them but here on the ground there was air to breathe.

Rowthorn was coughing violently, and then vomited black bile onto the grass. A loud crack came from the house behind them and then a shuddering bang.

'Come on.' Kowalski crawled to Rowthorn and she put her arms around Rowthorn's shoulders. Together they managed to lift Rowthorn up. The effort sent shooting pains through Loxton's chest and she coughed uncontrollably.

'Not far,' Kowalski said.

They dragged Rowthorn towards the little gate and through it onto the pavement. A crowd of neighbours had gathered and looked at them with stunned expressions. A young man was filming everything on his mobile, his face a blank mask.

Loxton's lungs burned and her head was light. Sirens called to her from afar, clamouring louder. Tears pricked the corners of her eyes. She helped lower Rowthorn to the floor. He was clutching his neck and coughing. She sank down next to him, sitting on the cool pavement. Her throat was tight and she couldn't speak. The effort of moving Rowthorn had finished her. She couldn't believe they were alive.

Kowalski was standing above her, his face black with grime, his eyes bright blood-red. Police cars were pulling up and uniformed officers and detectives piled out. It looked like the whole of CID had scrambled into the back of police cars to get here.

'Get back,' Kanwar ordered the crowd.

'Who else is in there?' Patel asked Kowalski.

'Julia and Emily were in there,' Rowthorn managed. 'And Lucy.' His voice cracked.

Loxton felt her heart throb as she imagined them still in the house. The blistering, agonising heat that she'd felt, they were still suffering. She got up and Kowalski stood with her.

'We'll tell the fire brigade there's still three outstanding.' Patel put a hand out towards Loxton and Kowalski. 'The fire's too strong for anyone to go in now. It'd be suicide.'

'I'm going to evacuate the surrounding houses,' Kanwar called to them. 'You need to move further back.'

Loxton glanced at Kowalski, whose eyes were bright against his grimy face. He pressed his lips together and shook his head. 'It's too dangerous. The fire brigade is their only chance now.'

Loxton nodded, knowing that they would be dead already. The fire was too ferocious for anyone to have survived any longer in there. She felt her legs weaken under her as the world span for a moment. Kowalski put his arm around her shoulder, steadying her.

Two uniformed officers lifted Rowthorn and carried

him towards the other side of the road. Kowalski led Loxton after Rowthorn and out of harm's way.

Rowthorn was struggling to breathe; the uniformed officers were sitting him down and loosening his shirt.

'Ambulance is on the way,' one of them said.

Great black columns of smoke billowed off the house. The roof was almost gone. Burning timber and plastic fell from the walls.

Charred grey pieces of cloth floated down around them like dirty snow, some still glowing red. She recognized part of Webb's bedroom curtains drifting to the ground. No one else came out.

Rowthorn was coughing violently. Loxton knew there was nothing she could say to help him, so instead put her arm around his shoulder.

'Is there anyone I can call for you?' she asked.

Rowthorn shook his head through the coughs. He managed to raise his eyes to hers. 'She came to save me.'

Loxton wasn't sure which woman he was talking about. He was wheezing and his breath ragged, and then the fight suddenly went out of him as his eyes rolled backwards, leaving only the whites visible.

'Mark!' She caught his head as his body fell backwards. The other officers sprang into life, lowering Rowthorn onto the pavement.

'Stand down,' one of them said, before checking Rowthorn's airway.

Kowalski pulled her away. 'Let them.'

She couldn't move. She was rooted to the spot. An overweight officer knelt down and shoved his ear near Rowthorn's mouth. After a few seconds, he began CPR.

Kowalski's mobile rang and he answered it. 'Hello, sir.' Kowalski walked away from Rowthorn and the unfolding scene. 'We've found Rowthorn. He's alive.' He grimaced at Loxton. For how much longer, none of them knew. 'He was trapped in Lucy Webb's basement. Talbot, Webb and Hart are still in the house.' Kowalski listened for a moment. 'Yes, I know the house is on fire, sir, but I can't go in and get them.' His brow creased in concentration as he focused on what Winter was saying, then he held the mobile further away from his ear and shook his head at Loxton.

'Does he know that I'm here?' Loxton asked.

'He knows,' Kowalski said, bringing the mobile back to his ear. 'He's hung up.'

Loxton's mobile began vibrating in her pocket and she saw Winter appear on her screen. She switched her phone to silent and slid it back in her pocket.

The uniformed officer was still performing CPR on Rowthorn as two fire engines pulled up. Fire officers jumped out and started arranging equipment.

'Three women are still in there,' Loxton said.

'Understood,' the fireman said. 'This one's code red,' he said to the fire crew around him.

Sorrow spread through Loxton's chest. If they had come here first, instead of heading to Talbot's house, maybe they could have prevented all this.

Not long after the fire engine, an ambulance arrived, fighting its way through the growing crowd that slowly dispersed onto the pavement. It eventually reached Rowthorn. The paramedics climbed out, wary of the crowd.

'You'll need to come in too,' the young paramedic said when he reached them. 'We need to make sure your lungs aren't damaged.'

Loxton and Kowalski glanced at each other. 'No problem,' Loxton said. There was no way they were

letting Mark Rowthorn out of their sights. An officer
needed to go with him in case he gave a dying declaration.
And she wanted to be there to hear it, if it came to it.
More uniformed officers were turning up.

'I'll follow in the car,' Kowalski said.

'Best you don't drive.' The paramedic was attaching a
defibrillator to Rowthorn. 'You can all get in the back,
officers. There's room.' Kowalski handed his car keys to
Kanwar.

'We'll sort you out a lift from the hospital once you're
done,' Kanwar said.

'Thanks,' Kowalski said. He climbed into the ambulance
and turned to help lift the stretcher, which Rowthorn had
been put onto.

'You need to sit down,' the paramedic ordered.
Kowalski's face had paled and he stepped back and sat
down heavily on a seat, listening for once. The paramedics
manoeuvred the stretcher into the ambulance and Loxton
followed them into the crowded space.

The paramedic injected Rowthorn near his heart with
a clear liquid and attached an oxygen mask. The high
hiss of the tank irritated Loxton's ears. Rowthorn's body
thrashed about for a second and then went still.

'His body's clinging on.' The paramedic strapped him
in as the ambulance pulled off. 'Can you hold this up?'
He handed Loxton a clear bag of liquid and then stuck
a cannula into a vein on Rowthorn's wrist.

'You're going to be all right,' she said to Rowthorn,
laying her free hand on his arm.

The paramedic glanced at her but didn't say anything.
She braced herself as the ambulance swerved through the
crowded London roads.

Chapter 47

Julia Talbot

Friday

I couldn't stop coughing. There was black smoke everywhere. I crawled forwards, but I had no way of knowing which way I was going. For all I knew, I could be heading deeper into the house. I couldn't see my hand in front of my face.

There was something in front of me. I patted the object; it was wide and tall, and higher than I could reach. It blocked my way. A surge of anger stabbed though me. Where the hell was the door with Mark trapped behind it?

The heat behind me increased. I pushed at the object but it wouldn't move. I tried to get around it but then realized it was a wall. I moved along it. Heat and noise surrounded me and always the black smoke. The wall was long. I tried to picture Lucy's house in my mind, but I couldn't focus. I kept crawling. The carpet under my hands became stone tiles. I was in the kitchen. I prayed Lucy had left the back door unlocked.

I could hear a man shouting behind me, but I couldn't go back towards the heat and smoke. I had to get to air now or I'd – *we'd* – die here. I'd failed at everything so far, but I wasn't going to fail at being a mother. I scrabbled forward and reached the wooden kitchen units. The sink was halfway along and above it the window. If I could just reach that . . .

Sweat trickled down my forehead and into my eyes, which stung with the smoke and salt. I was lying on my front now, trying to escape the smoke that billowed above me.

Rachel danced in front of me. Was I already dead? I didn't deserve any better. I hadn't been able to protect my little sister and now my baby was going to die.

Stand up. Stand up.

The thought leapt into my brain and I tried to obey it. I reached my hands up into the heat and grabbed the top of the cabinet. The metal of the sink seared into me and I ripped my hands away.

The pain blocked everything else out.

My palms were red raw and blistering in front of me. A crash behind me pulled me back into the room. I put my bubbling palms on the floor and pushed up with my arms and legs, using every bit of energy I had left.

This was my last chance.

I crawled onto the surface; everything was darkness around me. I threw myself against the window, my hands scrabbling for the handle. My throat constricted and I couldn't breathe. My hand knocked against something sticking out from the white wooden frame and I crouched down next to it. The heat on my back was immense.

I managed to push the button in and yank the handle up, my hands screaming in protest. I threw my weight against the window, but it wouldn't budge. I was knocked backwards by the force and for a moment I was balanced on the sink, but then I tumbled backwards, falling onto the kitchen floor.

My lungs were burning from the inside, every breath agony.

I could hear a voice, but I didn't know where it was coming from.

I tried to call out but only a hoarse croak came out of the back of my throat. I managed to haul myself up onto my knees, every muscle screaming with pain. I needed to get back onto the sink and to the window, but the harder I tried, the darker everything got. The voice became muffled.

Hands grabbed my shoulders, pulling me roughly upwards. Thank God. I tried to help by pushing up with my legs, but the sensation of being carried was slipping away, until there was only darkness.

Chapter 48

Alana Loxton

Friday

Loxton stared up at the clouds, which were like brush strokes swept across the darkening grey sky. She should head home; she was suspended after all and technically had no right to be there. Yet she couldn't drag herself away.

Webb's house was a wreck, the inside burnt out. The old Victorian terrace had a wooden framework within its walls, which had helped fuel the fire. It had taken the fire brigade a couple of hours to put it out and get it cool enough to hand over to the forensic team.

A few figures dressed in white suits were now picking their way through the shell of the house. A handful of residents were still watching, as if hoping more drama would unfold, but they reluctantly retreated indoors as the temperature dropped. The downstairs that she had crawled through to save Rowthorn was covered in rubble and burnt debris.

The rescue might all have been for nothing. Rowthorn was in intensive care, fighting for his life, machines sounding out his failing heartbeat. There were thick plastic tubes coming out of his throat which were attached to a ventilator, breathing for him. The doctors had told his parents and the police that Rowthorn might never regain consciousness and she shivered at the thought. A life sentence in a prison of flesh with no chance of escape but death.

A white suit paused and crouched down to inspect a piece of charred remains and then discarded it as rubbish. It was painstaking to watch.

'They've found burnt remains of one female,' Kowalski said. 'They reckon it's Emily Hart from a piece of jewellery welded to her neck.'

'We've been there before with McGregor's body,' Loxton warned.

'I know,' Kowalski said. 'Reynolds reckons we might never find anything more. The petrol and concrete basement acted like an oven in places, which could have caused any other bodies and bones to be cremated into nothing but dust. It depends where they were in the basement.'

Loxton shook her head. A human life reduced to ash and charred bones, indistinguishable from blackened burnt wood. It was all so pointless.

'You ready to go?' Kowalski started heading to the car.

'I'm going to stay here for a bit. I'll hitch a ride with one of the forensic guys.'

'I'd hang on, but a takeaway's calling.' Kowalski held his stomach. 'I've barely eaten all day.'

'Go ahead.' Eating was the last thing on her mind. She plonked herself on the garden wall and watched the white suits carrying on their silent vigil. It was going to be a long night for them.

She looked at the space where her life had nearly ended.

It'd been reckless to go into the house. Worse than that, she'd endangered Kowalski, who'd been forced to follow her. If something had happened to him, because of her, she'd never have been able to live with it.

A forensic officer walked past, carrying a plastic bag. A glint of gold caught her eye.

'Can I see that?' She held the bag up, examining it. Inside was Talbot's wedding band. Or it could have been Rowthorn's. She lifted it closer. It was small enough to fit on her finger, so it was Talbot's.

'Where did you find it?' Her mind was racing with possibilities.

'In the back garden, near the fence.' He motioned behind him.

She was on her feet before he had a chance to stop her and heading towards the back garden.

'You aren't allowed back there.' He jogged after her.

'Where was it?' Loxton was scanning the area. It was a neat little back garden with a small lawn and a flowerbed at the very back, next to the fence.

'Where that loose fence panel is.' The forensic officer pointed it out. 'But I heard that you were suspended? We've been told you're not to be allowed to go into the scene.'

Loxton ignored him, crouching low, looking at the bedding plants. They were crushed, as if someone had dragged a bag of soil over them. She saw one set of footprints. 'There's a back gate here.'

'It leads onto an alley which runs between the houses. It's an old estate. Everyone would have been in and out of each other's houses back in the day, not anymore though.'

She was on her phone, pressing Kowalski's name.

'I'm not there yet.' Kowalski's voice was muffled; she could tell he was trying to drive and speak on the phone.

'I don't think they're dead,' she said.

'What?' Kowalski's voice was loud.

'Talbot and Webb. I don't think they're dead. Webb's car's not here.'

'You know I'm starving, right? The Chinese is just around the next corner.'

'I'll get Patel to run Webb's registration through the live ANPR, but I think I know where they're going.'

'I'm turning back.' His voice sounded heavy with disappointment. He thought she was chasing ghosts.

She hung up and took the ring in the plastic bag from the perplexed forensic officer.

'I'm not going to find any more remains in there, am I?' He glanced back at the gutted house.

'No, I don't think you will.' Maybe she'd got a second chance after all.

Chapter 49

Julia Talbot

Friday

The wind whipped my hair around my face and into my eyes. Mark had been with me, but he wasn't here now. I tried calling his name, but no sound came out. I opened my eyes, but whichever way I tried to look, there was only darkness.

I could hear the whoosh of the sea, lapping against the hull. The ocean. But instead of salt in the air there was a strange smell, as if something was rotten.

'Time to wake up.'

Who was that? I thought I'd been on the sea but there were no waves – only a sharp pain behind my eyes. Everything was black.

'Wakey, wakey, sleeping beauty.' *Lucy*. Her voice muffled. 'We're nearly there.'

I was rocked from side to side as if by waves. Maybe I was inside a boat? Sick rose in my throat as I remembered. *Lucy. The fire.* I couldn't breathe. There was no air in here and what little there was choked me with the stench of sickly-sweet blood and something rancid.

Hot tears fell from my eyes. Lucy had tried to kill me. She had murdered Rachel. For a moment my head span with images of the raging fire, Hart's screams and Mark's feeble knocking at the basement door. I had to get out of here or I would be next.

I checked the cut on my forearm with my fingertips. Cloth was tied round it, and it seemed to have stemmed the bleeding, as the outer layer of cloth was dry. Lucy must have applied it.

My seared hands felt cold metal above me and to my sides. The space was small and I couldn't stretch out my legs. I felt the hum of an engine and the roar of traffic as something went past us, fast. I must be in the boot of Lucy's car.

I breathed hard through my nostrils, counting to five in my head, and then kicked the boot lid. It didn't budge, but the movement sent a burning sensation through my chest.

'Stop fucking about.' Lucy's voice was cold and strange.

I kicked out again, my legs jarring with pain. Futile. I was going to die in here.

A thumping beat vibrated through the car, deafening me. Lucy had turned the radio on to block me out. I tried to hold back sobs. I crashed sideways into the wall of the boot as the car swerved. I couldn't tell if I was upside down. I wriggled around until my back was on the floor.

We hit a bump and I was thrown up, crashing back down. I covered my stomach with my hands but they gave little protection. Nausea welled inside me. The car swerved and stopped with a jerk, throwing me forwards.

Silence.

I heard the car door open and then slam shut. 'We're here.' Light from her torch streamed over me as the boot was opened. 'Are you going to behave, or am I going to have to hurt you?' She held up her steering lock, ready to strike me. Above her was a black sky with white pin pricks twinkling down.

Ancient oak trees surrounded me. I was back in that green prison.

'Get out.' She stepped back, too far for me to try to grab the steering lock. Her face was dirty with the grime of smoke and dried blood. I dragged myself out of the boot. Every muscle burned from lack of oxygen. We were in a small deserted car park, the floor made of soft woodchip. It was so dark I could only see the small area around us, lit by her torch. But I didn't need to see any more to know where I was.

Ashurst Wood.

The playground of my childhood until that day, and the last place in the world I wanted to be now. I hadn't been here in twenty years. I realized it was almost to the day that I'd last been here. Had she planned it this way?

I dry-retched, the stench from the boot too much to bear.

'Don't worry about it.' She waved her hand dismissively towards the boot. 'A tramp was in there.'

'A tramp?'

Her brows knitted together and I knew not to ask any more. 'Do you remember the way?' She tilted her head at me.

I felt the soft woodchip underfoot as I unwillingly headed up the single track in response to her question. It was as if I'd been here only yesterday.

'I knew you wouldn't have forgotten.' She was right behind me, keeping pace. I could try to outrun her, but she seemed strong despite the cut to her head. I could barely see, her light only illuminating half a metre in front of us. If I bolted and she caught me . . .

'We should go to a hospital,' I said. 'You're bleeding.'
The trail went uphill, and my breathing became more
ragged. The trees' foliage blocked out the cloudless night
sky.

'It doesn't matter.'

She was going to kill me where she'd killed my sister.
And she'd murdered Mark, cooked him alive in her
basement. The Lucy I knew was gone – had never even
existed. I didn't know who this person was.

We followed the trail, and the trees became denser, the
undergrowth thicker. It was unlikely anyone would be
here at this time, but if someone came down the path
towards us, I had a chance.

'This way.' Lucy stood off the path. 'We go off-road
now.'

'I'm sure it's just a bit farther along the trail.' I motioned
towards an oak tree.

'When was the last time you came here?' Lucy shook
her head at me. 'It's this way.'

I didn't want to push her, so I reluctantly left the safety
of the path behind.

She waved me onwards, forcing me to stay at the front.
'Stop dawdling.' Her voice was strange. There was an
edge to it I hadn't heard until today.

We left the path and civilization behind and the wood
completely swallowed us. My legs were heavy. I stumbled
over tree roots and staggered around bracken. Every
single step I took brought me closer to where Rachel had
died. Brought me closer to my own death. *At least I
would be with her at last.*

Chapter 50

Alana Loxton

Friday

'Webb's car was picked up near Caterham. She's heading to Ashurst Wood. From the ANPR footage it looks like she's the only one in the car.'

'Shit. It'll take us twenty minutes to get there and she's got a couple of hours' head start on us.' Kowalski put his foot down, cursing the other drivers' slow responses. The blue light attached to the top of the car roof made little impact on their progress and the siren wailed mournfully. They were going to be too late.

'*Kurwa*.' Kowalski hit the steering wheel with his fist.

'I've got Kent uniform headed there.'

Kowalski pressed the horn, changing the tone of the siren to a staccato scream, and half-mounted the pavement in his effort to push through the traffic.

'Aren't you meant to go on the outside of the traffic?' Loxton grabbed the internal passenger door handle and closed her eyes. As a response driver herself, she knew damn well you were never meant to go on the inside.

'It's fine.' Kowalski went through a red light, missing the traffic control pole by millimetres. He urged the car onwards and she opened her eyes as he turned right onto a side street.

'Side roads will be quicker until we can hit the A22. It'll be clearer on there.' He surged forward, faster than she would have dared, oblivious as he hit the speed bumps at forty miles an hour. Loxton's back ached as she was lifted and then slammed into the seat. She checked the map on her phone, barking instructions at him. It was still going to take them fifteen minutes.

She dialled Kanwar's number. 'Kanwar, it's Loxton. On my desk is the murder case file for Jonathan Cane. Can you find out exactly where in Ashurst Wood Rachel Hughes was murdered and send me the coordinates?'

'You're suspended for leaking news to the press, Alana.' His voice was hard down the phone. 'What sort of fool do you think I am?'

'I'm with Kowalski.' She shook her head in frustration, even though he couldn't see her. 'We haven't got time for this.'

'You're not a police officer anymore.' Kanwar wasn't listening to her. 'I'm not telling you about any cases.'

'Kowalski, tell Kanwar to do his fucking job.' Loxton put the call on loudspeaker.

'Just get us the damn directions and stop fucking about,' Kowalski shouted towards the mobile.

'Fine, I'll send them through, but I'm reporting this.' With that, Kanwar hung up.

'Why is she going back there?' Kowalski asked.

'I don't know, but it's not going to be good.' Loxton prayed a car didn't come from the other direction. Kowalski would never be able to brake in time.

'Gówno.' Kowalski's brow furrowed deeper as the car sped up.

Chapter 51

Julia Talbot

Friday

Lucy pushed me onwards, deeper into the darkness. Her torch lit up the trees, which grew taller as we went further into the heart of the wood. This place was where my nightmares always brought me, and now it was where I was going to die.

'Everyone will think we burnt in the fire,' I said.

'When they don't find our bodies,' she said, 'they'll come looking.' She was moving quickly and we weren't far from the brook now. The tree branches were bathed in moonlight but for a moment I saw sunlight filtering through the leaves. I could almost see us as children again, running between the trees, laughing.

'We could go to an airport right now.' I stopped and turned to face her, trying to hide the desperation from my voice. 'You and me. Hop on a plane and leave it all behind. Start again.'

She stopped too. 'Where would we go?'

'We used to talk about Australia. Do you remember?' Maybe she would get tired. She had to sleep eventually. Then I could make a run for it or grab something heavy.

'We wanted to get away from your parents and the

idiots around here,' she said. 'Remember the way they used to look at us afterwards . . .'

'We wanted to be like the characters in *Neighbours*,' I said. It was so long ago; a different life.

'That was it.' She was excited, her voice bright. 'Endless sun and barbecues at Christmas. We were going to escape to the other side of the world.'

I nodded. My throat hurt and it was painful to talk. The hike was taking it out of me.

It had been a lie. All those rainy afternoons fantasizing about endless summers and white beaches weren't real. She'd been pretending the whole time. She was the one who had killed Rachel.

'Get a move on,' Lucy suddenly said as she brandished the steering lock at me, as if shaking herself free of the spell I was weaving. We carried on into the woods.

'Why didn't you just kill Mark? Why wait all this time?' She was never going to let me walk away, but at least I could try to get the truth before I died.

'I just wanted him out of the way, but things spiralled. I wanted Mark's death to look like a suicide. I needed him to write a suicide note first, but it took more time persuading him to do that than I thought it would.'

I shuddered as I thought of Mark, tortured and killed because he'd fallen in love with me. I'd never hear him laughing or feel his arms encircling me again. He was really gone.

Suddenly I heard the gentle sound of rushing water. For most people it was a relaxing, hypnotic sound, but it had always brought me out in a cold sweat since Rachel.

We'd reached the brook.

There was the old willow, unchanged despite twenty

years having gone by. This was the clearing where Rachel had drawn her last breath.

Looking at it now, it was as if it had never happened. Everything was peaceful, an ethereal forest bathed in moonlight. There was no trace of the violence that I'd seen when I'd last stood here, only the sharp ache that I could never put into words, gnawing inside me. I thought I could almost hear Rachel's giggle as she hid nearby, watching us from behind some bracken.

'Rachel, I'm sorry.' I let the tears fall. I didn't have to keep it together any longer; soon it would all be over. At last I could let myself fall apart.

'You're sorry?' Lucy looked incredulous 'You *wanted* her dead.' She gripped the steering lock tighter.

'I never wanted her dead. That was all you.' The anger and grief, always underneath the surface, rose up. For years I'd been biting my lip when I saw sisters together or women my age with their mother or father. I'd felt ashamed at myself for the jealousy I felt towards them – the hate. But all along that rage had a real home – Lucy.

'Do you know how desperate you sound?' Lucy said. 'I killed her for you and you're pretending you didn't know!'

'You didn't do that for me.' My voice was a croak. We were right by the spot where I'd found her. Rachel's frozen face came back to me, her lifeless eyes. Had she thought of me at the end? Had she been hoping I'd save her? 'You're insane.'

'You were bored of me.' Her eyes looked sad.

'What are you talking about?'

'You and Rachel were sisters. I was just your friend, and you were moving on from me. You told Jonny.'

'I didn't.' But then I remembered, in the wood that

day, I had told Jonny I was fed up of everyone. Rachel, my mum, even Kayleigh.

'I heard you talking to Jonny that day like I was nothing to you. Like you didn't need me.'

'You followed us?'

'Of course I followed you. I thought you would pick me over him, and when you didn't, I just couldn't believe it. It wasn't hard to follow you into the woods. The three of you were so noisy.'

'But why kill Rachel?' Disgust burnt through my veins.

'I didn't plan it. I went to watch her and there she was, moaning and crying as usual. I don't know what happened.'

'What did you do?' Panic rose in me. I didn't want to hear this.

'I crept up behind her. I had a rock in my hand.' She stared at her right hand, still holding the steering lock. 'And I struck her with it. Her head was so fragile. It cracked open like an Easter egg, all this pink goo seeping out. She fell forward and was twitching on the grass, her head turned to the side, her eyelids flickering and her mouth moving as she tried to say something. She wasn't dead.' She looked away from me, as if seeing it all again. 'I hit her again and again until my arm burnt. I remember hearing this howling noise, like an animal. And then I realized it was me.'

I was cold and the edges of my vision became darker. 'You never said a thing. Not once in all those years.'

'I thought we were both pretending it was Jonny. You were the one who put your ring on Rachel. That was the final nail in the coffin for him.'

Blood was pounding through my head. *Jonny had been innocent, and I'd condemned him to prison and a shattered life. And then I'd killed him.*

'I couldn't go to prison,' she said. 'I'd suffered enough as it was, what with my father. It was an accident really.'

I ran, throwing myself at her. I was going to kill her. Lucy's eyes widened, and she tried to lift the steering lock, but I was already lashing out at her face with my fists. She fell backwards as she tried to get away from the blows, the steering lock falling to her side, and we both landed hard on the ground, me on top of her.

I punched her hard with my fist and tried to reach the steering lock with my other hand, but Lucy pushed me off, rolling me backwards. She kicked out at me, connecting with my stomach. I feared for my baby, as the pain seared through my midriff.

Lucy turned onto her front, scrabbling for the steering lock. I got to my feet, but she'd already grabbed it and was now standing up.

My breath was ragged and I didn't have much left. I lifted my fists up and bent my knees, like I'd been taught at the gym. One blow from the steering lock and it would be over. I could try running but I knew I wouldn't make it far.

She was on her feet again, facing me with the metal lock high above her head. She ran at me and I threw my hands up, trying to catch it, but it was too heavy, smashing into my wrist and sending a sharp white pain through it.

I staggered backwards. My wrist was at a funny angle and white lights jumped in front of me. I looked up at Lucy and she scowled at me as she pulled back the steering lock. I put my left hand up to ward off the blow as I pulled my useless right arm into myself. It wouldn't be long now. All I could think of was my poor baby.

'Police! Stop!'

It was Loxton, in the clearing, her hand outstretched. They'd found me and the relief was overwhelming.

'Fuck off!' Spit flew from Lucy's mouth.

'Put the weapon down.' Loxton put her palms up.

'Take one more step and I'll kill her.' Lucy waved the lock towards me.

'I'm going to stay right here.' Loxton still had her hands up, she hadn't moved. 'You're in control.'

I looked from one woman to the other. 'She killed Rachel! She killed my sister!' I shouted to Loxton. Whatever happened, Lucy wasn't going to get away with this.

Loxton ignored me, only looking at Lucy. Her voice was surprisingly calm. 'What do you want to happen, Lucy?'

She laughed. 'How the hell should I know? Everything's fucked up.'

'No, it's not.' Loxton shook her head. 'We can talk about this.'

'I killed Mark. What's there to talk about?' Lucy shrugged. She still had the steering lock above her head and her eyes kept flicking between me and Loxton. 'You're just going to lock me up for ever.'

'Mark's alive,' Loxton said.

Relief flooded through me – I couldn't believe it. Tears sprang to my eyes.

'That's just great.' Lucy's voice got louder until she was suddenly shouting. 'That dickhead's not dead. Are you sure?'

'He's in a coma, but he's alive.'

'I still killed Rachel and Jonny. You can't bring them back to life, can you?' Lucy's eyes focused on me.

She'd killed Jonny?

Loxton looked taken aback for a moment.

'Don't bullshit me that I'll be out in a couple of years, because I won't. I'm not an idiot, Loxton. There's no way out for me.'

'You need help.' Loxton took a step forward. 'The courts are very understanding.'

Lucy shook her head and waved the steering lock at Loxton. 'You stay back. You think I'm mental? I'm not mad. It's the world that's mad.'

'What do you want?' Loxton asked.

'All I wanted was for her to love me. It wasn't much.' She glared at me. 'But no, instead she used me, and as soon as her life was complete, she tried to toss me aside.'

'Toss you *aside*? You were my *bridesmaid*.' I wanted to kill her, but my wrist throbbed so much I felt sick.

'I know you'd have ended up going to America. You're so fucking weak. You do whatever that dick tells you to do. You would have put him before me, no danger.'

'That's not true.' I couldn't believe I was arguing with her like this. After everything she'd done.

DC Kowalski came into view. He was behind Lucy but a good ten metres away.

'You always put men before me. You kept saying our friendship was everything, but I should have known you'd let me down. Just like everyone else.'

'You're like a child. You never grew up. The rest of us moved on with our lives,' I shouted at her.

Loxton threw me a look of frustration; she was silently telling me to shut up. 'Who let you down?' Loxton asked.

'My father,' Lucy's voice dropped. She hadn't spoken about him in years. Had refused to talk about it. 'He put booze before me. He used to beat me.'

'So, you're going to blame all of this on your father?'

I couldn't help myself. 'None of this is your fault . . .' I didn't want to hear her excuses. Kowalski was creeping towards her. For such a big man, he didn't make a sound.

'You've muddled everything up, made it sound all wrong. All I've ever done is try to make your life better, like you made mine better. Before you came into my life, I had no one. I didn't know what happiness was until I met you. Remember that first day of school, when I'd caught that butterfly in the playground and you saw me with it. You came over and I let you hold it.'

I did remember.

'You were the only person who ever tried to protect me from my dad,' Lucy said. 'My mum didn't. My parents didn't like me and yours ignored you. I thought that meant something, all the things we went through together.'

'I did care.' Our eyes met. I saw all the years of pain we carried between us.

Kowalski was five metres away now. Loxton was motionless, watching Lucy like a lioness ready to pounce.

For a second, Lucy's resolve seemed to fail. 'Why are we talking about all this? We can't go back.' She lowered the steering lock.

'It's never too late,' I lied.

At that moment Kowalski grabbed the steering lock and Loxton sprinted towards Lucy. Kowalski wrestled it from Lucy's hands, and she lashed out in retaliation, scratching at his face. Loxton grabbed hold of her wrist, but Lucy punched her in the face, pulled free and ran towards the brook. Kowalski threw the steering lock behind him and chased after her. Loxton was faster, racing past him, and tackled Lucy to the ground. Kowalski kneeled down on Lucy's body and snapped handcuffs on her. She thrashed against them but then all the fight drained out of her as she realized it was over.

I staggered over to them and stood looking down at Lucy. Her eyes met mine. 'Betrayed me again,' she said.

'You murdered Rachel.' I cradled my broken wrist with my good hand. 'Every awful thing that's ever happened in my life is your fault.'

'Not everything.' She glared up at me. 'Mark was all yours.'

Chapter 52

Alana Loxton

Friday

Loxton sat next to Webb in the back of the car, the woman who had hidden in plain sight, as Kowalski drove them back to Walworth police station. Lucy was handcuffed with her hands behind her back, but Loxton still kept her eyes on her. Kowalski had made sure the child safety locks were on, too.

'Julia needs to understand that everything I did was for her,' Webb said. 'I want you to tell her. It's all been muddled up by you lot. I killed them to protect her.'

'You're under caution,' Loxton said.

'But I've not been able to speak to my solicitor yet, so this will all be inadmissible in the end.' Webb gave her a little half-smile.

Loxton hated to admit it, but Webb was probably right – the courts were so weak. 'You're still under arrest; anything you say can be used as evidence at court.'

Lucy gave a bitter laugh. 'Still playing your part. I heard another officer say you were suspended, so you can drop all that crap. When I walk into that interview room, I'm going "no comment", so this is your only chance, Alana.'

Loxton kept her face impassive. It'd been a mistake taking her in the car, but she hadn't wanted to leave Kowalski to transport Webb back to Walworth on his own.

'How did you do it?' Kowalski asked, quietly, clearly aware that he was breaking police protocol. 'How did you get Mark into that basement?' Loxton's eyes met his in the rear-view mirror. They shouldn't ask Webb, but they both needed to know.

'I waited for him outside Emily Hart's block of flats and used a syringe of ketamine; he never saw me coming. Then this homeless guy came towards me. He attacked me and I had to defend myself, so I hit him with my steering lock.'

'Robert McGregor. He was old and no threat to you.'

'Not much of a loss then. I did the world a favour. It threw you lot off the scent for a while, putting Rowthorn's watch on him.'

Loxton winced inwardly. 'Robert McGregor had children.'

'They're probably glad he's dead. He was a drinker, wasn't he? He stank to high heaven. You know he was covered in shit. Not just from when I hit him. He hadn't washed in weeks – disgusting. I gave him his first proper bath in a long while.' She smiled.

'He was still alive when you threw him into the river. He drowned.' Loxton imagined McGregor clawing at the surface, trying to get a gasp of precious air as it felt like his lungs were exploding. Fear and confusion and the icy-cold water his only company.

'Tough as an old cockroach, that one. All drunks are cockroaches; my father certainly was. They're a drain on society.' She spat the last words out.

'What did Mark do?'

'Just opened and closed his mouth like a goldfish. The fight just left him and he passed out.'

'No surprise after you'd injected him with a horse tranquilizer.' Kowalski's voice shook with anger.

'What did you do then?' Loxton asked, glaring at Kowalski to quieten him. They needed to keep Webb onside, keep her talking.

'I loaded them both into the boot of my car. I thought they were both dead. When I got to Surrey Docks, I pushed the homeless guy into the river, hoping the police wouldn't care too much about him.'

Loxton felt sick. She longed to be out of the car and away from Webb. Just her presence was intimidating.

'Then I drove Mark home. It was just starting to get dark; everyone was inside having their dinners. He was heavy but I got him inside, pretending he was drunk and I was his girlfriend. I thought pushing him down the basement stairs would have finished him off, but it didn't.'

'Why didn't you kill him?'

'Killing the homeless man spooked me. It wasn't part of the plan. Mark was meant to go in the river, not the old man, but two bodies would look odd. Less like a suicide. And then you were all running around looking for Mark, more than I thought you would. I was worried if I killed him in my house the stench would alert the neighbours. That's how people always get caught – the smell. I had enough ketamine left to keep him quiet until I figured out how to make it look convincingly like he'd killed himself. I was thinking of a bag over the head in a secluded wood and hope you didn't question the ketamine, assuming he'd taken it himself. I even got him to write a suicide note. It's amazing what people will do to avoid pain.'

Kowalski shook his head slowly in disgust. Webb didn't miss a thing and slammed her feet into the passenger seat in front of her. 'That womanising cokehead didn't deserve to breathe the same air as Julia. He deserved everything he got.'

'Lucy, I want to understand.' But Loxton wasn't sure that she *did* want to understand. How had she missed what was right in front of her?

Webb turned to Loxton and eyed her suspiciously, but she calmed down.

'How does Jonathan Cane fit into all of this?' Loxton asked.

'Julia's fault. She had to drag him out of his little box. She wouldn't listen to me. She never does and that's why we're here. She went to see him without telling me, but I followed her. I had no choice.'

'What did you do?' Loxton had to know, even if she couldn't use anything Webb said in evidence.

'Julia had done half the job for me. They'd had a fight and she'd knocked him out. His head was quite bad. Once she'd left, I administered the ketamine. Couldn't have him calling you lot, dragging up the past, going on about being innocent.'

Loxton felt lightheaded. She'd spent her career trying to prove that women were as capable as men. This felt like the universe was playing a sick joke on her. Webb was the perfect murderer, as capable as any man she'd ever investigated.

'I thought you wouldn't examine another dead junkie dealer too hard. Guess I was wrong.' She rolled her eyes at her own mistake.

'How did you even get ketamine?' Kowalski asked.

'I bought it through the dark net. It came in skin rejuvenation bottles. It's unbelievable, right?'

'How did you pay for it?' Kowalski was struggling to keep his voice calm.

'With Mark's money, which I transferred into Bitcoin. Idiot told me his hidden bank details after some persuasion.'

'I don't suppose you'll give us access now?'

'I was going to use the Bitcoin for me and Julia to get away. It can rot in cyber space now.'

'And what about Emily Hart?'

'She was a whore. I worked out Mark was cheating months ago. It was obvious. Julia suspected, but the more I tried to show her, the less she wanted to see. I sent Mark some threatening texts before the wedding, telling him I knew what he'd done. That he'd burn for it. It didn't stop him though. He just carried on as normal. That's why I had to intervene.'

'But why kill Hart?'

'She's the same size as me – similar hair colour although hers was dyed. I wanted to conduct an experiment to see if Julia would save Mark over me. I sent her a WhatsApp from Mark's phone and she came running, thinking he'd chosen her at last, and had just gone missing to escape the wedding. She didn't see it coming at all. I drugged her and tied her up. I set up a choice for Julia: save Mark from burning or save me. And I got my answer.' Lucy looked down at her hands and for the first time Loxton saw pain in her eyes.

'What were you going to do in the woods just now?' Kowalski asked.

'I don't know, do I?' Webb shrugged. 'You showed up.'

'Were you going to hurt Julia?' Loxton asked.

'I wanted to.' Webb's face was contorted in anger and confusion. She shook her head as if she was being torn in two. 'I could never do it for real. That's why I saved her from the fire. It's always been like that. She drives me mad sometimes, but in the end she's all I've ever had.'

'You have no problem with killing,' Loxton said. 'You took Julia to the woods to kill her just like you murdered her sister.'

'Rachel was an accident. All I ever did was try to protect Julia from the world. But it looks like the world won.' Lucy turned her face away and stared out of the window. It seemed she was done talking.

'Patel's going to interview her.' Kowalski sat at his desk. He looked about as bad as she felt.

'Alone?' Loxton asked. She liked Patel; she didn't want her to be on her own with Webb.

'Winter thought it was the best idea. A woman-to-woman chat.' If Kowalski was disappointed at being pushed aside by his boss, he didn't show it.

'Is she taking over the case?' Loxton wished she could be in that interview room.

'Kanwar is,' Kowalski said. 'You're out and I've fallen from grace after continuing to work with you.'

'I'm sorry,' she said just as Kanwar marched into the office and headed towards Kowalski. 'Ready to watch a pro nail this at court?' Kanwar barged past Loxton, forcing her to step back.

'Be our guest,' Kowalski said. 'But, remember, we got her to custody.'

'Plenty of suspects have been in police custody and walked at court. It's the final kill that counts.' Kanwar

grinned at Kowalski and threw Loxton a sideways
glance. Loxton kept her face neutral, but her jaw
clenched involuntarily. The corners of Kanwar's lips
raised slightly.

'Just make sure you get her.' Kowalski looked too tired
to argue.

Kanwar turned his back on Loxton as he talked to
Kowalski. 'What is she doing in here?'

Loxton's face and chest heated up but there was nothing
she could say. Kanwar would never believe her that she
hadn't been the leak.

'If Winter finds her here, you'll be in even more shit
than you already are, Kowalski.' Kanwar shook his head.
'Why are you messing up your career for her? She tipped
off the press. I don't get it, mate.'

'It was Loxton who realized Webb and Talbot were
still alive. There wasn't much time, so we headed there
together. Anyway, we were just leaving.'

'Good. I best get on. Catch you later, Kowalski.' Kanwar
strode out of the office, his expensive aftershave lingering
in the air long after he'd left the room.

Kowalski rolled his eyes at Loxton.

'It's not his fault,' Loxton said, although she couldn't
help but feel hurt by Kanwar. She began gathering up
her belongings.

'I'll keep you updated with what happens with the
Webb case.' Kowalski helped her pack. 'And I know a
good federation representative who can help you with
this news leak thing.'

'Thanks, Dominik, that's—'

But she was interrupted by Winter charging into the
office. 'What is *wrong* with you?' He looked incandescent
with rage.

Kanwar must have called him as soon as he'd left. Loxton hadn't realized how much he hated her.

'I was just leaving.' Loxton felt her shame twist into anger. She hadn't done anything wrong.

'You're not allowed to be on police property.' Winter's voice shook with anger. 'You don't work here anymore. You're trespassing.'

'It just all happened so fast,' she said, pulling her jacket on. 'I'm sorry.' She didn't want Kowalski to get in trouble.

'This isn't going to look good for your disciplinary board, sneaking around the police station when you're suspended.' Winter shook his head at her.

'I'm sorry, I wasn't thinking. I—'

'Save it, Loxton. There's no reason for you to be here. Get out before I do something I regret.' He glared at her, a disgusted look on his face. Was he so angry because he thought she was looking for evidence to identify the leak and he was worried she'd find out it was him?

Kowalski stepped forward. 'Sir, without Loxton, Talbot might not be alive. It was Loxton who made me look for Webb.'

'Kowalski, I've known you a long time. I never thought you were capable of this. Both of you get out of my sight. I don't want to see her anywhere near this police station again.'

Loxton didn't care what Winter thought. It looked like he was out to ruin her anyway, pinning the leak on her. But she'd got to the truth of what had happened to Rowthorn. And she was going to find out who the police leak was, however long it took.

Chapter 53

Kayleigh Webb

Monday 24 July 2000

Kayleigh watched Rachel running round and round the clearing, calling Jenny's name – but Jenny didn't answer. Jenny wasn't here.

Rachel was crying to go home, but she didn't seem to know which way home was. She would set off in one direction, and then stop, turn around and hurry back to the clearing snivelling.

The trees towered above Rachel's tiny figure, their branches reaching down to try to tug at her hair. All around, shadows were forming. Rachel was clutching that bloody toy rabbit and her face was full of snot and tears.

Rachel's sobs got louder. She must have realized that Jenny wasn't coming back for her. They'd left her behind. Kayleigh knew how she felt. She'd been discarded for Jonny too.

She observed the pathetic child blubbing in the woods and it made her angry. Is that what Jenny thought of her? That she could be dropped just as easily as Jenny had abandoned Rachel?

Kayleigh felt a lump in her throat and tears forming.

She swiped them away. She wouldn't get upset. She wasn't a stupid little baby.

Rachel had wrapped her arms tightly around herself and she was looking wildly around. Kayleigh stayed hidden in the bush. The sun had sunk lower, so Rachel couldn't see that she was here. That was good. Kayleigh didn't want to be seen. Not by anyone. She didn't want them to know that she'd followed them to the woods, like a lost puppy, when Jenny had gone off with Jonny.

'I know you're there.' Rachel's voice wavered. 'You might as well come out.'

Kayleigh stayed perfectly still. Silent. The dark was setting in, making it harder to pick out shapes. Soon Rachel wouldn't be able to see anything at all.

'Come out, it's not funny.' Rachel's voice grew loud. She span around in a circle, peering into the growing darkness, and Kayleigh smiled.

Rachel didn't have a chance at spotting her. It was so dark now.

'I'm not playing anymore.' Rachel sat down right where she was, crossing her legs and folding her arms like Kayleigh used to do in assembly back in primary school. Things had been easier then. She'd had Jenny's whole attention. Now everything was changing and she was getting left behind. If only it was just her and Jenny, like it used to be. An idea flashed into her head. A way to make it like it was before.

Kayleigh crept from her hiding place over to the brook. It was hard to see anything, so she moved carefully. She crouched down next to the brook and reached inside, trying not to make a noise. She felt around the bottom, her fingers becoming cold, until her hand came across what she was looking for – a large rock.

She slowly retraced her steps. The wood around Kayleigh felt different now. The birds had stopped singing and the evening air was chiller. All she could hear was Rachel's ragged crying.

There was a snap.

Kayleigh silently cursed the twig. She was so close now. Rachel was shaking and turned her head towards the sound, but Kayleigh stepped quickly to the side, so that Rachel couldn't see her in the gloom. It was like playing 'What's the time, Mr Wolf'.

Rachel stopped holding her breath and, turning to face forwards once more, gave a noisy sigh of relief. It was short-lived.

Kayleigh lifted the rock high and then brought it down in a swift motion, as hard as she could, smashing it into the back of Rachel's stupid head. That would teach Jenny. That would teach them all.

Rachel's head cracked and the rabbit toy fell to the floor as she fell forward onto her face. Her body jiggled on the grass like a broken wind-up toy, so Kayleigh lifted her arm and struck Rachel's head again – anything to stop her jerking body.

She heard a roaring noise as she delivered another blow. The back of Rachel's head exploded, red and pink everywhere.

Kayleigh stared at the mess.

Rachel had stopped moving, but she could still hear the noise. Kayleigh realized it was her. She dropped the rock and clamped her hands to her mouth. She stood there, waiting for her own breathing to quieten as she stared down at the dead child.

Kayleigh had to be quick. First, she picked up the rock. Then she saw the toy rabbit's eyes staring up at her, as *if a silent witness. She grabbed it too, just in case, before running over to the brook and wading in, heading up stream and away from the direction Jenny and Jonny had gone.*

When she was a good five minutes up stream, she paused to wash the rock, rabbit toy and herself carefully in the water. She made sure all the blood was gone. She carried on splashing upstream, knowing that it would take her out of the east side of the wood. Then she could swing back and head towards home.

Her legs were cold, and she couldn't feel her toes inside her trainers, but she didn't care. Rachel was dead. And now Jenny would be sad and would turn to her best friend for help. Jonny would be no use and Jenny would grow to hate him. She would blame him for distracting her, when she should have been looking after Rachel.

Kayleigh struggled in the dark, but she knew she would still be home before her dad was back from the pub. He stayed until kicking-out time. And he would be so drunk, he wouldn't notice anything wrong anyway.

Mum was on night shift, so she wouldn't get home from the hospital until morning, and then she would sleep for hours. Kayleigh would be able to hide the rock in the back garden in the rockery tomorrow morning and the toy rabbit she would destroy, so that no one ever knew it was her.

It was perfect.

Chapter 54

Julia Talbot

Monday

It was the meeting I'd been dreading. The last time I'd seen him was on the stairwell with the fire behind him. It felt like a lifetime ago, but it had only been a few days.

The monitors by my bed beeped and whirled. I was attached to them by two pads that were stuck to my stomach. They were monitoring my baby – *our* baby. I was mesmerized by the lines leaping up and down; nervous they would change from a healthy jagged peak to a flat line.

A nurse poked her head through the door. 'Are you ready for a visitor?' She was smiling at me, thinking I'd be thrilled to see my fiancé and the father of my baby. I nodded, managing a weak smile.

Mark was wheeled into the room and the nurse left us alone. He was dressed in a white and blue hospital gown and was clutching a bunch of pink and white roses. He handed them to me and tried to kiss my cheek, but I pulled away. He looked crestfallen. He sank back into his wheelchair. An unpleasant silence filled the room. I gingerly put the flowers onto the bedside cabinet, trying to avoid touching anything with my bandaged palm.

'How are you?' I asked. He looked like a prisoner of war, his skin grey with bandages on his neck and arms.

'The doctors said I should be fine. Minor burns, smoke inhalation. They've got me on heart meds. Just have to take it easy. You?'

'A few bumps and scrapes.' I lifted up my plastered wrist. 'Nothing serious.'

He gazed at my stomach and the monitors. 'Is he all right?'

'He?' I smiled to myself – of course Mark thought it was a boy. He'd want to play football with him and drag him to games. I stopped myself, remembering that everything had changed between us. 'The doctors say the baby seems fine, despite everything.' I thought of the fire and how close we'd all come to death.

'I'm sorry—' he said.

'No, I'm sorry. I left you down there.' The words tumbled out of me; the guilt I'd been carrying making me ready to burst.

'It wasn't your fault,' Mark said. 'You couldn't have saved me. We all would have died. The police nearly didn't make it out themselves.' He lowered his head.

It'd never occurred to me that he felt ashamed. It was me who'd brought Lucy into our lives. Me who had put the people I loved in harm's way. I saw Rachel's smiling face, forever seven years old.

'I didn't know I had it in me to save myself over another person.'

'You were saving our baby.'

I looked out of the window, watching a few white clouds drifting through an impossibly blue sky. An idyllic day.

'So, what happens now?' He lifted his face and met

my eyes. I saw his desperation and fear. Was it fear of losing me or fear of losing his perfect family unit?

I shrugged and shook my head.

'What do you want to happen now?' he asked.

I had no idea. A few weeks ago, I'd been about to marry the man of my dreams. Now I was pregnant by a man I didn't even know, who had hurt me more than I had ever thought possible. The past few years had been a complete lie. Had he ever loved me at all?

'I've been an idiot.' He reached his hand out towards me, but I didn't take it. He put it on top of mine. I felt numb. 'I love you, Julia. More than anything. I can't believe I nearly lost you.'

'What makes you think you haven't lost me?' I turned back to the window.

'I never loved her,' he said. 'You know that, don't you? I was just scared. Forever is so final. Can you forgive me?'

It was a question I'd been asking myself over and over again. Perhaps I could have forgiven an affair, but it wasn't just that. He'd been lying about everything: the drugs and the money. The thought of being a single parent scared me, but not as much as trying to go back to him. I would never trust him again. I would never trust anyone again.

'It wouldn't work.' I fiddled with the edge of my plaster cast to avoid looking at him. 'It wasn't working.'

'Only because of Lucy.' He leaned towards me. 'She was constantly there, pulling us apart. Everything I did she would criticize. Now I understand why. She was in love with you. Completely in love. She got between us.'

'This wasn't Lucy.' Sharp anger in my voice. He couldn't lie his way out of this one. 'You did that all by yourself with the coke and the other women.'

'There was only one.' His cheeks were colouring but there was a pain deep inside his eyes. He had loved Emily Hart. In that moment, I knew it would never work, however hard we tried.

'It's the truth.' His hand pressed harder onto mine. 'I wouldn't lie.' Lying to me was all people had ever done.

'It doesn't matter.' I pulled my hand from under his and crossed my arms. 'It's over between us.'

'But the baby.'

'What about the baby?' Anger rose in me.

'Don't you want to try to be a family for the baby's sake?'

'You can be a father for the baby but it's over between us.'

'How are you going to cope financially?' He cringed a little as he said it.

He had to be kidding. 'Easier without your debt.'

'You can't do this on your own. You can't even book a holiday by yourself, for fuck's sake.'

When he didn't get his own way, he always berated me, but not anymore. 'I'm tired. I need to rest.'

'You haven't given me an answer.'

'How many times do I have to say it? You and me are done.' I picked up the assistance buzzer and pressed it, calling for the nurse.

'You're upset,' Mark said but his voice wavered with uncertainty. 'You need some time.'

The nurse entered and smiled at us both.

'I'm tired,' I said. 'Can you take him back to his room?'

'Of course,' the nurse said. 'Come on, you, it's probably time you rested too.' She wheeled Mark to the door and pulled it open. He glanced back, but he was looking at me differently. Everything had changed and he knew it.

I was left on my own. But not completely alone. I placed my bandaged hand gently on my stomach. The lines on the monitor leaped higher as it picked up both our heartbeats.

Chapter 55

Alana Loxton

Saturday

Loxton sat in Mamuśka Café in a corner, watching the world go by. She took a deep breath in, savouring the coffee flavours and baked bread. It was quiet, the breakfast rush just finishing up.

Kowalski came through the door, spotted her and strode over.

'I ordered you a latte.' She motioned at the mug opposite her.

He took a sip. 'Perfect, thanks. How are you doing?'

'Not bad,' she replied, trying not to think of her suspension. 'The smoke inhalation cough has just about gone. You?'

'Still coughing up black crap in the night.' He shrugged and took another sip of his latte.

'You should go back to the doctors,' she said.

'I'll give it a couple more days.' He picked up the menu, his eyes running down the photos.

'How's the case?' she asked.

'They're going to charge Webb this afternoon with everything, including Rachel Hughes's murder,' he said.

'Jonny Cane might be acquitted in the end. Shame he didn't live to see it.'

'I really thought Webb loved Talbot like a sister.' Loxton shook her head. She always prided herself on spotting the suspect before anyone else. Rowthorn had nearly died and Emily Hart hadn't been as lucky, all because of her mistakes.

'She must have loathed Talbot to do all of that to her.' Kowalski looked away.

Loxton suspected the opposite, that Webb loved Talbot, but that love was unforgiving. 'I think she got a taste for murder. Once she'd crossed a line with Rachel Hughes, that line was rubbed out for ever. There was no going back. Webb reverted to her old ways of coping when Talbot began to slip away from her again.'

'What happened with David Steele?' she asked.

'He was arrested at an airport trying to get out of the country in a complete panic. He wanted to get out of the country before the insider trading and money laundering caught up with him. He's been charged for both those offences now and he's looking at serious time. Rowthorn will be as well, once he's recovered.'

'And Jonny Cane was involved in all of that too?'

'Yes, he was in terms of the money. But it looks like he'll be acquitted after death of Rachel Hughes's murder. The team are looking at the owner of the Night Jar, too. Seems he was paying the bankers for the insider information and doing very well out of it.'

She shook her head. 'I bet the bank director isn't happy.'

'The media have gone crazy for this case,' Kowalski said. 'The trial will be a circus.'

'Is Winter letting you back on it?'

'I'm not in Winter's good books. He hasn't forgiven me.'

She shook her head at him. 'He'd be an idiot not to get you involved. You'd be officer in charge if it wasn't for me.'

'And Talbot would be dead. Don't worry about it.'

'It was a complicated case,' she said. 'We all made mistakes.'

'All we can ever do is our best,' he said. 'Are you getting breakfast?'

'You and your stomach – you never stop,' she said with an amused smile. 'I've already eaten.' The truth was she didn't feel like eating. She couldn't stop the nervous energy rushing around her stomach long enough to eat. She kept going back to who had leaked the press information. That person hadn't cared that she'd been suspended. Was it Winter, or had it been someone else?

She hated goodbyes but she knew that when she walked out of that café door she wouldn't be coming back. She'd only known Kowalski for a couple of weeks, but she was going to miss him. It was rare to meet someone you could connect with as easily as they had.

'It's been good working with you . . .' She put her hand out towards him.

He ignored her hand. 'Are you ready to take on the leak now?'

'Yes,' she replied, retracting her outstretched hand, 'but it's not going to be easy. I'm suspended. I'm not even allowed in the building.'

'I hate a loose end too,' Kowalski said. 'It's time we found out who's responsible for the mess you're in.'

'And remind me how we're going to do that?' His optimism amazed her.

'I got the phone records for Saunders's mobile. Got

someone to check calls coming in at the time we found the body and when Talbot was arrested.'

'How did you do that?' She knew as soon as she said it that she didn't want to know the answer.

'Let's just say it was through a friend.' He winked at her. She shook her head at him, amazed.

'You want to have a look?' Kowalski pulled out an unmarked envelope from his inside jacket pocket.

'You don't know who it is yet?' Her mind was racing over all the officers she knew at Southwark CID.

'I wanted us to look together,' he said. 'It's your career they're trying to ruin.'

It was Kowalski's career he was risking as well. Her eyes lingered on his for a moment and she was grateful she'd met him.

'Let's get this over with.' She ripped open the seal and pulled the sheets out, scanning the phone data; a number was highlighted at the important dates and times. A two-minute phone call to Saunders when they found the body in the river. Long enough to tell him about the body and where to find Talbot for an exclusive.

'Whose number is that?' she said.

Kowalski pulled a sheet of paper out from behind the phone records. She took it and read the report. The phone number was attributed to someone she knew.

Kanwar.

Loxton's eyes widened. *It couldn't be.* She rushed through the phone record to the time when Talbot had been arrested. It was the same number. The papers shook in her hands as she tried to control her fury.

Kowalski shook his head in disgust. 'I didn't think Kanwar was capable of that. How much was Saunders paying him to leak information?'

'Alec would be pretty desperate to get his career back on track after everything that happened.'

'It explains why Kanwar was so against you when you were suspended,' Kowalski said. 'He wanted to make himself look innocent by being so incensed about the leaks. And when he saw you in the station with me, he must have worried that we might try and find out who had really leaked the information.'

Loxton slid the papers back into the envelope, her anger growing. 'This is damning. But now we have to prove it properly.'

'No, we don't.' Kowalski said. 'I'll tell Winter I found this envelope left on my desk. Job done.'

He was right. She would be off the hook and it would be up to the DPS to deal with Kanwar. Loxton could go back to the real work of catching killers instead of corrupt cops.

'Thank you,' she said.

'Don't mention it – ever again. We could both lose our jobs.' He smiled at her.

She nodded. 'I still might. I disobeyed Winter's orders.' She folded her arms in front of her chest. She felt cold suddenly as she considered the repercussions for her career.

'There's only one way to find out.' Kowalski downed his coffee and stood up.

Winter stood up when she walked into his office behind Kowalski, his face reddening and his hands balled into fists. He turned his cold gaze on Kowalski. 'What are you playing at?'

'You need to read this.' Kowalski handed it to Winter. 'It shows Kanwar was the one calling Saunders. Not DC Loxton.'

Winter eyed them suspiciously, grabbed the envelope and leafed through the pages. Winter checked his mobile to be sure the number was Kanwar's and then stared at Kowalski in amazement. 'How did you get this?'

'It was left on my desk.' Kowalski shrugged.

'How did you *really* get this?' Winter held Kowalski's gaze.

'As I said, sir, it was on my desk.'

Winter eyed Kowalski and Loxton warily. She didn't flinch.

'I thought you should see it straight away,' Kowalski said. 'Being as you've put Kanwar in charge of the Webb case and the first hearing's on Monday.'

'Shit.' Winter rubbed his face with his hands, he looked suddenly tired. 'Kowalski, you're in charge of the Webb case. You go to court on Monday.'

Kowalski nodded. 'It's a big case, boss. I could do with a deputy. Someone who knows the ins and outs.' Kowalski glanced at Loxton and then back to Winter.

'You never spoke to Saunders about this case?' Winter asked her.

'Never, sir,' she said.

Winter sighed and shook his head. 'Kanwar was with me when the uniform called me about the body in the Thames. And he knew Talbot had been arrested. I didn't think for a moment it would be him. I'm usually a good judge of character, but this time I got it wrong. If you want a transfer after all this is over, I'd understand.'

Loxton glanced at Kowalski. 'I'd like to stay on the team.'

Winter smiled. 'Good, I'm glad to hear that. There'll still need to be a formal investigation into the leaks to the press. The DPS will need to interview you and finish interrogating your phones.'

'They won't find anything, sir.'

Winter nodded as he sat down and opened his desk drawer. He held Loxton's warrant card in his hand. 'You're on light duties for now, until you're formally cleared by the DPS. And you're to be supervised by Kowalski. You can assist him with the trial, but nothing more. Help with the case papers, getting it all finished off.'

'Thank you, sir.' She held out her hand, willing it to stay steady.

He handed her the warrant card. 'Remember: light duties only, so no running around chasing suspects. And don't say a word of this to anyone. Let's keep this in-house. I'll update DPS now.'

Loxton slid her warrant card into her inside pocket and tried to hold back tears. All the fear and stress dissipated and she realized she'd been wound so tight she'd been close to breaking.

'Monday's going to be a busy day for you both,' Winter said. 'You should head home.'

'Thank you, sir.' Kowalski turned and headed out of the office. Winter gave Loxton a single nod and she returned it before leaving. She felt shaky inside, as if she'd escaped near death.

She caught up with Kowalski, who was striding towards their bank of desks. 'He didn't apologize outright,' she said.

Kowalski laughed. 'You didn't expect him to, did you?' He began digging around his desk, shifting paperwork and stained mugs. He stopped for a moment. 'Winter is sorry, trust me, and that should be enough. Let me take you home if I can ever find my car key.'

She reached past him and grabbed it from where it had been lodged behind his monitor and passed it to him.

They headed out of the police station and were met by the press. The journalists surged forwards, but Kowalski stepped in front of her. The bodies stopped short when faced with his large frame.

'We don't have a press statement,' he said. 'When we have one, you'll be contacted.'

'Officer, can you tell us if anyone has died?' A female journalist pushed her purple glasses up her nose, pen poised ready as she hung onto his every word.

'Miss, we can't tell you anything. Your understanding is appreciated.' He headed towards the exit doors, and Loxton had a hard job keeping up with him. As they went outside, a figure followed them.

'Still on the case? I thought you'd been suspended, Alana.' Saunders's eyes were gleeful. He popped a cigarette into his mouth and held the packet out to her and Kowalski. 'No hard feelings?'

She put her hand out for a cigarette, and then knocked the proffered packet out of Saunders's hand. She placed her foot on top of the box and ground it into the pavement. 'If you ever come near me again, I will do that to your scrotum.'

Saunders's smile dropped. 'You two are going to be in serious shit when your boss finds out you're still on the job. And then your new friend here might get suspended too.'

'You run along and tell him,' Kowalski said. 'That's what you've both been doing this whole time.'

Saunders laughed. 'That's right, me and Winter. How did you guess?'

'We're not detectives for nothing,' Kowalski said. Loxton saw what Kowalski was doing – he didn't want Saunders destroying the mobile, he wanted him to think they were clueless.

'You'll never prove it,' Saunders said, enjoying himself.

'We will though,' Kowalski said. 'Winter will slip up at some point. Come on, Alana, you've wasted enough of your time on this piece of shit.'

'What? Are you two lovers now? Pull the other one. It takes longer than that to get over me.'

Kowalski grabbed Loxton's hand and strode away from Saunders towards the car, which was parked across the road. He stopped after a few steps and turned quickly around to face her, leaning down as he pulled her to him. His face tilted to the side and he pushed his lips into hers, kissing her deeply.

A shiver went down her spine, and a light grew inside her stomach. He pulled away, and she was left breathless, looking up at him. He then put his arm around her waist and led her to the car, opening the passenger-side door for her. He climbed into the driver's side. Saunders was still staring at her from where they'd left him. His cigarette was hanging out of his mouth and his arms dangled by his sides.

'Sorry,' said Kowalski. 'I shouldn't have done that, but it showed that prick, hey?' He glanced at her nervously.

She could still feel his warm lips against hers, and her stomach tingled. 'Of course, it's fine. It did show him.' She stole a sideways look. His face was as flushed as hers. He revved the engine hard and pulled out of the space, spinning the wheels. Then he raced out of the car park and onto the London roads.

Chapter 56

Epilogue

Jenny Hughes

18 months later

'Rachel,' I said. 'Rachel, come back here.'

Mum laughed. 'She's so much like you; I can't believe it.'

The early spring sun broke through the thin clouds, but its light wasn't strong enough yet to warm my skin. I pushed my hands deeper into my pockets.

'How did you cope?' I said. 'It's so hard.' Rachel had turned around and was crawling through the sand towards me.

'You get used to it.' She cooed at Rachel, encouraging her. 'Heard from Mark recently?'

'He called at the weekend. He won't be able to come at Easter after all; he can't get a prison day release.'

'That's a shame.'

I shook my head at her. 'It's a good thing, Mum. It's too soon. I'd rather not see him at all, but then there's Rachel.' I struggled not to raise my voice.

Rachel was making steady progress through the sand.

She stopped and threw her head up to check I was still there. Then her head lolled forward as she carried on her marathon.

'You don't think you'll ever get back together, you and Mark?'

'Never.' A wave of anger threatened; it surprised me. I thought I'd got past all that.

She nodded and we sat in silence, the weight of the past pressing down on us. There was so much I wanted to say, but I didn't know where to start. It would take time, a long time, but as my mum and I sat together watching Rachel crawling in the sandpit, somehow I knew we would get there. Rachel had come along and brought us all closer, had helped to heal, to make us live again.

Rachel dug into the sand with her hands. Occasionally she would laugh loudly, thrilled as the sand sprinkled around her. The noise made my stomach flip with joy, but a sadness was always behind it. I missed my sister.

'Thanks for all your help. I can't imagine doing this without you and Dad.' The words were feeble, but between them were the vast amounts of money they'd used to bail my business out after Mark had got us into so much debt, and the endless babysitting. They'd uprooted their lives, selling their house in Milton Keynes and downsizing to be nearer to Rachel and me. They were trying hard to make up for all that lost time and so was I.

'We wanted to help. To be part of your life again.' She took my hand, gently squeezed it and let it go.

'I'm sorry I pushed you out. I've missed you.' I couldn't look her in the eye, afraid that I might start crying.

'How's the business going?' she asked.

'Great, now Mark's not leaching the profit from it.' I

couldn't mention his name without feeling disgusted at myself for letting him run the books for me. All that time I thought my business was dragging us down, taking too long to get off the ground, but it had been him.

'Dad said you were starting an Open University course?'

I nodded. 'Accountancy and business. I always let other people do it for me but it's about time I did it for myself.'

'It's a lot to take on, love.' My mum was about to say more but thought better. 'Do you need us to take her next week?'

'If you could have her Monday and Tuesday, that'd be great.'

Mum nodded. I knelt to scoop Rachel up. She'd reached the end of the sand pit. In front of her was the asphalt floor of the playground, too rough for her soft knees. She wriggled for a moment, frustrated by being restricted, but then settled on my lap. I kissed her red cheek, brushed sand off her hands.

'You're getting hot, little lady.' I peeled off her winter coat.

'She looks just like you when you were that age. It's uncanny.' Mum shook her head as she stroked Rachel's blonde curls from her forehead. Mum's eyes were shining but she managed to hold back the tears. We both knew what she meant when she said that.

Rachel looked nothing like me, but every bit like her namesake.

Acknowledgements

Without readers, there would be no books, so thank you for taking the time and energy to read this one. I hope you enjoyed reading it as much as I enjoyed writing it.

I'm eternally grateful to the Write Here, Right Now competition run by Simon & Schuster UK, Darley Anderson Literary Agency and the Bradford Literature Festival; without it, none of this would have happened. I'm indebted to the judges – Anne Perry, Jo Dickinson, Camilla Bolton and Tanera Simons – for giving me this opportunity.

A special mention to my brilliant editor, Bethan Jones, for your patience and expertise. Thank you to everyone at Simon & Schuster UK, for your endless enthusiasm for this book and the beautiful cover.

Thank you to my amazing agent, Camilla Bolton, for your faith in me and for championing DC Alana Loxton. Thank you to everyone at Darley Anderson for their continued support.

To my colleagues in the Met Police, it was a privilege to work alongside you. A special thanks to the Met, for allowing me a career break to pursue this dream. And to DC Fiona Loxton, thank you for letting me borrow your surname – Alana is forever grateful and so am I.

Thanks to my excellent teachers at City University London for passing on their writing secrets: Claire McGowan, Laura Wilson and William Ryan.

Thank you to the wonderful Alex Marwood, for being the best mentor I could have wished for and generously sharing so much writing wisdom, wine and time. It's not every day you get to meet one of your heroes and be taught by them.

I'm so grateful to the other writers on the City Crime Writing MA, especially to Finn Clarke, Paul Durston, Fraser Massey (thanks for the title of this book!), Vicki Jones and Jane Phillips. Thank you for your continued insightful criticism and our get-togethers that keep me sane.

To all of my friends and family, for your patience, encouragement and support – you know who you are. But especially to Kalynda Bradley for being a fantastic early reader. To Anna Kosiorowska for assisting with the Polish and for showing me around your beautiful country: *dziękuję serdecznie!* To Rosie White and Mel Wilson for being the best cheerleaders a girl could wish for. And to Alex, Fi and Becky for the Prosecco, the laughs and for keeping me up-to-date with the police world.

Arigatou gozaimasu to Andy Niewiarowski (Grammar Panda), for meticulously reviewing this book more than once; you're the best. And for the lunches, endless cups of coffee and grammar advice.

Thank you to my brother, Pete, for being my first teacher in storytelling. You taught me the limitless capability of the imagination when our toys would embark on epic adventures through time and space and glittering alien cities built in the sandpit.

A special thank you to my twin sister, Alison. You believed in me long before I believed in myself. Thank you for dragging me to the City University London MA Open Day, even though I'd missed the closing date, and encouraging me to apply anyway. It changed everything. Thank you for reading this book numerous times and for loving it as much as I do. You will always be my 'Ideal Reader'.

And finally, thank you to my husband, Mike. You kept your promise, supporting me in my dreams, however crazy they seemed. I love you for your patience, calmness, humour and optimism. You make every day an adventure.